Lake Overturn

Also by Vestal McIntyre

You Are Not the One: Stories

Lake Overturn

Vestal McIntyre

HARPER
An Imprint of HarperCollins*Publishers*
www.harpercollins.com

Dedicated to the memory of my mother,

ALICE EVANS MCINTYRE
1935–2004

FIRST EDITION

Designed by Renato Stanisic

Library of Congress Cataloging-in-Publication Data is available upon request.

ISBN: 978-0-06-167116-6

09 10 11 12 13 OV/RRD 10 9 8 7 6 5 4 3 2 1

Step One:
Problem

High in the mountains of Cameroon, West Africa, there was a small lake surrounded by green, treeless cliffs—Lake Nyos. No river emptied into Lake Nyos; it was fed by rain from above and springs from below, leaving the surface utterly still—a blue jewel set in a mountaintop, penetrated by slanted bars of light. Water trickled gently from it into a valley that held three small villages of cattle herders.

Summer was usually the rainy season, but the August of 1986 had been dry. Then, on the evening of the twenty-first, a warm, pelting rain began to fall. Children came outside to run through the grass and slide in the mud, while cows lumbered into the shelter of the great, waxy-leafed trees.

The cattle here were of an African variety that Idahoans would never have seen: giants with great wide horns and spines that hung like suspension bridges between humps at the shoulder and hip. As majestic in unblemished white as Idaho cows were humble in brown inkblots, they looked more like wild things—water buffalo or wildebeest—than anything you'd raise and eat. Those Idahoans who saw the news reports in the following days, which showed these animals twisted languidly in death, imagined that, in life, they had moved regally, their muscles rolling and twitching under their sleek coats. The Idahoans fixed their minds on the death of these cows rather than the cows' owners. A cow lying dead with flies in its eyes was a common enough sight.

The rain died off at sunset. Then, in the middle of the night, a gust of wind blew through the villages and up over the mountains. This wasn't a howling tempest; it didn't have force enough to snap limbs off trees, just to flap the leaves and send down a second, lesser shower. Nobody even woke up. But the wind moved the blanket of rain water across the surface of Lake Nyos. Like a tablecloth that one pushes across a tabletop, which gathers momentum and falls of its own weight to the floor, the warm water collected in one corner, then slipped down the side, past the still strata of frigid water, to the depths where something lay sleeping. The villagers, who regarded Lake Nyos alternately as a benevolent mother and a sanctuary for evil spirits, would later say it was the Lake Witch. She awoke, swam up the opposite side of Lake Nyos, and emerged from the water with a groan and a rumble. A few villagers woke and sat up in bed, wondering, *Was it a dream?* Seconds later their breath was taken from them, and they fell back onto their pillows. Their family members sleeping across the room didn't even awaken, but made a few gasping snores before they died. Outside, cows fell on their knees, surged to heave themselves back up, then rolled onto their sides. Birds dropped like black fruit from the trees. A bat swooped to catch an insect that had fallen dead, but failed, died, and tumbled through the air. Strangely, though, another bat flying at a higher altitude didn't die, but flitted away to find a fresher meal elsewhere.

Farther down the valley, the Lake Witch seemed to tire. She allowed the people of the next village to rouse their children and make it outdoors before they fell. She let them feel the struggle of their children gasping for air under them before taking their lives.

Dawn came hot and steaming. A man used a switch both to drive his five cows up the road and to swat the biting flies from his own ankles. He entered the trail of the Lake Witch where there were no more flies, but he did not notice this. The buzzing and chirping, which never stopped, *had* stopped, but until the man came upon that first dead cow, he couldn't name the chill.

A similar, though much less ominous, disorientation—a gap between feeling the chill and naming it—was experienced only days later by Connie Anderson in Eula, Idaho. Temperatures had reached one hundred degrees every day for a week. At dusk one Thursday, when husbands were plugging in their Weedwhackers to charge them up for the weekend, and wives were turning on their sewing machines, and everyone was tuning their TVs to *Hill Street Blues*, which was thought to be set in New York City (where few Eulans had ever been but which seemed gritty and fascinating and made their own lives seem dull, yes, but clean), the electricity, already overtaxed by air conditioners that had been running all day, went out.

Connie happened to be leaving First Church of the Nazarene at that moment. She and some women from her group, the Dorcas Circle, had volunteered to change the decorations in the sanctuary. They had taken down garlands of plastic roses from the stained-glass windows, replaced them with bunches of Indian corn, and propped up sheaves of dried cattails and corn stalks in the corners. The last to leave, Connie stepped out of the church and opened her purse to look for her keys. She found them, looked up, and everything had changed. She reached for the handrail in case she was fainting. A dog's insistent bark echoed in the distance. A car passed, and its tires on the smooth road made a sound like breath. Above Connie, clouds hung like knotted wool blankets that had been dipped in gold on the edge closest to the horizon, behind which the sun had dropped. The scarlet haze on the horizon and the faint odor of spice were due, Connie knew, to the wildfires that had been burning steadily for several days in the brush lands across the Snake River from Eula. Small clouds suspended above the haze in the west shone like nuggets. Then, before Connie could name the difference, the streetlights flickered on, and the windows of the houses glowed, and something buzzed—the power line that entered the church building above Connie's head, which she never would have noticed otherwise.

Nothing more required Connie's attention, so she went to her car. It was as if whatever had turned the lights on had turned the sky *off*; it still hung there but was no longer something to admire.

The African man came upon the first cow, whose white body made a dazzling U in the grassy arms of a creek bed. Another cow lay among the bushes farther up the meadow. The man had been swatting at his ankles with the switch out of habit, but now he stopped. In the silence, his swallow was a brief melody of ticks and gurgles.

Step Two:
Research

CHAPTER 1

A warm breeze rattled the venetian blinds as it entered the classroom and brought with it a tingle of mint from the nearby fields. Mr. Peterson made an announcement: "The Snake River District Science Fair will be in the field house in Chandler on November 18. Anyone can enter."

In the front row, Enrique was jarred by a hiccup of excitement at the idea of pink foam flowing down the slopes of model volcanoes, fronds of exotic plants unscrolling under bright grow-lights, tadpoles, guppies, sea monkeys darting in jars, shedding fins, sprouting green hands, mutating, and blinking a cluster of intelligent eyes up at him from the palm of his hand. It was the nature of Enrique's mind to fire off images in rapid succession—images that lit others like a string of firecrackers, or like popcorn whose first promising pops seemed to set off subsequent ones, until they multiplied into a cacophony of buttery explosions.

There was a flip side to these ecstasies, however. Any insult, no matter how slight, lodged in Enrique's heart, then burrowed like a worm, leaving Enrique no choice but to dig after it until he found himself in a hole so deep and dark he could do nothing but hide his face and cry. "Sensitive," his mother had called him when he was little, and he had considered this a distinction that set him above other, brutish boys. Then one day, his older brother, Jay, had called him "sensitive," but said it with a lisp, and Enrique had hated the word ever since.

"The winner from each grade will go on to the Idaho State Science

Fair in Boise." (In Enrique's mind: gleaming trophies, applause, the dark lenses of local TV news cameras confronting him from the crowd, *Speech! Speech! Speech!*) "The winner *there* will go on to National."

Enrique saw Miriam trying to catch his eye from a few seats away. But instead he nudged Gene, next to him. *Listen!* Enrique said to Gene with his eyes.

"Start thinking about projects, all right? It will be an assignment due a week from Friday to come up with a project proposal, whether or not you plan to enter the science fair, so it's not too early to get started on a hypothesis. Who can tell me what a hypothesis is?"

In raising his hand, Enrique used his arm to momentarily block Miriam out. Miriam was Enrique's friend, but Gene, whose beady eyes still rolled after something in the air only he could see, would be the better partner.

"Enrique?"

"An educated guess."

"Correct. And can anyone tell me what the seven steps to the scientific method are? Miriam?"

"Problem, research, hypothesis—um—experimentation, analysis, results . . . and presentation."

"You are absolutely correct, Miriam. Thank you."

Miriam now sat stiff and didn't look Enrique's way—very purposefully, it seemed to him.

JUST ACROSS THE lawn, in Building C, Fred Campbell, the principal, sat at his desk, sweating and wringing his hands. Then he stood and paced. This was ridiculous. How could he be so weak? He had to do this. It was his job. But when he imagined approaching Coop, putting his hand on the man's sloping shoulder and saying, "Coop, my friend, let's sit down. I have somethin' I wanna discuss with ya," he felt a chasm of horror open beneath him that he could fall into and become nothing. He wasn't man enough to be principal. Why had they hired him?

They had used a classroom for the interview on that day last June, since Eula Schools didn't have a conference room. An unsettling *psst-psst* of sprinklers on the football field filled the quiet moments as school board members, with their reading glasses riding low on their noses, sifted through papers.

"You realize you'll be responsible for discipline among the kids, both junior and senior high," said Brenda Simon, the school board president. "That means chewing them out and calling their folks, since they're too old to paddle."

"Alas!" said the English teacher, always the joker.

"Well, Brenda," said Fred, "as you know, I have five little ones of my own, so I've done plenty of chewing out in my time, not to mention paddling some fannies good and red from time to time."

This was a lie. Karen alone disciplined the kids. Sometimes they would even run behind Fred, using him as a shield against their mother's anger.

"And you'll do the hiring and firing, in conjunction with the board," Brenda said. "Basically, you'll be the bearer of news both good and bad."

"I'm your man," Fred said. He had uncrossed and recrossed his legs easily.

What a fraud he was! Never, ever would he be able to tell other adults, fellow teachers, that they were fired. Look at him now, and he didn't even have to fire Coop, just confront him.

He was qualified on paper at least. He held a master's in education, concentrating on driver's ed., from Brigham Young. He had taught driver's ed. and world history at Eula High for eight years, and this put him at a great advantage, since the last principal had been a Methodist from Oregon. This time (it was whispered in the teachers' lounge) they were looking for a Mormon from here in town.

Fred never dreamed he'd get the job, but he was obliged to apply. Karen was pregnant again.

So, this was his first test. Last night he had worked himself up into tears—tears!—about it. Karen had awakened and muttered, "What is it?"

He had slowed his breath and forced ease into his voice. "Sorry, honey, just a bad dream."

Karen had rolled toward him and laid her arm across his chest. "Poor little quail," she had said, falling back asleep. She and the kids said he was like the Papa Quail of the family that foraged in the backyard. It had to do with the abrupt way he jerked his head toward the source of any unexpected noise.

Now Fred stopped pacing and sat down at his desk. How could he get a hold of himself? He decided to call Dean, an elder in his church, his prayer partner and confidant—the only one who knew the magnitude of his self-doubt.

"Dillon Auto Parts."

"Dean, it's Fred."

Dean, who had a million things to do, clenched his jaw and wished he had let the receptionist get it.

LINA TWISTED THE long nozzle onto the vacuum hose, knelt, and ran it along the carpet under the skirt of the sofa. *You sound like a fuckin' wetback*—it had been in her mind all day. It wasn't fair that she had heard, but she hated Jay a little for it. That's what he wanted, though, to make her hate him, to be a stranger in her house. Usually Lina filled her workday with old songs—songs from the Mexican dances at the field house in Chandler she attended when she was young—whistled in a way audible only to herself, through her widely spaced teeth; but today it was Jay's words that kept her company.

This bright room was the parlor of the Halls' house. The sofa was upholstered in a natural linen—stiff, not so comfortable to sit on, but beautiful. Last March they had had all the furniture professionally cleaned, and the little grayish impressions left by rear ends of the Halls and their company, who must have sat upright—there were no impressions on the backs or the armrests—vanished. Lina turned off the vacuum cleaner and paused before she stood. She pushed herself into a squat and let the weight settle into her heels. She couldn't just stand anymore; everything required planning. Her hips were so heavy, and she wasn't even forty. She took in a breath to say *Dios mio* as she stood, and, in her mind, Jay prepared to answer her, *You sound like a fuckin'*— but then she felt the presence of someone else in the room and stopped mid-breath. A footstep fell like a whisper on the carpet. She stood and, although she expected to see someone when she turned, she still jumped.

"I'm so sorry," Mr. Hall said, raising his palms in surrender. He had the shiny bald crown and ring of hair that made Lina think of a monk.

"That's okay, Mr. Hall," she said from her squat. Using the armrest of the sofa, she pushed herself up to stand.

"I didn't mean to startle you, Lina," he said.

Lina waited a moment to see if he would say anything else, and when he didn't, she pulled the plug from the wall and gathered the cord. "I didn't know anyone was home," she said.

"Yes, I decided to come home for lunch." Again, he stood and stared. "Sandra is in Salt Lake with her parents."

Lina nodded.

"Have you had lunch?"

"Yes, I ate before I came."

"But you've been here for hours."

Lina nodded patiently, but said nothing.

"I have an open bottle of chardonnay from last night. I'm having a glass with lunch. Can I offer you some?"

"No, that's nice, but no thanks. I got to finish up."

"Of course. Well, if you change your mind . . ." He made a shrugging gesture toward the kitchen.

Lina wiped down the upstairs showers. She had understood from the day she first cleaned this house and saw wine in the basement and Coke in the fridge that the Halls were Jack Mormons. Bend-the-rules Mormons. But what did he want to give her wine for? Maybe he just wanted company. He was a strange man. He had books about trains in the library, train magazines in the bedroom, and toy trains all still in their boxes down in the basement. "Lina," Sandra had said last year, "we need to cut back a little. How much would you charge if you didn't do the basement every time?"

Lina had been thinking of raising her rate, but now she wouldn't. Money embarrassed her, and for that reason she always undercharged. "I don' know . . . forty?"

"Great, let's do it," Sandra had said, patting Lina on the shoulder like it was an idea that they had struck upon together. And it was done: she'd work a half hour less every other Thursday. That was nowhere near enough time to fit in another house, so Sandra had effectively tricked her into a pay cut.

Lina threw away her gloves, washed her hands in the bathroom, and put on her shoes. She gathered all the bottles and rags and put them in the broom closet, then hesitated. It would be rude to just leave when Mr. Hall was in the kitchen. So she poked her head in. "All done, Mr. Hall. Tell Sandra hi."

"Are you rushing off? You won't join me?" He had an empty plate and a folded newspaper on the table before him, a bottle and two wine glasses, one half-full.

"You know, I don' really drink."

"It's just wine."

"And the boys will be home soon."

Mr. Hall lifted the wine bottle, offering to pour.

"Well, maybe one glass." She left her duffel bag in the foyer.

"How is Jay?" asked Mr. Hall. "I haven't seen him in a while."

Two nights ago, after Mass, someone (maybe Connie, her neighbor, had had company) took Lina's spot, so she had to park a few units down. As she approached the porch, she heard Jay's angry voice and stopped to listen. "Why do you talk Spanish to her, Enrique? Talk English."

"Why you care?" (Enrique's sad little voice.)

"See? You sound like a fuckin' wetback. '*Why you care?*' Say, 'Why do you care?' "

"Guys, I'm home," Lina had called. She climbed the stairs and stood at the screen door. Enrique was on the floor surrounded by his homework. Jay sat on the coffee table looming over Enrique's shoulder. He was shirtless, his long brown torso leaning forward, elbows on knees, his big hands hanging.

"Jay?" she said now to Mr. Hall. "He's good."

"Still playing basketball?"

"He will once season starts."

"And what's your younger one named?"

"Enrique."

"And . . . the boys' father?"

Two sips of wine were enough to make Lina bold. Instead of scrambling for an answer, she pursed her lips and wagged her finger scoldingly.

Mr. Hall dropped his head and squeezed his eyes shut. "Sorry," he half-coughed.

For a while they talked about the townspeople they knew in common. "You know Dr. and Mrs. Barnes just celebrated their fiftieth," Mr. Hall said.

"Yeah, big party." Lina knew this because she had cleaned their house the next day.

"Fifty years. You know, Lina, Sandra and I . . . our marriage isn't so much of a marriage anymore. We love each other for what we once had, and for Abby. But we don't love each other . . . passionately anymore." He said this matter-of-factly, as if it followed what came before. Like a car with bad alignment, his conversation kept turning this way, and it seemed funnier now than at first, because he was so clumsy, and she was so tipsy. She would never let him in.

They talked on and Mr. Hall refilled her glass. "Not so much, Mr. Hall. I have to drive home." He was a nice man, just lonely. She would have used his first name if she could remember it. But he didn't seem to notice enough to say, *Oh, Lina, please call me . . .* whatever. A lawyer for the city, he was certainly used to everyone calling him Mr. Hall.

"My husband, he got a job in Nevada," Lina offered when conversation failed.

"And that's where he lives? Nevada?"

Lina nodded.

"When was the last time he . . . lived here?"

"Long time ago. He'll come up here around Christmas." Lina didn't know why she added this little lie. She didn't know when Jorge would come around, or, for that matter, if he still lived in Nevada. She called him her husband—she always had; he was the father of her two boys—but he had never married her in the church. Jorge hated priests.

"Do you want to see something really amazing?" Mr. Hall asked in a brisk voice, as if to clear the air.

"Um, sure."

"It's upstairs. Bring your wine."

"I don' know . . ."

"Come on," he said, picking up her glass, "you'll like it."

He led her up the bright staircase under the skylights and down the hall to the bedroom. He set her glass on the bedside table and sat on the edge of the bed.

"No way," she said, laughing.

His face was like a baby's, searching your face and copying your expressions. He laughed, too. Then he remembered. "No, it's right here." He opened the drawer, took out a magazine, and patted the bed beside him.

Shaking her head, she sat down and reached over him for her wine as he opened to a page that he had marked with a colored paper. "There's a new type of train they're building in Japan. It's just incredible. The maglev train, they call it. Magnetic levitation. They don't have wheels. They use electromagnets to levitate over the track." He pointed to a diagram. "They go superfast. Imagine going three hundred miles per hour, completely smoothly, without a sound, just whizzing by." He flipped through pages. "They're going to make one from Los Angeles to Las Vegas. A six-hour drive will be a half-hour train ride."

Lina burst out laughing, and again Mr. Hall copied her faintly. "It's so stupid!" she said.

He looked hurt. "What?"

"To pretend that train's what you brought me up here for."

He smiled again. "Okay," he said. He closed the magazine, touched her face, and kissed her.

She laughed and shrugged away. "You shouldn't kiss me," she said.

With both hands he gently turned her face toward him again, like Enrique used to when he wanted her attention. He kissed her. She closed her eyes. It stirred her, even though he wasn't handsome, and she didn't really like him. She pulled away and looked down. The trembling in her chest had caused her wine to come up a little. She turned away and burped.

He turned her back to him, and went to kiss her, but she pushed him away. Maybe he didn't take the rules of his church seriously, but she did hers.

"Why you want to do that?" she said.

"Well, I think you're very beautiful, and . . ."

"And what?" She didn't believe him.

"And you are like me. We both need to kiss."

All right, then, she let him kiss her again. A little sadness came with his honesty. She did need to kiss. They lay down on the bed and he kissed her neck and buried his face in her breast. This was so stupid. How far would she let this go? He ran his hand up her leg. That was it.

"Come on, Mr. Hall, let's stop this." She grunted to lift herself.

"But why?"

"You know why."

She left the room and walked down the soft, carpeted steps. She picked up her duffel bag and paused, looking up at the skylights above the stairs. This two-storied room was like a chapel, and it amplified the fluttering of her own breath. Mr. Hall didn't come to look down at her from the railing. Was he waiting for her to turn weak and come back? Sacrifice her pride for the feeling of being kissed? Give in to sin? She left the house. At least she'd have something to confess this week—kissing a married man. It was so stupid.

The bell rang, and school was out. Now Fred Campbell had missed his chance to speak with Coop before he headed out with the kids. Fred had built up some resolve during his conversation with Dean. They had prayed together, and he had felt like he could do it. He should have gone out to the garage right then, found Coop, and sat him down. But now he'd have to wait another two hours until Coop returned, during which he'd certainly lose his nerve. In the meantime, Karen would have to get dinner on alone. Fred buried his face in his hands and again called on Jesus to help him.

John Cooper, whom everyone, child and adult alike, called Coop, was unaware of the anguish he stirred in the frail heart of his new boss, and if anyone had told him, he would have laughed long and hard. Coop's hair was gray at the temples, his face was ruddy and usually fixed in a grin that exposed his one false incisor that stood straight and white as a piano key in the jumble of chipped, coffee-stained teeth.

There was tension now in his voice as he laughed, gripped the wheel, shook his head, and whispered, "Son of a bitch." This wasn't an expression of anger any more than his laugh was of amusement; they were both tics.

Coop's route took him out toward Lake Overlook to drop off the rich kids first, before it headed back into town, passing the schools again, for the town kids. This irked him, but it wasn't his decision, so all he could do was laugh a little. Also, the kids were beginning to act up. The ones up front were quiet as usual, but farther back a couple of sixth-grade boys were playing a game—not much of a game, really—of flinging themselves across the aisle on top of a few girls, who would scream and kick them off but who weren't so bothered as to change seats. A few bits of paper had sailed through the air, and when you had driven the bus as long as Coop had, you could read the signs that it would be a hard ride. Paper in the air before you even reached the subdivisions was like thrushes chattering in the treetops: a storm was brewing. He might have to stop on the empty stretch and do his little song and dance, but he'd wait and see.

Close behind Coop sat Gene and Enrique, the only seventh-graders who rode the bus on sunny days. "C'mon, Gene," said Enrique, "help me think about this. What could we do? Something about outer space? The *Challenger* explosion?"

The idea must have been sour, for Gene's face puckered. Despite his obsession with space travel, Gene had shown little interest that January when the space shuttle exploded over Florida. Enrique suspected this was because coverage of the disaster pushed the space probe *Voyager 2* from the papers, just as it passed Uranus and sent back detailed pictures of its moons.

"The environment, then," Enrique went on. "Acid rain, solar power, erosion—"

"Hey, Gene. Hey, Gene." A boy tapped Gene on the shoulder, a sixth-grader, younger than Gene and Enrique, but tall.

"Yes?" said Gene.

"What's *Gene* short for?"

"Eugene."

The boy and his friends broke out in loud, barking laughter and ran back to their seats.

Enrique was quiet for a moment, then said, "Why do you tell them, Gene?"

"He asked and I answered. I can't help it if he thinks it's funny."

"Next time just tell them to bug off."

When Coop reached the empty stretch, he braked hard, causing a couple troublemakers standing in the aisle to stumble forward. Coop had only two speeds: laughing patiently and putting his foot down. He pulled the lever to put out the stop sign, just to make it legal, and stood. The children were all quiet now.

"Listen up, kids," he said. "I've had enough of your screamin' and runnin' around. We're a long ways from anything. See that silo? That's the closest little bit of civilization. I'm perfectly happy leavin' you all here if you'd prefer to walk clear acrost all those corn fields to that silo and see if whatever grumpy old goat roper lives out there wants to give you a ride rest of the way home. You ever done corn toppin'? Well, I have, and this time of year those corn stalks are good and dry and'll give you plenty of cuts 'long the way.

"This is the first time I've had to stop this year. I was under the impression a few of you was growin' up, but I guess I was mistaken.

"Well, do I have any takers? . . . No? . . . It looks like you're dependin' on me to gitcha home, then. I want you to sit there like little ladies and gentlemen until I let you off this bus."

Coop stood there for a long moment looking at their contrite, downturned faces before he sat down, took in the stop sign, released the brake, and drove on.

The bus was quiet for a minute. Then, starting at the back, there began a soft chant: "*Chicken Coop . . . Chicken Coop . . . Chicken Coop . . .*" A few of the children made clucking noises.

Coop's face reddened, and he laughed a desperate laugh. He could handle this as long as it didn't get so loud.

Lina drove down the smooth, black, winding road between the saplings, around the bend by the golf course, then up over the ridge, from which she could see Lake Overlook shimmering under the white sun. Why did Mr. Hall have to say that? Before, it had just been a kind of game. Kid stuff. She had played along; no big deal.

Then he had said it: *We are people who need to kiss.* That made it desperate, like they were addicts of some kind. Lina pulled her crucifix out by its chain to kiss it—as she always did when she felt tears rise—but to do so now, with lips still hot from a married man's kiss, would be sacrilege. She dropped it back into her collar.

Now that she thought of it, her lips felt roughed up, as if they were torn in a hundred places, as if she could press a napkin to them and leave a lipstick-kiss of blood. When she touched her mouth with her hand, though, it came away dry.

She reached the fork in the road where she had to make the decision and, as usual, took the detour to drive by Carl and Janet's house—the Van Bekes'. She had always done this—kept her face forward as she glanced up the line of poplars past the fountain to the big white house with yellow trim—when Jay lived there, and ever since. It was a magnet to her. Today, Jay's car wasn't there.

Lina pulled into her spot at the same time as Connie. The two exchanged tired smiles, and Connie put her hands to her hair, which had loosened a little from its bun. "How are you, Lina?"

"I'm good. You?"

"Fine. Were you cleaning today?" Connie flinched, as if her own question embarrassed her.

"Yeah, all day, south of town. You know, I can't just stand up anymore if I'm kneeling on the floor. I have to make a little game plan." She patted her thighs and laughed.

Connie laughed too, lifelessly. Lina felt sorry for her. So stiff. Lina's uncle Mario would have said she had a *pedo atraptado*, a trapped fart. "Well, the boys will be home soon," Connie said as she climbed the stairs to her trailer.

"Do you want to send Gene over for dinner? You seem tired."

"Oh, that's so nice, Lina, but his grandfolks are coming over tonight."

"Any time," said Lina.

They had been neighbors for over ten years, and their boys were best friends, but still Connie always kept her distance. In the past, Lina had suspected that this was because she cleaned houses (but Connie herself was a nursing-home aide) or because she was a Mexican (but Connie had had Mexicans from her own church over for dinner). Now Lina knew that it was because she was Catholic. But today there had been something different in Connie's eye . . . could she tell that Lina had been kissed?

Gene and Enrique walked along the cinder-block wall of the fabric store, through the hole in the chain-link fence, and into the trailer park.

"C'mon, it'll be fun. We'll get to work with Mr. Peterson. He's nice, right?"

Gene was silent, his brow knotted.

"We can do something on flowers if you want."

"I'm done with flowers," Gene said.

"Well, then, anything. Anything you want. I'll be your assistant. We'll do experiments. I'll write the paper all alone, if you want. You can do drawings, and I'll do the presentation. We'll win, I promise."

Since entering junior high only two weeks earlier, Enrique had been wondering what he would do to keep from falling between the cracks. He was too short and chubby for sports, and until high school there would be no school play in which to act. His mom couldn't afford art lessons or piano or gymnastics, so he never asked, and being first altar boy was something to be hidden rather than flaunted. He did have a good singing voice. Once he sang the Doxology a cappella at Mass, and some old lady had told Father Moore afterward that it made her think there should be a boys' choir. But now an eighth-grade girl had sung a Christian Rock song at assembly, and even if Enrique mustered the nerve to perform at school, it would now seem like he was copying her. But this—a science fair! Gene was super-smart, especially when it came to science, but shrank in front of groups, and was generally awkward and abrupt. Speaking was Enrique's talent. Together they could win.

Finally Gene said, "Maybe a nova. I'd like to research a nova."

Enrique's heart leaped, although he wasn't sure if Gene meant the car or the TV show. "It'll be so much fun. If we win, then we go to State. I think we get money, too."

Locusts buzzed away as the boys made a place in the shade of Enrique's house to sit.

"Or a supernova," Gene said.

Enrique had the vague realization that Gene was talking about outer space but, not wishing to seem stupid, he skirted the issue. "I'll bet Miriam's already got some idea," he said. "I'll ask her tomorrow. No, I'll wait until we have our hypothesis, then I'll ask her. I wonder who she's gonna get as a partner."

Enrique explored one scenario of victory after another until Lina called, "Enrique! You out there?"

"Yeah, Ma."

"Dinner."

"Think about our project," Enrique said, brushing seeds off his pants.

When Connie came to find Gene an hour later, he was still huddled against the wall, brow wrinkled and features pinched, staring at the grass with such concentration it seemed he would set it ablaze.

Coop drove into the lot that separated the grade school from the junior high, hooked the bus up to the gas pump, and walked toward the garage. Fred Campbell was there, sitting on an upside-down five-gallon bucket. He stood as Coop approached.

"Howdy, principal," said Coop.

"Howdy. Nice afternoon it's turned out to be."

"Yessiree."

"Was wondering if I could have a little chat with ya."

"Goodness. By the look on your face it looks like I'm up fer detention."

Fred laughed breathlessly. A wetness in his nose made the laughter sound like weeping.

"Let's go in and sit down," said Coop.

They entered the large, cool garage which doubled as the junior high's wood shop. In the back corner was a dented old office desk with file drawers that wouldn't open—Coop's desk. Coop sat in his chair and put his feet up. Fred sat across from him on a wobbly stool that some kid had made long ago.

"What's on yer mind, Fred?"

Fred took a deep breath and in a voice that wavered, but had volume, said, "A parent called me yesterday, Coop. Said she saw you at Albertson's buying beer. That's your choice, of course, if you care to imbibe, but her concern, that she made mine, was the amount. Said your shopping cart had case upon case of beer and not a whole lot of anything else, and they weren't regular beer cans either, but the extra-tall sort. Now, as I said, if you care to imbibe, that's one hundred percent your business, and I'd never bring it up if you were a math teacher or a gym coach or a janitor. But as this parent pointed out, you're picking our kids up in the morning and riding them home at night, which makes you a special case."

Coop took his feet down and folded his hands, but said nothing. Strange, though—he still had a pained smile on his face.

"I'm hoping," Fred continued, "that you're going to tell me you're planning a barbecue this weekend and everyone's invited, including me."

After a few seconds, Coop said, "Well, principal, I guess I have three things to say in response to your question. One is that I'm pleased by your concern with the safety and well-being of the children. I've been drivin' the bus for many years and I've seen three principals come and go, and watched 'em struggle to put ideas in kids' heads when that's no longer their job. Principal's job is to maintain order and ensure safety, so I thank you for doin' it. Second thing, I haven't had a drink since my daddy died twenty-seven years ago, and I was a kid back then who didn't do much drinkin' anyhow."

Fred Campbell nodded vigorously as if he were the one being disciplined.

"And thirdly, what I buy at Albertson's is my own goddamn business, pardon my French, and next time you talk to that parent you can extend an invitation to her to come over and visit sometime and meet my uncle, who's the one I was buyin' all that beer for, and the one I buy the same heap of beer for every week. I do it because if he didn't have his drink, I'm fairly certain he'd just lay down and die. Everyone needs somethin' to hold on to and, sadly, for him it's his drink. Most folks know a little bit of the Cooper family history, but my guess is this parent is a newcomer from California who don't. So I'd be pleased if you'd extend an invitation to her to come over and meet my uncle and maybe have a beer with him, 'cause that might cure her of nosin' in other folks' business."

Light-headed with relief, Fred continued to nod. Coop's ire was directed at the parent, not him, and its impact was mitigated by the strained smile. Still, Fred felt accused. He was from Utah originally, and didn't know Coop's family.

Coop came around the desk and put his big hand on Fred's back. "Thank you, principal. You're doin' a good job. Don't worry so much."

"Thank *you*, Coop. You put my mind at ease." Fred rose and shook Coop's hand. "And I'm sorry about your uncle. You'll both be in my prayers."

This made Coop laugh. "That's very nice. Yes, pray for us," he said.

ENRIQUE TOLD LINA about the science fair as they ate. "And if we win, we go to State, and if we win there, we go to National."

"Oh my God, *mijo*, that's exciting. What are you going to do?"

"I don' know. Maybe something on supernovas."

"Is that a really fast car?" Sometimes she liked to play dumb to let him feel smart.

"No, Ma, it's in outer space."

They had the same posture, hunched over like dogs protecting their dinner.

"You know," Lina said, "there's a new train they're making in Japan. It's called a maglev train and it doesn't touch the tracks. It goes three hundred miles an hour." Why did she want to plant little clues? She wanted to seem different to him.

"What does that have to do with anything?"

"It's science. Maybe you can do it for the science fair."

"What, make a train that flies?"

"I don' know, *mijo*, it's just an idea I heard about today is all."

The ringing clap of a basketball being dribbled up the walk made their laughter die. The door swung wide and Jay kicked the basketball into the corner of the tiny living room.

"There's plenty of food, Jay. Sit down with us," said Lina in a different voice.

He said nothing, but loaded a plate, turned on the TV in the living room, and went into his room, leaving the door open. He had turned the TV to be at such an angle that he could see it from his bed.

Lina and Enrique didn't look at each other, didn't say much, and soon Lina rose to clean. Through the window she could see Connie's car alone in its spot. No voices emerged from the trailer. Gene's grandparents clearly hadn't come after all.

Later, Enrique lay in bed and Lina next to him on top of the covers. This was their habit, which had begun in their old trailer when Enrique was afraid of the dark. Together they would open the pullout couch, and Lina would lie with Enrique until he fell asleep, then go to her own bed in the trailer's tiny bedroom. She knew she was spoiling him, but she didn't care. Her frustrated love for her first son, Jesús, who was being raised by the Van Bekes and liked to be called Jay, had turned her love for Enrique into something wild. Back then she worked so hard cleaning at the hospital and topping corn in the fall that she'd nod off next to Enrique and sleep there half the night.

Darkness no longer frightened Enrique, and he had his own bedroom in the doublewide. Now this was simply their time to talk privately.

"You'd tell me if Jay said mean things to you, right, baby?" she said in Spanish.

"I guess," he said in English.

"Does he?"

"I don' know."

"All right."

She stroked his hair.

"Today," she said in English, "a man kissed me."

"What? Who?"

"It was nothing. A man. I clean his house. I didn't let him do nothing."

"Why'd you do that, Ma?"

"I don' know."

"You're not supposed to."

"Why?"

"Because!"

"Do you think it's a big deal?"

"Yes."

"*Cariño*, don' be upset. I shouldn't have done it. I'm lonely, I guess."

"You're not going to do it again, are you? When do you clean his house?"

"Don' cry, baby. I won't do it again."

They both gazed at the ceiling. Lina wondered if Enrique was still crying.

"Why does it bother you so much, Enrique?"

"I don' know."

"I'm lonely, *mi vida*." That was her name for him—"my life."

He threw his arms around her and they both cried for a moment, then Lina lifted herself from bed. "No more blubbering. Time for sleep." She kissed him, and went to the living room. Jay had come in from his bedroom to lie on the couch. Lina wiped her eyes. "What's on?" she said, sitting in the recliner.

"Just news," Jay said, turning away slightly, embarrassed, it seemed, by her tears.

In his bed, Enrique still cried. It seemed so dirty, this kiss from some old man who liked watching her clean his toilet. She should have said no.

He thought back to a night the previous summer, before Gene quit Boy Scouts. "Don't kiss me," Gene had said.

"Why?" They were in their tent and had zipped up their sleeping bags together as they always did. It was very dark.

"It's what boys and girls do. It's for reproduction."

"All right." Enrique was disappointed, but not really ashamed. Gene felt no shame or regret about anything; it was a capacity he had been born without. So their friendship was one of a kind: the forces of fear and guilt that buffeted Enrique about in the rest of his life were quiet here.

Enrique listened to the crickets and waited for Gene to start snoring, but then he did it again—he touched Enrique's hair, searched out his earlobe, and rubbed it lightly between his thumb and forefinger. Then his hand made a padding journey to Enrique's mouth. The thumb glided back and forth across Enrique's lips, while the fingers rested on his cheek. That was what Gene had done minutes earlier that made Enrique decide to try to kiss him.

Enrique rolled away from the hand and went to sleep.

CHAPTER 2

The bun in which Connie kept her hair and the boxy blue dresses she wore on her days off led people in the street to think she was a Mennonite. But she wasn't. All her life she had attended First Church of the Nazarene, Eula's largest. When she was a child, First Church had been a traditional small-town, white-steepled structure that stood at Eula's center point, the corner of Twelfth and Main, like a dignified old gentleman waiting to cross the street. That building was still there, but now it housed First Church's ministries for Hispanics and its senior center. The congregation now met two blocks away in a huge, modern, semicircular structure of white plaster painted to look like marble. First Church now had three ordained ministers: the senior pastor, who gave sermons, traveled on church business, and ministered to the dying; the worship leader, who organized the Sunday service, met with congregation members in need, and oversaw the church's administrative office; and the youth minister. The block between the new and old churches contained a parking lot and a sports center. If Connie had still been a deaconess when they proposed that sports center, she would have voted against it. Basketball courts, when people here in Eula and around the world were dying without Christ—it smacked of vanity.

On a Sunday morning, Connie and Gene sat in their pew, which was not a proper pew but something more like a row of movie-theater seats. "Mom?" said Gene, scratching at his wrists, as he tended to do when he wore his nice shirt.

"Yes?"

"Can we go to Boise?"

"I suppose so, if you're quiet during the service and you don't fidget."

Gene rocked to one side, then the other to sit on his hands.

The sermon that morning was on Christ and the lepers. This made Connie happy. She loved sermons drawn directly from Christ's life and words, because they brought to mind images of her savior strolling the countryside in his robes and because they seemed more appropriate than, say, last week's sermon on how the church should stand behind President Reagan through these arms-for-hostages accusations, just as the disciples stood behind Christ when the Pharisees accused him of violating the Sabbath. "And you," said Reverend Keane, "how do you treat Eula's lepers when they come begging? Do you embrace them and take them in, or are you so concerned with your own health and safety and the contents of your own wallet that you spurn them?"

With the nauseating wave she always felt when God was talking to her directly, Connie remembered how she had treated Wanda Cooper the day before. With the exception of Coop, who drove the school bus, the Coopers were bad news, so when Connie saw Wanda in a coffee-stained undershirt with her raw knuckles approach in the mini-mart parking lot, she had quickened her pace.

"Pardon me, ma'am," Wanda said. "I'm tryin' to buy some formula for my baby. Could you maybe spare a dollar or two?"

"I could," Connie said without slowing her pace, "if I didn't know what you'd do with it, seeing's you have no baby, Wanda Cooper." Wanda stopped abruptly, but Connie went on: "And if your mind was intact, you might remember telling me the same story last year."

Just as Connie reached the entrance, Wanda called her a name—a horrible name—in a voice just loud enough for her to hear. She called her a *twat*.

Connie could now see that she had been proud and sarcastic, and in spurning Wanda she had spurned Christ Himself. She deserved Wanda's rebuke. Well, not that word, of course, but . . .

A woman in the next row shot an irritated glance over her shoulder. This made Connie realize that Gene had been noisily crumpling his bulletin while she had been lost in thought.

"Eu*gene*," whispered Connie, "quiet, or no Boise!"

Gene froze like a mannequin, still holding the bulletin. Another mother would have thought he was being willful, making a joke of his mother's order by obeying it so instantaneously and dramatically, but not Connie. Gene didn't make jokes.

Eugene. People called him Gene, except for Connie, when she was angry, and his schoolmates, when they were making fun of him. *Eugene* seemed to his schoolmates a very funny name, and to Connie, a very serious one. It had been the name of Gene's father, who had left her.

Gene had always been strange. When he was a toddler, Connie's keys fell again and again into his clutches. Rather than jangling them and throwing them, as any other child would, Gene frowned at them critically and ran his tiny fingertip along their jagged edges. As he grew and Connie wrenched things one by one from his ball-like hand, he turned his focus from objects to the empty space in the air about a foot in front of his chest. In the mornings he walked to the bus stop with his head bowed, focusing on this spot, which seemed to have become an imaginary scratch pad. He would scribble across it with his finger or, if frustrated, swat at it. He even seemed to talk to the space, although he never opened his mouth. His lips stayed bunched up under his nose, but his jaw lurched and his short, blunt eyebrows rose and fell independently of each other, as if they were fighting over the small patch of hair between them. There usually seemed to be a battle, or several battles—a war—going on in Gene's face. When his gaze rose from his scratch pad, it was never to the path before him but to something in the air—a bug, fairy, or idea—that swirled around him and caused his head to pivot and crane.

Socially, things had gone better for Gene back in grade school. Although he was single-minded in his play, stubborn with his rules, and miserly with his toys, the other children took him or left him without branding him an outcast. And he had a buffer: Enrique, who had a natural understanding of Gene, embraced the role of translator between the boy who didn't care to be understood and the world, which only became less understanding with time. Enrique apologized to the little girl whom Gene had made cry by yanking back a toy he had lent, then quieted the storm in Gene's face by whispering something into his ear. But come fifth grade, it seemed that even Enrique couldn't save Gene. The boys began to notice and comment on his stunted height, his pumpkin head, his shuffling, pigeon-toed gait, and the pimples that were sprouting too early on his tiny, upturned nose. A mere acorn tossed across the playground was enough to draw Gene suddenly out of his reverie. His head swiveled, eyes squinted as his attention cast wildly about like a fly fisherman's line. The boys laughed and laughed. It was *so funny.*

In the sixth grade Gene added to his collection of odd traits an aversion to walking under the open sky. He began to walk in the shade of tree branches rather than cross an open field, even if it doubled the distance. At recess he played under the concrete canopy that extended from the building, or in the grove of maples at the center of the schoolyard, and cast a suspicious squint toward the sky as he darted in-between. Enrique indulged this new foible and rode the bus home with Gene, even on warm afternoons.

Given Gene's strange behavior and the white baseball cap he took to wearing with the bill pulled low to shelter his eyes from the sky, it was little wonder people often assumed he was mentally retarded. Idaho's State School and Hospital for the Developmentally Disabled, or "the State School," as it was commonly called, was in Eula, so the town had far more than its share of "special" citizens. When Gene opened his mouth, though, his voice was high-pitched, precise, and intelligent.

Would his voice ever change? He already had a little fuzz on his upper lip. His mother would do good, said the concerned ladies at church, to give Gene a razor and encourage him to use it, not only on his upper lip, but on that tuft between his eyebrows, too. Then the concerned ladies shook their heads. It was so hard for single mothers.

But she had. Connie had taken Gene into the bathroom and told him he had to start shaving. He had gazed grumpily at the water swirling down the drain. Connie soaped up her hands and lathered his face. He squirmed a little, and Connie's pink disposable razor caught his attention as it approached—he seemed apprehensive—but nothing prepared Connie for his reaction when he felt the blade drawn down his cheek. His arm shot up as if of its own volition and knocked the razor across the room. He dropped to his knees and released a bawl that was loud and barely human. Connie backed away, frightened of Gene, frightened that the neighbors could hear.

Then one night, as Connie straightened up after dinner, a program on PBS caught her attention. The narrator, who was English, was talking about artistic children. But the facts presented about these children became more and more extraordinary, and at last Connie sat down, paid attention, and realized this was something else: the program was actually on *autistic* children. Connie had never heard of autism, but here it was; here *he* was; here was Gene. She felt both horrified and liberated. It wasn't her fault! She had always suspected that she might have hurt him without realizing it when he was an infant and, as a result, he had developed wrong and with a built-in resentment against her; this is why his eyes never met hers. But it wasn't her!

After the program Connie called her prayer partner, Myra, who, before retiring, had worked as a nurse at the State School. Myra had heard of autism, although they hadn't had any autistic kids on her floor. She doubted Gene was autistic, because, as she put it, "Those kids tend to raise Ned when they don't get what they want."

You haven't seen Gene when I try to put a scratchy sweater on him, thought Connie. Still, it was true that the kids on that show had seemed barely functional. Was that a result of autism, though? Connie and Myra prayed together, and before they said good-bye Myra gave Connie the telephone number of the doctor under whom she had worked at the State School—a fine, Christian man.

The State School was located on the hill north of town, where, legend had it, the cavalry had finally tracked down and killed Chief Eula, for whom the town was named. Connie had driven past the hill and peeked up the willow-lined lane innumerable times, but had never driven up it until now. She parked atop the hill, where there were five box-like brick buildings arranged around a cul-de-sac and a chapel at its farthest end. A vegetable garden at the plateau's edge was visible in the gap between the buildings, and in it several adults in straw hats stood on their knees in a line, staring at her. Connie waved. One hand shot up and waved back emphatically; another rose in a vague acknowledgment. A woman nodded at Connie and turned to the others, said something, and went back to digging with her trowel. Whatever she said, the others didn't obey, but continued to stare at Connie until she passed out of their line of vision. It occurred to Connie that this place was a humane sort of prison.

She entered a large, open hall with shining floors that reflected the light from the windows and empty walls that echoed the sound of her footsteps. The odors—bleach, feces, and aerosol air freshener—didn't bother Connie, as they also filled the nursing home where she worked.

The room number the doctor had given her was 210. Connie expected on her way to encounter a receptionist, or a nurse, or even an inmate, but there was no one. She found room 210, knocked, and a voice from within told her to enter.

The doctor who sat behind the desk was very old. Older, even, than Myra. He wore a crewneck cotton sweater with no undershirt. This was the way the old men at the nursing home dressed when they were in their last stage of unassisted living; they selected their clothes for the ease with which they could be put on and taken off. Connie suspected (though she couldn't see, as the doctor remained seated behind his desk) that he wore no socks and his shoes were slip-ons.

"So," said the doctor after they had introduced themselves and chatted for a minute about Myra, "you have some questions about your boy?"

Shyly, at first, Connie told the doctor how Gene never looked her in the eye, and never embraced her, and when he told her that he loved her, he said it as if it was something he had memorized. Although the doctor's bottom eyelids sagged open like a Saint Bernard's, revealing the red veins inside, his gaze was focused. She told him how he would take things apart and put them back together when she wasn't around, and she would only know when the phone receiver felt different in her hand, or the answering machine's buttons were a little crooked, or the toaster, the doorbell, the curling iron behaved a little differently. And how, recently, he had taken to tearing flowers apart. If she brought home a bouquet from work, she'd have to give him one rose, and put the rest by her bed where she could guard them. Connie didn't mention the obscene details of how Gene would lay his flower under the desk lamp and slowly peel back its petals to expose the powder-tipped shag, dig for the inner parts with his thumbs, then turn away to sneeze.

"He checked out Bach records from the library and sat right in front of the speakers to listen to them. I asked him why, and he told me, 'Bach is talking to me.'" Connie didn't say what Gene had said next. She had asked him how Bach could be talking to him, and he had replied, "He asks questions and I answer." Then he had shaken his head wildly, a gesture he used frequently, implying both a clearing of the head and exasperation at having to waste his time explaining when he certainly wouldn't be understood. "I mean, Bach poses a question, and I predict the answer."

Bach poses a question. A sixth-grader. Connie couldn't string together all his habits for display, even to a doctor. She was embarrassed on Gene's behalf for doing such things and on her own for putting up with it, for having been defeated by him. She had witnessed children defeat their parents before, but never using such roundabout tactics. It didn't seem fair.

"His teacher called me just last week," she said. "Gene is putting the date on his papers in the Hebrew or Chinese calendars. He refuses to use ours. These things frighten me a little, doctor. It seems wrong to refuse to date things from the Lord's birth." She stopped.

The doctor said, "Mrs. Anderson, sounds like you've got yourself a unique little feller."

Connie nodded.

"Let me ask you, what was Gene's first word?"

"Phone," Connie said. "My husband used to call out 'Phone,' when the phone rang. Then one day Gene called it out, too."

"How old was he?"

"Very young," said Connie. "Ten months." She knew the age because when Gene was eleven months old her husband had left.

"And at that time, did he know his name? Would he look up when you called him?"

"Yes."

"About when did he begin speaking in sentences?"

"Around two, I suppose. He's always been bright. That's not the problem."

"Interesting. Has Gene ever tried to hurt himself?"

"Oh, no," said Connie.

"Does he throw fits where he hits you or hugs himself and rocks back and forth?"

"No, but he does throw things."

The doctor nodded. "A unique little feller who throws things."

Suddenly Connie saw what the doctor saw: a lonely woman, frustrated that her son didn't love her enough. Because he suspected her of this, she suspected herself.

"Maybe I should bring him here to meet you," she said meekly.

"There's no need for that, Mrs. Anderson. I just asked you if your son displayed any of the three cardinal indications of autism. Does he have delayed or impaired speech development? No. Does he show evidence of delayed or impaired cognitive development? No. Does he show violent or self-destructive behavior? No. The patients who live here, Mrs. Anderson, are disabled—mentally disabled, profoundly. Your son is not."

Again, something snapped into focus for Connie: it was this doctor's job to ward off parents who came attempting to dump their children here merely because they were difficult. Connie bowed her head. "I don't want to bring Gene to live here, doctor, I just want to find out what's wrong with him, and help him."

The doctor smiled kindly. "Perhaps you can help him by focusing on what's *right* with him. That is my suggestion. Do you know why Bach wrote his music, Mrs. Anderson?"

"No."

"He wrote every piece, and there are hundreds upon hundreds of them, for the glory of God. Be glad your boy listens to Bach, Mrs. Anderson. It's better than the garbage my kids listened to." He took a deep breath, apparently pleased with how the meeting had gone. "It was a pleasure to meet you, Mrs. Anderson. You'll forgive me if I don't get up to see you out. The old knee's been acting up."

"Of course," Connie said, rising. "All of this is just between the two of us, right, doctor?"

"Yes. Completely confidential. Always."

Connie worried—not that people would learn the details of Gene's strange behavior, which had been her worry before the meeting, but that they would say that Connie was trying to have him committed.

"Show me the way, Lord," Connie whispered as she drove home. "Send someone to show me the way."

And God had answered her prayer. She had had her spiritual awakening. That had been over a year ago.

Gene behaved himself through the rest of the service, so in the car after church Connie allowed him to punch the button on the dashboard that realigned the mileage meter to a row of zeros (as he insisted he must before any trip), and they headed to Boise. Eula sat in a slight depression in the countryside, a basin in which, this time of year, the molasses-smelling smoke from the sugar factory pooled with worse odors from the stockyards along the railroad tracks. To drive out of town felt a little like elbowing yourself up out of a bed that was cozy, yes, but which smelled of a night's worth of sweat and digestion. Connie mounted that first gentle ridge where twin wheat fields rose slightly, then lay flat on either side of the highway like the yellowed pages of an open book. The wildfires had been extinguished weeks ago. The haze had cleared, and now blue sky whitened where it met the earth in a crisp line that was interrupted by a ship-like butte, then again ran perfectly flat until turning jagged with the distant mountains ahead, beyond Boise. In the rearview mirror Connie could see beyond Eula's jumble of trees and rooftops and billboards advertising cheap accommodations to the pale, treeless folds of the Owyhee Mountains.

Twenty minutes of driving north or south would have taken Connie through the irrigated belt that lined the Snake River, up to where the green ceased and the scrub took over. The earth seemed to lose its meat here and become dry, as if a vast rock—a skull—rose underground, leaving only the thinnest skin of soil. That was a lonely territory of jackrabbits and coyotes and dying ranch towns populated by leathery-skinned cowboys. Driving to Boise, however, she stayed parallel to the river, so the comforting patchwork landscape littered with houses and silos continued for forty-five minutes, until it disappeared behind walls meant to shield the subdivisions from the highway's noise. Then the city opened before her with its two tall buildings like sentries guarding the gleaming white egg of the capitol dome.

Connie drove downtown and parked in front of the magazine store, which was actually a smoke shop. It seemed as old as Boise itself; the same neon cigarette had glowed in the window on the Sundays thirty years earlier when Connie would come with her father to buy tobacco and papers. He quit on doctor's orders years ago, but the fingertips of his right hand were still yellow. He now kept a toothpick at the corner of his mouth, as if holding the spot for his beloved cigarette, should it ever choose to return.

Connie and Gene entered the store, which smelled like her father. Connie read a gardening magazine while Gene, on his knees, rifled through pages of newsprint. After twenty minutes, he came and stood before her, holding a great pile: three big Sunday newspapers and two glossy science magazines. "Now, Gene, don't get used to this," Connie said as they walked to the front. "It's even more than last week. We can't afford it." But Connie was secretly glad to do something so normal for her son. She would have preferred magazines about cars or airplanes—these science magazines, she imagined, might include propaganda like evolution and the "Big Bang"—but still.

Connie put the pile on the counter, caught a glimpse of pornography behind the register, and turned quickly away.

"Excuse me, sir," Gene said. Even when he followed Connie's rules about how to speak politely, his voice sounded abrupt.

"What kin I do for ya, little feller?" The old man peered over the counter. He had a face that bulged in parts, then pinched at the eyes like a lopsided potato. The tube of a hearing aide entered his head at the ear. Connie could imagine him looking at dirty pictures when there were no customers.

"Please set aside one *New York Times* every day this week for me. I will buy them next Sunday."

"*Gene!*" said Connie with an airy laugh. She made a quarter-turn toward a man standing behind holding a box of cigars. "Don't pester the nice man."

"How 'bout this, little feller? We usually have extras that I toss at the end of the day. If you're a good boy and mind your ma," he winked at Connie, "I'll save 'em and give 'em to ya fer free."

"That's very nice," said Connie.

Gene appeared to be confused by the man's offer, and said nothing.

Connie paid the man. "Come on, Gene," she said. She loaded his arms with his purchases and guided him toward the door.

"THANK YOU!" said Gene, too loudly, as they left.

GENE GOBBLED HIS food at dinner, in a rush to get to his reading. "May I be excused?" he asked.

"You may."

Gene raced to the sink, washed his plate by running water over it, squirting it with dishwashing liquid, and rubbing it quickly with his bare hand. Then he went down the hallway and closed the accordion door that shut his room off from the rest of the trailer. Only when he pressed the handle against its magnet did his movements become ginger and precise.

It was all right. Connie would give the plate a good cleaning later.

At bedtime, Connie came into Gene's room, and told him his time was up. He got under the covers, and she knelt by his bed. "God in heaven," Gene said, "thank You for this earth that we live on and the force of gravity that keeps us here. Thank You for the living things—people, flowers, and animals—and the nonliving things—oceans, houses, and computers. Forgive me for the sins I committed today and bless my mother. In Jesus' name, amen."

It was the prayer she had had him compose years ago, and he had repeated it monotonously every night since. She bent to kiss him. "I love you, Gene," she said.

He touched her hair, then felt her earlobe, just as he had done when he was a baby. It made her smile. His eyes didn't meet hers, but looked up, perhaps at the hairs that had escaped her bun and caught the hall light.

She closed the door and sat down on her bed. This was her room; her bed was divided from the rest of the trailer only by a dresser, and from it she could hear the refrigerator's hum and click. Now she would read her Bible, then her devotionals, then spend her half-hour or so in prayer.

In the middle of the night, it rained.

Rain was unusual in Eula. All through the summer the lawns had been kept green by hose-connected sprinklers that created a fan-shaped plume that slowly waved back and forth, making a split-second rainbow with every pass, or by a man who sprayed back and forth as mechanically as a sprinkler until his thumb grew numb. It was simpler for those living among the fields outside town. They would shove a dike into the ditch on irrigation day, and the whole lawn (and, possibly, driveway and basement) would be flooded. Their kids and the neighbor kids and even some friends from town would race across the sun-speckled lawn kicking the water high into the trees, then bend to gather it in their cupped hands and toss it in each other's faces. They'd run and slide until they made a mud slick, and their fathers would holler from the porch, "You kids stop that! You're wreckin' the dang grass!" while the quieter ones would gather into buckets the earthworms that had been flooded to the surface. Later, they would sell these worms to the Bait Shack on the boulevard for a dollar a pound. (The excitement of watching the big, mucusy mass roll into the metal tray on the scale—*How much will I get?*—would usually turn into disappointment: only enough for McDonald's and a matinee.) Their mothers would always steal a handful of worms to toss over the fence into the vegetable garden almost superstitiously, as if they were charms.

Those who lived in the hills near Lake Overlook didn't have to bother, as sprinkler systems that had been embedded in their lawns before they bought their houses would turn on automatically, controlled by a timer or by someone at the property-management company, no one knew.

The people in the trailer parks had no lawns.

So on this September night warm enough that Eulans had their windows open but not so warm as to make them turn on a fan, the rain drew everyone at least partway out of sleep.

Connie, who was a light sleeper, registered the tiny *tic tic tic* as the smallest sound there was, the aural equivalent to a pinprick at the tip of your finger. Then quickly it increased so there was nothing specific about it anymore: it was a wash, a huge sound like wind in a wheat field or (she imagined) the ocean. And then like a solo backed by a symphony, another individual sound rose—the splatter of a stream falling from the corner of the roof onto the asphalt. She thought of blind people. She had read something written by a blind man who said that the different sounds made by the rain against surfaces made it so he could see those surfaces, in a way. When it rained, he could see his garden. And this made Connie think of Marlene Bailey, the church organist whose parents were both deaf. At an ice cream social in the church gymnasium, Marlene had been telling a story and couldn't remember the name of a family friend. "What was his name!" she said, looking around, until she spotted her mother. She gave the floor a quick, deft stomp with her heel, not loud but firm, and her mother immediately looked over. In sign, Marlene asked what the person's name was, and her mother spelled it out using one hand. "Of course!" Marlene said and continued her story.

Connie was sleepy enough to admit that Marlene Bailey was a hero to her, someone who had achieved a degree of holiness in her daily life. And Gene had something missing, like a blind or deaf person, but harder. *If only he were deaf,* she thought, and before she could catch herself wishing such a thing, she fell back asleep.

Next door, Enrique and Lina were both such deep sleepers that the rain only lifted them from dreams they would never remember to ones closer to the quiet roar and lovely fragrance of the world. Lina dreamed that she was driving on a dark and rainy road, and Enrique dreamed, as he often did, of giant birds—storks and cranes with yellow leathery legs as tall as telephone poles, flamingoes with their backward-working knees—all marching across the Earth. The strange undulations of bird-walking—the thrust forward of the beak, the dip of the curved neck, the slow heave and settle of the body—looked even stranger from down here, lying in the grass. Their huge feet tented as they lifted, then they sailed through the air to flatten on the ground many yards away. But in this dream, he was safe. They wouldn't pluck him from the grass, as they had before, to fly him off to their huge roosts in the red wall of a canyon.

Coop was asleep, not in the house in Eula that he shared with his uncle, but in another out in the country, halfway to Homedale, where the rain arrived some minutes later. He was in the arms of Maria, the woman he had quietly loved for over ten years now. The beautiful sound was not rain, but *her*, and he pressed her to him, from face to hips to knees, and she kissed him without waking.

So it rained, and Eula rustled in its beds for a little while, enjoying something that was beautiful because it was rare.

Eulans were quietly perplexed by cousins in Northern California, where the fog crept in and out daily and August nights were cold, by uncles in Oklahoma towns outfitted with tornado sirens, and by grandchildren in the South, where the thunder rolled from one side of the sky to the other—"God moving His furniture." Eula was very cold in winter and very hot in summer, but the air was so dry that neither extreme got inside one's skin. Eula pumped water from Lake Overlook up into the water tower (a canary-yellow mushroom labeled "Eula" as if that were the name of water itself), then let it flow over the fields and lawns and into the Snake River. Weatherwise, there was no place simpler.

CHAPTER 3

Dress kind of old." That's what Winston had said to Wanda over the phone the day before. At the time, it had stirred her vanity a little, and she had smiled. What he had meant was that they would never believe that Wanda, at thirty-one, was the mother of Winston, a high school senior, unless she made herself look older. Now, as she flipped through the stained tops in her closet and rifled through the jeans in her bureau, all of them snug-fitting, she wished she would have listened to what Winston said and actually considered what she would wear, rather than collapsing onto the couch with a Newport Menthol, a glass of sun tea, and her last pain pill, settling into the happy truth that she'd have a hundred dollars to buy five more pills tomorrow, and, as part of the deal, get to spend the afternoon with Winston. She wished she would have listened to him, because now she realized that she had nothing at all motherly to wear.

Then the phone rang. It was Winston, calling to make sure they were on. From the echoing shouts in the background Wanda could tell he was calling from the stairwell pay phone at Eula High. Wanda had once used that phone to call in a bomb threat to the school in order to get out of a geometry midterm.

"When you said I should dress old," she said, "what did you mean?"

"I meant that you should try to look older than you are. Like, responsible," Winston said.

"Well, I looked through my clothes and I couldn't find nothin' like that."

"And you're telling me this an hour before we're supposed to leave?"

"Sorry."

Winston was quiet for a moment, then he made a sound that showed that his throat had been tensed in exasperation and had at last released his breath—a tiny, grumpy dam-break. "Think of what *your* mother wears," he said. "It can't be that hard."

This caused a flutter of panic in Wanda's heart. First came the memory of her mother's pants, jeans with an elastic waistband that she wore nearly every day. They gave room to her belly, which was round as a bowling ball and low, a grotesque bulge, though her arms had become spindly. This was the body drinking had given her—that of a wizened old woman, pregnant not with something living and growing but something dead. Her mother had been wearing these jeans when she died. Wanda had awoken on a Sunday morning not long after her eleventh birthday and went downstairs to find her mother curled up on the couch, facing away from the blaring TV. This was not unusual. But on this morning there was a nasty, unfamiliar odor in the room—the caustic smell of bile or something else from deep in the body, some essence, some ugly fuel that had kept her mother living and was released only with her ghost. Wanda walked toward her mother. She put her hand to her mother's hip, the elastic waist of those jeans, and shook. The whole body rocked as one, something living things cannot do. Wanda climbed onto the couch to look into her face. Then she was wild, running to one window and then the next, throwing each open with a bang. And—did it occur to her then, or only now as she remembered?—how *alive* the curtains looked, billowing into the room with the cool breeze, turning up their hems in graceful gestures!

This memory was followed quickly by the realization that Winston didn't know that her mother was dead. Should she tell him? Of course not! But she pitied him, as if she already had: for the shock of the news, for the remorse he would undoubtedly feel for bringing it up, and even for the imaginings of his own mother's future death it might kindle. This pity for Winston, even though she hadn't told him, outshone her memories and became the prevalent emotion of the moment. Then she scrambled unsuccessfully for a response.

This was how her heart cast about in fits when she was out of painkillers—twisting and flipping like a fish that had slid out of her grasp and onto the hot aluminum floor of her uncle's fishing boat.

"What do you wear to church?" Winston asked.

"Of course!" she said. "I know just the thing. I'll see you at noon."

Using the stepladder from the kitchen, Wanda got down the box from the top of the closet, took out the dress, and laid it out on the bed. The fabric was silky rayon with a floral print; a bit springy for late September, but she'd wear her black overcoat, too. This coat was coming apart in the back, but she'd take it off in the courtroom and fold it over her arm. When she tried on the dress, though, the seams hung off her shoulders, and the lacy V-neck plunged farther down between her wide-set, cone-shaped breasts than she remembered. ("They look like party hats," Hank had said once, holding both breasts out by the nipples. Wanda had laughed, even though it hurt.) In the mirror she could see the hard plate of bone in the center of her chest, from which her ribs radiated like the spokes of a lady's fan. The last time she had worn this dress, two years ago, she had been fuller, meatier, and prouder. Oh, well. It would have to do.

She found the overcoat in the back of the closet and went out to the porch to smoke while she waited for Winston.

"You shore look nice!" yelled Darrell from across the street. "What's the occasion?" He was bent over, burrowing into some piece of machinery in his driveway. Was it a furnace?

"Nothin'," called Wanda. "Just goin' to Boise with a friend."

A kid rode by on a bicycle, and Skeet, Darrell's dog, came charging off the porch, barking his head off. The kid stood up to pump madly on the bike pedals. Darrell swiftly threw a pipe that rotated in the air and hit the dirt just in Skeet's path, sending the dog in a quick U-turn back to the porch, where he shifted from paw to paw and groaned.

"Good shot!" said Wanda.

"Only kids on bikes!" said Darrell. "Leaves the mailman and everybody else alone 'cept kids on bikes. You'd think they'd learn not to ride by here."

Darrell went back to his burrowing and Wanda blew out a stream of white smoke that disappeared against the white sky. Her porch wasn't really a porch. Every unit in her block-long two-story complex had its little box of a balcony that accommodated an easy chair or a bicycle, not both. The upstairs neighbors' balcony hung over hers. They were boys who commuted to Boise State University, although it seemed they rarely attended class. Last January they had thrown a keg party (Wanda had taken a pill and slept through it) and had left the keg out on the balcony overnight. The beer had expanded in the cold, seeped out of the keg, leaked down, and formed long icicles over her balcony that cast a pretty amber light on Wanda's sliding glass door in the morning. However, not knowing what these yellow icicles were and worrying that they might contain a dangerous chemical, Wanda phoned the boys. One of them staggered down, red-eyed in his sweats and ski jacket. He broke off a thick icicle and licked it. "Want one?" he asked.

Winston's big Buick pulled up. Wanda ran inside for her purse and keys, and jogged down to the car. There was a boy in the passenger seat she had never met before. Wanda got in the back.

"Is that what you're wearing?" asked Winston.

"Yeah. What?"

"I don't know, it's just kind of . . . revealing."

"Oh." Wanda looked down between her breasts, then quickly up at the boy in the passenger seat, who looked away. "It's a church dress," she said.

"It's just real summery," said Winston, "and it's not summer anymore."

"I thought I'd wear this coat, too."

"Yeah, but not in the courtroom. Do you have anything else?"

"No."

"Shit." Winston put the car in drive and sped, bouncing, down the street and around the corner onto the boulevard. "We'll have to get you something, then." He drove toward the interstate that would take them to Boise, then veered swiftly into the parking lot of a strip mall. The store largest and farthest from the boulevard was a Dress Barn. He pulled into the fire lane and left the car running.

"Gary, move the car if somebody makes you. Gimme twenty bucks."

The boy dug in his pocket for a bill.

"Wanda, this is Gary," said Winston. "You're gonna play his mom, so maybe you two should get acquainted. I'll be right back."

"I thought I was gonna play *your* mom," Wanda said.

"Didn't you listen to anything I said?" Winston demanded. "I'm eighteen. I don't need to bring a parent. I paid my fine. I'm done. Gary's seventeen."

Winston slammed the door and disappeared into the store, and the car was quiet.

"Hi," Gary said over the top of the passenger seat. He was big, like Winston, but softer, chubbier, and more sloped in the shoulder. He had the longest eyelashes Wanda had ever seen on a boy, and for a moment he appeared to her a frightened forest creature peering over a tree root.

"Hi," said Wanda.

Gary heaved his backpack into his lap, which made Wanda remember that he and Winston were cutting school to go to court. "Here, I took this from my mom's wallet. I was afraid to take her driver's license, 'cause she might miss it. It's her sports club ID. She never goes."

Wanda took the card and looked at the tiny photo. It was the face of a real mother—round, generous, and exhausted. "It doesn't look like me," she said.

"Yeah, I know. Winston says they won't ask you for an ID, but I thought, just in case."

"It'd probably be better if I just say I forgot my purse," said Wanda, giving him the card back.

He nodded.

Wanda took out her cigarettes and began searching the complicated door for a way to open the window. Gary pushed a button up front that did it for her. "Wow, electric," Wanda said. She lit the cigarette and blew the smoke as far out of the car as possible. Then she sat leaning against the door and dangling the arm that held the cigarette out the window.

"So, what do you do?" she asked Gary.

He stifled a laugh. "I go to high school," he said.

"Yeah, I mean, in high school, what do you do?"

Gary shrugged. "I dunno."

"Do you wrestle?"

"Yeah."

"Are you on the team with Winston?"

"Yeah."

"Well, there ya go. That's what you do," Wanda said, and she took another drag.

"I took photography last year," Gary said.

"Oh?"

"Yeah. I was supposed to be on yearbook, but I couldn't fit it in."

Something in the tone of this last sentence told Wanda that one of his parents had forbidden it. Maybe it had come down to yearbook or wrestling.

"Sorry," she said.

Gary shrugged and looked off toward the store. "For what?" he said.

"Do you have a girlfriend?" asked Wanda.

Gary blushed. "No," he said. The blush climbed his neck, then spread like a mottled rash onto his cheek, as if bloody fingers had left their prints on his white skin. Wanda was fascinated. She had never watched someone blush in so detailed a manner, and it reminded her of an old book she had read where young ladies "coloured"—with a *U*—then hid behind their fans when men looked their way.

"You're shy!" Wanda said, and she reached out to pinch his shoulder, which wasn't as soft as she expected.

"Stop it," said Gary.

"You're a big enough boy to get in the type of trouble you need to go to court in Boise to fix, but you still blush around girls."

"Don't tease me, please," he said.

There was something old-fashioned about this kid. It was cute. His mother had taught him manners.

"Okay, I'm sorry." She smiled in such a way as to let him know she wasn't, really. "Do you have brothers and sisters?"

"Two little sisters."

"And what about your mom?" said Wanda.

It seemed Gary remembered he was preparing her for a role. "Oh, right. She answers phones in the afternoons at Eula Feed and Supply."

"What's her name?"

"Theresa. Theresa," then he said a last name that sounded to Wanda something like "void check house key."

"What was that?"

"Theresa Void Check House Key. My dad is Polish."

"How do you spell that?"

Gary handed her the ID again.

The car door opened and Winston tossed a bag onto the seat next to Wanda. "We're gonna be late. Don't smoke in the car." They tore out of the parking lot, back onto the boulevard, then onto the highway toward Boise.

Wanda dropped the cigarette out the window, opened the bag, and took out a navy-blue-and-white dress. She knew at a glance it was too big for her. It had long sleeves with white cuffs and a white yoke that tied in front like a sailor's scarf. She tugged at the scarf to see if she could remove it, but the knot was stitched. A paper tag covered in two red clearance stickers, whose prices were scratched out and halved, then halved again, was attached to the label with a plastic tab. The last price was $5.99. Winston hadn't given Gary his change. Attached to the sleeve of the dress with the same type of plastic tab was a floppy white hat.

"There's a hat," Wanda said miserably.

"Yeah, I think you should wear it," said Winston.

"Why?"

"You're so *blond* right now, Wanda. I thought it would be better to cover it up. Not that it looks bad. It's just, you know."

She touched her hair, which felt like hay. It did look bad, she knew. She had bleached it on Monday, and had been meaning to give it the conditioning treatment that eased the color from straw to caramel, but she hadn't gotten around to it. All the aches in her joints and the craving in her chest that had subsided while she interviewed Gary now returned, and she felt tears coming on.

Would you trade two of the pills you'll have later for half of one now?

Yes.

Would you give the hundred dollars to have a better dress and pretty, conditioned hair?

Well, no. But I would give twenty-five.

(All her life Wanda had bargained with this power who, in school, had been God: *Would you shave off your eyebrows if it meant Billy would ask you to the dance?* No. *Would you shoot a stranger in the head if it brought your mother back to life?* Yes. The power had long since lost his name.)

"Maybe you should put it on now," Winston said gently. "We'll be in kind of a rush once we get there."

Wanda retreated into the corner of the seat, hiked up her dress, and pulled it off over her head. She sheltered her chest with one hand as she used the other to open the new dress from underneath and determine which was the front and which was the back. She was careful not to look up at Gary's mirror. Her body looked ugly and crumpled, her belly creasing as she dressed in this cramped space, and she didn't want to know if Gary was watching her. And if he was, she didn't want to embarrass him by catching him. She pulled the dress on, and tried to smooth it. She had never worn anything so stiff, starched, and ugly. She began to cry.

Winston looked over his shoulder. "It's pretty," he said, and looked back to the road. On his second look he noticed she was crying. "What are you doing? Don't cry."

Gary turned to look at her.

"It's so ugly," Wanda whimpered.

"It's not ugly, it's pretty," Winston said. "I told you so already."

Wanda looked down at herself. The front of the dress showed squares as regular as floor tiles—the creases where the dress had been folded and placed into a plastic bag, which was then shipped in a box with the fifty other dresses exactly like it from the distribution center to the Dress Barn. Wanda had once worked in the stock room at K-mart, so she knew how this worked. Wanda would hang and tag the garments, then quickly steam away the creases. Dress Barn didn't even bother to steam their dresses. This was why no one shopped there, except Mexicans. Wanda was sure neither of these boys' mothers would ever be caught dead in a Dress Barn dress.

"Seriously, Wanda, don't cry. This is important. You can't get weird about this."

"I'm not cryin'," said Wanda. "And I know it's important."

Wanda quickly ran her hands over the fabric, then she wiped her face, rested her hand over her mouth, and looked out the window.

Winston softened his voice. "Really, Wanda, you look *so* pretty. Doesn't she, Gary?"

Gary didn't want to lie. Wanda could tell he agreed with her and pitied her. But he lied anyway: "You look pretty," he said.

"You two just shut up. I'm sure you think I'm cryin' just to get you to say that."

"No, Wanda, you look really pretty. Blue is your color."

"Winston, I'm gonna do my job. Don't worry. I'm gonna play the part, and I'm gonna do good. There's no reason to lie and say it's a pretty dress when it's ugly as homemade sin."

"It's pretty and it'll do," said Winston. "And if everything goes right, Gary will take you and buy you a better dress after."

Wanda looked to Gary, expecting him to protest, but he didn't. He grinned and nodded.

"You're sweet," said Wanda. She felt like she was done crying.

For a while she watched the countryside go by. It was a busy time. Monstrous machines lumbered slowly through the fields gathering food off bushes the way whales filter krill from the ocean. The biggest creatures ate the smallest—she had seen this on *Nova*.

"Theresa Wojciechowski," Wanda practiced. "Theresa Wojciechowski." Then she tried a more conversational tone: "*Theresa Wojciechowski.*" It was an interesting name, and had dignity. It came from far away on a boat and kept its chin up against the battering winds of the sea. Gary's mom probably had to spell it out for people several times a day.

Wojciechowski? I never heard a name like that. What kinda name is that?

It's Polack. My husband is a Polack.

Gary's friends probably called her Mrs. W, even though it sounded like a V. Theresa Wojciechowski.

"I think you've got it," said Winston.

"Huh?"

"You can stop saying that name over and over."

Wanda gave it one more try in a cocktail-party voice. "Ther*e*sa Wojcie*chow*ski."

Both boys laughed. Gary shook his head guiltily.

"Do your friends call her Mrs. W?" Wanda asked.

"No."

"What do they call her?"

"Theresa."

Wanda hardly felt older than these boys, but here was a difference: she would never have called a friend's mother by her first name.

As they approached Boise, Winston gave Wanda a brief description of what had happened. They had gotten stoned with some friends on the Boise strip on a Friday night, and their good time had gotten a bit out of hand. Wanda listened, but not closely. How much of these details would Gary have told to his real mother? She didn't want to over-prepare, especially since, although Winston hadn't put it into words, it seemed her job would be to sit and contritely accept whatever punishment the judge handed down.

They took the City Center exit, and Wanda felt a thrill that overcame both the craving and the nervousness. Even though she was grown-up and had been to Portland, it still excited her to see the tops of Boise's two tall buildings peep over the horizon. The highway was landscaped here on the entrance to downtown, with red lava rocks and spider-shaped juniper bushes that seemed never to grow from year to year.

"Okay, Wanda, are you ready?" Winston asked when they reached the courthouse.

Wanda pulled the hat onto her head and opened the door. The dress was too long, and as she climbed out of the car, she stepped on the skirt. She bent over to brush dust off the hem and put her hand to the car for balance, the very moment Winston was closing her door. He reached out to stop it from slamming, but only managed to slow it. The door banged Wanda's thumb and bounced back open. Wanda yelped.

"Oh my God," Winston said. "Are you all right?"

She stood upright, and a stoic look came over her face. She held her thumb in her other hand. Winston took this bundle in his own two hands and squeezed. His eyes were desperate and penitent. Wanda clung to her role; it helped with the pain. "I'm okay," she said.

Winston slowly opened his hands and cupped Wanda's fist like a captured butterfly. Then Wanda opened her hand. It wasn't so bad—just a little smear of blood and a mark that looked like a smudge of blue ink.

"It's fine," she said. And it was. She was a mother now.

She turned to Gary, and took from him the wad of tissues he had found in the car. "Thank you, Gary," she said.

They entered the courthouse. The woman at the front desk looked up their names ("Theresa Wojciechowski," Wanda said with an emphatic nod, then she spelled out the last name fluently as if she were singing the alphabet) and gave them a card with their assigned courtroom number. "Now, you just go right on up there, have a seat and wait to be called, 'K?" the woman squeaked in the over-enunciated voice women use with children. Did she talk like this to the hardened criminals who came through here?

Wanda led the boys up the wide limestone staircase, found the courtroom, and quietly went in. It was two o'clock; right on time. They sat in the back row and waited. Wanda held a tissue around her thumb in such a way that it was almost unnoticeable.

To her surprise, the judge was not an old man with white hair. He was a Mexican, and only perhaps in his early forties. He did, though, wear the kind of reading glasses she expected judges to wear, low on his nose. He had no accent. *A judge!* thought Wanda. *He must be the most powerful Mexican in Idaho.*

The judge heard one case after another, all men, all drunk drivers. Sometimes the arresting officer was in court to report the details of the case but, more often, the clerk read aloud from an officer's statement. The sad men told their lies, gave their excuses, and made their apologies. The judge nodded patiently and unbelievingly, then elevated his eyebrows and handed down harsh sentences as casually as a doctor writing a prescription. The men reacted by dropping their heads, stunned. When he permanently revoked a repeat-offender's license, the bent old man whimpered, "How'm I gonna git home?" This was the one moment the judge's temper flared: "You're going to have to start thinking about how you're going to get anywhere, sir, because you're not driving." The old man was shaking visibly as he walked down the aisle and out the door.

Wanda was a bit disappointed. There was no gavel to slam, and none of the offenders took the witness stand. They just sat at the long table in front. She had been hoping to take the stand, like the mothers of murdered children did on *L.A. Law*. On the other hand, it would be good to sit with the table blocking the horrible dress from the judge's view.

After an hour, Wanda's attention began to wander. From her place between the boys she imagined she could feel warmth from Winston's shoulder. She resisted the temptation to look over at him. She wished that he was again desperate and apologetic, squeezing her hands in his. Wanda lay her hand, with its thumb wrapped and dully throbbing, on the bench next to his. She knew he would never hold her hand, but she wanted it to be there, available, even for an unintentional brushing, a spark.

Winston inspired in Wanda a quiet, blinking respect. He seemed to confront and move people aside as easily as someone flips through garments in a closet—as if he owned them. She had met him at the apartment of Gideon, a pot dealer who lived in her complex. Who was this good-looking kid sitting on the floor, smoking pot, and playing a race-car game on Atari? He seemed completely at ease with Gideon's friends, some of whom had done time. He called them douche bags when their cars tumbled and burned. Then he looked at his watch and said, "Shit, I've got to get home." He didn't say it, but it was dinnertime. He leaped up, paid Gideon for a bag of pot, which he threw in his gym bag, then left, having failed to notice Wanda.

"Who's Junior?" Wanda asked Gideon.

Gideon screwed his face up and smiled with his rotten teeth. "Some rich kid. Why you want to know?"

Wanda slugged him in the arm. There was something perverted about Gideon. Wanda had always wondered if he had bent over for the men in prison.

The clerk called them. "Gary Waj . . . Waj-check—?"

"*Wojciechowski!*" Wanda sprang up and dragged Gary forward. Before sitting, she smoothed her dress and registered on her face a look of humility and perseverance.

A few moments passed as the Mexican judge read some papers. Then he looked up. "Is Officer Smith here?"

"Here, Your Honor." A policeman rose from his seat and came up to occupy a spot at the other table.

Then the judge looked over his glasses at Wanda and Gary. "Forgive me. Could you tell me how to pronounce your last name again?"

Gary inhaled to answer, but Wanda cut him off. "Wojciechowski, Your Honor. I'm Theresa, and this is my son, Gary. It's a Polack name, Your Honor. My husband is a Polack."

Everyone laughed, even the policeman. Wanda glanced around the room quickly and tried to smile. What had she said?

The judge stiffened for a second, then he relaxed, took off his glasses, and folded them. He allowed this moment of levity before getting down to business. "Thank you. Tim, why don't you give us your report? No need to stand."

"Well, Your Honor, about eleven p.m., Friday, September fifth, we got some calls about kids raising hell on the strip, turning over garbage cans, a coupla car windows smashed. Officer Reade and I was standing on the corner of Ninth and Idaho, and we hear a disturbance mid-block. A business owner, Mr. Merrick of the pharmacy down there, was arguing with a buncha kids, knocked over the city trash outside his store. Some of the kids run off, but Officer Reade and I apprehended two of 'em: one's this young man, the other was over eighteen. There was no blood alcohol level. We ticketed the boys and let 'em go."

"Thank you."

Gary, now under the judge's unbroken attention, looked down at his hands, which were twisting and knotting, his fingers bright red.

"Young man?"

"Yes, sir."

"Did you overturn a city waste receptacle?"

Wanda detected the slightest smile behind the judge's stern expression.

"No, sir."

"It's customary to address a judge as 'Your Honor.'"

"Excuse me, Your Honor."

"Would you mind telling me who *did* upset the receptacle?"

"This kid Carl."

The judge looked away impatiently, then quickly back to Gary. "And did you or *this kid Carl* or any other member of your party overturn any other waste receptacle or break any car windows or damage any other property that night?"

"No, Your Honor."

"Do you mind looking at me when you answer?"

"Sorry, Your Honor."

The judge eased himself back into his chair. "Tim," he said without looking away from Gary, "I don't know if I believe this young man."

The officer smiled and looked down.

"Your Honor, might I say something?" Wanda said.

The judge looked a little wary. "Yes, Mrs. Wojciechowski."

"I would never dream of interrupting the proceedings, it's just that we've played out this scene in our living room about a hundred times over the past two weeks, and I thought I'd save you some time. Gary swears up and down he didn't do it, and so does Winston, Gary's friend, the over-eighteen kid. Well, there's been days when we've believed them and days when we didn't. Finally one night, after praying and thinking it over, things became perfectly clear to me. I turned to my Lawrence and I said, 'Honey, whether he did it or didn't, the punishment's the same. Whether he overturned one receptacle or he smashed them car windows too, I want to soundly punish Gary in a way he won't forget.' Lawrence agreed with me, Your Honor.

"See, Gary's always been a sweet, gentle boy who minds his manners. That's the type of boy I raised. Not some ruffian who barrels down the street in Boise raising Ned. The biggest animals on earth, Your Honor, whales, eat the smallest, little bitty shrimp. I will not let my Gary become some monster that eats and destroys without thinking. I've seen it happen to other men. They hurt and kill and damage property, then go on their way without looking back. I'd rather Gary be a shrimp who fights fair. The meek shall inherit the earth, that's what I've always taught him."

The craving in Wanda's heart and the pain in her thumb throbbed in unison now and overcame her. She choked back tears and lifted the tissue to her face, until she realized it was speckled with blood. She wiped her eyes with her other hand. Gary placed his hand on her shoulder.

"I'm sorry, Your Honor. I'm almost done. Gary won't tell us the names of those other boys. Says he just met them that night. Carl. I don't know no Carl. Well, whoever it was, Gary won't be seeing them for quite some time. Gary's been grounded since that night, and will be for the next two months. He lost his car privileges except to and from school. He does his homework, spends some family time, then goes to his room.

"We, as a family, volunteer every Saturday at the Mennonite soup kitchen. Have for years. Lawrence and I decided Gary should work there Sundays after church as well, and go to the Wednesday administrative meetings. Sure, he griped at first, but he's done real good. He'll keep on after his punishment's over."

Wanda allowed herself a glance at Gary, whose jaw hung open like a broken drawer.

"Your Honor, my friends think me and Lawrence are being too hard on Gary. I tell them that if I have any power at all as his mother, Gary will never darken the door of a courtroom again. He will never damage another person's property. He will never harm a person littler than himself."

Now Wanda broke down and hid her face against Gary's shoulder. Then she lifted herself. "Thank you, Your Honor."

The judge sat for a long time, holding the tip of his reading glasses in his teeth. A fear gripped Wanda's heart. What if he put down the glasses and said, "Miss, you don't seem old enough to be this young man's mother"? Instead he put them on again, leaned forward, and wrote some words on the forms. Then he stacked them and pushed them away.

"In cases like these," he said, "I usually levy a fine and require that the offender spend some time in community service. However, I would guess that you, Mrs. Wojciechowski, and your husband would be burdened with the fine, and not your son. I certainly don't want to punish you when you appear to be raising the boy right. And as far as community service, you've already got him involved in projects more worthwhile than painting hydrants. So," he turned to Gary, "young man, I have two requirements of you. Are you listening?"

"Yes, Your Honor."

"One, honor your mother, just as it says in the Bible."

Gary nodded.

"And, two, tell that Polack he's a lucky man."

Back in Eula, Winston's sister, Liz, walked back and forth in front of the high school entrance, her thumbs hooked into the front pockets of her jeans. She was waiting for Winston, and had been for a half-hour. Her car was in the shop, and he was her ride home. All her friends had left already, and his car wasn't where he had parked it that morning. Maybe he had gone to McDonald's for lunch, and parked it somewhere else when he returned, or maybe he and Jay had decided to cut school. He was such a show-off, sweet when they were alone, braiding her hair as they watched TV, then disowning her when the guys showed up. She'd give him five more minutes, then call her mom from the pay phone.

Liz and Winston were easily identifiable as twins, but their sharp features, so delicate they could have been sculpted with a toothpick, made the boy somewhat elfish and the girl simply beautiful. And while Winston's hair was plain brown, Liz's was chestnut with strands of real red. Faint freckles splattered her cheeks and forehead like dried rust water on a window.

A Maverick pulled up in front of her, driven by Jay. He hoisted himself up to sit in the car window so he could talk to her over the roof of the car.

"Hey, Liz."

"Hey, Jay. Have you seen Winston?"

"I was going to ask you the same thing."

"Great," she said, looking down at the toe of her sneaker, which was grinding into the concrete sidewalk as if Liz were crushing an insect.

"Do you need a ride?"

"Yeah."

"Hop in."

They drove out of the parking lot, past the cow field, onto the road that headed out toward Lake Overlook. Eula Schools had been built on the eastern edge of town in the late 1950s, since it was in that direction (toward the interstate and Boise) that the town was predicted to expand. But instead, the town had stretched south toward Lake Overlook, where the rich people lived, and north toward the sugar factory, where poor people worked, leaving Eula Schools still on the edge of town. There was a field next to the high school parking lot that contained what may have been the most abused cows in Idaho. They had been chased, ridden, pelted with rocks, and, once, spray-painted and herded by kids from a rival high school onto the Eula High football field during a game.

"So, how have you been?" Jay asked.

"Fine, you?"

"Fine."

"You're living at your mom's, right?" Liz asked.

"Yep."

"How's that?"

"Oh, excellent. We get along great. She lets me do whatever I want. It really feels more like living on my own than anything." Liz had never heard such wild insistence in Jay's voice. He must have heard it too, for when she glanced at him, he jutted his chin up and turned briefly to watch a passing car. Then he added, "I still go to the Van Bekes' a lot."

"Sounds good," said Liz. She had only asked to be polite. She didn't really care.

They crested a hill and Lake Overlook lay sparkling before them.

"Wonder what happened to Winston," said Jay.

"Yeah. I figured he was with you and the guys."

"Why?" Jay asked.

"Why?"

"We're not, like, married."

"Okay," Liz said with a whatever-you-say laugh.

"No, really," said Jay. "I actually feel like we're kinda, I don't know, growing apart. I'm feeling more . . . serious these days. Maybe it's moving out of Carl and Janet's, or maybe it's being a senior. Don't tell him I said that."

"I won't," Liz said, then added, turning toward him and nodding condescendingly, "We don't really talk." They had reached the Padgetts'. "Thanks for the ride," Liz said. She leaped out of the car and ran up the lawn.

Jay pulled away and left the subdivision. He drove calmly until he reached the open road. Then, as if his fist had been set on a spring, it shot out and struck the dashboard. When he withdrew it, there was a crack running between the two air-conditioning vents. A drop of blood collected on his knuckle and fell, but his face never changed.

IN THE WEEK since Mr. Peterson had announced the science fair, Gene and Enrique had failed to agree on a project. Enrique had come up with dozens of ideas that had provoked little or no response from Gene. Now, as they zigzagged down the sidewalk from the bus stop, Gene taking care to keep awnings and tree branches between him and the sky, Enrique tried again: "Gene, I know you don't want to do erosion, but it could be really neat. We could make a landscape out of dirt with little miniature trees and stuff. And we could have a fan blow it. We could show how the soil holds together when there's roots in it. What do you think?" With this, Enrique stepped forward slightly, and bent to be in Gene's line of vision.

"Erosion is boring," said Gene.

"I know erosion is boring," said Enrique, "but a model of erosion with a fan blowing dust around is neat."

"It would be boring because erosion is boring. A model of something boring is boring. A model of something neat is neat."

"Well, then, what is neat, Gene?" Enrique's voice rose into a whine. "I come up with these ideas, and you shoot them down, but you don't come up with any yourself. We only have a few days left. If we don't come up with something we both like, I'm just going to do it on my own."

They circled the car-wash parking lot and stepped through the tear in the chain-link fence to enter the trailer park. On Meadowlark and Goldfinch Lanes, the deepest corner of the trailer park away from the boulevard, bushes huddled against trailers, carports extending toward the lane like hands offered in greeting, frilly curtains hung in the windows, lawn statues and pinwheels peeped from flower beds, and an American flag hung from a pole that rose at an angle from one vinyl-sided garret. This was the quiet, respectable part of the trailer park, to which the long-term residents had migrated. The front spokes of the star-shaped trailer park—the only part visible to passing cars—was the rowdier neighborhood. For the more-or-less transient residents of these lanes, Robin and Sparrow, nothing seemed to stick to its intended purpose: cookouts became brawls; refrigerators died, moved outside, and became anchors for clotheslines; a broken-down, doorless car became a pirate ship for the children, complete with a Jolly Roger hanging from the antenna. The trailers here exposed the jacks and stilts and wood blocks that held them up off the ground, while on Meadowlark and Goldfinch Lanes, vinyl skirts modestly covered these underpinnings. It was to avoid walking down Robin or Sparrow that the boys' mothers encouraged them to enter the trailer park the back way, through the hole in the fence.

The previous spring, Gene had become interested in the mechanics behind all of those spinning brushes in the car wash. Every day the boys had peered into the building on their way by, eventually lingering and hiding when cars entered. They got home with their shirtfronts damp and smelling of ammonia. Enrique had already got bored of watching the car wash when, one afternoon, one of the men who worked there decided to come around back of the building and run them off. "I'm going to design car washes when I grow up!" Gene had shouted in defense once they were safely through the fence. Enrique had shushed him. He could be so embarrassing.

After this, Gene went through a period of stopping to examine the morning glories that grew on the fence. He began by opening the flowers—which, by the afternoon, had twisted themselves closed like hand-rolled cigarettes—then turning the flowers inside-out. Sometimes Gene picked them and took them home to perform experiments on them. He put them in his closet to see if he could make them open and close by shining a bright light on them.

Once when Enrique was over watching TV with Gene, Connie had come upon a pile of withered flowers under the kitchen sink. Her body stiffened. Then she bent and grabbed the bunch of brown sticks and crumbling petals. Enrique had feared that she would yell—that's what his mother would have done—but instead Connie came into the living room and turned off the TV, causing Gene, who hadn't yet seen what she had found, to grunt angrily.

"Gene," said Connie, holding out the sad bouquet, "give me your eyes. Give me your eyes, Gene. Give me your eyes." Finally he looked up enough to satisfy her. "Clean up after yourself, and stop destroying flowers. Do you hear me?"

Connie rarely disciplined Gene; this was one of the few times Enrique had witnessed it. (How many times had Gene seen Lina yell at Enrique about something trivial? Her outbursts were always followed by a brief period of angry cleaning, then a hug.) It occurred to Enrique, as he watched, that Gene had trained her. She was addressing him exactly in the way he wished to be addressed—quietly, clearly, from across the room.

"I'm going to be a botanist," Gene said, as if this would close the subject.

("I'm going to build a submarine." "I'm going to work at the water tower." It seemed that each new interest not only replaced the last, but consumed Gene wholly, future and all.)

"That's fine, Gene. In the meantime, clean up after yourself. Stop destroying flowers," Connie had said.

Now, as they walked down Meadowlark Lane, Enrique put aside his anger to give it another try: "Halley's Comet?"

Gene sniffed, as if the comet had personally offended him. In March the two had spent a few nights in sleeping bags in the dewy grass between their homes, and the most they had seen of the much-anticipated comet was a tiny yellow shape like a fingernail clipping among the stars.

"We could show those photos from Japan—it was brighter there—and make a diagram of its orbit."

"Come inside," Gene said.

"Why?" Enrique said.

"I want to show you something."

"Is it for the science fair?"

"Yes."

"Something we can do as a project?"

Gene didn't answer, but climbed the stairs to his trailer. Before following, Enrique called across the empty lot, "Mom?"

"Yeah?" Lina called from inside.

"I'm going to Gene's." Ever since his mother had told Enrique she had been kissed, it had been important for him to know when she got home. He paid more attention to which homes she cleaned on which days. He couldn't help it.

"Great," Lina responded after a curious pause.

The boys went into the trailer, angled their bodies to pass Connie's bed, and entered Gene's bedroom. Gene opened a drawer in his desk—it only opened halfway before it hit the bed—and pulled out a pile of newspaper clippings. He handed the first to Enrique. It was from the front page of the *Free Press*, the local newspaper. "Hundreds Poisoned in Cameroon," said the headline.

"This was last month," Enrique said. "It was a rebel attack."

"It wasn't a rebel attack," Gene said.

"What was it?"

"No one knows."

WINSTON BLASTED Def Leppard on the way back to Eula, and Gary was jubilant. Winston couldn't stop going over the details, retelling the glorious story. "Shit, Wanda, you deserve a fucking Academy Award! You cried for the judge. Gary, you got off scot-free! What a cheat! I had to pay a fine! *The meek shall inherit the earth.* Wanda, you are a master bullshitter. I fucking love you."

Gary didn't join in, but bounced gleefully in his seat.

Wanda smiled, nodded, even managed a chuckle, but she was in misery. Pain smoldered in both her thumb and chest, and occasional bolts shot up and down her arm between, just as the earth and the clouds volley bursts of electricity in a thunderstorm. It was intense, in part, because it would so soon be soothed. Without the prospect of relief her suffering would be less, she realized, but that's how life worked. And although she had gotten swept up in the lie's momentum—it had eased the pressure inside to let the story gush from her mouth—she now felt guilty. It must have taken a lot for that Mexican to become a judge, and he obviously regarded himself as hard-boiled and unflappable. How embarrassed he would feel if he knew how gullible he really was! And Mrs. Wojciechowski! The idea of this nice lady ever finding out she had been imitated, made fun of . . . Wanda couldn't bear it. She felt as if she had torn down everything right in the world.

"God!" Winston said. "The soup kitchen! How did you come up with that one?"

"Dunno," Wanda said. Never, ever could she admit that she ate at the Mennonite soup kitchen when she was broke.

She sat and watched the back of Winston's head as he babbled on. She lifted her uninjured hand and waved a little bye-bye to him, low enough that neither boy could see. He loved her now because she had lied. She hadn't even known, really, how much she wanted him until she won him—and lost him—by playing his game. By damaging property. Now she realized that she firmly believed every word she had said as Theresa Wojciechowski. She needed a pill.

"Uh, Winston," she said, "would you mind stopping by my friend's house on Garrity on the way back? I need to pick something up."

This broke Winston's mood. "Shit, Wanda, I've gotta get home or my mom's going to start calling around. I barely have time to drop you off at *your* place."

"Well then, just leave me at my friend's. It's on the way. You don't have to wait."

"How will you get home?"

"Don't worry."

Wanda wasn't worried. She'd walk if she had to. Nothing after that point was problematic. As Gideon, the pot dealer down the street, liked to say, *Drugs will provide*, referring to the lovely way things seemed to come together when you were high. It was a motto of his.

Winston drove to the house on Garrity and turned to Wanda. "Well, thanks, Wanda. That was a totally brilliant performance. Sorry we can't wait around."

"That's all right."

Gary was stiff in his seat, fiddling with something in his lap. Then he swiveled quickly and held out some bills rolled tightly into the shape of a cigarette. Wanda understood that paying her embarrassed him.

"Thanks a lot," he said.

"You're welcome."

She pulled on her overcoat, got out of the car, and walked up to the house, carrying her purse in one hand and the hat, into which she had stuffed her church dress, in the other.

Tammy made her living by caring for elderly and mentally retarded people in her home. The state paid her so much per person (more for the retarded, she had once mentioned), and so there were usually four or five people living under her care. Before Wanda knew her, Tammy had been a hospice nurse—she had lived in people's homes and eased them into death. Tammy had observed the very depths of human misery, and her heart seemed neither darkened nor enlightened by the experience. She was a regular, cheerful gal, and this alternately comforted and frightened Wanda. The pain pills (along with innumerable other medications) had been prescribed to two of Tammy's "folks," as she called them, who had died. Their deaths had been reported to the state—everything was aboveboard; old people die—but the state had never gotten around to cutting off their Medicaid, so Tammy was able to fake prescriptions and resell the pills. "The extra money improves the quality of life for my other folks," she had once said, and Wanda bought this excuse. Tammy wasn't living large. She drove an old maroon El Camino with one green door.

Wanda rang the doorbell. A dog barked next door. Wanda heard Tammy holler, "Vincent, don't answer that door!"

Vincent answered the door anyway. He stood, one eye squinted, his mouth hanging wide, his tongue slowly rising to touch the roof of his mouth, then lying back into the bed of his jaw. His tongue did these calisthenics, up and down, endlessly. Vincent always answered the door, although he wasn't allowed to, and never recognized Wanda, although he had seen her many times.

"Well, howdy do, Wanda," said Tammy, crowding her huge frame into the doorway, pushing Vincent aside with one prodigious hip. "Come on in."

Wanda followed Tammy into her living room, where the seats were arranged around the TV set. Here sat two white-haired old women dozing, and one very aware-looking young woman, whose eyes darted between Wanda and the TV screen as she rocked back and forth. The room smelled of urine and cinnamon potpourri.

"Everything all right, hon?" Tammy asked. Her arms were short, like flippers that rested on her sides.

"Well," said Wanda, "I banged my thumb. It's killing me." She took away the tissues and showed Tammy. The smudge had spread into a blackish bruise that ringed the midsection of her thumb, and there was a crust of blood.

"Sweetie!" cried Tammy. "Let's gitcha cleaned up!"

She led Wanda to the kitchen, walking with effort—not the effort of carrying a heavy load (she actually seemed strangely light for her size, balloonish) but an effort of balance similar to that of a person on stilts. She climbed a stepladder and, from the top of the cabinet, retrieved a first-aid kit. Then she sat Wanda down and cleaned her thumb with hydrogen peroxide.

"The cut isn't so bad," Wanda said with a wince, "it's just sore."

"I'll just bet it is! How'd ya do it?"

"Car door."

Tammy gasped and shook her head. She got a Ziploc bag from a drawer and filled it with ice. "Now, you just keep this ice on it, and you'll be good as new."

How many cuts and scrapes did Tammy have to mend day by day? She had once had a woman here who pulled out her own eyebrows, then, when they were gone, continued to pluck at the skin until she had horrible eyebrows made of brown scabs. That one ended up back in Blackfoot, the town in southeastern Idaho where the psychiatric hospital was.

"Thanks so much, Tammy. What I really need is some pills."

"Of course you do!"

"You know, the pain."

"Hush," said Tammy, with a squeeze on Wanda's knee. She rose from the stool (such a slight difference in her form, between sitting and standing!) and went to the back porch. Wanda had never seen where Tammy kept the pills; Tammy had never let her. She returned with a little yellow prescription bottle. "How many ya need, hon?"

"Ten. Thanks so much, Tammy."

Tammy got the wax paper from a drawer, ripped off a square,

and shook ten pills out of the bottle onto it. Wanda took from her purse the bills that had loosened a little in their roll. Despite the craving, which had reached a relentless, screaming intensity, Wanda smiled at the memory of Gary, that polite and embarrassed boy. She flattened the bills and counted them, then nearly burst into tears. He had given her $120. He had tipped her! Now she had $20 to buy groceries tomorrow.

She gave five of the bills to Tammy, who pocketed them without counting and handed over the folded square of wax paper. "You need a glass of water?" Tammy asked.

"You know," said Wanda, blushing with shame, "the pain is so intense I might need to . . ."

"Of course," said Tammy, squeezing Wanda's knee again. "Come with me."

She led Wanda to the bathroom and, from under the sink, took a handheld mirror and a razor blade. She set these on the counter and gave Wanda a tight-lipped smile accompanied by a squeezing shut of her eyes. This was the clumsy smile of sympathy old women at church used to give Wanda. Wanda hated it but endured it, reminding herself that to Tammy she wasn't the poor little orphan girl, but a friend in pain.

Tammy left the way nurses leave exam rooms to let you undress, closing the door respectfully behind her.

Wanda settled onto the fluffy green shag that covered a foam-padded toilet seat cover. With trembling fingers, she unfolded the wax paper and dropped four pills into her coin purse. Then she folded the fifth back into the wax paper and looked around for a tool. She picked up a decorative glass bottle and with its rounded base she crushed and re-crushed the pill. Then she unfolded the paper, dumped the powder onto the mirror, and, with the razor blade, arranged it into a line. She had never done this at Tammy's house before, and she was ashamed of herself, but she couldn't wait those long minutes after the pill would go down her throat and before it would take effect.

Wanda had crossed this border about four months ago. Back when she swallowed the pills—even after the doctor refused to renew the prescription, and she began to buy them from Tammy—Wanda still felt that they were medicine. Once she crushed and snorted them, however, they became drugs. She hated that Tammy knew now.

Wanda rolled the twenty-dollar bill—that wonderful bill—back into its cigarette shape. Then she paused and counted. For five seconds she observed in herself a complex sensation: agony and anticipation folded together and flowered into a horrible, gorgeous moment. It was like being on the verge of coming. Then she snorted the line.

She roused herself. How much time had she spent sitting happily on the soft toilet seat? She looked down at the hand mirror and noticed a few grains of white. She licked them up, right off the glass. They tasted wonderfully bitter.

She put away the mirror and razor blade, threw away the wax paper, and stood up. In the big mirror over the sink she saw herself, a girl playing dress-up in her mother's clothes. She smiled down at the blue dress. *I hate you*, she said—aloud?—and felt not hatred but, rather, forgiveness, contentment, and, strangely, music. Dancing a little, she took the dress off. Should she stuff it in the trash or give it to Tammy? That green plastic hamper in the corner would make a perfect new home for this dress. *Drugs will provide.* She took her own dress out of the bowl of the hat and put it on, lifting her arms and letting it fall around her body. Then she opened the hamper, which now resembled a yawning frog, and placed into its belly both the blue dress and the hat. A message in a bottle. Where would it end up? Clothing one of Tammy's folks. With a beneficent smile, Wanda pulled on her coat, imagining that darting-eyed woman from the other room donning her new outfit and proudly, jerkily, walking downtown. All was well now between Wanda and that dress.

As she moved through the house, Wanda thanked the walls for setting everything right. Tammy wasn't in the living room. Maybe she was giving Wanda room to leave uninterrupted. Wanda came upon Vincent pacing the empty foyer. He retreated a bit into the darkness upon seeing her.

"Bye-bye," Wanda said.

Vincent ducked his head to the side.

"Vincent," Wanda said, "why do you always answer the door? Are you waiting for someone?"

He said nothing. His tongue was busy with its exercises, and there was a suspicious slant to his brow.

"It's just your job, isn't it? It's what you do."

Vincent hugged himself and turned farther to the side. Wanda didn't want to frighten him. "Bye-bye, Vincent," she said.

Walking down the street toward her part of town, Wanda wondered whether there was a job out there that she should be doing, and whether she would be happy if she found it. Then she realized: she had. She was doing her job. It was nothing so simple as answering the door, but she had a job and she was doing it every moment of the day. Her overcoat felt comfortable and warm as a blanket, a magic blanket that supported her and helped move her forward. She imagined that she could stop using her feet and this coat would carry her home.

Wanda floated through rooms of sunlight that narrowed and widened at the direction of the elm trees lining the street. This was a pretty neighborhood of clean, humble houses whose flower beds had withered over a few recent frosty nights. In the lawns, yellow leaves had been raked into piles. Some of them were neat as igloos; others had been smeared across the grass by children's play. In an upcoming shaft of light Wanda saw a sphere of busily flying gnats, and she ducked so as not to disturb them.

Wanda imagined that another force besides her coat was helping her forward: behind her, over her left shoulder, a huge, benevolent cat prowled along. A tiger or panther, but bigger, as big as a car, protected her as she walked. Then she realized the cat was real, and it was a car. She turned toward it, and it stopped. Gary was the driver. Wanda got in.

"Hi, Wanda," he said, smiling with effort. "I totally forgot I promised to buy you a dress."

"I don't need a dress," said Wanda. "But thank you."

"Well, then, maybe just a ride home?"

"That'd be nice."

Wanda looked at Gary's hands as he steered. His fingers were bright red. His body radiated a nervous heat. Poor Gary. He needed to find his job.

"You seem like you're in a good mood," said Gary.

"Do I?" said Wanda.

"Yeah, you're, like, smiling."

"I am in a pretty good mood," said Wanda. Then she looked around the car. "You changed cars."

"Oh. This is my car. We were in Winston's before."

"I know," said Wanda.

When they reached Wanda's complex, Gary said, "Um, can I come in and use your bathroom?"

"Sure," said Wanda. She led Gary up the walk and into the apartment, which she never locked. She showed Gary to the bathroom, then went to the kitchen to pour herself a glass of the sun tea she had left brewing on the windowsill. Then she sat down and turned on the TV, completely at ease.

Gary came out of the bathroom and strolled around the periphery of the living room as if it were a playing field he mustn't disturb.

"You wanna watch some TV?" Wanda asked.

"Yeah," he said, and came to perch on the couch's edge. He spread his fingers and rubbed the flats of his palms together.

Wanda closed her eyes and drifted for a while, thinking of nothing at all. When she opened her eyes, Gary was seated on the couch, watching her. She smiled.

"Wanda?" he said.

"Yes?"

"Remember when I told you I don't have a girlfriend?"

"Yes."

"Well, it's more than that. I've *never* had a girlfriend."

"Why not?"

Gary shrugged. "I dunno." He seemed a little less nervous now that he had resolved to tell her these things. "I've never even had sex."

"I'm sorry," Wanda said.

Gary shrugged again. "For what?"

There was silence again. Did Gary want to have sex with her? She didn't want to. She didn't feel like being jostled around. She did enjoy having a visitor, though, this polite boy sitting on her couch. He could tell her his secrets if he wanted. Wanda opened her eyes and realized that they were watching a news program about that woman in New Jersey who had carried a baby for an infertile couple and now refused to give it up. To protect the child they called it only Baby M. Had this been on the whole time? How boring this must be for Gary! Wanda reached for the remote and started to search for something better to watch.

"Um, I was thinking . . ." said Gary.

"Yes?" Wanda said.

"Well, Winston told me that he did stuff with you . . . that he paid you for . . . and that was cool with you—to get paid."

Wanda's heart felt as if it were suddenly under attack, like a little troop of feelings dispatched from the other side—the world of ache that she had left behind at Tammy's house. She turned to Gary and was about to say, *He never paid! I never charged him! Why would he say that?* But something stopped her—another dispatch from the world of ache, but this time from herself—a message from the Wanda that lived in pain, saying, *You need the money.*

"I'm sorry! I didn't mean to insult you!" Gary said, starting to stand.

"It's all right. It's all right. Everything's all right." Wanda swallowed the sob, took Gary's hand, and pulled him back onto the couch. She had promised herself on her birthday last March that she wouldn't do this ever again—take money for it. But now she saw that this, like everything else she did, was part of her job.

She touched Gary's soft skin. She stroked him like his mother must have when he was little. Gary hid his face against her and became a nameless baby.

Wanda moved to turn off the TV.

"Oh, don't," said Gary. "It helps."

Wanda lay back, carrying Gary with her. She felt his soft bulk over her, ignored the hardness underneath, and listened to his halting breath.

Big baby. Poor baby.

CHAPTER 4

Lina rang the doorbell and allowed a moment for someone to answer while she groped around her duffel bag for her keys. When no one came, she unlocked the door and entered the bright, chapel-like entranceway where, two weeks earlier, she had stood waiting to see if Mr. Hall would come out of his bedroom after her. She looked up at the second-floor railing. As if the house had been holding its breath while Lina came in, it released a long, quiet exhalation—the heat had kicked on. She took off her coat. It was hot in here. She would have opened a window, but the Halls, like the rest of her clients, preferred to keep their climate-controlled house sealed. Instead, she set down her things and looked around for the thermostat. When she found it in the parlor (which was what the Halls called their second living room), she saw that it was set on seventy-five degrees. What a waste! She turned it down to sixty-eight.

She changed her clothes and went to the broom closet, where she saw that the Halls were low on cleaning supplies. Sandra usually kept an eye on this. Lina would have to make do. She'd dilute the Pine Sol more than usual and leave Sandra a note.

"We both need to kiss." In saying that, Mr. Hall had spoiled the kiss, made it an endeavor against loneliness. But over the intervening two weeks, Lina had come to be touched by his honesty. He was sad, and could see that she was, too. He could just as well have said, "We both need happiness."

This didn't make it right, however. Neither did it make Mr. Hall handsome, or strong, or whatever it would take to make her want to kiss him again. She had entertained herself with imagining the come-ons he would use the next time they were alone in the house, and how she would shoot them down.

Can I show you my train set?

Mr. Hall, it's time to grow up. Stop playing with trains and stop kissing women other than your wife.

Can I offer you a glass of chardonnay?

Mr. Hall, it would take a lot more than a glass of wine to make me break the Sixth Commandment.

Yes, she was armed and ready, but he was not here.

The order in which Lina cleaned rooms had to do with the way dirt particles fell. She dusted first, from the highest point to the lowest, then vacuumed, upstairs, then down. She cleaned the bathroom and kitchen fixtures, and, finally, mopped. Sometimes when she left, she shuffled across the still-wet floors on paper towels, then put her shoes on outside. It made her feel like she was sealing closed a pristine chamber, like the incubator Jesús had lived in for the first days of his life. He had been frail and yellow, and they had still wanted to circumcise him. "Leave him alone. Can't you see he's sick?" "Of course, Lina, of course. It's your decision," the doctor had said. It was this kind doctor who told the Van Bekes about Lina's situation. An older couple whose children were grown, they had visited her in the hospital the next day. Carl Van Beke had been a banker. The community had given them so much, Janet explained, they wanted to give something back. They had the room, the means, the stamina to raise one more child. Lina would remain the boy's mother and could visit when she liked, and teach the boy Spanish, even. Lina had been numb and dry-eyed when they took him. It would be weeks before she broke down and cried, months before she visited, much longer before she looked the boy in the eye. She was poor back then. She ate stale bread from the day-old outlet and bought gas two or three dollars' worth at a time. She couldn't have given Jesús what he needed.

Lina climbed the stairs and walked down the softly carpeted hall. She was tempted to go into the Halls' bedroom for a moment, just to be where he had kissed her, but before she decided whether or not she would, the door opened and someone stepped out.

Lina jumped.

It was Sandra. "Lina," she said, "sorry to startle you. I heard the doorbell ring and I knew it was you. I figured you would let yourself in."

"Oh, it's okay," Lina said.

Sandra had a tired look around her eyes, as if she had just awakened from a nap. At the same time, though, her face looked strangely drawn-on, her eyebrows very arched, as if she had just made herself up to go out.

"Well," Sandra said, "I'll try not to be in your way."

She walked slowly past Lina, down to the parlor.

Lina went to Abby's room and began to dust. Usually Sandra greeted her brightly and gave her a little hunched-shouldered hug that Lina never resisted, but certainly never enjoyed. The two women would not put their arms all the way around each other, but just to each other's backs. Lina could feel the ridges of Sandra's shoulder blades and, at the same time, was aware that Sandra could feel her soft rolls. Lina would have preferred a handshake.

Damas. That's what Lina's mother had called white women. She said it sharply, pushing the word to the front of her mouth, while *mujeres*, her word for Mexican women, sat comfortably in the back.

But Sandra hadn't given her a hug today. Was she tired? Or did she know?

Lina dusted the upstairs bedrooms, the downstairs living rooms (Sandra had either slipped back upstairs at some point, or left), and, since she hadn't last time, the basement. Here, in the dimness, she simply ran a feather duster over shelf after shelf of toy trains: engines, cabooses, cars loaded with tiny logs, cars loaded with coal, cars painted with the flowery logos of old-fashioned companies. Boxes of track, too, and railroad crossings. Trees, houses; even, in a big box, a pond.

"Don't use Pledge down here," Sandra had said while giving her the introductory tour. "These boxes are very valuable. Just use a feather duster." She said this loudly, and made a feather-dusting motion to make her meaning clear. As if Lina didn't speak English.

The first years, Lina would wonder, as she dusted the boxes, how much were they really worth? If you sold them, how much money would you get? Enough to make a down payment on a doublewide? But then Lina had saved her money and gotten a doublewide, and now she was tired of wondering about the worth of Mr. Hall's trains.

The maglev train, they call it. Magnetic levitation. They don't have wheels.

Lina smiled. *What a weirdo.*

She went to the broom closet, got the vacuum, and took it up to Abby's room. After she had been vacuuming for a few minutes, in the corner of her eye she saw Sandra, who stood in the doorway waving apologetically in an apparent attempt to avoid startling her again. With her toe, Lina pushed the button to turn off the machine.

"I'm sorry, Lina. I have a little headache," she said. "Would you mind not vacuuming?"

"Sure, Sandra."

Sandra returned to her room.

Lina yanked the cord from the wall and began to coil it. For some reason she *did* mind. *If you want to get me out of here early*, she thought to herself, *fine! You still have to pay me the same.*

Lina brooded as she mopped. Sandra knew. She would call sometime in the next two weeks and tell Lina not to come back. She'd make up some lie, *We need to cut costs*, or whatever, but it was because Lina had kissed her husband. Because her husband had kissed Lina.

BEFORE LINA WAS born, her parents, aunts, and uncles had established something of a homestead out near Payette, more than an hour's drive from Eula. They called it "la Hacienda," which was a joke, as the house, though roomy, was in a state of perpetual disrepair. The roof leaked, and once Uncle Mario got around to nailing down a few new shingles, the pump gave out, and the family had to start contributing to the coffee can to buy a new one and, in the meantime, drink from jugs of water they bought at Albertson's and shower at a cousin's house in Chandler. Slowly, over the years, as the family's fortunes improved, as more babies were born in Idaho and more parents got their papers, the house became sturdier.

Lina's family still lived at the Hacienda—distant cousins who spoke no English. It was their first stop in Idaho. Lina had rarely visited since *Mamá* died. The Cortezes of her generation all had their own places now, mostly in Payette, but a few in Chandler, and Lina in Eula.

Lina used to go on holidays. She'd pick Jay up from the Van Bekes' and make the long drive out, Jay pouting all the way. Once at the Hacienda, he refused to speak Spanish with his cousins. He would pick at his dinner, claiming to hate spicy food, while *Mamá* glowered at him from her wheelchair at the head of the table. She resented the fact that Lina had given him to the Van Bekes instead of her to raise, and found it easier to take this resentment out on the boy than on his mother. Lina was her youngest, her favorite, the child of her old age, and the only one born in the United States. *Mi americana*, she liked to call her.

Eventually, Lina gave up and stopped forcing Jay to go. Now she had Enrique, who loved the Hacienda. He would play for hours outside, hiding-and-seeking with his cousins under the porch and climbing apple trees in the orchard while Lina helped with dinner. Later, he'd crawl into the broad lap of his grandmother, whom all the other children feared, and fall asleep. If only Lina's father could have seen it!

Papá was rarely mentioned, and this was not because he had been cruel, although his sternness did sometimes border on cruelty, but because they feared that he had been lost to the fires of hell. The sound of his name, *Papá*, had a chilling effect on everyone at the Hacienda; it was better saved for prayers.

Back when he was a young man, *Papá* had worked his hands to bleeding in the corn fields. He had no family here, and the other migrant workers shunned him, fearing he'd take work from them and their families. His heart ached for his brothers and his wife and three children, who were in Mexico, unable to cross over, and for his parents, who were too old to make the journey. Having little to eat, as he sent his money back home, he became ill. One feverish night he wandered far out into the sugar-beet fields, calling out to God for help. He knelt down in the dirt and prayed to God yet again to deliver his family to him. The night was starless and moonless and he felt that God had drawn a black curtain between them, despite *Papá's* prayers and his weekly attendance at Mass.

So he prayed to the Devil.

"Satanas, traeme a mi familia y danos un hogar. Give us a home. *Después puedes tenerme."*

That's all he said, and for some minutes he felt silly, like a child who had been playacting. It was so quiet and dark it was easy to believe that there was no heaven or hell, and that his words had traveled only as far as he could see, then settled into the furrows like the dust raised by his steps.

Then he heard something coming toward him swiftly from across the field. He leaped up and ran. He could hear hoofbeats gaining on him. The creature, close behind him, grunted menacingly. *Papá* looked over his shoulder to see a huge pig chasing him, its evil eyes shining like black pearls. It bit at his ankle, and he tumbled through the dirt. He pushed the pig off, and ran again. He ran and ran until he saw the lights of the barracks. When he reached the door, the pig had vanished.

The next morning his fever was gone and he was able to work. A few months later he had his brothers with him and, a year after that, his wife and children. Then the Hacienda.

He confessed his sin and did penance many times over, but still feared that his soul was lost. All his life he worked with fatalistic determination. He rarely smiled and never sang, and he died young.

Lina's mother once told her that *Papá*'s soul was trapped in purgatory—forever, she feared. God had forgiven him, but the Devil had him by the ankle and wouldn't let him go. She knew this because she had dreamed it. There were tears in her eyes as she told Lina this; it was the only time Lina ever saw her cry.

On Lina's last visit to the Hacienda before *Mamá* died, two nieces, having heard that *Mamá*'s health was in decline, had visited from Mexico with their children. The house was full to bursting. Enrique, who was growing up and turning shy, especially around all these cousins he didn't know, would venture out among them, then return to Lina's side. He slowly washed leaves of lettuce as Lina diced chilies with a plastic grocery bag covering her left hand like a glove. Her eyes watered, and she raised her wrist to her nose, letting the knife dangle.

Enrique's aunt approached with a steaming pot. "Enrique, *muévate*, I need that sink!"

"There's nothing for you to do, baby," said Lina. "Go sit with *Abuela*."

Enrique's grandmother sat under blankets in her wheelchair. She nodded when Enrique sat down, but then closed her eyes and said nothing. Someone played a guitar on the back porch, sang a call-and-response song with the children in Spanish.

A horizontal bar repeatedly licked the fuzzy image on the screen of the old television in the corner. *Abuela*'s head nodded and she seemed on the verge of sleep. (A week later Enrique would wonder if she had been on the verge of death, testing the waters of the black river, *el rio negro*, and then retreating. Old Mexicans, he felt, died in a very different way than old white people, who slipped away quietly in clean hospitals.)

After dinner they all gathered on the steps out back for a family photo. *Abuela* squinted, let her jaw hang slack, and seemed to wonder, *Who are all these fools?* A cousin from Mexico named Julio sat on the step behind Enrique. Enrique had watched him roughhousing with the other boys earlier. He didn't earn their respect by hitting or pinching, but by carrying himself with utter confidence, shoulders thrown back and a white smile blazing forward.

At one point he had come over to Enrique. "You live here?" he asked in Spanish. Unlike the others, he wasn't ashamed that he only spoke Spanish.

"No, I live in Eula."

"But you live in the United States?"

"Yes."

"I live in Juárez."

"Yes, I know."

"But I'm going to move here."

And with that he had run off.

Enrique had watched him for a while and fantasized that, when Julio moved here, they would become best friends.

Now Uncle Víctor said, "*A ver, sonrían.* Say cheese!"

Enrique leaned back against Julio's knees. The group said "cheese" with the hardest *ch* and the softest *s* ever: "Tcheeees!"

Uncle Víctor snapped the picture and said, "Hol' on, don' move, I got another camera here. *Momentito, por favor.*"

All the kids squirmed except for Enrique, who couldn't move for the thrill of being supported—even gently clutched—by Julio's knobby knees.

"Okay, *sonrían*!"

In a brash moment, Enrique leaned farther back and draped an arm over Julio's knee, and—rapture!—Julio lay his hands on his shoulders.

Julio never ended up moving to Idaho.

That night *Mamá* didn't say good-bye, even when Lina took her hands and repeated "*Adiós*," and "*Te amo, Mamá*," until her voice broke. Lina couldn't stay over—all the rooms were full, and it was a school night for Enrique—but neither could she tear herself away. Finally she embraced her mother and said, into her ear, "*Mamá, tus diamantes* . . . the earrings I gave you for your birthday when I was little, the ones you called your diamonds—I stole them from the drugstore." *Mamá*'s eyes fluttered uncomprehendingly.

Lina cried and cried as they drove across the dark countryside, and Enrique stroked her shoulder for a while, then fell asleep, his head resting on the soft armrest that divided the driver's seat from the passenger's in their squeaky old station wagon. Then he was awakened by his mother whispering, "*Shit! Shit!*"

"What is it?" he asked, afraid she had run over an animal.

"I'm going to run out of gas. I forgot to fill up in Payette."

"Can we go back?"

"No, baby, it's too far. There's that Texaco just before Parma. I just hope we can make it."

Now Enrique watched the dark road, wide-awake, anticipating the moment the engine would give, while Lina murmured prayers to Saint Christopher. After several minutes she said, "We're going to make it." But then, when the gas station came into view, its lights were off and a CLOSED sign hung in the window. Lina pulled in anyway, parked, and turned off the car. The silence was scary.

"Enrique," she said. "I'm sorry, but we have to sleep here until they open. Otherwise, we'll never make it home."

They put down the backseat and covered themselves with a scratchy woolen blanket. Lina shivered, but Enrique felt warm huddled up next to her with her arm as his pillow.

Now she cried again. "I'm so sorry, Enrique. I'm a bad mommy. I'm a bad mother and a bad daughter, both."

"No you're not."

"I am, *mi vida*."

"Stop it! You're a good mother!" She was making him cry, too.

"Arright, arright, I'm sorry. Let's go to sleep."

And Enrique had gone to sleep. But Lina stayed awake, listening to the sounds of crickets. There was a rumbling, and the car was illuminated by white shapes panning like searchlights, then the semi passed and, again, it was dark.

I'll do better, Lina thought. *I'll make more money. I'll get a doublewide and bring Jesús home to live with us.*

CHAPTER 5

"Our project is entitled 'You Are Totally Infected,'" April Martinez began. "All over your body, microorganisms are living and growing. For example," she held up a drawing of what looked like a fur ball, "tiny mites live in your eyelashes, just like squirrels live in trees."

"Ew!" squealed some of the girls.

April attached the drawing (which was backed with double-stick tape) to the head of an outline of a boy's body, which hung on the wall. This body was the same height and proportions as Tommy Hess, April's partner. Above the diagram, YOU ARE TOTALLY INFECTED! was written in Magic Marker. The last word was spelled in warty, oozing green capitals.

Enrique had always liked these two. He and April often sat together at Mass away from their mothers, playing tic-tac-toe on the bulletin. She had jagged teeth and a severe slant to her brow that masked her sweet nature, while Tommy had an appealing, if somewhat Muppet-ish, face—blue-eyed and shovel-jawed—under a curly blond mop. He had been gangly and inappropriate in grade school, often making strange bids for attention. Enrique remembered a time he turned his eyelids inside-out and chased the girls around, fluttering those pink, veiny lids. Tommy had now dropped these antics but still seemed to have the most tenuous control over the volume of his voice: he would bark the first words of a sentence, shyly mutter the next, and wrangle his voice into his service only when he was nearly done. Perhaps this was why he was silent now, smiling and shifting from foot to foot as April spoke.

"Not all of the creatures that live on and in your body are bad. It's like a city block where some of the neighbors are nice and helpful, while others are troublemakers. One of the helpful neighbors is the bacteria that lives in your small intestine. There's about five hundred species down there." She attached a drawing of several hairy blobs to the diagram's belly. "Without it, you wouldn't be able to digest your food."

While some in the class made further expressions of distaste, Enrique began searching through his script. How could he jazz it up? April and Tommy's project was good. It held the attention of the entire class and was scientifically sound, and April had apparently memorized the whole thing.

"Dandruff is more than just flakes of dead skin in your hair; it's caused by a fungus called malassezia. It eats your skin!" Having gained confidence by grossing out the other girls, April slapped a drawing of a voracious, wide-mouthed monster onto the head of the diagram.

April profiled a few more residents of the bodily neighborhood while Mr. Peterson watched from a seat at the back of the room, his fingers steepled before his mouth, perhaps to hide an amused and approving smile. The presentation reached its climax: "Every cell in your body is like a machine, with an engine called a mitochondrion." She stuck a drawing of a blob containing a smaller blob onto the center of the body. "Mitochondrions have DNA of their own, which are closer to bacterial DNA than to human DNA. Some scientists think that this proves that at a cellular level, we are totally made up of outsiders."

This last bit puzzled some in the class who were braced for a final, supreme gross-out, but they applauded anyway. April and Tommy bowed.

"Miriam, would you like to go next?"

Miriam rose and went to the corner near the windows where her sheet of paper hung. At the beginning of class, everyone had posted their project mock-ups, drawn on long sheets of craft paper that Mr. Peterson had provided several days previous. This gave Enrique a mysterious preview of what was yet to come: a waterfall covered in Jesus-fish, a caterpillar-cocoon-butterfly cycle prettily drawn with pastel-colored arrows in-between, two volcanoes, and Enrique's own poster, which, he now realized, looked like a third volcano, but one dotted with ants and palm trees.

Miriam's drawing seemed to depict several ponds linked by streams. "The digestive system of the *bos taurus*, or domestic cow, is as puzzling as a maze," she began. Enrique felt relieved. Miriam, who should have been his and Gene's best competitor, had chosen a subject that was boring beyond words. Then a searing guilt took over. Poor Miriam. Who was her partner? No one had been absent at roll call. "Why should we care that cows spend eight hours a day chewing? Or that they have four stomachs, or that it takes them seventy to one hundred hours to digest a meal? One reason is that, in part, the future of our planet depends on cow digestion. Methane, a colorless, flammable gas, is one of the main culprits behind a phenomenon scientists call the 'greenhouse effect.' In their digestive process, cows release as much as a pound of methane a day—"

Miriam was interrupted by a loud and very realistic imitation of a fart. The class erupted in laughter.

This lit a flash of protective fury in Enrique. He turned toward the source of the noise, Jake Wilson, and inhaled to say something in Miriam's defense. Before he could speak, though, Jake lifted his wrist, placed his hand to his chest like a prim old woman, and mimicked Enrique's indignant gasp.

"Enough, Jake," Mr. Peterson said. "Miriam, you may continue."

Injured and in a hurry to return to her seat, Miriam limped through the remainder of her presentation.

Enrique was crushed, maybe more than the situation warranted. Jake had been Enrique's friend in Boy Scouts. Only last year they had spent an hour alone together, panning for gold in a creek where water-skippers made tiny dimples with their feet on the surface. The boys had lined up the grains they found on an overhanging tree branch and fantasized about the boat they would buy with the gold and the distant islands they'd sail to. In the disorienting scramble for allegiances at the beginning of this school year, Jake and some other boys had dropped Enrique. It seemed to have had something to do with entering junior high. Now that they were in the same building complex as the high school, they sensed (or imagined) the critical eye of the big kids following them.

The authors of the caterpillar diagram went next. There was no project here, only information that was as readily available as the nearest textbook. Next came the first volcano. These boys had at least done their homework. The volcano would be built from papier-mâché and would feature a small container at the top, which would hold a mixture of water, vinegar, and dish soap. One of the boys would drop in a packet of baking soda, setting off the "eruption."

Enrique's mouth felt dry, and he wondered if he would gag when he went to speak. In grade school he had taken every opportunity to get up in front of the class, whether to read the teacher a poem on her birthday or to lead the class in the Pledge of Allegiance. He had been well liked. In fifth grade he had served as representative on class council. The position had no responsibilities other than to sit quietly at a few meetings, but he had been elected to it by the rest of the class. Justin Watts, his campaign manager, had hung up VOTE FOR ENRIQUE posters in the hallways. Now Justin sat in the back with Jake, egging him on. Enrique took deep breaths and concentrated on memorizing the last paragraph of his script, so he could, at that point, lay down his notes and speak directly to the class.

Jake and Justin went next. Theirs was the second volcano and, unlike the first, it was clumsily drawn, perhaps hastily completed over lunch. As Justin described the project, Jake shrugged the whole thing aside, looking off, acting bored and put-upon. Justin borrowed phrases from the boys who had just gone and who now sat glaring from their seats.

Now it was Gene and Enrique's turn. They took their places on either side of the diagram. Enrique cleared his throat and began.

"On August 21 of this year over seventeen hundred people died in the middle of the night. They were villagers in the mountains of Cameroon, a country in Africa. Many people died in their sleep. Some made it outside before they dropped dead on the ground. Imagine if everyone in Homedale suddenly died—it was that many people. Although the Eula High football team might benefit, it would be a huge tragedy."

No one laughed at the joke. Enrique swallowed, and went on.

"Were these people poisoned on purpose, as the newspaper said that first week? Was it a rebel attack or a gassing sponsored by the government? If so, why would nearby Lake Nyos turn red and muddy afterward? Why would the level of Lake Nyos drop by three and a half feet and its temperature rise? And why did the same thing happen at another lake in Cameroon two years ago, killing forty people? That mystery was never solved. This time scientists are determined to find out if something in Lake Nyos killed those people.

"Lake Nyos is a crater lake at the top of an extinct volcano." With a pencil, Enrique pointed to the top of the volcano. "Every human and animal in a fifteen-mile radius of Lake Nyos was killed." Enrique made a sweeping gesture across the surrounding land. "Some have hypothesized that the volcano erupted, emitting a poisonous cloud. If so, then why didn't anyone hear or feel the eruption? Why didn't anyone see the cloud? An eruption powerful enough to kill seventeen hundred people could not have happened so quietly. Remember Mount St. Helens? We had ash on the cars here in Eula, over five hundred miles away. And the blast at Mount St. Helens only killed fifty-seven people. There was no ash at Lake Nyos, no lava, and no fires. The volcano appears to be dead.

"So what killed all those people?

"Lake Nyos is very deep and very cold. There is no current in the lake, so the water is very still." Enrique set down his notes and held his hand flat halfway down the mountain. "Some scientists think that poison gas might have seeped slowly into the lake from cracks at the bottom." He indicated a cloud of gas with a fist under the flat hand. "The weight of the water held the gas at the bottom. On the night of August 21, the gas got to be so much that it bubbled up through the water and escaped."

Another loud fart noise came from the back of the room, and the class roared.

"Jake!" barked Mr. Peterson. "One more interruption and I'm sending you to the office."

Enrique flushed red. He picked up his notes in trembling hands, but couldn't remember what came next. Gene stood still as he had before, but his features drew into a tighter knot at the center of his face.

"Enrique, please continue," said Mr. Peterson.

"Um, that's our project. To illustrate what might have happened at Lake Nyos."

"How are you going to illustrate it?"

"We're going to make a model of the mountain in a Plexiglas box. We're going to have ants in there. Gene already has ant farms. Then at the science fair, we're going to uncover a jar full of cotton balls soaked in nail-polish remover. It will kill the ants." This was a blunt conclusion, but Enrique had lost the graceful wording he had planned and was desperate to return to his seat.

"Thank you," said Mr. Peterson.

Other groups described their projects, but now Enrique was deaf to everything. He sat looking at his pencil in its little gutter at the top of his desk, and with the tip of his finger rolled it from one flat side to the next. Getting up in front of class, in junior high, was risky. *Don't speak in front of class,* Enrique told himself. When he had an important thought like this, he stated it in a short sentence, hoping it would ride the tempest of his imagination like a message in a bottle. It was like the orders he had seen Connie give Gene: *Stop destroying flowers.*

If Enrique's classmates cared to look at him as he was thinking these thoughts, they might have wondered if he was having an allergic reaction, his face was so red and mottled. But they were all watching the presentations.

Unable to hate Jake—he still held up the fact that they had until so recently been friends—Enrique focused his hatred on junior high. *I hate junior high.* He felt tears rise, and looked up, searching for a distraction. He found his drawing of the mountain and suddenly paper butterflies shot out of Lake Nyos—hundreds of them, in every color offered in Magic Markers. Their wings crinkled as they flapped. The butterflies swarmed the room, swirling in a great whirlwind. Then they burst out the windows and flew over the town. Now in the millions, they filled the sky and choked the sun, yet still more flew out of the mountain. And then clouds rolled in, and rain sent the butterflies down to carpet the ground—soggy bits of paper with bleeding colors like the waste of a parade. And no one would ever believe that Eula, Idaho, had been overwhelmed by a sudden, miraculous infestation of paper butterflies. It might be on *That's Incredible!* but it would be one of those stories you weren't supposed to believe.

How's that, Mrs. Cuddlebone?

Enrique hadn't addressed Mrs. Cuddlebone for a long time. For much of his childhood she had been a kind of imaginary friend. Her hair was coiled and piled into the shape of a great heart and decorated with dangling jewels, and she never rose from the fan-back chair in which she sat. Recently Enrique had seen a portrait of Queen Elizabeth I in a history book, and realized this must have been Mrs. Cuddlebone's origin, just as her name must have been based on "cuttlefish bone," something his aunt gave to the parakeets she kept at the Hacienda. Enrique never played with Mrs. Cuddlebone, he presented artwork to her: sometimes finger-paintings or Play-Doh sculptures (*Not quite to my liking*, she'd say, or, *Well done, my boy; I'll take it*) but usually creations that were purely imaginary. If Enrique's mind wandered from his grade-school teacher's math lesson, say, to something dirty, the boys he had seen naked in the dressing room at the pool, he'd catch himself. Suddenly the dressing room's back wall was rent in two, drawn back like curtains, and out of the pool would charge dozens of dolphins, their arcing dives landing them in the children's pool, which was now an orchestra pit, with tuxedoed musicians standing waist-deep in water. The dolphins would slosh around, slapping the cranky violinists with their tails and sending into chaos the overture that led anyway to the arrival on the diving board of—what?—an enormous whale, three stories high, teetering on its back fin and blinking its tiny eyes. Fireworks bloomed in the sky, then rained a glowing pink and yellow dust over the audience, who applauded, not with hands but flippers, tentacles, and claws.

How's that, Mrs. Cuddlebone?

A little silly, Enrique.

Part of why he didn't make offerings to Mrs. Cuddlebone anymore was that he had grown weary of distracting himself from dirty thoughts.

The bell rang.

"Those of you interested in actually competing in the science fair," said Mr. Peterson, his voice increasing in volume to stay above the fray, "come back to my desk for a quick meeting."

Enrique, Gene, Miriam, and several others gathered. Mr. Peterson quickly scanned the group. "All of your presentations were very good. You all get *A*s. Now. The science fair has a different set of criteria from classroom assignments. Guys," Mr. Peterson turned to presenters of the first volcano, "you seem to have a handle on the volcano project, but be warned: The science fair judges have seen about a thousand volcanoes in their time. Okay? You might consider a different project altogether. If you stick with the volcano, you'll have to find some new angle. April, Tommy, the plural of mitochondrion is *mitochondria*, all right? Tommy, are you going to have a part in the presentation?"

"Yes," he answered. "We're going to make three-dimensional germs and parasites, and April's going to stick them to my body with Velcro."

"That's good," said Mr. Peterson. "Kids get higher scores, I've noticed, when both play a part in the presentation."

This bit of news penetrated the fog and worried Enrique. Although Gene had gathered all the information for the project and would be responsible for the ants, there was no way he would ever take part in presenting the project to the judges.

"Enrique, Gene, interesting stuff," said Mr. Peterson. "No ants, though. They don't allow live animals in the science fair, even insects. I should have told you."

"Oh," Enrique said with some ambivalence. He had not wanted the ants either—it had been Gene's idea and seemed cruel—but the death of the ants comprised the whole of their demonstration.

"Also, Cameroon is a long way from Eula, and it sounds like they haven't even figured out what's behind all this. You might want to rethink the whole thing. The winning project is almost always something of local relevance, okay? Miriam, do you have a partner?"

"My little brother is my partner," Miriam said. She lifted her chin proudly and refused to look at Enrique, who, again, winced under a stab of pity.

"Well, your project is very relevant. You've done good research. But you have to have a *project*. You have to do something, grab the judges' attention. You're a smart girl and I know you can do it, okay? Talking about cow farts isn't enough." With this Mr. Peterson smiled kindly, to let Miriam and the others know he was joshing.

No one laughed.

"Anyway, kids, some members of the high school science club have generously offered to mentor you through the science-fair process. These are excellent students who have competed in science fairs before. Some of them have won. I strongly suggest you take advantage of their offer. If you are interested, you should go to the science club meeting Thursday at three in room D204."

The kids looked to each other with wonder and apprehension. Years later, the high school would move to a new building with a clock tower on a sunlit hill west of town, and the junior high would take over the entire ancient complex. But until that day, the two would remain separated only by a lawn. The room Mr. Peterson mentioned was in a high school building none of these kids had yet had reason to enter.

The happiest day in Enrique's life so far had been the previous June, when men came with a semi and hauled away the tiny trailer with dents in its aluminum sides, then returned to fasten together and secure in its place something that resembled a real house—the doublewide that he himself had helped his mom pick out. Now Enrique had a real bed in a real room, although both were tiny. With sunlight pouring in his big new window and lighting the sawdust still in the air, Enrique hung all his Garfield posters. In a place of honor above his bed he hung the oversized chart showing all the different species of whales. He had been collecting these posters for years in anticipation of the move. When he got thirsty and went to the kitchen where his mom was happily wiping down the walls, he realized that this doublewide wouldn't teeter like the old trailer did. In the past, when Enrique had to pee in the middle of the night, he'd walk from the pullout couch to the bathroom at the trailer's farthest end. He'd sit down to pee, because his weight would shift the balance, and cause the trailer to slowly tip onto its other feet with enough of a jolt to send his urine splashing across the toilet's rim, if he was standing. In the new doublewide, he would be able to pee like a boy.

A few days later, Jay had arrived with a duffel bag, having refused to bring all his belongings from the Van Bekes'. Enrique stayed in his room with the door ajar as, with a few slams, Jay set up his room, then turned on the TV and threw himself across the couch. The next morning, he swaggered into the kitchen as Lina was scraping burned toast over the sink to make it edible. "I hope that's not for me," he said. The way he cut his eyes at her like she was a washerwoman—like she was a Mexican—made Enrique hate him.

Gene, on the other hand, was completely awestruck by Jay from first sight. About a week after moving in, Jay pulled up and walked from his car to the house, dribbling his basketball with angry blows past where Enrique and Gene sat in the grass. Gene's jaw hung. "Don't stare, Gene. He's a jerk." Of course, Enrique wasn't blind. He could see why Gene stared. Jay had dark, deep-set eyes, long arms with dents along the biceps, and a taut stomach with a belly button set in it like a brown pebble. And all of this was embarrassingly on display, as Jay seemed to think that wearing a shirt around the house would be too much a show of respect. The shade of his nipples, brown bordering on gray, surprised even Enrique, whose skin was nearly as dark. It looked as if they had been licked and dusted with cocoa.

"Hey, faggots." Those were Jay's first words to Enrique that summer.

Enrique's first words to Jay, when they came a few days later, were ones of gentle assistance, despite his hatred. Enrique came upon Jay slapping the TV on its side, then taking both antennae and working them back and forth like ski poles. Enrique showed him how, to get channel seven, you had to turn the dial just a hair toward eight and push it in so it stuck. Of course, Jay didn't thank him.

Jay filled the house with the hard rock Enrique despised: Van Halen, Ratt, Quiet Riot. Jay's old tapes, Enrique discovered when he snooped in Jay's room, were originals, but the newer ones were dubbed onto blank cassettes. This made sense; Jay no longer had the Van Bekes' allowance to buy what he wanted, so he had to copy from his friends. Snooping further, Enrique found a box of condoms, their packages attached in long strips. He took one to the bathroom and tried it on. It came coated in its own lubricant and, in it, Enrique's penis reminded him of a snake shedding a pale, wrinkled skin. After he removed it with a shudder and flushed it, a gummy residue remained.

Soon, though, Enrique found escape, for this was a season of trips to the mountains with Gene and the rest of the Boy Scouts, and to the mall with Miriam. Enrique's two best friends didn't like each other, or, rather, Miriam was frightened of Gene, and Gene refused to acknowledge her—or any girl's—existence. Enrique was happy to keep one friend in the mountains and the other at the mall.

A visit to the mall began with a quick "lap," or trip up and down the mall's short length, lost in conversation about what junior high would be like. Then, if they had money, Enrique and Miriam might get a drink. They cautiously became friendly with the head-banger girls who hung out at Orange Julius—girls who blackened their eyes with makeup, sprayed their hair to rise like haystacks and cascade down their backs, wore heavy metal band T-shirts that usually featured a rotten corpse playing an instrument, smoked cigarettes, and used the F-word. Aside from that, they were like Enrique and Miriam, harmless kids with nothing to do. Enrique and Miriam would visit with these girls until they finished their juliuses, then move on.

Miriam liked to shop for clothes. She didn't buy them, she took them off the rack to squint critically at their stitching and sometimes tried them on. Later, she'd copy them; at Miriam's, they made their own clothes. Some of her copies were good, but most were too big in the collars and cuffs and looked clownish. Enrique praised them nonetheless.

Enrique didn't like clothes-shopping, so this was the point when he'd go off to the video arcade, where he played Space Invaders. There were newer and funner games, such as Donkey Kong and Ms. Pac Man, but Space Invaders was easy, and Enrique could stretch a dollar out for almost an hour. The male counterparts to the Orange Julius girls were here at the arcade—boys with zits and stringy hair, who would slip out the emergency exit to the parking lot, then return, coughing conspicuously and smelling of pot. They slammed the buttons of the games with their open palms and cursed at the screens—"Die, motherfucker!"—while their friends who were out of quarters hung from the top of the game (causing their T-shirts to rise a few inches from the tops of their jeans) and sniggered at their defeat. Pinball machines lined one wall of the arcade, winking and shuddering. Long past their prime, they were like old bums waiting for a handout. No one gave them a quarter.

One afternoon midsummer, when Enrique was out of money, he wandered into the bookstore. In the psychology section, he found a book of interviews with women about their sexual fantasies. This entertained him for a while, less as a turn-on than because it relieved some of his boundless guilt to know that women (whom he had always assumed to be the purer, higher-minded sex) had even dirtier minds than he. Then someone came around the corner, and he quickly put back the book and walked deeper into the bookstore. In the health section, he found a book called *Working Out*, an exercise manual filled with photos of men demonstrating different ways to lift weights. The shocking thing was what they wore: tiny bathing suits that barely covered them, like the ones the divers in the 1984 Olympics had worn. (Enrique had loved the diving competition; he had never seen men wear so little. At Eula's public swimming pool the boys always wore roomy, ballooning bathing suits that revealed nothing.) He came to a chapter on hygiene, with men bathing, shaving, applying creams to their skin. The men in this book were more handsome than anyone Enrique had ever seen in person, and their bodies . . . Enrique didn't see them as beautiful so much as *detailed.* There were gouges down the front of their thighs and along their arms; their abdominal muscles fit together like puzzle pieces; and the various patterns of body hair were fascinating—a fan at the armpit, a whorl under the navel, a ring around the nipple.

Enrique stood for a long time, far too engrossed in the pictures to devise a way to hide his erection. It poked straight out, tenting the front of his shorts. Light-headed, he walked back into the mall, the thing leading him like a divining rod to the bathroom, where he locked himself in a stall and did the sin which he had learned in confirmation classes was called "masturbation," the wasting of one's own seed. (He had learned this name after having believed, for a year, that the act was his own invention.)

Now Enrique had his own destination while Miriam went clothes-shopping: the bookstore, then the bathroom.

It was wrong to masturbate, and it was super-wrong to masturbate thinking about men from *Working Out*, but this seemed to Enrique a sin that rose from a featureless perversity rather than being specifically "gay." The men were exercising, not touching each other, and, in his bathroom-stall fantasy, they crowded the locker room, barely noticing the short, pudgy Mexican kid moving among their hard, hairy thighs. Enrique admitted in confession that he had masturbated and quietly added that he had a "dirty mind," but the specter of homosexuality was so unimaginable that Enrique still felt clean of its touch.

"Gay," in grade school, had been a rude word that meant "lame." "*Fantasy Island* is so gay," kids—but never Enrique—would say. Among the older kids, Enrique saw, it was an insult that could become attached to you. But being called a pig didn't give you hooves and a snout. He had not yet discovered that among adults there were men who had sex with men.

One afternoon late in the summer, Enrique looked up from *Working Out* to see Miriam standing at the end of the aisle, watching him.

"Oh!" Enrique said.

"I've been looking for you," Miriam said with a cross expression.

"Oh!" He crammed the book back onto the shelf.

"You were late."

They stood searching each other's face in a mute guessing game. Was she admonishing him for being late or apologizing for finding him? Had she seen the book? What did she know?

They made only one more mall-trip that summer. Miriam turned blouse sleeves inside-out, and Enrique stuck at her side, bored but eager to prove he wouldn't sneak off on a dirty mission again. Then school started, and they hadn't returned since.

One day in early October, the two sat together in the lunchroom.

Everything was fine between them, as long as neither mentioned the science fair. The previous week Enrique had made a mumbling, inarticulate apology for choosing Gene and not her as his partner; Miriam had tossed her head and answered, "That's okay; he needs you more than I do."

Miriam rose before the end of lunch period. "I have to go over something with Miss Holly before class," she said. "See you there?"

"See you there."

Enrique broke his cookie into bite-sized pieces, which he began to dip one by one into his milk, then pop into his mouth.

Pete Randolph approached and flashed a big smile. "Hey, Enrique," he said.

"Hey, Pete," said Enrique. He felt a little thrill. Pete was new, and Enrique had been wondering if they would become friends. He wore expensive clothes—shirts with epaulettes snapped on the shoulders and pants riddled with zippers. Enrique had seen kids wear clothes like these on *American Bandstand*, but no one in Eula had previously had the nerve. Some of the Mexican dropouts who wore red bandannas around their wrists to look like gang members and liked to break-dance at the roller rink—kids Enrique's mom called *cholos* and told him to watch out for—wore cheap imitations, but Pete's were the real thing. Pete was already popular, even though he had only moved here from Boise at the beginning of the school year.

He straddled the bench, and Enrique noticed that he was flanked by a few other boys. "I was wondering if you could help me with this report I'm writing for health class."

"Okay," said Enrique.

"It's on AIDS. I was wondering if I could ask you some questions."

The other boys snorted and kicked at each other's shoes.

Enrique looked down.

"First of all," Pete said, "do you have AIDS?" Enrique said nothing. Some of these boys were his friends, or had been. "Okay, what else? Does it hurt when Gene puts his dick in your butt? Do more Mexicans have AIDS than white people? Do you think you'll always be gay, or do you think it'll go away?"

Enrique's heartbeat rang in his ears. Inside, he became very quiet and small. He was like an animal in the woods, for whom stillness is the first defense. *Don't move.*

"Okay," said Pete. "Thanks for your help." He got up from the table and walked away, followed by the other boys, who now laughed loudly.

Enrique sat quietly looking at his tray, wondering if everyone had seen. How loudly had Pete been talking?

The bell rang.

Enrique quickly took his tray to the window, then rushed outside with his shoulders hunched and his arms taut at his sides, like an escape artist who walks away from his challenge with his arms still bound. He didn't look at the other kids running to class but kept his eyes on the pavement.

Then, suddenly, trees were exploding out of the lawn—huge trees with trunks the size of silos. Redwoods, giant sequoias, ancient trees, shooting up a mile high, throwing chunks of earth over the school buildings. Like Jack-and-the-Beanstalks; like volcanoes erupting, but erupting tree trunks. The thunderclaps they made as they exploded from the earth, which were really Enrique's own heartbeats banging in his ears, drowned out the echoing of Pete Randolph's questions.

"What's wrong?" Miriam asked when Enrique sat down next to her in English class.

He didn't answer. He didn't hear another word that Miriam or Miss Holly or anyone else said for the rest of the day.

CHAPTER 6

In order to play a sport or join a club, a kid had to have either a car or a ride. The bus left at two-thirty sharp, the time most extracurricular activities started. So the school-sponsored groups, be they debate team, French club, or football, were made up mostly of rich kids, and the afternoon bus passengers were mostly poor. To take advantage of the science club's offer, Enrique and Gene would either have to make the hour-long walk home afterward under the open sky, or find a ride.

"Jay," Enrique said without looking up from his supper Sunday night, "could you give us a ride home after school on Thursday?"

"I got football practice."

"I know. We have a meeting after school, so we can't take the bus."

"You and E.T.?"

"His name is Gene."

"Yeah. I'll pick you up in front of the junior high at four-thirty."

"We're going to be at the high school. Building D."

"Look, I'll pick you up in front of the *junior high*, all right?"

Enrique, who had been hoping Jay would ask what he would be doing in the high school building, now understood that he didn't want to be seen with him. "Okay," he said.

If either boy had looked up from his plate, he would have noticed Lina smiling to herself. This was less from the satisfaction that Jay had agreed to do Enrique a favor than relief at not having had to broker the deal herself.

On Thursday, Lina went to the Halls' house and cleaned. She had not received the call from Sandra that she had expected. The anger Lina had felt when Sandra had asked her not to vacuum had faded, and Lina could see that it had been silly: Sandra had been tired; of course she didn't want a vacuum roaring in the next room. She didn't suspect that her husband had kissed Lina and wasn't going to fire her.

Lina cleaned well, making up for the last time. She wiped down the high shelves in the breakfast room and—even though it was an off-week and she wouldn't get paid for it—thoroughly dusted the train boxes in the basement. Usually she gave these a quick once-over with the feather duster out of disdain and the knowledge that, even if Mr. Hall ever came down here, he would never be able to see dust on the boxes in this dim light.

Later, when she was deep in thought, vacuuming the Halls' bedroom, Mr. Hall stepped in. Lina stood and, with her toe, turned the machine off. There was silence. Lina opened her mouth once, then closed it. She couldn't think of what it was she had prepared to say.

Mr. Hall walked toward her. Lina felt a little panic. He took the vacuum hose out of her hand and laid it on the floor. He took her face in his hands like a boy who had learned to kiss from watching TV, and kissed her. There was warmth in the kiss. It was unrushed and deliberate, as if he had been searching the world for Lina these past weeks, all the while thinking of how he would kiss her when he found her. Now he had.

The searing argument that Lina had practiced, the scolding hand gestures, the indignant tone—all of this was lost. She hadn't planned what she would do if he didn't say anything.

They kissed and held each other. With a kind of distanced fascination, Lina realized that this event—sex with this married man—was going to happen. She was going to let it. She was going to watch.

Slowly, without releasing each other, they made their shuffling way onto the bed. Mr. Hall got up and closed the blinds. Then he pushed a button on the wall, and slats over the skylight buzzed closed, darkening the room. Lina had never noticed that button before. Then Mr. Hall returned to the bed and said, "Lina, are you all right?"

"Yes," she said.

"Can we undress under the covers?"

They pulled up the comforter and wrestled out of their clothes. Now she was naked with this man. They kissed again and again, because they needed to.

Everything they did felt completely different from what Lina had done with Jorge, the father of her sons—so different that it seemed to be another act entirely. This was lovemaking. Although Jorge had disavowed the Catholic faith and all its rules, his approach to sex still bore Catholicism's regimented mark. He refused to use condoms. He claimed to have a physical need to ejaculate every other night, and Lina usually had sex with him to avoid the displeasure of lying there in the dark listening to the persistent wet thud of his masturbating. It sounded, she couldn't help thinking, like a dog licking a wound.

This felt different, but she would wait and list the ways afterward.

Mr. Hall went down under the covers. Lina shifted a little and squirmed, embarrassed (although he surely couldn't see) of how hairy she was down there. He rested one hand on either of her bulging, dimpled thighs. He put his head between her legs and started to lick her. She knew some men did this to women, but Jorge had certainly never done it to her. It tickled. This was too much. She tried to pull him back up, but he clutched her soft flesh. The licking tickled more, but in such a way that, to make it stop tickling, she had to let him do it harder. So she held the back of his head and crushed him into her.

WHEN ENRIQUE AND Gene arrived at the meeting of the science club in room 204 of Building D, Miriam was already seated next to Cam Pierce, and they were conversing with ease. Enrique figured that Cam was a friend of one of Miriam's older siblings. Miriam interacted with members of her family's wide-reaching circle, both kids and adults, without formality, rivalry, or discomfort. They didn't trade in *cool*. Enrique was learning that *cool* was the gold standard in high school. One had to act cool. "Is he cool?" kids would ask each other, meaning, *Do we accept him?* They would glance at each other to take a quick vote. "Yeah, he's cool." Or, more often, "No, he's lame" or "gay" or "retarded" or "a spaz" or "a shit-kicker," which meant that he was a farm kid and therefore not cool. Enrique and Gene were not and would never be cool; the question was which of its many opposites they would be.

But, Enrique noticed as he and Gene joined their classmates in the corner, neither were these members of the high school science club cool. Some were outright nerds, but others were regular smart kids who were neither popular nor unpopular but had managed, as it were, to dodge the draft. Liz Padgett was here, the twin sister of Winston, Jay's best friend, but the others Enrique didn't recognize and hardly remembered having seen before, they kept such a low profile.

"Ahem, I call to order this meeting of the Eula High School Science Club," announced a boy—one of the true nerds present—after the room had filled with fifteen or twenty high school kids. Mr. Peterson and Mrs. Christiansen, the high school science teacher, had taken their seats near the junior high kids in the back. The boy speaking had feathered hair that fell over his ears and down past his collar. Even Enrique knew this style was hopelessly out of date. His horizontally striped Izod shirt was tucked too firmly into his tightly belted jeans.

"I am Kevin Fry, president. Our main item of business today will be planning next weekend's trip to Craters of the Moon National Monument. But first, we have present with us some seventh- and eighth-graders who will be taking part in the Snake River District Science Fair. Can we take a moment to welcome our junior brethren?" Laughing at Kevin's choice of words, the high school kids turned and applauded. Enrique's spirits were actually lifted by this. He imagined for a moment being inducted into this secret society: learning powerful chants in ancient languages and receiving a special ring. "Each team has been assigned a mentor," Kevin continued. "We're going to break into small groups now. You can meet your mentor and explain your project, then you're free to go, since the rest of our agenda doesn't concern you. Ten minutes, all right?"

A few of the high school kids stood and approached the junior high kids, who remained frozen in their seats; the rest leaned forward over desktops attached to chairs to chat with each other.

"Hi, are you Enrique?"

The girl smiling down at him had straight hair the color of cardboard. Her solemn face was long and narrow, as was her body. If it weren't for a beak-like nose, she would have been pretty. Her round, heavy-lidded eyes were set in their sockets like those of a doll that sleeps when you lay her down. Their weary expression seemed at odds with her lips, which smiled freely.

"Yeah," said Enrique.

"I'm Abby Hall," she said. "And you must be Gene."

Slumped sideways in his seat, Gene nodded and gazed away at the floor. It looked as if his round head would roll off his shoulders.

Enrique saw in Abby's expression that she was registering the oddness of this boy. He had witnessed this look many times before. Abby turned back to him. "You're Jay's little brother, right?"

"Yeah."

"I know your mom."

Enrique understood: his mother cleaned her house. Abby was trying to be polite by not mentioning just how she knew her.

"Oh, right, the Halls," Enrique said.

"Why don't you tell me about your project?" Abby said, sitting down.

Enrique took out the special Trapper Keeper he had devoted to the science-fair project and, with a loud rip, opened its Velcro flap. From a hot-pink folder he took several newspaper articles. He handed these to Abby, who lifted them one by one carefully, as if they were pieces of lace. He told her what had happened at Lake Nyos.

"I remember hearing about this last summer. Wasn't it Agent Orange or something?" Abby asked.

At this Enrique perked up. "That's what everyone thought, but that's definitely not it." He explained the theories of poisonous gases from the lake.

"Wow," said Abby, handing the clippings back to Enrique, "good research."

"Yeah, Gene's been going to Boise for articles."

Abby took on a mock-stern expression and gave Gene a thumbs-up. Enrique could see she was one of those girls who would try different methods of reaching Gene. He liked those girls.

From a chartreuse folder, Enrique took Gene's sketches and handed them over. "Nice," murmured Abby, sifting through the drawings as Enrique explained the project: "We're gonna make a model in a Plexiglas box. We *were* gonna have ants in there, and demonstrate how the poison worked by uncovering a jar with fingernail-polish remover."

"But," Abby said, "no ants."

"Right."

"Plus," she added, "no one wants to see a bunch of ants killed for no reason, even though they're just bugs."

"Uh-huh."

"It's kind of macabre."

"See? Macabre," said Enrique to Gene, who responded by tightening the fold of his arms.

"So, it looks like you've got good information, you just need to figure out another way to demonstrate it. Do you have any other ideas?"

"We haven't gotten that far," Enrique said. "Mr. Peterson said to try to make it about Idaho. But this happened in Africa."

"I suppose you could try to tell what it would be like if this happened in Idaho, as a motivation for solving the mystery." Abby lowered her voice and added, "You could also ignore what Mr. Peterson says."

Enrique and Gene both smiled.

"What else could you do? You could show the different theories of what actually killed those people, the right and the wrong ones."

"Or we could find out other lakes where this could happen," Enrique said.

"We can solve the mystery!" said Gene.

Abby appeared surprised by his soprano voice.

"How are we going to do that, Gene, go to Africa?"

"People? People?" Kevin called. "Can we reconvene?"

"You guys are on the right track." Abby took out a pen and wrote down her phone number.

"Our junior brethren are free to leave at this point," Kevin said. "You are invited to our meeting two weeks from today to present rough drafts of your projects to the club."

"Call me if you want to practice," Abby said, pushing the paper toward Enrique as she stood. "This is going to be a cool project." She went back to her seat next to Liz Padgett.

"She was nice, huh?" Enrique said to Gene as they walked toward the junior high along the wall of the gymnasium in order to avoid crossing the naked lawn.

"Yes," Gene said.

"What did you mean, we could solve the mystery?"

"I meant that we can find out what actually happened."

"Before the scientists?"

"Yes."

"I'm so sure, Gene! How are we gonna do that? They're in Africa, and we're in Idaho."

"We'll use the scientific method," Gene said.

They passed between the junior high buildings and went to the parking lot. Enrique looked at his digital watch and saw that it would be nearly an hour before Jay came to get them. The boys put down their backpacks and sat down on the curb in the shade.

"I'm going to join the science club when I'm in high school," Enrique said. "Did you hear? They go on field trips and stuff. Are you going to join?"

"I don't know."

"It sounds like Boy Scouts, but better. I wish they let junior high kids join."

They sat quietly. Enrique picked up a leathery yellow leaf and folded it into tiny squares, while Gene traced a pattern on the concrete with a stick. Then Gene became restless. He got up and walked a strange walk, two short steps, then a long one, balancing atop the short wall that held the bank of landscaping against the wall of the school. Enrique got up and followed, kicking off the yellow leaves. Then he heard laughter and looked up to see a group of boys walking toward them. Junior high football practice had just gotten out.

"Let's go this way." Enrique turned Gene around by tugging on his shirt. They hopped off the wall and walked away from the approaching boys.

"Enrique!" one of them sang in falsetto. "Sweetie!"

The other boys whistled and made kissing noises.

"Come on, Gene!" said Enrique, and they walked faster.

"Hey, Enrique, come here!" yelled one of the boys. It was Pete Randolph.

Enrique outwalked Gene, who remained in the shade, apparently confused by the boys' attention.

"Enrique, I want to ask you something!"

Enrique slipped between the cars out into the parking lot.

"Hey, fag, are you deaf? I said, come here!" By the sound of Pete's voice, Enrique could tell that he was running to catch up with him. Then Enrique felt a hard shove from behind. He hit a car and fell onto the pavement. Pete stood over him. "Don't be a pussy, all right? When I call you, you come!" The look of anger on Pete's face was less that of a bully than a disgusted parent. He seemed to want to discipline Enrique, to teach him a lesson, but one Pete himself didn't know. "Fuckin' Mexican fag," he sputtered in frustration. He kicked Enrique's shin. It was a half-hearted kick, but strong enough to hurt.

Enrique would see, when he examined his shin in the bathtub that night, a gray smudge with dots of red where the tiny soft hairs grew out of the skin. Holding his knee close to him and examining the bruise and remembering Pete Randolph's face would make Enrique's penis start to grow, and he would quickly do it—masturbation—letting his seed, as Father Moore had called it, squirt under the water, unfurl and drop to the bottom.

Enrique lay on the pavement until he was sure Pete was gone. Then he got up and brushed himself off. Gene came around the car, pulling the bill of his white cap low over his eyes. "Are you okay?" he asked.

"Yeah," said Enrique.

"Did he beat you up?"

"No."

"Did he hit you?"

"I'm fine, Gene. Stop asking."

They walked back to the curb.

"We should go to the office," said Gene.

"Shut *up*," said Enrique, and he heard the whine in his voice. It sounded girly. *You must change your voice*, he told himself.

"Where's our stuff?" Gene asked.

"Oh no, did they steal it?" Enrique said. Then he saw his backpack, and Gene's, empty, hanging in the bushes. Their books were scattered. "Those buttholes!" Enrique said. (He still followed Lina's rules about bad language; he didn't say "asshole," even when she wasn't present.)

They gathered their things and put them back in their backpacks. The Trapper Keeper containing the project remained safely Velcro-sealed. Nothing was damaged.

Then they sat back down on the wall and waited.

Finally Jay pulled up in his car. It was a cool car, a Maverick with racing stripes. The Van Bekes had bought it for him when he was fourteen and learning to drive.

"Hey, faggots," said Jay.

"Screw off," Enrique muttered as he got in.

Jay smiled.

AT THE NURSING home, an old woman named Adele Burnham sat in a wheelchair angled toward the white wall. She pushed, but her curled foot just turned her more toward the wall. Adele's breath quickened and, like wind catching a sail, took on tone to become a whimper. With each gust of breath the whimper loudened, becoming a grunt, then a bawl.

"Mrs. Burnham, there's no reason to make a ruckus," said the new aide, turning her away from the wall. "Look, hon, now you can see what's goin' on."

Adele continued to make her short, hoarse calls.

"Sweetheart, you're gonna upset everyone if you keep this up. You're fine. Are your feet cold?" She placed the free foot onto its rest and tucked the blanket around it.

Adele's bawling only became louder.

"Sweetheart," she said, laying her hands on Adele's shoulders, "I need you to quiet down a little. Oh, now look. You've upset Mr. Ellis."

The man limped down the hall toward them with an expression that asked what he could do. He stopped short of them and put a crooked hand to his brow.

"Hush now, Mrs. Burnham," the aide said.

"She likes to be put in the light," Connie said. She took the handles and wheeled Adele down the hallway. The new aide followed. Adele furled her voice and breathed. Connie wheeled her to the crafts room and put her into the warm light before the sliding doors.

Adele tipped her head to the side so that despite the permanent crook in her neck the light struck her eye. Here, in the light, she could remember running up the sloped lawn after the picnic, tripping on the hem of her skirt—a bright green stain punctuated with brown dirt, *darn it!* And walking down the dirt road between yellow walls of grass, frightening a grouse who exploded into flight, causing other grouse to explode into flight, and they all flew, warbling as they went, over the irrigation ditch and back into the grass. And opening the curtains of her children's room on the first day of summer vacation to let the sun wake them, and sneezing.

Adele's voice warbled and her head nodded. "You learn these things over time," Connie said with a stern look. She'd have to keep an eye on this girl. Aides who showed so little restraint in placing their hands on the shoulders of their charges might shake them roughly before long. Connie had seen this happen, and worse.

The new aide nodded and looked around for an escape.

A wasp, in silhouette, slowly, lethargically climbed the window blind. Lina was always vacuuming up dead wasps. There must have been a nest under the eaves or in the attic. The wasp took flight and went from one window to the next, its body swaying like a heavy bag.

"This is nice, isn't it?" Mr. Hall said, stroking her hair.

Lina said nothing, but moved her hand under the covers to find a part of him. The part she found was his soft thigh. She squeezed it.

"When do you have to be home?" he asked.

"Today's Thursday? Five."

"Good. We have a little time."

"Do we?"

"Abby has a club meeting. Sandra is in Salt Lake."

"Well, Mr.— I want to call you by your name. What is your name?"

Mr. Hall pulled away. "You don't know my name?"

"No."

"How could you not know my name?"

"How could I know it? You never told me."

"But what do you call me?"

"Don' be stupid. I call you Mr. Hall."

"I . . . I never noticed." His expression, which was so easy to read, went from wonderment to amusement to a deep remorse. It occurred to Lina that somewhere in becoming an adult most people put on masks. How had he avoided this? Then his face changed again and he pulled her to him. The strength with which he did this surprised her, and she gasped. He put his hand to the back of her head, drew her near, and, in a low voice directly into her ear, said, "What do you think my name is?" It tickled.

"I don' know." Lina laughed and tried to push him away.

"Guess," he said.

"No. Lemme go."

"Not until you guess my name."

"Rumpelstiltskin?"

"No."

"Cory?"

"No."

"Tom? Dick? Harry?"

"No."

"I give up."

He continued to hold her close, breathing hard with the effort of holding her still. She could feel that his erection had returned and was throbbing against her hip. She stopped struggling and put one arm around him.

He whispered, "*Charles.*"

They kissed.

Then he pulled back and their eyes locked. He said, "But you can call me . . ."

He didn't finish. Did he want her to guess again?

"Charlie?" she guessed.

He shook his head. "Darling."

Lina groaned and turned away from him. She sat up and fumbled with the sheet to remain covered as she reached for her bra.

"Lina, what is it?"

"You always do that!"

"What?"

"You go too far. We're not kids. We're married. We shouldn't do this. I'm not going to call you 'darling.'"

Lina got dressed, and Mr. Hall stayed in bed. He wasn't the type of man who would stop a woman from leaving. He was weak. Before she left the room, she turned to him and said, "Tell me what I'm really supposed to call you. Is it Charles?"

"No." His voice rasped a little, as if there was something in his throat. He coughed. "Chuck."

"Thank you, Chuck. Good bye."

She went downstairs and gathered her things. She hadn't mopped. Before she left, she looked up to the railing of the second floor, her hand poised on the doorknob. Would he be there?

Of course not.

When Liz Padgett opened her locker after the science club meeting, she found a tightly folded note on the floor. Someone must have slipped it through the vent in the door. Liz unfolded the note and revealed the typewritten words: I LOVE YOU!

Each letter was made of faint lines anchored by black dots that nearly pierced the paper, and the short sentence got darker as it went, as if the writer's emotion became more ardent and his fingers stronger as he wrote. The bar and point of the exclamation point nearly met. I LOVE YOU! Clearly, this had been typed on one of the ancient manual typewriters in the school library.

Liz cast a glance around. No one. The hallway was lined with lockers interrupted here and there by dark gaps of classroom doors.

She read the sentence one more time. Then she laughed in its face. He didn't love her, this stupid Eula boy. Whatever dirty-nailed farmer or meathead jock or suicidal dirtbag had written this was confusing his lonely jerk-off fantasies with love. No one loved Liz, because no one but Abby knew her, and she wouldn't have had it any other way. Liz wished that Abby hadn't rushed off after the meeting. Liz would be laughing now rather than feeling angry tears rise. *Fuck you*, she said to her secret admirer. She refolded the note and looked for a trash can. Not finding one, she tossed it on the floor with the other debris. The janitor would be through soon.

Then she thought better and picked it up again. She put it in her pocket, a token of her unloved state, and went to her car. She set her jaw and drove south past the fields, over the ridge, to the grand house where she lived with those three strangers—Winston and her parents—who didn't, couldn't, love her.

On the way, Liz's smart compact car passed the dusty, dented clunker driven by Lina. A bit shell-shocked, Lina still felt in all her creases the residue of that man, whose name she had just learned and who she felt *loved* her (it was crazy, she knew) even though he didn't know her. Lina headed north through the town, to the doublewide where her sons—the one who had always been a stranger and the other, who was becoming one—sat watching TV in silence. Later, Jay would take off in his car, and Lina and Enrique would sit down to dinner, their secrets humming in their chests: *I was lifted up today*; *I was beaten down.*

Across town from the trailer park, past the thinning globes of trees, the dark-shingled roofs, and the white blades of church steeples, Connie sat in her car outside the nursing home. It was time to go home, but somehow she couldn't summon the will. Who would push her into the sun when she could no longer speak? Someone who loved her, or some stranger who was paid to do it? Or would she be left to kick the wall alone? She wondered, as she did so often, if Gene loved her and if she loved him. Then she quieted herself with this thought: *At the very least, I love him in God's way.* She lifted her chin and turned the key in the ignition.

In Eula, everyone loved everyone in God's way, or at least that was the story. If a grade-school boy was taunted by his friends with two-little-lovebirds rhymes, he might protest, "I don't love her!" then quickly amend, "I mean, I love her in *God's* way, but I don't *love her* love her." It was forbidden not to love everyone. Love was a light you directed not only in a narrow beam at your husband or son, but—differently and at the same time—you flooded over friends and strangers and, as Christ decreed, your enemies as yourself. The world lost its color in the light of such a love, as the houses did in the noonday sun. It was easier to find your way home in the evening, as Connie did now, when the windows glowed blue with TV light, and the sun's last rays lit the white smokestack of the sugar factory like a beacon.

After Lina left, Chuck dressed and opened the skylight, but then lay the remainder of the afternoon as the square of sunlight crossed the bed, bisecting him. His mind traveled over all his life and the faraway places he had been. The trash-strewn beach in Pattaya, Thailand. Kimmi was a masseuse, a prostitute. He stopped going to meetings of the convention to lie in the hotel room where she brought him mangoes. She couldn't believe that he had never eaten one—to her, it was as if he had never experienced any pleasure at all. She started the mango with her teeth and let the juice drip into the sink of the wet bar as she peeled it. That was love—taking that slick, fibrous mango from her and tasting it. He had written her letter after letter afterward, and she had sent him only one, at the office—"Miss You!!!"—and then, nothing.

Then his mind wandered back to his grandmother's house in Illinois, where his great-aunt, who never came downstairs, sat on the balcony and called, "Kids! Kids!" until he left the game and ran up the lawn. "Shake the rosemary for me!" He stepped carefully through the herb garden, bent, embraced the bush and shook it, then ran back down the lawn. His aunt's head fell back as she breathed in deeply. That August, after they left, she died on that balcony.

Sandra was in Salt Lake City, having her treatment.

Lina.

"Daddy?" Abby said softly from the doorway. He hadn't heard her car. It was dark outside now.

"Yes?"

"Are you taking a nap?"

"No, thinking. Are you just getting home?"

"I had science club, then I went to the library." She paused. "Have you been taking your medicine?"

"Yes, sweetheart. Heat something up. I'll be down in a minute."

Abby walked down the hall. "Smells clean," she said.

CHAPTER 7

For a moment Connie was captivated by the sparkling of dust in the projector light. All those things in the air that we never see—do we just breathe them and swallow them all day long? When Gene was a baby, his eyes always seemed to be following dust motes. She'd move her face into his line of vision, but his eyes wouldn't fasten on hers, they'd keep following the path of something else.

Then the guest speaker began and Connie looked to the screen and saw gray streaks of dawn over the African savanna. "Um, it's been four years since I've been in the States," he said, "so you'll have to forgive me if my presentation's a little rough." The women of the Dorcas Circle—the Dorcases, so named after the female judge in the Old Testament—gave him a reassuring murmur. "You ladies will be my guinea pigs; I'm going to show these slides at a few churches in the area. But anyway, I thought I'd start with something pretty. This is the view from the roof of our hospital."

"Ahh," said the women, as if his words only now released the beauty of the image, although it had been on the screen for several minutes as he had adjusted its focus and piled workbooks under the projector to bring it up.

"This is the hospital itself"—a two-story cinder-block cube next to a white goat—"and these are some of the children at the orphanage"—a group of laughing children, their skin blacker than any of the Dorcases had ever seen in person.

"Cute," cooed one of the women, and there were some affectionate laughs. Connie, though, did not laugh, because to do so seemed disrespectful of the direness of the children's situation and the importance of the missionary's work.

"And this—oops, I'll have to fix that—well, this is me with some of the children." The slide was upside-down.

The women all laughed; some tilted their heads one way, then the other. "We'll stand on our heads!" said Kaye, who was always quick with a loud, dumb joke.

"We have a hospital and an orphanage in our compound, two doctors on staff, seven nurses, three teachers, and I don't know how many gals work in the orphanage." Images lifted and dropped into place. "And two missionaries, one of which is me. Here's the church." In the reedy voice of someone more used to action than words, he described his mission. He seemed in a rush, as if he couldn't imagine anyone ever finding this interesting. He couldn't have been over thirty-five.

"These next slides might be a little disturbing. I put them in just to show the kind of things we deal with every day. I'll go through them quickly." On the screen appeared an old man whose arm was mottled purple and half rotted away from gangrene, then a baby whose mother lifted a dirty bandage to reveal a tumor which had overtaken one eye socket and resembled a neatly rolled ball of hamburger. The women gasped. When it came time for questions, he seemed surprised that the women were so interested, and his voice became more confident and his answers longer. Then Bess Morgan raised her hand. The other women exchanged worried looks.

"I have more of a comment than a question. It goes back to Paul's vision of the unclean foods being offered him in a sheet from heaven. This is the sign from God that we are to spread the Gospel, not only to our own people, but to the people of the world, and if missionaries are our equivalents nowadays of someone who has stepped out of his community and country and gone to a place where they don't even speak the language—or, I don't know if they speak English in Africa—but I'm sure partaking of foods that we would consider repulsive, or not repulsive, that's too strong of a word, but outside our experience, outside who we are, like how they eat crickets in Mexico . . ." When Bess went on these bizarre wanderings, her eyes would follow her words off into space, and her voice would become quieter, almost as if she were talking to herself. This had the annoying effect of making the others strain to hear words they didn't want to listen to. ". . . and in Egypt, it's no longer the ancient gods they worship, but Mohammed, just like they do in Saudi Arabia—but I know we're talking about a different part of Africa . . ." Again and again she reined herself in, but never so much as to bring the monologue to a point resembling a conclusion closely enough that one of the other women could gracefully interrupt. They just had to wait it out. Kaye, sitting next to Bess, was smiling and looking for someone with whom she could share a significant look, but the others considered this too mean. ". . . So what I'm saying, really, is thank you for doing something that others of us don't have the opportunity, or not the opportunity but the resolution, to do. I'm sorry I went on so long."

"That's quite all right," said the missionary. "I'm flattered. Thank you."

Pamela, the president of the Dorcas Circle, said, "I think we should have one more question, then close with prayer. Is that all right with you, Reverend Howard?"

"Sure, and please call me Bill."

"Connie, didn't you have your hand raised earlier?"

She hadn't, but she saw what Pamela was trying to do: bring the discussion to an end with something thoughtful.

"I think we're all wondering what we here in the States can do to help," Connie said. She used the phrase *the States* the way he had. The other women all nodded.

"Well, most importantly, keep us in your prayers. Send us letters of encouragement, remember us. Of course, you can also give us money; but really, ladies, your ministry is here in Eula, and it's as important as mine."

"Bill," Connie said. "I think I speak for all of us when I say that if you should need anything while you're in town, we'd be glad to help."

Pamela smiled and nodded. "Let's pray," she said.

Connie felt that she had handled that well. If Bill knew her, he would see that she didn't take things lightly. The gravity of the offer would counterbalance Bess's foolish speech and save face for the group. Maybe this had taken place even without his knowing her.

THE PHONE RANG during dinner. "I'll get it," said Lina, rising.

Jay didn't turn from the TV. His chair was pulled slightly away from the table so he could eat and watch the game at the same time.

Enrique gazed at the TV too, but with a far-off expression. Today he had gone to his locker between classes to find the words ENRIQUE HAS AIDS written in thick black marker on the door. After covering this with a scribble that left it still legible, Enrique had packed all his books into his backpack and avoided his locker for the rest of the day.

Lina answered the phone.

"Lina, it's Chuck."

"Oh."

"I'm sorry to call you at home, but I didn't know how else to reach you."

"Yes?"

"I'm sorry about how it ended . . . last week . . ."

Lina said nothing. Wouldn't he understand her boys were there?

"I was wondering if I could see you tomorrow."

"Oh, that's no good. I'm at the Hamiltons' tomorrow."

"Afterward, Lina. In the afternoon."

"No, sorry. I'm going to have to look at my calendar and call you back."

She went back to the table.

"Who was that?" Enrique asked.

"Mrs. Hood," Lina said.

"You don't like her, do you?" Enrique said.

"Why wouldn't I like Mrs. Hood?" Lina said. "I like her a lot."

"Your calendar?" Enrique said, a smile tugging up one corner of his mouth. "You don't have a calendar."

"*Diablito*," Lina grumbled, relieved that she had pulled it off.

Later that night, Enrique worked up the courage to call Abby Hall. Her dad answered.

"May I please speak to Abby?"

"Hold on," said Mr. Hall.

"Hello?"

"Hi, Abby. It's Enrique Cortez."

"Hey, Enrique," she said.

"I was wondering if Gene and I could show you our project before the science club meeting."

"Sure. How about tomorrow?"

"Okay."

"Um, I'm busy after school," said Abby, "but I have study hall during junior high lunch period. Would you want to do it then?"

"Sure."

"I'll just find you in the lunchroom."

"Okay. Thanks."

Enrique hung up the phone. A high school girl was going to come eat lunch with him and Gene while all the junior high kids looked on, including whoever had written that on his locker. Enrique was going to give her an update on the project. And he would win the science fair and be on TV and everything would be better. He was so excited, he couldn't help mentioning it to his mom and Jay, even though he knew Jay would make fun of him.

"The high school science club is helping us with our science-fair projects," Enrique said, standing next to the television.

"Really, *mijo*?" Lina said. She wriggled her toes, in their socks, on the coffee table. "How nice!"

"Yeah, the girl who's helping me and Gene is really neat."

"What's her name?"

"Abby Hall."

The look on Lina's face shifted. It wasn't a mere look of recognition (Enrique knew that his mother was acquainted with Abby, since she cleaned her house); it was recognition followed by a shade of concern, then obscured behind a smile like a curtain quickly drawn. Enrique immediately knew that it was Abby's father, Mr. Hall, who had kissed her. Now his good mood was ruined.

"I know Abby Hall," muttered Jay without turning from the TV.

Enrique felt he must defend Abby, who had been wronged by her father, just as he had by Lina. "She's nice!" he barked.

"*She's nice*," Jay mimicked, bobbling his head and bugging his eyes.

"Come on, Jay," said Lina.

Jay emitted a low, rasping laugh. "Enrique, do you have a crush on Abby Hall?"

"No."

"You do! You have a crush on Abby! Good boy! Hot nerd-on-nerd action!" Jay started making sex noises.

"Mom, make him stop," Enrique said. But when he looked at her, he saw that she was smiling. Betrayed, he opened his mouth and released a breath that, had he not checked himself, had he not been on his guard not to sound girly, would have been a whimper. He ran to his room.

"Enrique, come back," said Lina. There was suppressed laughter in her voice.

Enrique slammed his door and threw himself onto the bed, causing the springs to squeak. It seemed that his mother, having done something dirty with Mr. Hall, wanted to make things between Enrique and Abby dirty as well, to ease her guilt. But they *weren't* dirty.

Back in the living room, Lina said quietly to Jay, "Don't tease him," and they both chuckled.

The next morning, before Lina went to the Hamiltons', she called Chuck at his office.

"You can't call me at home," she said. "I have kids."

"But how am I supposed to contact you?"

"You're not supposed to contact me. You're married."

Chuck allowed for a silence, then he said, "Do you want me to leave you alone, Lina?"

"No."

"This afternoon?"

"Four o'clock."

COOP SAT BACK in the glider and Wanda, in a rusted old lawn chair, wrapped her coat tighter around her. The glider was Coop's favorite possession. It was an extravagance, having cost $150 at Greenhurst Nursery, but since Coop often entertained on his porch those visitors who were hesitant to go into the house where Uncle Frank sat drinking in front of the TV, the glider saw plenty of use. Soon, Coop would haul it down to the cellar so it wouldn't rust over the winter—that was always a sad November day—but tonight was brisk but not cold, and the air was scented with burning corn husks. Coop glided back and forth, his foot resting on a stool, the wicker of which was punched through like a circus net that had seen an accident.

"Things are getting better," Wanda said at last. "I have a plan. I just need to get through this rough patch. And I've got to go to Portland."

"Why Portland?" Coop asked.

"Well . . ." said Wanda, then she released a little sigh, and gave up. She always forgot how much she feared Coop and craved his approval until she was face-to-face with him. Coop rubbed his great, yellow palms together and stared up into the trees. His shoulders were sloped at the angle those of a mountain would be, washed away by rain. "I'm registering with this agency," Wanda continued. "It's a way to make money. Honest money. I'm not with Hank anymore. I can't go back to him ever again, Coop. He's mean, Coop—meaner than I've told you."

Coop shook his head. "What kind of agency?"

"Let me explain before you say anything, okay? And don't make fun."

"Okay."

"Promise?"

"Wanda—"

"It's an agency that matches couples with surrogate mothers. I want to be a surrogate mother." Wanda cringed.

Coop smiled a smile of pain, silently.

"I want to carry a child, Coop. I'm never gonna have one of my own, I can just tell. I'm thirty-one and I've never even come close to meeting Mr. Right. I missed my chance; they're all gone. I don't know, Coop, they never liked me anyways, the good ones. But I want to carry a child. I don't want to die with that regret, that I never did that with my body. I feel like my body wants it. There's so many of these poor, infertile couples . . ." She paused, ashamed of showing emotion, and worried that it seemed, to Coop, disingenuous. "And I'd get paid ten thousand dollars."

"Wanda, they give you a physical before they let you do that. They check you out good. Can you pass a physical?"

"Yes, Coop, I'm clean. Totally clean for months, I swear it."

This was true, in a way. It had been months since she had done illegal drugs. Even pot. She still bought the pain pills from Tammy, but she swallowed them like she should. The last time she had snorted one was that day when she had gone to court in Boise. The day Gary came over.

Something went wrong in Wanda that day. She woke the next morning with a discomfort in her belly and a yawning sadness in her heart. I'm pregnant, she thought. This is what that feels like.

A cautious certainty took hold even though her period had been out of whack for years. She would go four months without menstruating, then they'd come all in a rush in one miserable, cramped month. She attributed this to not eating right. A friend told her if she ate raw spinach her periods would become regular. In any case, Wanda had been boyish in adolescence—her breasts, when they finally came, were small and cone-shaped—and she had suspected since then that her apparatus down there wasn't functional.

As the days went on, she became more and more certain. Should she drink lighter fluid? Another friend had once been pregnant, and the fluid from one plastic disposable lighter had caused her to abort. Wanda went so far as to smash a lighter with a rolling pin and allow its contents to trickle into a coffee mug before the smell made her reconsider. Instead she swallowed a pain pill, thereby putting an end to her thinking for that day.

After two weeks of mild morning sickness and worry, mainly concerning how bad an abortion would hurt, Wanda decided it was time she confirmed what she already knew. She bought a pregnancy test, the kind where you pee on a stick. After a few minutes it gave a faint pink minus sign. Negative. She bought a different brand the next day and tried again. It too told her she wasn't pregnant.

How could this be? She felt the little thing growing inside her. She had even come to suspect already that it was a girl. Was it still too early to show? She read and reread the insert from the pregnancy test. The next day, still wondering whom to believe—the tests or the baby inside her—proof came: she lowered her underwear to see a crease of rust on the white fabric. Either the baby had never been there to begin with, or it was coming out with her period. Wanda knew she should feel relieved, but she felt more miserable than ever before. Or, rather, her fundamental misery, which had been set off by her father's death and deepened by her mother's, and that Wanda had daubed for a few days with the idea of a baby, was laid bare again, and it was hotter and throbbed more for the treatment.

Why? She knew she couldn't care for a child.

Then she saw a *Donahue* on "The Real Face of Surrogacy." In reaction to the Baby M controversy, which was all over the news, several surrogate mothers took Donahue's stage and insisted that nearly every surrogate pregnancy ended with a smooth transfer of the baby to the "intended parents," or IPs. The surrogates were treated with the utmost respect by the IPs. The couples flew them in for visits, made sure they ate right, bought them gifts. Some let them play roles in the children's lives, like aunts. Several couples came on and described their plights—the years of trying and failing, the tens of thousands of dollars spent on treatments that didn't work, the decorated nurseries that remained empty until they found their surrogate mother. It touched that part of Wanda that had felt so guilty for playing the role of Mrs. Wojciechowski—that good woman, that rightful mother—and she stayed on the couch long after the show was over, blowing her nose into a dish towel, crying deliriously for those poor people who had been saved from suffering, and for herself, who, it seemed, never would be.

"I even quit smokin'," Wanda offered.

"Well, I'll be damned."

Wanda blushed with pride. "It was easy. Easier than I thought."

"Still, Wanda, you might be gettin' yourself in more than you can bargain for. It's a real live baby you'll have in your belly. That's nothin' to sneeze at."

"I thought it through, Coop. I haven't been thinkin' about anything else."

Coop squinted out at the street for a while, his eyes moving from side to side as if he were reading an answer written there on the pavement. Wanda was tempted to say more to convince him, but she quieted herself and let him think.

This was not the first time Wanda had hit Coop up for a loan, not by a long shot, but there was something different this time. It was evident to Coop that she was clean and had been, if not for months as she claimed, at least for weeks. Her complexion was clear and her face was full. And if Hank was truly gone for good, all the better. The man had always scared Coop, even though he was as scrawny as a wet poodle and flinched when Coop went to clap him on the back. There was something in the lines that framed Wanda's eyes—age or weariness—that allowed Coop to look into them and not look away. Strange, that wrinkles would be attractive on a person. Well, when he was used to seeing those wild, hungry eyes and skin tortured with hives . . .

Fundamentally, the idea of carrying a baby for ten thousand dollars seemed crazy to Coop, but he had seen the same *Donahue*, so he knew that surrogate mothers got mandatory checkups before they became pregnant and after. He had noticed Wanda use the same phrase one of the surrogate mothers on the show had used: "My body wants this." He didn't fault Wanda, though, if she borrowed feelings from people on TV on her way to becoming real. Ten thousand dollars to go through a kind of enforced detox? Wanda could do worse.

"I tell you what," said Coop. "You take a couple weeks to think about this. If you're still sure, then come back, and we'll talk about the money."

Wanda inhaled to protest, then thought better of it. Once Coop made a decision, he never changed his mind. This was a lesson Wanda could never learn when she was high. She'd whimper, wail, lie, make empty promises, and finally call him a traitor, but Coop would never budge. Neither would he ever show his anger. From a distance, he'd let her hiss and sputter like a campfire you mustn't leave burning, then he'd walk wordlessly back into his house. What an idiot she had been!

Coop leaned forward in the glider to rest his elbows on his knees. "Good night for food shoppin'. Care to join me?"

They went to the grocery store, where Coop gave Wanda her

own cart and told her to get whatever she wanted. She tried to keep it cheap: packages of assorted lunch meats, popcorn in disposable tins, milk, eggs. Coop filled his own cart and stopped in the beer aisle for several cases of the cheap stuff. Coop and Wanda were quiet as he loaded these onto the rack under his cart. Neither Coop nor Wanda drank; these were for Uncle Frank.

Then Coop dropped Wanda off at home. Unloading her groceries, she discovered that Coop had slipped her a packet of T-bones and—Wanda caught her breath—a bag of frozen chicken livers. Their mother had made the most delicious chicken-liver gravy. It had been Wanda's favorite but, of course, she hadn't the faintest idea how to make it.

From the back porch of the house in which Coop and Wanda were raised, one could see band after band of decreasing width and fading color—the thick, mossy ribbon of an alfalfa field, a lighter one speckled with cows—leading to the ragged strand of a tree-lined canal. Beyond that the bands became threads, then the sky.

On an evening when he was only six or seven, Coop had been sitting there imagining he could hear the earth turning (it was really just the wash of soft sounds—distant running water, the wind's hiss on grass, and the whir of the windmill) when a crash shook the house. Coop sprang to his feet and ran inside. Again: *Chop!* In the kitchen there were two chalky scars in the yellow wall, and his father stood grinning and weighing a long-handled axe in both hands. "Get the boys; we're gonna make a door." Maybe the beauty of the evening had inspired him to make the porch accessible from the kitchen. Whatever the reason, he was ecstatic. Coop, delighted as he always became when his father was in such a mood, got Paul and the two began to carry chunks of drywall to the back porch, leaving a trail of white dust through the living room.

Then their grandfather arrived, their mother's father, who was a preacher. Their mother had called him. He put his hand on Coop's father's shoulder between chops, causing him to turn, his face bright, then confused, then desperate—quickly it darkened, just like that. Coop wondered if he had done something wrong by helping his father. Coop's grandfather took the man out across the fields, where they talked and prayed.

The wall stayed open like that, the drywall torn away, ribs exposed, for months, as Coop's father sank into silence and slept most of every day. Finally a stranger, someone from his grandfather's church, came and repaired the wall. His mother painted it a yellow that didn't quite match.

Wanda didn't remember their father; she had been too young when he died. She remembered Alan, though, their stepfather from when she was five until she was eight. Under Alan's tutelage their mother became a true drunk. It was like a daylong theater piece the couple performed, a passion play, which began quietly, Alan making whimpering requests of the children—"Bring me my coffee," "Give Daddy a hug"—which would be grumpily reinforced by their mother from her easy chair in front of the TV. Then, in the afternoon, they would abandon their chipped coffee cups for Mason jars of iced tea and whiskey. "Look at Katherine, she's gettin' her boobies," Alan said, and everyone laughed, except for Katherine, who folded her arms and ran outside. As the afternoon wore on and their mother and Alan howled at each other's half-fictional stories and danced to country music, the children felt they had two big, sloppy playmates. But, like monkeys among elephants, the children were always sure to have an escape route open, because their mother and Alan weren't like other parents—they didn't look where they stepped. When the sun went down, it was best to go upstairs or to a friend's house, because that's when the drama's climax took place. The two would go to the bedroom, forgetting to close the door, and rustle around, emitting mysterious bursts of laughter, grunts, and moans. Or, more often, there was a hollering, figurine-throwing fight.

Usually Coop, who had become a tall, heavy-set teenager, kept his distance from these silly, maudlin games in which neither his mother nor Alan could successfully complete an insulting sentence, but those times Alan grabbed their mother by the hair and slammed his open hand into her face as she thrashed and screamed, Coop intervened. He dragged Alan at arm's length outside as the man swung and spat and cursed until he exhausted himself and crumpled, whimperingly. Once, though, Alan threw a good punch that landed squarely on Coop's jaw, jarring him to the base of his spine. (Coop's jaw was crooked for days, and he could barely chew until the swelling receded.) Coop responded with a powerful slug to Alan's middle, which sent him staggering backward, releasing a spew of yellow, whiskey-scented vomit that splattered across Coop's boots. Alan stood with his hands on his knees, shaking his head like a sick cat, until he was able to manage one huge gasp. "Sum-bitch," he croaked, then there was a long pause as his windpipe seized again. He squeezed his eyes shut and managed another gasp. "Kill-you-sum-bitch."

Coop's mother rushed out and threw her arms around Alan, sheltering him. "Are you trying to kill him?" she screamed.

Coop held his aching jaw and laughed. What could he do but laugh?

Alan caught his breath, hid his face in his wife's breast, and cried. He really was a coward.

"Go on!" Coop's mother screamed.

Coop turned and wandered off down the dirt road. It was not until hours later, as he stood at the spigot on the back of the shed cleaning the yellow crust off his boots, that he cried a little.

Coop moved in with his uncle, his dead father's brother, in town—another drunk, but of a different, quieter type. For the season that Coop lived there, none of his siblings spoke to him, partly because they felt abandoned, but mostly because they all, even the younger ones, hated their uncle because he had killed their father, albeit accidentally, on a hunting trip.

It was a few more months before Alan left for good. None of the children knew what unforgivable thing came to pass, but at the end of a fight, which was more hushed and urgent than usual, the children heard their mother say, "Leave, Alan."

"I ain't leavin'. This is my house much as yours now. I been payin' the mortgage. And these kids is much mine as yours too."

"Leave, Alan, please!" Her voice cracked with a fearfulness unfamiliar to the children.

"Why don't you just go, if you need to be rid of me?"

The children heard the rustle and bump of their mother gathering some things. Could she actually be leaving? Wanda slipped out of bed and ran across the room to crawl into Katherine's bed. The two held each other and cried.

"You're a fuckin' whore," said Alan. It sounded as if he was sitting at the kitchen table, probably sipping straight whiskey, as their mother went up and down the stairs in a frightened rush. Then she left. Wanda could hardly believe it, but the old station wagon revved and sped down the driveway, leaving the children all hiding in their beds. There were minutes of quiet, without even a sound from the kitchen, until Alan announced loudly, "Your mother is a fuckin' whore. You kids know what that is? Somebody fucks men for money." Then he crossed the kitchen and opened the freezer for ice.

Wanda cried softly, and Katherine said, "Go to sleep. It'll be all right." But there was no confidence in her voice, only a scared tremor.

Then Alan's footsteps were on the stairs, climbing up. He opened the door to their room, and Wanda and Katherine clung to each other, shaking—their bodies actually shaking—with fear. "Look at me," said Alan, "or else I'll give you both a spanking."

Neither of them moved.

"Look at me," he said and pulled the covers from over their heads.

Katherine let out a little shriek.

"Your mother is a fuckin' whore," said Alan. "You know what that means? Means she sucks men's pricks for a dollar." Wanda saw that his pants were open and he held himself with his hand. "Look. This is gonna be yer livelihood." Sickened and fascinated, Wanda caught a glimpse of a little white nub peeking out from a black mass before she turned to hide. She had seen the neighbors' horses mating once, so that was what she thought men's penises were: black poles like the nightsticks that dangled from policemen's belts. But this was nothing so powerful; it looked, especially in the haze of memory, like a tiny, ugly face.

(The thought would return to her years later, when her foster brothers crept to her bedroom and forced themselves on her. What was it that tormented men and boys in the middle of the night? Why couldn't they just sleep? She imagined herself mouthing those ugly little faces, sucking their Pinocchio-noses. This didn't make it any better, just different.)

Paul, who, at thirteen, was the second-oldest brother, appeared brandishing a baseball bat in the doorway, flanked by the two other boys. "Get out of here!" he hollered at Alan. "Leave them alone or we'll kill you!" The boys' eyes were white in the dimness, and Louis, the youngest boy, only a year older than Wanda, was holding high some little weapon from the kitchen with a bravery his tear-streaked face belied. This was the part of the memory Wanda might rush over, to avoid the pang in her heart. Louis, that sweet and haunted boy, would spend his life in and out of Blackfoot. The last time he checked himself out they found his body days later on the shore of the Snake River a few miles and a rapids downstream from the psychiatric hospital.

Alan laughed and stumbled toward the boys. "You little bastards! You gonna beat yer daddy?"

"You're not our daddy!" they screamed as they ran down the hall.

There was the sound of a car in the driveway, and Alan crossed the room quickly to look out the window. Relief gushed from Wanda's heart and warmed her body. Had her mother come back? Was it the police?

No, neither. Wanda's mother was on parole and therefore wouldn't call the police. She had swallowed her pride and, for the first time since her husband's death, driven to the house of his brother, in town. It was Coop who alone got out of his uncle's truck.

Alan rushed downstairs and locked himself in the bedroom. Wanda knew Coop by his shuffling but determined steps against the gritty floorboards in the foyer. "It's Coop," she whispered to Katherine, and she started to crawl out of the bed.

"Stay here!" Katherine said, seizing Wanda's arm.

Something strange was going on. It was certainly Coop down in the kitchen, but he was doing something only their mother and Alan did, something patently grown-up: he was making coffee.

"Lemme go!" Wanda said, squirming.

"Don't go down there," Katherine said. "Go to sleep."

Wanda yanked her arm free and ran down the stairs. There was

Coop at the kitchen table, and, sure enough, coffee was percolating on the stove. Wanda jumped into his lap, and he held her as she cried.

"Did he hurt anyone?" Coop asked.

Wanda shook her head without lifting it from his shoulder.

None of the other children came down. Relieved that Coop was there, no doubt, they still regarded him as a traitor.

After a few minutes, Wanda stopped crying. Coop got up, carrying her with him, and poured himself a cup of coffee. This frightened her a little, as coffee was the awful medicine that lifted Alan and her mother from their stupor and put into motion the day's drama. She hated its bitter smell. The third cup always had a dash of whiskey in it. Would Coop drink until he danced, then dance until his mood turned and he hollered? Who would he holler at?

There was a scrambling in the living room as Alan dashed out to his car. The engine roared, and he was gone. Coop's shoulder, shaking in laughter, jarred Wanda's chin. "Son of a *bitch*," he said.

Then he kissed Wanda's head in apology for having disturbed her, but she had quickly fallen asleep, the way children do when they are safe. He freed some strands of her hair from his lips, sipped his coffee, and stared at the discolored patch in the yellow wall.

CHAPTER 8

It seemed that all of Enrique's competitors had altered their projects according to Mr. Peterson's advice except for April and Tommy. Still riding on the success of their presentation in class, they basically repeated it for the science club. "Tommy's going to be wearing a black outfit. I'm going to stick three-dimensional representations of the germs and parasites and stuff to his body." Tommy stood ready—smiling with his funny underbite, his feet apart and his hands slightly raised—although it didn't seem that April was going to demonstrate.

"That's a good idea," said one of the high school kids, "but remember, the judging takes, like, two hours, then the public viewing lasts for two more. Even longer if you make it to State. Are you going to want to stand around for that long? It's good to have a stationary display you can leave and come back to."

"Good point," said Mr. Peterson.

Stumped, April and Tommy both turned questioning expressions on their mentor, who sat at a desk in the front row. He lifted his hands and gave a nod, a gesture which seemed to mean, *It'll be all right*, and perhaps, *We'll discuss it later.*

Next, the volcano boys presented their project, which now focused on the 1980 eruption of Mount St. Helens. "We're going to have poster boards with before-and-after pictures," one explained, "and then we'll set off the model volcano during the judging."

Kevin, the president of the science club, stood leaning against the wall. "They've seen a million Mount St. Helenses," he said flatly. "What are you going to do to make yours different?"

Some of the science club members rolled their eyes. Kevin, who was so mercilessly taunted by the jocks in the hall, liked to play king here.

The boys looked at each other. They had already differentiated theirs from other volcanoes. Now they had to further differentiate it from other Mount St. Helenses?

Miriam went next and stood alone before the group. For a moment Enrique wondered if her little brother was still serving as her partner, and why she hadn't recruited one of her girlfriends to join her. But then the screen, which Enrique hadn't noticed was down, lit up, and a picture of a fish slid onto it. Cam Pierce, Miriam's mentor, was operating the overhead projector. "The sockeye salmon is an ancient species native to Payette Lake and other lakes around Idaho," Miriam began. "But only seventy percent of our river species and fifty percent of our lake species of fish are native. What is the impact of the high numbers of introduced species on our bodies of water and the native species that live there?"

Enrique again felt a dim and conflicted sense of relief; Miriam had scrapped her cow project, but the one she had chosen instead was even more boring. During her presentation, the audience read their own notes or turned to the window, which afforded only a bleak view, as it was filthy and covered by a grate. One girl mercilessly clicked the buttons on a four-color pen, apparently unaware of the loud sound it made. When Miriam finished, no one had any questions, so she sat down.

Now it was Enrique and Gene's turn. Coming up with a second draft of the project had been a balancing act. Enrique had to appease Gene, who had resisted the removal of the ants, seeming not to care if the project would be disqualified. Enrique had been too excited by the fact of Abby's lunchtime consultation to remember afterward much of what she had said. (The lunchroom din *had* quieted somewhat as she walked through; Enrique imagined the faces of his tormentors burning with envy.) Gene had gone to Boise again on Sunday and returned with updated clippings from the *New York Times* and a science magazine. All of this served to make the project stronger, so it was with new confidence that Enrique explained to the science club what had happened that night in Cameroon.

"Were these people poisoned on purpose by rebels, as the newspapers suggested that first day? This hypothesis has already been rejected. A man-made poisonous gas would have left a residue and might have damaged plants as well as animals, as mustard gas did in the First World War. No plants were damaged in the least, and there was no odor.

"Was it a volcanic eruption? No. There was no noise reported, no explosion, no smoke, and no ash.

"Some scientists have suggested that gases stored up over years under Lake Nyos could have reached such a mass that they bubbled up out of the lake and flowed down over the villages. But what gases? Hydrogen sulfide is a gas commonly produced by volcanoes. It's the same gas you smell when you crack open a rotten egg. At a concentration of one part per thousand in the air it can cause immediate collapse with loss of breathing after one breath.

"So, why should we here in Eula, Idaho, care?

"Two years ago, in another lake in Cameroon, the same thing seems to have happened, killing forty people. If we don't find out exactly what happened at these two lakes on the other side of the world, how do we know it can't happen here? Say, for example, at our own Lake Overlook?"

This was the angle that Enrique and Gene had arrived at, together, three nights before. Enrique liked the idea of creating a model, and Gene was interested in calculating the possible magnitude of the disaster in a different lake, based on volume or surface area.

Enrique now held up a large drawing, in marker, of their planned model. "The gas that escaped Lake Nyos appears to have traveled down the valleys, getting weaker as it went along. This means it's a gas that is heavier than air. Gene and I are going to make a model of Lake Overlook and Eula. We're going to fill Lake Overlook with dry ice. The visible carbon dioxide mist will flow over the town." Enrique pointed to a group of buildings in the foreground of the drawing. "At Lake Nyos, every human and animal in a fifteen-mile radius was killed. Our model will make it clear how, if the same phenomenon took place at Lake Overlook, everyone in Eula would die."

Enrique smiled. When a stunned silence greeted him, he gave a little nod to indicate that his presentation was over.

"Enrique," Miriam ventured, "the demonstration . . . it's like you're gassing our town."

"It's meant to be shocking," Enrique said, "so people realize how important it is for us to solve this riddle. It makes our project very relevant."

"It's creepy," said a high school boy.

Enrique could see that Abby, sitting in back, bit her lip in a pained expression. She had gently warned him and Gene at lunch that this might be the group's reaction.

Kevin finally broke the silence. "Let's thank our junior brethren for their fascinating presentations." The high school kids applauded, and the meeting was adjourned.

Enrique quickly headed out, as they were late to meet Jay for their ride home, but Miriam called out his name in the hall.

"What?" he said, turning.

She marched up to him. Cam Pierce waited by the classroom door. Apparently, he was her ride. "Enrique, don't do that project."

"Why not?"

"You'll never win."

"Yes, we *will* win. It's a good project."

"Enrique, it's a bad thing to do."

"You're just jealous."

"I'm trying to do you a favor. It's wrong, and you'll never win by telling people they could all die."

"*You'll* never win with your stupid, boring fish!" Enrique said.

Miriam's eyes narrowed. She inhaled to say more, stopped herself, then spun around and walked back to Cam. The oversized collar of her blouse bounced with every step.

"Come on, Gene. We're late." When they reached the lawn, Enrique tugged on Gene's sleeve, indicating that this time they had to walk directly across. Gene made a grumpy, wordless noise.

"She's just jealous that we have a neat project," Enrique said once they reached the shade.

"She's afraid," said Gene.

"Afraid of what?"

"Of dying."

"Don't be weird, Gene. Nobody thinks this lake thing is going to happen here."

"Why not?"

"Hurry up," Enrique said. "Jay's probably waiting."

They passed between the buildings, and Enrique saw the junior high football team waiting for their rides in front of the entrance. Beyond them, Jay stood leaning against his car.

"Great," said Enrique.

In the past week, the low murmur of taunting and name-calling had risen in volume. An anonymous catcall, *En*-ri-*que!*, sailed through the hall as he ran for class; a muttered *faggot* rose from somewhere in the group of boys when he dropped the ball in gym class. His taunters had an uncanny ability to strike a perfect balance: loud enough to reach Enrique's ears and tip him over the precipice into the blackest of moods, quiet enough to be anonymous, leaving Enrique to wonder who and how many his enemies were.

Now he tucked his chin, steeled himself, and walked quickly forward.

"It's Enrique and Gene!" said Pete Randolph, and all the boys turned. "Hey, Enrique, are you guys on a date? Are you gonna go butt-fuck?" The boys laughed. A foot stuck out from the group as they passed. Gene stumbled over it, then broke into a jog to catch up with Enrique, who was already climbing into Jay's car.

"Let's go," Enrique said, but Jay remained outside leaning against the car with his arms folded. "I'm sorry we're late. Can we go now?"

Jay paused, then launched himself from the car and walked slowly over to the group of boys. One by one they noticed his approach and fell silent. Jay stood looking down at Pete Randolph, who chuckled, glanced at his friends, and said, "Hello, can I help you?"

Jay grabbed him roughly by the front of the shirt, causing his head to whip back. "Listen, you little piece of shit," he said, "don't talk to my little brother. Don't say a fucking word to him, or I'll kill you."

The other boys stepped backward into a large, loose ring that threatened to come apart altogether. Jay released Pete's shirt and started to turn away, then apparently changed his mind and decided to allow himself one slug. He made it fast and hard to Pete's shoulder.

Pete stumbled backward, then squeezed his eyes shut and held his shoulder. Without producing a sound, his mouth made the large, round shape of *owwww!*

Jay turned slowly away, spat into the bushes, and walked to the car.

Enrique wondered, on the way home, why Jay had done this. Did he like him after all? And would this episode make life at school easier or harder? Easier, most likely. But what if it only served to confirm that he was a sissy who couldn't fend for himself? What if Pete sought his revenge by increasing the taunting, or even by beating Enrique up? Enrique would not be able to fight; he had never even hit anyone. He'd have no choice but to roll into a ball on the floor that Pete would kick and kick until a teacher pulled him off. For days he'd limp from class to class covered with a camouflage pattern of bruises. But even these images couldn't diminish the delight of having watched Pete Randolph take a punch from his brother. As they descended from the overpass into the north side where the leaf-matted lawns were littered with broken plastic toys, Enrique gazed out at the passing houses to hide his smile.

Apparently wishing to change lanes, Jay looked to the rearview mirror. "Stop gawking at me, faggot!" he said to Gene.

Gene's face knotted and dropped.

THE NEXT DAY, Connie pulled into her spot and climbed the steps. "Gene, are you home?" she called. No answer. He couldn't have been far, though: while the screen door was closed, the front door hung open into the living room. She went to Lina's porch and called him again.

"Yes?"

"I'm home, Gene."

"Come on in, Mrs. Anderson," called Enrique.

"My goodness, what are you boys building?"

The living room was carpeted with newspaper. Gene stood

holding a long strip of Plexiglas that was two feet wide and nearly as tall as he was. Enrique was squatted on the floor glue-gunning the edge of the strip to another at a right angle. The house smelled of newsprint and burned plastic. With a twinge of envy, Connie glanced around the relatively spacious, wood-paneled room and saw a crucifix, a garland of silk flowers, several candles in glass cylinders decorated with images of saints. *Idolatry.* A seam where the house's two parts had been joined ran along the ceiling and down the middle of the kitchen wall to disappear behind the cabinets.

"It's our project for the science fair," said Enrique.

"You boys are in a science fair?"

"Uh-huh."

"Is your mother okay with this?"

"Yes, Mrs. Anderson, she knows all about it. Gene, hold still. It's almost dry."

Connie walked back to her house. She was glad they were using Lina's living room and not hers, but then she wondered, why weren't they using hers? They hadn't even asked. Was it because Lina's was roomier, or because they felt more at ease there?

The tiny red light on the answering machine blinked. Connie slipped out of her shoes, sat down, and pushed the button. Then she began to gently work her fingers into the aching muscles of her jaw.

"Oh, hello, this is a message for Connie. This is Bill Howard. I spoke to your group last week. I work at a mission in the Ivory Coast." How charming, that he would think he had to remind her! "Well, I was remembering your offer, that you'd be able to help me while I was in town, and wondering if I might take you up on that. Please give me a call." He gave his phone number.

For a minute Connie was dizzy and unable to move. Could this be the Lord's calling for which she had been waiting? Finally she took a deep breath and dialed the number. She got a machine with another man's voice, not Bill's. He must be staying in the visitors' apartment above the garage of the parsonage.

"Hello, Bill, this is Connie Anderson. My offer is certainly still open, and you can call me any time. I'll be home all night. Thank you. I look forward to your call."

She slammed down the phone and cringed. Had she sounded too

eager? Then she chided herself, *Settle down, Connie. You're acting like a silly girl.* But she couldn't help it. She felt that this might be what she had been praying for.

Connie had barely had time to get to know her husband—not nearly enough to start to love him—when he took all his things (and some of hers) and disappeared. She spent years praying for someone to love, until, a little over a year ago, she had her spiritual awakening. First Church put on a week of revival meetings in the evenings, featuring a popular speaker, Reverend Raleigh Wells the Painting Preacher. Reverend Raleigh wore a small microphone on his wide lapel, and his voice was broadcast throughout the darkened sanctuary, even though these revival meetings were attended by only around fifty congregation members who, in order to have a good view, filled the first few pews. Connie still thought of them as pews even though they were comfortable padded seats whose bottoms popped up, like those in a movie theater, when you rose to sing. The unique thing about Reverend Raleigh was that as he preached he painted a beautiful picture that illustrated the sermon. The first night's program was entitled "Scaling the Heights." Reverend Raleigh spoke of overcoming obstacles on the steep climb toward redemption and painted several peaks that might have been the Tetons, swiftly adding snow to the slopes with a blade. Night two's sermon was on the "Fruits of the Spirit," and the reverend painted a peaceful apple orchard, deftly sprinkling leaves onto the waiting branches with a large round brush dabbed in green. The congregation responded to such elegant touches with an approving sigh. Each night's picture grew in beauty and detail as the sermon built upon itself. Blank shapes that appeared meaningless were, with a few magical brushstrokes, transformed into lakes, clouds, meadows.

Connie best remembered night three's sermon, "Finding Your Joy." The picture was strange and less beautiful than those that preceded it: a forest overhung with vines, darkening at the center of the canvas into a thicket. "People today have lost their joy, or never touched it in the first place," the reverend said as he created a tangle of green shapes. "I see these folks who are wandering around, numb. They're dependent on drugs, alcohol. They're slaving away in an endless quest for material wealth. They're angry at their folks, their brothers and sisters, their kids, even. They cling to resentment from old arguments until it's the resentment clinging to *them*, binding them, wrapping them up like spiders trapped in their own webs. They're lonely, lonely, lonely," and with this he turned to the congregation, still holding his brush, his eyes the very picture of sympathy, his apron a battlefield of colors. "I've traveled all over the country, my friends, and do you know the most common problem I find in the lives of the folks I meet? More common than addiction, anger, and all manner of sin? Loneliness. I met a man in Texas with eight children, dozens of grandchildren, a loving wife, and many friends. And still he was lonely, lonely, lonely to the brink of despair. People hugged that man and told him they loved him every day, but still his heart was like a piece of meat packed in ice.

"Why? *Why?*" Reverend Raleigh seemed on the verge of tears. "Why does this happen, when it's so simple? When the escape from life's traps, when the balm for all of our wounds, when the *cure* for *pain* is offered us at no cost whatsoever?" He dropped his head and allowed for a lengthy silence among the congregation members, some of whom touched handkerchiefs to their faces. Then he threw back his head, heaved a deep breath, and tuned again to his painting. "Christ has a store of joy for each of us, not just in the afterlife, but in *this life*." He set down the green brush, picked up a clean one, and dipped it in white. "Paul says, 'Neither death, nor life, nor angels, nor principalities, nor powers, nor things present, nor things to come, nor height, nor depth, nor any other creature, shall be able to separate us from the love of God.' And that love, my friends, is the source of the purest, realest, brightest, and most enduring joy to be found in this world." With this he drew the brush down from the top of the thicket, creating a shaft of brilliant sunlight. At the edges the white paint blended with the green, creating streaks of shadow—a stab of warmth through the cool mist of the forest. "Could it be simpler? Ask Jesus Christ for joy. Make yourself His, and follow His laws. And He will flood you with joy. It's the simplest message I will give you this week, my friends, one you've heard a thousand times, but have you ever really listened? 'Ask and ye shall receive.' Why aren't you asking?"

Connie wept. At the end of the service they sang "Just as I Am" and Connie came forward, knelt, and prayed with the reverend.

The Nazarene church taught that there were two transforming moments in every Christian's life: the first when one invited Christ into one's heart and was born again, the second—this was the more difficult one and could happen years later, if ever—was sanctification, when one was freed from one's sinful nature. The church taught, and Connie believed, that everything could change in a moment. The light could be thrown on. Connie had felt the call many times and had gone to the altar and prayed on her knees, and every time she had felt a euphoric cleanness for a few days before she again fell to sadness, anger, covetousness, and self-pity. During the wonderful periods of sanctification she had wished to die in an accident in order to be truly free of sin when she met God, but even this wish was a fall from grace.

This time was different, though. Her motivation was clear: to have joy in this life. On the few occasions she had seen joy, she had been afraid to reach for it, suspecting that to do so would constitute a sinful lust. Now she recognized this fear as her mortal nature at work, refusing to let her truly give herself to Christ. Reverend Raleigh taught her that she could have joy *and* be sanctified—that the two were one.

On Sunday morning, the six paintings were displayed in the narthex and sold at silent auction, the proceeds going to help fund Reverend Raleigh's traveling ministry. Connie had taken part, bidding much more than she could afford on the painting of the thicket with the glorious shaft of light, but someone outbid her.

After this awakening, Connie's past came into very sharp focus, and although she was determined to claim her joy and live without regret, she did wonder where her life had gone. Had she never bothered to make one? Had something been missing in her? Or had she been cheated, and, if so, by whom? Her husband? Gene? What if she had awakened to the Lord earlier, maybe during her teen years? Maybe she could have studied music, developed a lovely voice, and had a ministry like Marlene Bailey, the church organist. Connie entertained these thoughts briefly, then drove them from her mind, the way her mother used to feed the neighbors' dogs scraps, then chase them from the back porch. One thing was clear, though: she must stop waiting for someone to love her and start focusing on God's laws if she were to access the store of joy that Reverend Raleigh had spoken about.

Could it be that now, through Bill Howard, God was offering Connie a ministry? One that would sanctify her?

Connie let Gene stay at Enrique's for dinner, thinking that his presence might make her self-conscious when Bill called back. She warmed up leftovers, and no sooner had she sat down to eat, than the phone rang.

"Hello?"

"Hello, Connie? This is Bill Howard."

"How are you?"

"Just fine, and you?"

"Very well, thank you."

"Connie, I so enjoyed talking to your group last week. I'm calling to possibly take you up on that offer you made. I'm here for a couple weeks, and I have quite a few speaking engagements at churches in the area. To be honest, some of these towns, well, I can't even find them on a map. Murphy? Where on earth is Murphy?"

They laughed together.

"I have use of one of the church's minivans, so I'm not asking for a ride or anything, but I could use a guide, someone to help me find these churches, who wouldn't mind sitting through my presentation again."

"Bill," said Connie. "It would be my pleasure to serve as your guide. There's no reason to take up a church van. We'll use my car. It will be my contribution to your ministry."

"Are you sure? I have quite a few of these engagements. You might want to trade off with some of the other women."

"Well, if I can't do it some night, then I'll call one of the other Dorcases, but I would love to do it. When is your first engagement?"

"Tomorrow."

In the lovely hour Connie had to herself after the phone call, she allowed herself to indulge in a new fantasy. What if she had awoken to the Lord earlier in life and ended up in Africa? She would hold a little black child, a famine orphan, in her arms. In this fantasy her arms were strong, golden, and ropy, not thin and pale. *There, there, precious child. You're safe now. Christ loves you, as do I. We will find you your store of joy.* And the child would sniffle and gaze into her eyes trustingly, then lay his head on her breast.

IT WAS SWEET of Liz Padgett, who knew the severity of Abby's mother's condition, to show support in the ways she did. But Liz's gestures, such as draping an arm over Abby's shoulder as they walked down the hall at school, seemed luxuries that came with being the prettier friend. Abby hesitated to initiate them, out of a dim knowledge that it would look like she was hogging Liz, or attempting to rub off some of her beauty, or even trying to hurt her the way children do their infant siblings with hard kisses. So she simply enjoyed the warmth of her best friend's touch and, maybe, the little attention it brought her.

"Oh, another one," Liz said upon opening her locker one afternoon.

"What?" Abby asked.

Liz bent, hooking her hair behind her ear. Both girls wore their hair long and straight. They were the only ones at Eula High to do so and, without each other, neither would have had the nerve to be so behind the times. Although no one yet had the audacity to copy the wild frizzed, bleached, and ratted styles they saw on MTV, the gentle featherings of the early eighties now had higher peaks and wider sweeps and were cemented in place with hairspray and often given kink and volume by a perm. Even the boys were tentatively poufing out the wings of their middle-parted hairstyles.

Liz opened a tightly folded piece of paper, read it, and rolled her eyes.

"What is it?" Abby asked.

Liz handed the note to her. "I've gotten a few of them."

The typewritten note read,

REASONS TO BE SAD:
The Russians have hundreds of nuclear missiles pointed
at our heads and we could all die right now if
Gorbachev pushed a button.

REASONS TO BE HAPPY:
Liz Padgett exists.
You are beautiful!!!!!

"How sweet!" Abby said. "Who is it from?"

"I don't know."

"Who do you *think* it's from?"

"Come on, Abby. Honestly, do I care?"

"Sure, why not?"

Liz narrowed her eyes. Abby knew that they were supposed to be together in their disdain for boys at Eula High. Like their hair, it was something that set them apart. But the difference, which Abby hardly needed point out, was that Liz had until recently dated a handsome college student who would come all the way from Boise to see her, while the few self-conscious attempts Abby and her male friends had made at "going together" had always died of neglect after a few weeks, to the relief of both parties.

"So what?" Abby responded to Liz's wordless accusation. "I wish I had a secret admirer."

Liz shook her head and closed the locker, and the two walked down the hall. When they passed a trash can, Liz tossed the note in.

On the exterior, Liz was a good-natured, diligent girl, a favorite of her teachers and the first everyone called when they needed a babysitter. But what they labeled a fine work ethic—the fierce determination with which she studied, volunteered, played tennis, and wrote for the *Eula High Gazette*—was, in fact, a means to an escape. The quietest of rebels, Liz hated Eula secretly and with her every fiber. From grade school she had found teachers dull, the townspeople dim, the big sky that everyone claimed to be so beautiful desolate, and life under it boring beyond words. Once Liz had accepted, and then embraced, her odd tastes and disruptive thoughts, they had led her even farther from the Eulan mindset: she decided in junior high that she was a Democrat, and then, when she was a sophomore, an atheist. Liz would escape Eula, and do it in the right way. She would have a great life, the kind of which Eulans didn't even dream, because no version of it was presented to them on TV. With this type of motivation, getting straight *A*s was a cinch.

This escape was what Liz and Abby called the Big Plan. They seldom spoke of it by name, but it was an undercurrent in much of their communication. If a teacher praised Liz's work, Liz could, in bowing her head humbly, shoot Abby a quick glance that said, *Another one for the Big Plan*, and the corner of Abby's mouth would rise. The greatest step in the Big Plan was the one they had most recently taken: both had applied early-decision to Stanford. Liz often reflected on how lucky she was to have a partner in crime and an open-minded audience to her cynical views. She shared everything with Abby except for her atheism; that was her private, precious distinction. Abby still prayed.

When Liz got home that evening, the sweet, skunky smell of marijuana and the sound of MTV greeted her before she even opened the front door. Great. She'd have to study in her room. She had spent her whole life escaping Winston and his friends. There was no need for Liz to go through the living room, but Abby's curiosity about the secret admirer that afternoon prompted her to see which friends Winston had brought home and if any would offer her a hit of pot. She would, of course, sharply refuse any such offer. What she came upon resembled the scene of a massacre: near-horizontal bodies with splayed limbs in a trash-strewn room. Only Jay sat up when he saw Liz. He coughed—politely, somehow—and Winston finally noticed her.

"Hey, sis," Winston said in a cowboy voice, "git on into that kitchen and rassle me up a beer!"

Liz put her fist to her hip impatiently and rolled her eyes. Then she gestured toward the joint, which had gone dead in the ashtray. "That stuff causes impotence, you know."

"So they say, but my experience proves otherwise." Winston began grinding his pelvis.

Liz grimaced and turned. Before she mounted the stairs, she heard Jay say to Winston, "You're a fucking retard." Of all of Winston's friends, he was the least moronic.

Abby, at this moment, was with her father, taking one of their long walks along the lakeshore. It was the time in the evening when the lake glowed as brightly as the sky, and the trees created a mottled, black border between them. Curled beech leaves crunched underfoot, and the pop of a shotgun sounded, then echoed, causing the starlings that loaded a tree to take flight, rising like bubbles released upon the opening of a pop bottle.

"Pheasant season," said Chuck, in answer to Abby's unasked question.

She nodded. Then, after a moment, she said, "I miss Mom."

"I know, sweetie." Chuck reached over and put his hand to his daughter's head, then let it fall to her shoulder. "Would you like to go down there next weekend?"

"Is that all right?"

"Of course it is, Abby. I'll call tomorrow and reserve you a plane ticket."

"Do you want to come, too?"

"No, I've got work. I just went. I'll go down with you for Thanksgiving. I've already spoken to your mom about it."

"All right."

Somehow they had lost the trail. They walked through tall grass so thick and stiff it went up their pant legs and pierced their socks, then they stopped at the edge of the park to remove foxtails. This park was empty; the cement-and-plank picnic tables were bare and peeling. Concrete ramps led down into the water where, in the summer, people eased their motorboats in the lake for waterskiing. In spring the lake contained runoff from the faraway mountains, and was clear. But by the time the water was warm enough for swimming, it was also thick with green algae, a bloom caused by fertilizer washed from the fields into the creeks that fed the lake. "Frog nog," Mr. Padgett, Liz's father, liked to call it. It could give you hives.

The Padgetts owned a boat, and Abby had been out on it many times. She liked to lie on the bow and hold the rail, letting the wind whip her hair, as Liz's brother, Winston, and his friends water-skied—friends such as Jay Cortez, an unskilled but fearless water-skier who crashed through the wake but refused to let go, often returning to the boat with pink water-burns across his ribs. Strange, that a boy like Jay could have such a gentle younger brother.

"I'm helping Lina's son with a science-fair project," Abby said.

"Jay?"

"No, Enrique."

"Smart kid?"

Abby nodded vigorously, but her eyes became desperate with the awareness of another emotion overwhelming her. It won, that image that was always vying for her attention, of her mother telling her with clinical coldness in her eyes (although she held her hand tight), "It's renal cancer, Abby, kidney cancer. It's not good."

Abby's face crumpled; she was crying. They stopped and Chuck wrapped his arms around her. "I know, Abby. It's too hard. We weren't made for this."

They stood awhile, then Abby wiped her face with her hands, and they walked on.

The mention of Enrique had, in Chuck, brought on a brief rush of thoughts of Lina. It was like, in the shower, when the warm water finally kicks in. "Why don't you tell me about this kid's science project?" he said.

And she did.

CHAPTER 9

It had been with mixed pride and shame that Lina said in confession that first time, "I slept with a married man."

There had been a long pause. This was quite a departure from the unkind thoughts and foul language Lina usually confessed.

"That's a very serious sin. You've broken the sixth commandment," Father Moore said.

"I know, Father."

"Is this a one-time fall?"

"Yes, Father."

"Will you be in a situation with this man again? A situation of temptation?"

"Oh, no."

"Seven Hail Marys and seven Our Fathers."

But the next week, Lina said it again—quickly this time, like a child who believes a swift admission might diminish the crime and avert a spanking. "I slept with a married man . . ."

Father Moore, who had never before addressed her by name in the confessional, said, "Lina, not again!"

". . . twice."

"Lina, you've got to stop this. It's not right. It's a very dangerous sin."

"I know, Father. I'm weak. I tol' myself not to do it again, and then I did it."

Father Moore counseled her on ways to guide her mind back

onto the path of righteousness and entreated her to avoid being alone with the man at all costs. Finally his voice softened, and he said, "Pray for strength, my child, and I'll pray for you."

"What is my penance?"

"Twenty Hail Marys and twenty Our Fathers. Consider the wife, Lina."

For a moment Lina thought he meant the Blessed Virgin, but then—oh, yes, the *wife*, Sandra. "Thank you, Father," she said.

Neither Lina nor Chuck had been able to mention Sandra's name to that point. She had been staying with her parents in Salt Lake City, and Lina assumed that divorce was not far off. Maybe they were waiting for Abby to graduate, so she wouldn't have to endure the talk of the kids at school. But Lina didn't ask for details. The idea of Chuck as a divorced man alternately thrilled and scared her.

"I think she'll be back on Tuesday," Chuck muttered as they lay together one afternoon that week.

Lina nodded and allowed a few minutes for the woman's mention to fade. Then she carefully wrapped the sheet around her and sat up. Chuck pulled it away. "Stop it!" she hissed.

Chuck roughly yanked away the rest of the sheet and pulled Lina back onto the bed. She went to cover herself, but Chuck took her shoulders, turned her toward him, and cupped her face in his hands. "Do you know, Lina," he said, "that I love every inch of your body, that every part of you thrills me?"

Lina said, "Stop it. I'm not some kid. You don' have to say those things to me."

"It's true, Lina. I don't care if you don't believe me. I love to see you naked. You're absolutely beautiful."

"You're lying," Lina said. But she felt, deeply, that he wasn't. She could hardly believe it, as fat as she was, but Chuck did adore her completely and without reservation. And she wished she could say the same of herself. She liked Chuck, he was in her thoughts all day long, she might even be coming to love him, but those wisps of hair on the part of his back where wings would attach disgusted her, and there was sometimes an eggy smell about him that turned her stomach.

When she went to leave that afternoon, a car was pulling into the driveway next door, so Lina waited until it disappeared into the garage. She turned to Chuck, who was standing behind her, and said, "I can't keep parking in the driveway. Your neighbors know I don' clean your house this often."

Chuck shrugged.

"Maybe you don' care, but I do! We've got to stop this," said Lina, feeling tears rise. "We're breaking the sixth commandment. I'm rushing through my houses to come over here. It's no good. Mrs. Hood got after me. She could tell I didn't vacuum."

Chuck took her in his arms. His voice was very gentle. "Tell Mrs. Hood to vacuum her house herself."

Lina laughed through her tears and swatted his shoulder. "You think it's funny, but I have to make a living."

Chuck hesitated, then said, "I could—"

"Don't you dare," said Lina. "Don't even say it."

Chuck realized that Lina thought he was going to offer her money. This hadn't occurred to him. Having never been poor, he had no concept of the terror of collection agencies or the humiliation of food stamps. He was barely aware that things like these existed. Poor people, in his mind, simply lived in smaller houses. What he was going to offer was that Lina park in the garage next time. He didn't correct her, though. Savoring her anger, Chuck held her closer and felt the aching pulse of a returning erection. If he couldn't be that crass man who would offer her money, he could at least let her believe that he was.

As Lina cleaned the Sheltons' house the next day, she thought of her afternoons with Chuck, turning her favorite moments like jewels in the light. When he was on top of her, he liked to take her face in his hands and hold it and stare into her face, unaware of the lost expression on his own. Never had she been treasured like this. Then she admonished herself: *It's so stupid; it's so wrong.* Then she fell back to remembering how sometimes, lost in the pleasure and in her, he'd bite his lip, trying to get it just right.

Back and forth, it filled her day.

When she finished the Sheltons' and went out to her car, there, on the driver's seat, sat a gift box. She looked around and quickly got in. She drove out of the subdivisions far into the fields and pulled over near an irrigation ditch. A magpie dipped its Popsicle-stick tail to slow its flight, and lit on a cattail where it bobbed back and forth like a metronome. The box was covered with white velvet and tied with a red ribbon—the type of box that could hold expensive jewelry. She untied the ribbon and lifted the lid. Inside was another box, a small plastic one with a circular button on the top, the type of button people in the movies pushed to make something explode. She took out this little box, careful not to touch the button, then realized: it was an automatic garage-door opener. Underneath there was a note that said, "5:30?"

That week, Father Moore refused to give her penance. "Twice? Again? Lina, you must stop. There is no penance this week. Be strong. Stop doing this."

It frightened Lina not to do penance. Wouldn't the sin sit on her soul? She thought of her father with his bent back and staggering walk—results of having lived his life under the weight of his sin. She did the previous week's penance over again. Sandra returned. Lina didn't see Chuck that week, so in her next confession she allowed herself a false sense of virtue. She had very little to report.

THE BASEMENT OF Murphy Nazarene was wallpapered with a print meant to look like pine paneling. But it was so old that it had turned gray and begun to peel away at the corners. Connie stopped herself from judging. Did she prefer the pastel-painted walls and chrome fixtures of her church? No, it was vanity—she said so to herself every Sunday. The measure of a church was its congregation, not its house, and on this Wednesday evening Murphy Nazarene was full of life. There had been a potluck dinner of lasagna, homemade biscuits, and Jell-O salad, then the kids had been wrangled into their various youth groups. The men were having a special outing at a bowling alley down the road, and the women now occupied the main rec room. The comforting sound of dishes being washed came from the adjoining kitchen as Connie helped Bill set up the slide projector. The women sipped coffee, pinching together the tiny paper wings that served as handles on the disposable cups, as they waited for the presentation to begin.

Connie trembled a little in the light of all this attention. This group was far larger than the Dorcas Circle. But, then again, First Church in Eula had six or seven different women's groups to accommodate the varying ages and interests of the congregation. There was the Esther Circle for college-age girls; the Rebecca Circle for young mothers; Pet Outreach, a group of middle-aged women who worked with a youth group, taking pets to nursing homes; and the Knit Wits, a group of seniors who listened to inspirational books-on-tape while doing needlework.

There was also the divorcées' support group. This had been formed during a time when Connie had been serving as a deaconess. She had opposed its formation. It was one of the few times she spoke out at a meeting of the board of deacons. In his teachings Christ himself had made strict prohibitions against divorce, she said. It seemed part of the group's purpose to help these women find new husbands. To Connie this was tantamount to establishing a group within the church whose purpose was to facilitate adultery among its members. The other deacons and deaconesses sat in a silence of anger and guilt. Several of them had been divorced and remarried. It was a sobering speech, but a necessary one, and no one rose to rebut it—no one could have; Connie was too obviously correct. But they had gone ahead and voted the divorcées' support group into existence, along with a corresponding men's group, which then never really got off the ground, as it seemed that men either quickly remarried after a divorce or left the church.

Connie had, she felt, been proved right over the years, as the divorcées' support group, under the name of Naomi Circle, became a large, energetic group devoted more to gossip than prayer. Members of the circle who were unaware of Connie's opposition to its existence had invited Connie to their events, and Connie had politely declined. It seemed pathetic for these women to revel in their sin. One year, they arrived at the church picnic, late and en masse, all wearing floral-printed dresses they had bought at the same store. The congregation had erupted into laughter and then applause. "Let the party begin," said an old man at Connie's table who had tucked his napkin into his collar, like a child. Connie shuddered. It really was like the arrival of the whores.

Connie was more than happy to remain the one member of the Dorcas Circle without a husband at home.

"Thank you, Connie," said Bill quietly once the projector had been adjusted and an image of the African savanna appeared on the screen. The tiny fan inside the projector whirred and sent a warm air into the faces of Connie and Bill. "I guess you could take a walk or get some coffee if this bores you."

"Never," Connie said. "I've been looking forward to hearing you speak again."

Bill smiled, turned away, and said, "Thank you for your patience, ladies. If someone could hit the lights, I'll get started."

Connie made her way to the back of the room and sat in a folding chair against the wall. The metal was cold under her back and bottom. The lady seated in front of her turned, and, with an exaggerated look of concern, mouthed, *Can you see?*

Connie smiled, shook her head, and raised her hand slightly. It was a gesture that said not *Yes, I can see*, but *Don't worry, I've seen this before.*

"I thought I'd start with something pretty," said Bill. "This is the view from the roof of our hospital."

"Ahh," said the women.

Bill proceeded with his presentation in exactly the way he had the week previous, except that, by necessity, his voice was louder and, perhaps because of this, seemingly more confident. Again, when he reached the slide of himself with the orphan children, it was upside-down. "Oops," he said. "I'll have to fix that."

The women all laughed.

After she drove Bill past the moonlit field, Bill mentioning more than once that he was pleased with how the talk had gone, after she dropped him off at the parsonage and he quickly thanked her and bid her good night, Connie went home and took in the two boxes which, they had decided, could remain in the trunk of her car until the next speaking engagement. She reheated a meat loaf and called Gene over from Enrique's. They ate quietly, both deep in thought. Then Gene went to his room, and Connie opened the box marked number one, took out the carousel, and set it on the kitchen table. She carefully lifted the slides one by one to the light until she found the one of Bill and the children. She turned it right-side up and returned it to its slot. Then she continued through the rest, remembering what he had said about each.

Connie returned the carousels to their boxes and put them by the door. She heard the amused music of Lina's voice, as she did several times a night if the TV wasn't on, but didn't mind it. This happy noise reminded her that in an emergency she could yell and Lina, and possibly some other neighbors, would come running. Connie returned to the table with the envelope that contained her prayer-chain letter. She had received it the day before but hadn't yet decided on the wording of her prayer request.

The prayer chain was made up of fifteen Nazarene women around the country, and the letter—a bundle of fifteen notes written on everything from flowery stationery to recipe cards—made its way from one woman to the next. When you received it, you prayed for the other specific requests, removed your old note from the pile, added a new one, and sent it on. Some women wrote detailed lists—Claire from Reston, Virginia, used the prayer-chain letter almost as a journal of her family, thanking the Lord for her grandkids, praying that her son would find work and her daughter a husband; other women were brief—Susan from Phoenix, who had lupus, wrote the same thing every time: "Pray for healing."

Connie took out a small pad, sat back down at the table, and wrote, "Connie in Eula, Idaho, would like the members to pray for the Nazarene hospital in Savanes, Ivory Coast, and she would like to thank the Lord for giving her a small role in its mission."

After less than a week at home, Sandra Hall went back to Salt Lake City for another round of treatments. Chuck and Abby picked up burritos on the way home from the Boise Airport and ate them at the bar in the kitchen. Chuck flipped through the mail, then stopped. "Stanford," he said. "Big and fat."

Abby put down her burrito and took a deep breath before opening the envelope. "Congratulations . . ." she began, then was overwhelmed by tears. There were tears around every corner these days.

Chuck got up and embraced her from behind. "Call your mom. I'll clean up."

Later, as Abby stared into an open book, unable to focus, there came a knock on her bedroom door. "Abby?" called Chuck. "Can I come in?"

"Sure, Daddy."

Chuck held the handles of a large paper shopping bag in one hand. "I was just going through some things in the basement and—what was the name of that kid you were helping with the science project?"

"Enrique."

"Yes, Enrique," said Chuck. He sat on the edge of Abby's bed and put the bag down between his feet. "I don't need all these things. They're accessories to the train set—trees, houses, stuff like that. They've been sitting down there gathering dust. You said Enrique was building a model of Eula, right? Well, maybe he can use these."

"Are you sure, Daddy?" Her father's train set was his favorite possession. It was worth a lot.

"Yeah, I'm sure. I'm too old for this stuff anyway. See if he wants it."

"Okay."

Chuck remained for a moment. "You know I love you, right, sweetheart?"

Abby nodded.

"All right, then." He rose and kissed Abby on top of her head. "I'm off to bed. Good night."

"Good night," said Abby. Chuck walked out into the hallway. "Daddy?" He poked his head back in. "Are you all right?"

He knew what she meant by this, and he appreciated her concern. "Yes, sweetheart"—Chuck smiled and said this firmly, so she would believe him—"I am okay."

"Good night." When the doctor had his private meeting with Abby three years ago, he had told her to watch for "certain signs," one of which was the giving away of treasured possessions. He had been careful not to mention what such signs warned of, but Abby knew. Her father must have confessed suicidal thoughts.

His depression had been less sadness and more a general loosening of his hold. He lost weight and this was evident in his drawn face and in his walk: his feet touched the ground soundlessly as if he barely weighed anything. According to the cliché, happy people "walked on air," but Abby knew that, in real life, happy people stepped strongly and felt the world under their feet. She remembered leading him into the school gym for parent-teacher conferences when her mother was away. He squeezed her hand so tightly that it hurt, and turned a harrowed look from teachers to students to the basketball court beneath his feet, as if it would drop away, leaving him to float up to the rafters. It had been the most terrifying moment of Abby's life, to see her father so frightened.

But Abby wasn't concerned now. His feet were not lifting again away from the earth. In fact, despite his sadness about her mother, he seemed to be clutching life stronger than ever. And he was giving away only the accessories, not the trains.

The next morning Abby awoke too early, as she often did, and couldn't go back to sleep, so she ate a banana and decided to go for a drive before school. She took her father's bag out to the car and peeked in as she set it into the trunk. Tiny trees in boxes. She lifted one out. The tree trunk was painted in great detail—minute brown and black brushstrokes whorled at a tiny knot—and the leaves were rubbery flecks that seemed to have been sprayed on. She put the box back in the bag and closed the trunk.

Dawn lit the hazy gray sky pink, and the birds chirped in staccato, as if they, like Abby, were cold. Abby drove out of town, through the wheat and alfalfa fields, where children stood in twos and threes on deserted corners, waiting for the school bus. The closest house that must have been theirs was far away across the field. She passed the last field and entered the rippled landscape that led up toward the Owyhee Mountains. Here the sagebrush never changed color but remained forever the same silvery blue, a shade other plants turned only when they were dead. But while sage would have looked pale next to a plant that grew in a more generous climate, it looked positively lush in comparison to the tumbleweeds that tangled with it and the yellow cheat grass that sprang up between its branches. After a half-hour drive Abby looped back into Eula. The oaks and elms, which until a month ago had been the same earnest green as that tiny model tree, had now turned bold shades of red and yellow. All these extravagant colors had been borrowed from a state far from Idaho.

That afternoon Abby took the bag to the lunchroom, where all the junior high kids were eating and hollering and doing tricks with straws and milk boxes. Abby spotted the two sitting by themselves: Gene, poor kid, was a weirdo, but Enrique was like a little chubby-cheeked angel. He leaned forward across the table toward Gene, apparently giving him some sort of instruction. Then he looked up, saw Abby, and beamed. Abby went and sat down at their table.

"I have a present for you," she said.

"Really?"

"It's for your model."

She slid the bag toward Enrique, and he looked into it. "Neat!" he said, taking out a box of trees. "Can we really use them?"

"Yeah. They're yours."

"Are you sure?"

"Yeah."

"Do you want them back after?"

"No."

"Where'd you get them?" Enrique asked, taking out a boxed silo, then a house.

"They're my dad's. He collects train stuff. But he wanted to get rid of some of it, and I had told him about your project, so . . ."

Enrique's face turned, and it seemed to Abby that the fact of the gift had suddenly caught up to him and, seeming like charity, hurt his pride. He put the house, still in its box, on the table, and frowned at it.

"Anyway . . ." Abby said apologetically.

Enrique was torn. He had immediately fallen in love with these tiny things—the fact that they could be used in the science project had barely registered—but the idea of accepting a gift from Mr. Hall made his guts freeze. In the weeks since he had come to suspect that Mr. Hall was the one who had kissed his mother, he had grown to hate this man he had never seen, but to whom he had assigned, in his imagination, thick white hair and a carnation in his lapel—Blake Carrington on *Dynasty*. Now this underhanded tycoon was using his sweet, unsuspecting daughter to send Enrique gifts. Was it a way of moving in on his mother?

But this stuff was neat. *Really* neat. It was all Enrique could do not to open the box and lift out the house to see if its front door opened on tiny hinges, as it seemed it might. If Enrique was strong and refused the gift, how would he explain it to Abby? She might be hurt, and to hurt Abby was more than he could bear.

"It might help?" offered Abby. In the pause, she had come to feel ashamed of her family's wealth.

"Thanks, Abby. It'll help a lot."

Now it seemed that Enrique had simply been made solemn by the generosity of the gift. Relieved, Abby reached over and pinched his shoulder. He smiled. She turned to Gene, who tucked his chin and looked away, and gave him a thumbs-up he couldn't have seen. "Well, guys, good luck," she said. She rose from her chair and returned to study hall.

"Coop?"

He lowered the newspaper to reveal Wanda. "Well, howdy, little sister."

"I figured I could find you here. You know, I can walk here from my place." She seemed to be apologizing for having disturbed him at the Denny's counter, his daytime sanctuary.

"Well, have a seat. Gina?" he called to the overweight waitress who sat in a booth, balancing her checkbook. "This is Wanda, my baby sister."

"Hey," the women said to each other.

"You want somethin'?" Coop asked Wanda.

"Iced tea?"

"Iced tea for the lady."

"Shore thing," Gina said. She scooted out of the booth, leaving a cigarette burning in the amber glass ashtray.

Coop turned to Wanda, who looked pretty, her cheeks full and her eyes weathered but lively. With a twinge of sadness, Coop had a sense of all the things Wanda had seen with those eyes. It had started so early for her. Coop's childhood had already been over when their father died, but Wanda's had hardly begun. Funny—when she used to show up on his doorstep, high or needing to get high, Coop had never wondered what she had seen, he had just wanted to be rid of her.

Gina set a massive plastic glass of iced tea before Wanda and returned to her booth.

"So," Coop said.

"It's been two weeks," Wanda said. "I've been thinkin' and thinkin'."

"And?"

"I'm ready, Coop."

"Well, then, there you go."

"That's it?"

"That's it."

Coop didn't need to put Wanda through the wringer. He could see that she was clean, and that she was serious. "I don't have the money on me," he said. "I'll have to go to the bank. And I have one small requirement."

"What is it?" Wanda asked.

"While I'm at the bank, I want you to visit with Uncle Frank."

"Oh." Wanda had expected Coop to interrogate her, to take long breaks to stare off and consider, to make her work for it. But this surprised her. Wanda still blamed Uncle Frank for setting off everything bad that happened in her life by killing her father. Coop had somehow forgiven him, but he couldn't expect the same from her. Then again, it was only for a few minutes—a small price to pay, from Coop's perspective. "All right," she said.

"Gina?" Coop said. "Save my seat? I'll be back in an hour or two."

"Don't keep me waiting too long," Gina said without looking up.

"Do you want that to go?" Coop asked Wanda.

"No," she said. She took a long drink of the iced tea just so she wouldn't leave behind a full glass. It wasn't nearly as good as her own.

Wanda felt a little guilty. The truth was, she had already been to Portland. She had gone through a round of tests and two interviews with agency staff members, and now a couple had asked to meet her. She needed more money to get back to Portland.

After she had last visited Coop, Wanda had gone through the most difficult week since the death of their mother. She had cut her pills into tiny quarter pieces and allowed herself only one a day.

The difference between half and a quarter was surprisingly drastic. Wanda would pace the house in desperation, arguing with that side of herself that came up with reason after reason why she should be allowed one more chip of pill, then charge out into the street for a long walk. Wanda was careful not to walk past Gideon's unit, which was just down the block from hers. There was always a half-smoked joint in his ashtray awaiting visitors, and to walk by his door was to face the possibility of ducking in for a quick smoke. Instead she would walk around the corner past the empty lot where someone had set up a little shrine—a statue of Mary in a bed of plastic flowers, a knocked-over oil drum before it to sit on. She hadn't realized its purpose until she saw an old Mexican lady kneeling in the grass there, praying. Then she'd charge through neighborhoods where women in their curlers would turn from their soaps to watch her pass. No one went for walks, not around here. She'd reach the canal, where she'd throw in a handful of dirt to watch the red cloud roll along and disperse into the black water. The canal moved about as fast as she did, and gliding along it kept her mind off the ache. At night it took three sleeping pills to ease her into sleep—legal sleeping pills that she bought over the counter.

She felt she had earned the trip to Portland to register with the agency. She had earned the right to lie about her police record and her last name. *Wanda Coper*, she had written, and they hadn't noticed the missing *O*. She had earned the right to reverse two digits in her Social Security number. A friend had used these tricks to register twice for welfare. They had made a photocopy of Wanda's ID, but she figured that would just sit in her file. And she had earned the right to play a role in her interview with the psychologist—that of an independent country feminist, looking to do good for gals in need. In reality, she had a fundamental, if illogical, belief that once a couple's baby was growing inside her, she would no longer crave anything.

But Coop had told her not to come back for two weeks, and it had been only one.

Wanda looked up Wojciechowski in the phone book and dialed the number. A woman answered, bringing to mind the round face of Mrs. Wojciechowski on the sports club membership card.

"Is Gary there?"

"Just a sec. *Gary! Phone!* . . . No, it's a girl."

A girl. It was enough to make Wanda smile, despite her nervousness.

"Hullo?"

"Gary, it's Wanda."

"Oh. Hi."

"I was wondering if you could drop by. I have somethin' I need to talk to you about."

"What is it?"

"It's real important."

"I can't get away."

"Gary, I need three hundred dollars. To go to Portland."

There was a long pause. Wanda had inflated the amount a little, since she knew Gary could afford it. And she allowed *Portland* to hang in the air. Ever since she was little, Wanda had known what people meant when they said, in a certain tone of voice, that a girl had gone to Portland. It meant she had had an abortion.

"I'll bring it over tomorrow night," Gary said.

The grave and stony look on Gary's face when he handed her the envelope made Wanda regret it all for a moment. She had aged him. "Thank you," she said, and was going to invite him in, but he turned and walked quickly back to his car. She would have explained if he had come in!

Gary was the age, Wanda mused after he left, that he wouldn't doubt that he had gotten her pregnant with that one shot. These boys listened to their mothers' frantic warnings, and the message they received was this: *The girl will always get pregnant.* He didn't know the facts. Maybe Gary considered it a punishment from God. Maybe he would go through his life counting, year by year, the age his child would have been.

She soon put aside these remorseful thoughts. She had the money, and she construed things to make the ease with which she acquired it an indication that she was on the right track.

She did the same now, with Coop. He wouldn't be funding her first trip to Portland, but her second. What was the difference? She hadn't lied to him. She had been prepared to, but Coop hadn't required an explanation, so she felt, really, in the clear. This was what the Catholics called a "sin of omission." It was a term she had learned from an old boyfriend, Ricky, the only Catholic—and the only Mexican—she had ever dated.

As he drove, Coop gave Wanda an update on the condition of their uncle. He had never done this before and so it was awkward. "They say he's diabetic. Not so bad he has to take shots or nothin', but he's supposed to cut down on sugar, eat vegetables, whatever. He don't care, though. Gettin' a vegetable in him is about as easy as getting a camel up a cattle ramp, so I leave him be."

Wanda wondered if Coop might try to draw her into her uncle's care. The thought made her queasy. And when they pulled up in front of the house, with its roof that sagged a little over the porch, her queasiness turned to real apprehension. You need the money, she told herself.

The shades were drawn in the living room. "Frank?" Coop said. "Looks like you got yerself a visitor."

"I'll be," Uncle Frank said.

"It's Wanda."

"Well, don't she look purdy!"

As Wanda's eyes grew accustomed to the light, she saw her uncle. He sat among a pile of pillows and sofa cushions on the floor, the shape of an enormous egg. He wore a gray sweat suit; his long beard, which spread from his broad neck, was gray, and his face—perhaps from the television glow—looked purple. He held a tall, silver beer can. The air was filled with the intimate musk of orange peels left to rot in the kitchen trash. It occurred to Wanda that the sole purpose of his body now was to create this smell: to strain the alcohol from the beer and send it through veins to the skin, where it was released the way orange oil mists from pores in the rind when you peel it.

"Hi, Uncle Frank."

"I'll be. Wander. Haven't seen ya fer quiter while."

A sharp bang from the ceiling made Wanda jump.

"Acorns," explained Coop. "Now, I'm gonna run out on an errand, and Wanda's gonna chat with ya. I'll be back shortly."

Wanda perched on the edge of the recliner, the only seat whose cushions had been left in place. "How you been, Uncle Frank?"

"Cain't complain. No one'll listen. Now, watch this." He tipped his beer can toward the TV screen. It was *The Price Is Right.* A woman guessed the prices of household products, and Bob Barker pressed buttons beside them, causing a sign to flip open and reveal how far off her guess was. "Well, ain't you stupid! Everybody knows big thinger Windex coss more'n a dollar. Swear, I watch this show thinkin' I oughta go on there. Win a hunnerd bucks and a sailboat. Whud I do with that, though? The sailboat. Well, ain't you just stupid!" Uncle Frank sipped his beer. He had the same dismayed smile affixed to his face as Coop often did, his eyes had the same squint, but there was no light left there even as he laughed at the woman's guesses.

Periodically, a loud crack would come from above, followed by a rattle as the acorn rolled down the roof. Wanda was relieved that Frank didn't want to chat. The last time she had been stuck in this room with him, a couple of years back, he had asked after her brothers and sisters, oldest to youngest. When he came to Louis, she had said, "Louis is dead, Uncle Frank. He died years ago." That smile had stayed on his face, but his eyes had squeezed, and his head had turned back toward the television. "Guess I knew that," he had said.

Frank seemed to find *The Price Is Right* endlessly exasperating. When a man failed to spin the Big Wheel all the way around, Frank's bullfrog voice cracked like an adolescent's: "Aw, come on! Ya gotta do it hard!" Wanda leaned forward, her chin parked on the heel of one hand, her fingers cupped to shield her eyes from the sight of her uncle. The way his shoulders shrugged when he suppressed a burp nauseated her.

Finally Coop returned. "Mormon missionaries!" he called from the porch. "Anybody home?"

Frank made a rattling laugh.

"Well, Uncle Frank," Wanda said, standing, "you take care. I'll come see ya again real soon, okay?"

"I'll be right here," Frank said.

"Thanks for that," Coop said simply as he drove her home. He parked in front of her house and gave her the money.

"You won't regret this, Coop. I'm gonna do good."

"All right, little sister."

Coop kissed Wanda on the cheek, then glanced at his watch as she got out. Two o'clock. Time to head back to school. He'd have to pay Gina tomorrow.

THAT NIGHT, LINA came in and lay next to Enrique on top of the covers. They still spent these minutes together before bedtime, but they no longer spoke Spanish. Lina was aware that, in this, Enrique had obeyed Jay.

"Mom," Enrique said, "has that guy ever tried to kiss you again?" Enrique had put Mr. Hall's gift in his closet without showing his mother.

"Oh. No."

" 'Cause I was thinking about it, and I think it's okay. I mean you shouldn't *not* kiss someone just because he's married."

This was a lie, and Enrique said it just to test his hypothesis of what his mother would say. Mr. Hall was a subject Enrique couldn't help picking at, like a scab.

"Enrique, are you joking?" (She pronounced "joking" *choking*.) "Of course I shouldn't."

"I don't know," Enrique said.

Lina was quiet for a while. What did Enrique suspect? "Don' start changing your mind just because you're growing up, *mijo*. Right is right and wrong is wrong."

"I don't know, though. It's not always so simple."

"Who tol' you that? Jay?"

"It's like you said, you're lonely." Enrique felt tears rise as he said this. He had pushed the act too far and upset himself. And his hypothesis had been incorrect.

"Don' be mean," Lina said.

"I'm not being mean, Mama! I would never be mean!" He threw his arms around her. The sentiment was real, even if it had ridden in on a lie. "I just want you to be happy."

"Arright, baby, now go to sleep." Lina kissed him. To put a word to this hesitancy she felt toward her son—mistrust—would have broken her heart.

Once she was gone, Enrique allowed himself to rewrite the

episode. He had been encouraging her to be free, to find happiness. He had sacrificed his own moral code for her. How could she accuse him of being mean? He was indignant.

Of course, Enrique still only imagined that it had been one kiss. His mental image was his mother, in an apron and yellow rubber gloves, caught in Blake Carrington's arms upon turning from her task. Her eyes bulged in shock as the man's mouth mashed against hers.

The next afternoon, as Lina lay in the arms of the real Chuck—bald Chuck with black moles like currants in his soft, dough-colored shoulder—Lina said, "Enrique suspects something."

Step Three:
Hypothesis

CHAPTER 10

With trembling hands, Wanda flipped through an issue of *Parenting* magazine. It was all ads. That was okay, though, as she wouldn't have been able to concentrate on an article anyway. Then Helen rushed in and sat right next to her.

"Are you nervous?"

Helen *made* Wanda nervous. She tended to sit too close to Wanda and to look too directly into her eyes. And if Wanda looked away, Helen repositioned herself, chasing her gaze around the room.

"Yeah, a little," said Wanda.

"Well, take a few deep breaths through the nose. Exhale through the mouth. There's nothing to fear. These are very nice people. You couldn't ask for better, really—highly intelligent, both of them."

Few things Helen could have said would have put Wanda *less* at ease. Intelligent people had never liked her. And only now was Wanda able to put her finger on what was wrong with Helen: she talked like a man. Not that her voice was low-pitched (it wasn't), and she didn't look like a man—she would have been pretty if not for a small, reptilian nose whose open nostrils exposed, in profile, a wet septum—but her sentences, in their precision and power, were like a man's. Wanda would have wondered if Helen was a lesbian if she hadn't already made references to her husband and daughter, and if this strange behavior didn't seem to be a widespread problem. Many of the women Wanda had met at the agency, and in Portland in general, spoke this way. It was jarring, when you were used to the sugary chirp of Eula women.

"All right, should we go in?"

Wanda nodded.

Helen led Wanda by the hand into her office. "Randy, Melissa, this is Wanda."

The couple stood to shake Wanda's hand. Randy was bald on top, had a beard that was thinner on his cheeks than on his chin, and wore thick glasses that made his eyes look small and far away. A band that had been cinched tight around the back of his head held the glasses in place. A happy gasp caught Melissa, who was a full head shorter than Wanda, and she took back her hand to cover her small, heart-shaped mouth. "I don't know why I'm crying," she said. "I never cry."

Randy put his arm around her. "This process has been very emotional for Melissa," he said.

"For both of us," said Melissa.

Randy nodded and kissed the top of her head.

"Let's all sit down," said Helen.

Wanda gave Melissa a reassuring smile as they obeyed.

"This is just an introductory meeting," said Helen. "We've read each other's profiles, we've seen Wanda's test results. At this stage in the game we like to have a brief face-to-face. There's a lot to take in, so we keep it short. Of course, things are a little different since Wanda lives so far away. Wanda, I've made it clear to Randy and Melissa that you might be meeting with one or two other couples during your visit. So, like I said, just a brief meeting to put a face to the numbers. Okay?"

Everyone nodded and smiled at each other.

"Wanda, I think Randy and Melissa have a few questions they'd like to ask."

Wanda crossed her legs and turned toward the couple, like a guest on *Donahue*.

Randy said, "Well, Wanda, your profile said that you grew up on a farm?"

"Uh-huh. My dad was a farmer and my mom was a housewife. They died not too long ago—"

"In a car accident," said Melissa. "I was so sorry to read that."

"Thanks. But, yeah, we were farmers. I've lived in Eula all my life. Now I work at the K-mart."

"And do they know that you're doing this? That you'll have to take some time off down the road?" Melissa asked.

"Oh, yeah. I've worked there a long time. They're behind me on this."

Randy inhaled, then paused, then said, "What makes you want to do this, Wanda? I mean, it's such an odd situation"—he cast a sheepish glance at Helen, who had folded her arms and leaned her chair against the wall, as if she could melt into it—"and it makes perfect sense from our end, but, from yours . . ." His sentence trailed off, and his tiny eyes blinked.

"Well," said Wanda, "I'm thirty-one years old. I had a boyfriend Hank all through my twenties, and he was a good man. We talked about gettin' married and havin' kids, but we were just so busy, me at K-mart and Hank with his career, and pretty soon he got so high up that his company had to move him. He asked me to come with him, to Washington, DC, but I just couldn't, you know? Eula's always been my home. I have a sick uncle I take care of. Plus, I just knew Hank would never settle down and make a real family with me. So I broke it off. And now here I am at thirty-one, healthy and ready to bear kids. And I don't have a man, and I don't want a man. But I do want to experience pregnancy, to do that with my body. My body wants it. It's in my genes; women in my family have always had children. But, you know, I can't afford a kid, and I don't want to be a single mother. So I figured I'd do what the Bible says and give to the poor. Not that you two are poor, of course, but you need help. My friend Sarah gave her kidney to her brother. He died anyway, but that's not the point. I see this as a way of giving to the needy, even though I don't have nothin' to give. Does that make sense?"

Melissa glowed. "It makes perfect sense. It's the only reason anyone would ever do this, I think."

"Wanda," said Helen, "do you have anything you'd like to ask Melissa and Randy?"

"Um, sure. What do you do?"

"Well," Melissa said, "I'm an architect, and Randy owns a bike shop."

"We do a lot of cycling," Randy added.

"Wait, *you're* an architect?" Wanda asked.

"Yes."

"I never heard of a girl architect," Wanda said.

"Well," Melissa sang airily, repositioning herself in the chair, "there aren't too many of us around."

Randy chimed in, "They always said, a woman's place is in the home."

Helen guffawed. This was the first thing the couple did that felt canned; Wanda could tell they had said this a thousand times.

After a short pause, Wanda said, "Do you live here in Portland?"

"Pretty much," Randy said. "Out in the gorge."

"And do your parents live here?"

"Melissa's recently moved to Arizona."

Wanda continued asking them unobtrusive questions, and her mind wandered a bit during their answers. She had known what type of people they were since she laid eyes on them: They exercised regularly and watched very little TV. They used dental floss and voted in every election. There were people like them in Boise.

Nearly everything Wanda had said so far in this meeting had been a lie. She had told herself two weeks ago, before her first meeting with Helen, that she would lie about the drugs and that would be all. But then there had been questions about her parents on the form, and she knew that they'd never accept her unless she changed her family history a little. And once you change your family history, you change everything.

So, in this meeting, she was forced to tell those first lies, and after that she had had to keep going. A true answer would have sounded like a lie. Even when Randy had asked her why she wanted to be a surrogate, she had to lie—because she couldn't remember. She had known once, back before she had been asked to put it into words, but ever since that conversation with Coop on his porch, she had been quoting the women on *Donahue*. Once she was pregnant and everyone left her alone, the reasons would return to her. Until then, ten thousand dollars would be her reason.

"I hate to interrupt," said Helen. "I know you all have a million questions for each other, but, like I said, we try to keep these initial meetings short." She stood, and so did the others. "Melissa, Randy, have a seat for a minute. I'll be back to wrap things up."

Helen led Wanda back to the side lounge and sat down with her. "You all right, kiddo?"

"That was easy," Wanda said.

"No reason it shouldn't be. You did great. Now just sit tight for a few minutes, okay?" Helen disappeared back into the office.

Wanda picked up another magazine. Was there another couple for her to meet? Helen hadn't been clear about this part of the process. How many interviews would she go through, and, at the end, would she choose them, or would they choose her? After a few minutes, Helen came back into the room and plopped down with a satisfied sigh. She leaned toward Wanda and grinned. The grin implied that there was something Wanda should be expecting, hoping for—something about which she should feel in suspense.

"Did you like them?" Helen asked.

"Yeah."

Helen clapped her hands together and fell back in the couch. "I had a good feeling about this from the start. Somehow I knew." Then she leaned forward again and said, "They want to have you over for dinner, Wanda. Would you like to have dinner at their house?"

"When?"

"Well, you leave tomorrow, don't you? So it'll have to be tonight."

"What about the other couples?" Wanda asked, a little disappointed that she wouldn't get to order room service, as she had last night.

"Think of them as backups. You like the Weston-Sloanes, right?"

"The what?"

"Randy and Melissa. The Weston-Sloanes. Do you feel comfortable going forward with them? You can say no."

"I like them. They like me?"

"Enough to have you over for dinner and get to know you better. This is a very good sign, Wanda."

"And they don't mind that I live all the way in Eula?"

"Like I told you that first day, Wanda, that's going to work in your favor. Everyone wants a farm girl to carry their baby. They're a little concerned that you've never been pregnant before, that you've never carried a baby to term, but you can't have everything, can you?"

"Well, then," Wanda said, "I'll go over."

"*God*, I love my job," Helen said, with a force that startled Wanda. "I'm sorry, but this is the part that really excites me, when there's chemistry between a couple and a surrogate. *You* can help them make a family, Wanda. You have that power." Helen squeezed Wanda's shoulder and went back into the office.

THAT EVENING CONNIE took Bill Howard to Payette, a half-hour drive from Eula, to give his presentation to a board of deacons. The pastor of Payette Nazarene, Bill had explained to Connie as she drove, had approached Bill about giving a short talk during the Sunday morning service. The church would take a special collection for the mission, and this required the approval of the board of deacons. Hence, this presentation.

Connie remembered this sort of thing being presented to the board when she served as a deaconess. Still, by being Bill's guide, she was learning new things about how churches worked. The group at Melba Nazarene had made a collection after she and Bill had left, and someone had delivered a check to the parsonage the following day. It seemed this was the way large groups in small churches operated. Bill had been very encouraged by Melba Nazarene's generosity. Connie's group, the Dorcases, had left it to its members to quietly slip Bill a check after his talk. She wondered which method the smaller groups she and Bill were scheduled to visit would use, and she worried that they would shame the Dorcases by being more generous. Then she remembered Christ's words of the woman who put a penny in the offering: "This poor widow hath cast more in than all they which have cast into the treasury: For all they did cast in of their abundance; but she of her want did cast in all that she had." Bill would never judge one group harshly for having given less than another.

And so, here they were on a Friday evening, Bill giving his talk and Connie at the back of the room, listening to it for the third time. She loved it. She especially loved hearing the improvements he made each time. It seemed he was gradually realizing that people were interested not only in the fact of his work but the details of it, and he allowed himself to use the children's names and tell quick anecdotes about them. Connie would tell him, on the way home, just how well this worked. She had arrived at a decision during her evening prayer a few nights previous that it was her role not only to drive him around but to encourage him.

She sat in the back, quietly waiting for him to come to the slide that she had put right, hoping that he would pause, just for a second, and realize what she had done for him.

"And this is me with some of the children," he said at last. Then he looked up to the screen, and—he did!—he paused before he went on.

After Bill's talk, the deacons showered him with questions. It was clear that they were fascinated with his work.

"That went well," said Connie, once they were driving back to Eula.

"Yes, it did."

"Will you be showing slides Sunday morning, or just giving a talk?"

"I'm not sure. The pastor said he would leave me a message after the meeting lets out."

"I see," said Connie. She wanted to ask if she could accompany him Sunday morning, if he would need help finding the church again, but she worried that this would sound overeager.

"Connie?" said Bill.

"Yes?"

"Did you fix that slide that was upside-down?"

"Yes."

"Oh."

They were quiet for a long time. Wasn't he going to thank her? He cracked his knuckles and gazed out the window. Maybe he disliked that she had taken care of this. Maybe it embarrassed him. Gene sometimes tore his coat out of Connie's hands when she was helping him put it on; maybe Bill was feeling a grown-up version of this rebellion. The idea that she could have made a mistake so early in her position of assisting him made her throat seize a little in panic.

They were coming into Eula now.

"I'm a little embarrassed," Bill said, chuckling affably. He turned to her. His eyes were brown and close-set, and Connie could see from the lift in his brow that he was, indeed, embarrassed. Vulnerable. "See, Connie, you've found me out. There's a bit of the performer in me. That first night when I was speaking to your group, the slide was upside-down. You all laughed, and it kind of broke the ice, so I figured I would leave it that way."

"Oh," Connie said.

"Maybe you've noticed, on these church visits, it's had the same effect. It puts people at ease. Silly, isn't it? That it works?"

"Yes," Connie said, and she laughed lifelessly.

"I figure, a little showmanship never hurts, especially when it's in service of the mission."

"Of course, Bill. I'm sorry I changed it. I'll put it back the way it was."

"Please, Connie, don't trouble yourself. I'll take care of it. I've been meaning to change the order of some of the slides anyhow."

They arrived at the parsonage, where rosebushes lined the drive. Spindly at the base, they then ballooned into great masses of gray leaves and ragged flowers, which even now kept some of their petals, splayed away from their cottony hearts, which had long since been stripped of pollen.

"Well, until Wednesday?" he said. "Remind me, what is our destination?"

"Marsing."

"Marsing, Idaho." He shook his head in amazement, a gesture Connie couldn't quite interpret. "Thanks again, Connie." He patted her shoulder and got out of the car. Then he knocked on the window. "The trunk?" he said.

"Oh, of course!" She got out and opened the trunk with her key. He took out the slides, closed the trunk, and bid her good-bye. It hurt horribly to see him carrying away those boxes, as if she'd never see them, or him, again.

Driving away, Connie began to cry. "Darn it!" she said aloud and hit the steering wheel with her open hand. Why had she done that? Why hadn't she left well enough alone? She had embarrassed him, overstepped her bounds, made things tense between them, and placed an obstacle before Bill, whose ministry—whose calling in life—already presented such challenges. She wiped her eyes. "You are proud, Connie Anderson," she said aloud. "Proud and vain and stupid."

Melissa, in a jeep whose bumper was plastered with stickers—MONDALE/FERRARO '84 and SAVE THE WHALES—picked Wanda up in front of the hotel at the appointed time. "I forgot to ask if you were a vegetarian," Melissa said. She sat on a little cushion, Wanda noticed, but still had to tilt her head back to see over the dashboard and hike herself up to change lanes.

"Oh, no. I eat everything," Wanda said.

"Good. I think we'll have tuna."

"I eat tuna all the time."

They drove down a hill away from the tall buildings, then took a ramp onto the highway. The city disappeared behind them and the thickly wooded Columbia River gorge opened ahead. The forest here was different from the forest in the mountains above Boise. The same spindly pines were interspersed with the skeletons of aspen that had shed their leaves, but in Idaho there was a carpet of dry pine needles underneath that was always catching fire. The forest would then burn for days, and a dark haze would settle into the valley. Here, the forest floor was steamy and green, even now in November. Wanda could imagine lying on a bed of moss and pulling the feathery ferns around her and falling asleep. The day before, riding the bus down this same highway, Wanda had wondered about these houses among the trees. Now she was going to have dinner in one of them.

"In the meeting, you didn't ask about our problems . . . with getting pregnant," Melissa said.

"Oh. I didn't want to pry," Wanda said.

"I figured that was it." Melissa turned off the highway onto a narrow road that zigzagged up the side of the gorge. "I have *cervical incompetence*. Charming name, isn't it? The opening up there is just weak. I would get pregnant no problem, I'd reach the second trimester, and then everything would just fall out. It happened four times. I'd walk around on eggshells, like I had a house of cards inside, and when I miscarried . . . well, it was just unbearable. Twice they put sutures in but they didn't take, and I suspect they made the problem worse. It nearly did me in. Oh, look! Here's Randy."

Ahead of them, dressed in tight black cycling clothes and a helmet, Randy was laboring up the road on a bicycle, his head low over the handlebars, his torso rocking side to side as he threw his weight into every step.

"He bikes to and from work," said Melissa. She tapped a little greeting on her horn as she passed him, and he nodded breathlessly.

"Aren't you going to pick him up?" Wanda asked.

"Pick him up?" Melissa laughed. "No, it's his thing."

Wanda turned in her seat to watch Randy pumping with all his might. He looked in agony. Then the road turned, and he disappeared behind a wall of pines. Melissa drove a little farther up the slope, then pulled onto a gravel road that led into a hollow. "Here we are," she said. She parked the car and reached for a bag of groceries in the backseat.

The house—or what Wanda could see of it, as it was hidden behind trees and shrubs—resembled a bunch of tool sheds and greenhouses, piled on top of each other and linked with bulging joints. A spiral staircase led from a deck up to a balcony. There were panes of glass in all the roofs. Wanda wondered if it was finished. Melissa walked to the front door, which rattled with the scratching of dogs, and balanced the groceries on a knee while she got out her keys. "All right, already," she said. She opened the door and out they bounded—four mutts of all different sizes and colors, yipping and panting. They jumped on Melissa, who mimicked their whimpers—"Yes, I know, it's awful, isn't it?"—then jumped on Wanda, then ran out into the trees to pee. "Come on in," Melissa said to Wanda. "Make yourself at home."

Wanda slid onto a stool at a little bar that divided the kitchen from the living room, while Melissa put away the groceries and continued the story she had started in the car. "I felt that we should adopt. It seemed like the moral thing to do when there are so many kids who need homes, but Randy was adamant that the child should be connected biologically to at least one of us. He wasn't raised by his birth parents; he was raised in foster care, and it scarred him in certain ways. So we called the agency. That was in September. It's been a lot of appointments since then, paperwork, sperm counts. You're actually the first girl we've met." Then Melissa stopped. "Is everything all right, Wanda?" she said.

Wanda had been unable to focus on what Melissa had been saying. The room in which she sat was spacious like the interior of a barn, but a barn where she could stay forever—bright and clean, with a library where the hayloft should have been. The leaves of houseplants dangled from an archway, a hexagonal window revealed a lush bank, and a shaft of light slanted across a glass hallway. Wanda bowed her head. "I'm sorry. I've never been in a beautiful house like this before." She was ashamed, but it was true. The rich people in Eula lived in big, square houses where you were afraid to walk on the carpet. None of them would ever hide their treasure in the woods.

Melissa looked very solemn for a moment. "Well, that is the highest compliment anyone has ever paid me," she said.

It struck Wanda, and she was further humbled: Melissa, an architect, had made this house.

A shyness overcame the two women and they were quiet until Randy came in the front door, teetering on his cycling shoes. "One hour, seventeen minutes, my love," he said.

"Not too bad," Melissa said.

"Not too good either."

"He's been trying to get his time back down to where it was before he pulled his groin," Melissa explained. Randy came into the kitchen, and they bent in to kiss each other lightly on the lips, careful not to otherwise touch each other, as Randy was covered in sweat. Wanda could see that his buttocks were completely flat in his cycling shorts.

Randy turned to her. "Do you have a bike, Wanda?" he asked.

"No."

"We might have to fix that."

"What would I do with a bike?" Wanda asked.

"Ride it!"

Wanda laughed at the image. "Grown-ups in Eula don't ride bikes," she said.

Randy and Melissa laughed hesitantly, and Wanda was aware that she had been rude. She bit her lip.

"All right," Melissa said to Randy. "Hit the showers. Then fire up the grill. Wanda and I are going to take the dogs out."

"Aye-aye, sergeant," Randy said.

"You'll need a scarf," Melissa said to Wanda on the way out.

"It's not that cold," said Wanda.

"Oh, trust me on this." Melissa ducked into a little closet in the entryway and handed Wanda a scarf and mittens. Then they headed out onto a trail into the woods as the dogs trotted happily ahead. The smallest dog had a tail that, halfway down, kinked to the right in a perfect L. When the dog wagged its tail with extra vigor, the tip jabbed it in the side. Wanda pointed this out to Melissa.

"Yes, that's Simon. Poor thing. I think his tail got slammed in a door when he was a puppy. We got him from a shelter. Go run, Simon," she said. She threw a stick and Simon ran happily into the brush after it, his L swinging. "I'm not sure if this is a concern of yours," Melissa said, "but Randy and I are very solid, as a couple. As far as raising a kid, is what I'm getting at. We've been together, gosh, since we were barely more than teenagers. I can't imagine being with anyone else, and, I'm sure, he can't either. It's forever."

"You're lucky," Wanda said.

"Oh, I didn't mean to brag!" Melissa said. "Damn it, I forgot about Hank . . . the breakup. I'm sorry, Wanda. I just meant to put your mind at rest as far as carrying a child for us—that the child will always have two parents. That came out wrong."

Wanda couldn't believe Melissa was being so careful with her. Why would a woman who built a house worry about impressing *her*? "Melissa, forget about Hank. I can see how happy you and Randy are. It makes me feel very . . . secure."

"Good," Melissa said. "It's not an act we're putting on for you, just so you know. If we have a child, that child will have a good life."

The trail narrowed through a thicket, then opened up to an incline littered with boulders. "We're almost there, Wanda," said Melissa. "Don't turn around until I tell you."

A little out of breath, Wanda buttoned her jacket as she stepped over stones. It was a denim jacket, lined with fake lamb's wool and studded with shiny metal stars along the hems and pockets. Melissa wore the kind of jacket people buy to go hiking in. Wanda pulled on the fluffy mittens, which, on her narrow cuffs, seemed as big as oven mitts.

"All right," Melissa said, sitting down on a large, flat rock, "now you can look."

Wanda turned and witnessed the glowing Columbia bent into an S by the slopes of the gorge, which lay against each other like folds of fabric, each a paler shade of blue, off into the distance. The slopes plateaued into a perfectly flat horizon, and car lights twinkled here and there along the rim. In the haze under the sun, mountains appeared almost indistinguishable from the clouds. The idea of the time that it took for the river to carve this beautiful groove into the earth was, to Wanda, as awesome as the view.

"It's gorgeous," she said.

"There's a pun there," Melissa replied. "Sit down."

Wanda squatted next to Melissa, hesitating to put her bottom on the cold rock. The wind stung her ears, and she was glad now for the scarf.

"I was hoping there'd be a sunset," Melissa said. The sun lost its shape in the haze, and the sky above them glowed amber. "A good sunset, here, in the spring when all the waterfalls are going—you should see it." After a minute, she said, "Let's not get caught up in it. It's time to get dinner on."

Melissa and Wanda walked back down. The dogs, having spent all their energy, trotted along beside them until the house came into view. Then they ran to the patio and sat obediently waiting to be let in, all except Simon, the crooked-tailed dog, who whimpered and dug at the threshold as if he could tunnel under the door.

"Simon, stop that. What is it?" Melissa said. Then her face changed. "Randy!" she shouted, and she ran into the house.

When Wanda entered the barn-room, she saw a salad bowl and a cutting board on the bar. On the cutting board lay a cucumber. She didn't see Melissa or Randy.

"Wanda? Could you get these dogs off?" Melissa called.

Wanda came around the bar to see Melissa crouched over Randy and all the dogs crowding around. Melissa pushed one of them away and said, "Go on!"

"Come, dogs!" Wanda called, clapping her hands. Two followed her and she put them out; the other two she had to drag by their collars. Simon fought her all the way. Then she went back to Melissa.

"Grab me a washcloth," Melissa said.

"Do you want it wet?" Wanda asked, taking a cloth from beside the sink.

"No."

Melissa took the cloth and folded it. She gently pressed on Randy's chin to open his mouth, and lay the cloth on his tongue. Randy's head was cradled in her lap. His body was stiff and quaking. Melissa used one hand to firmly draw Randy's jaw up into an underbite, the other she laid on his chest. She bent over him, sheltering him, and whispered, "Shh-shh-shh." Now his body rocked back and forth, as if gathering momentum to roll over. "Wanda, could you move this stuff away?"

Wanda picked up a knife off the floor and dragged a nearby chair across the kitchen. Now Randy seemed to be trying to keep his arms straight. His fingers were curled tightly, and the heels of his hands thrust against the floor tiles. A drawn-out frightened sound came from his throat, like a trapped word struggling to get out.

A nightmare, Wanda thought—*he's caught in a nightmare, the kind where you're paralyzed and you can't wake yourself up.*

"Hush, sweetheart. It's okay," Melissa said.

Randy slackened and twitched. Then he was still. Melissa stroked his face. They stayed like that for several minutes, far longer than the seizure itself had lasted, while Wanda watched from across the room, unsure whether to give them help or privacy. Finally, she put down the knife, walked over to Melissa, and lay her hand on her shoulder.

Melissa looked up, her face surprisingly composed, and said, "Thanks, Wanda." She set aside the cloth and straightened Randy's glasses. Wanda knew now why he wore that silly band. Then Melissa said, "Could you help me get him into a chair?"

Wanda knelt and took an elbow, and they assisted Randy as he rose and walked into the seating area beyond the bar.

"Do you want some water, sweetheart?" Melissa asked.

Randy nodded.

"Let me," said Wanda.

They sat with Randy patiently as he took sips of water. Melissa said, "Simon always knows. Did you see him scratching?"

On Randy's face was an expression of deep sorrow. At last he looked at Wanda and said, "Sorry about that."

Wanda shook her head, no.

"Randy's epileptic," Melissa said in a confidential tone. "It's not severe. We haven't told them, at the agency, because it will disqualify us."

Randy corrected her weakly: "We *think* it *might* disqualify us."

"In any case," Melissa said, "we definitely planned to tell you—or whoever we ended up being matched with. I understand if this . . . disturbs you."

Wanda, overwhelmed and frightened of saying the wrong thing, shook her head again.

"Well, I'd like to ask you not to tell Helen. I'll understand if you feel that you need to tell her. But, as a favor to us, I ask you not to."

Tears clouded Wanda's vision—all those lies she had told them in the office!—and she said, "I won't tell."

"Thanks," Melissa said briskly. Then she leaned in toward Randy. It seemed she wanted to distract him so he wouldn't see the tears in Wanda's eyes. "Sweetheart, do you want to lie down for a bit?"

"I think I will," he said.

"He gets very tired . . ."

Randy rose from the chair and walked slowly across the room. Before he disappeared into the glass hallway, he reached up and touched the lowest-hanging leaf of a plant that overflowed from the balcony. Melissa had turned to Wanda to say, "Well, I guess you'll be helping me with dinner," and didn't see Randy touch that leaf, but the gesture moved Wanda. It was obvious to her that it was something he did habitually, maybe every time he entered that hallway, like how she herself always looked through the peephole before opening the door, even when she knew who it was, and like how her mother used to pull the lever and move the car seat back and forth to get it just right before starting the car, even though she was the only one who drove it. Habit. Wanda sensed that Randy had done it this time to mark that the seizure was over—to touch waking life after the nightmare.

"I'm happy to help," she said.

They went to the kitchen. "Wanda, could you rinse off the tuna? I get it at the Chinese grocery, and there's always lots of flies."

"Um, sure." Did Melissa want her to clean the cans, or to rinse the tuna inside? Either seemed a little excessive. But, wary of saying anything that would make her seem stupid or rude, Wanda began searching a shelf for the tuna.

"It's right there," said Melissa, indicating the counter. There was no tuna there, though, and Wanda gave Melissa a hesitant, bewildered shake of the head.

Melissa came over and opened a paper packet, revealing what Wanda assumed was a slab of sirloin. "Here," she said.

"That's meat," Wanda said, aware that she was stumbling, unaware of how.

"You've never seen fresh tuna?" Melissa marveled, laughing.

Wanda shrank.

"Of course you haven't!" Melissa said, suddenly businesslike. "You live far from the ocean. Treat it just like a steak. Rinse it off in the sink, then cut it into three."

Wanda took the package, sickened a little by the brilliant red color, the fleshy aroma, and the idea of a cow-sized fish. She had always assumed that tuna were smaller than the catfish she used to catch with her uncle and that the meat of one filled one can.

Later, as Wanda was setting the table, Randy walked in with a shy smile.

"Well, if it isn't Lazarus!" cried Melissa.

"Back from the dead," Randy responded.

Wanda saw that this was something they had said a thousand times, but this time it didn't seem canned, but sweet. She regretted having judged them harshly at the office.

Randy put his arms around Melissa, and she drew him down to

share some private words. Then she said aloud, "You're just in time. Sit down, both of you. Dinner's on."

"Wanda, I'm sorry you had to see that, before," Randy said.

"Please," Wanda said.

"It can really scare some people," Randy said.

"It's okay. I've seen worse."

Randy's gaze lingered on her for a moment as Melissa brought in a big plate with tuna steaks, crisscrossed with grill marks and surrounded by little potatoes. "Ta-daa!" Melissa said.

Wanda, when she said that she had seen worse, had meant finding her mother passed out on the floor—that had happened more than once. And, naturally, that led her thoughts to the morning she found her mother dead—the blaring TV and the cheerful breeze. They began to eat. Wanda didn't like the flavor of the tuna where it was red inside, and labored to eat only the cooked part without making a show. The three struggled to make conversation, and for Wanda it was as difficult to manage as the tuna steak. Every avenue dead-ended in something about which she had lied. She would curb her story abruptly, and Randy, who still seemed weak, would nod, leaving poor Melissa to come up with a fresh topic. Wanda's lies seemed almost to crowd her lungs and block her breath. Finally she said, "Can I tell you guys something?"

There must have been an alarm in her voice, because Melissa and Randy stopped eating.

"It's not just you," Wanda said. "I lied to Helen, too. My parents didn't die in a car wreck last year, they died when I was little. I can't even remember my dad. My uncle killed him in a hunting accident when I was just two. And my mom died when I was eleven. She had been . . . sick . . . a long time." Even now Wanda couldn't tell the whole truth, but this was a giant step toward it. "My life hasn't really been like I said. It's been pretty rough." She stopped herself. That was enough for now.

Melissa and Randy looked down and, after a moment, started to eat again. "I'm sorry to hear that," Melissa said.

"Did you go into foster care?" Randy asked.

"Yeah, for a year. I lived in this house in Chandler with these other foster kids, boys. Most of them ended up in prison."

"And," Randy said, "probably should have been in prison already?"

"Yeah."

Randy nodded gravely.

"Then I lived with my big sister awhile, till she moved to Boise."

"I was a foster kid," Randy said.

"Melissa told me."

"I was quite a mess until I met Melissa. It was Melissa that made me get my GED, and her parents that helped me open the bike shop."

Wanda looked to Melissa, who shook her head without raising her eyes. Wanda had always dreamed that someone would come and save her like that.

They were quiet for a while, then Wanda said, "I hope what I said doesn't change your mind. I mean, if you were going to choose me."

"Wanda," Melissa said. "Remember how I burst out crying when I saw you?"

"Mel, don't," Randy said.

"Randy doesn't want me to tell you, but I will. I never cry. The reason I cried when I saw you was because I *knew*, I absolutely *knew* that you were the one who would carry our baby."

Randy put his hand on Melissa's and said, "Wanda, don't let this make you feel pressured. It's just a feeling Melissa had, and we're both pretty wound up."

"He's right," said Melissa. "It's just a feeling . . ." Her eyes locked with Wanda's significantly, as if to say, *But it's true.*

Wanda smiled bashfully.

"All right," Randy said, "enough serious talk. Let's enjoy our meal."

"Oh, one more thing," Wanda said. "Earlier tonight, when I said that grown-ups in Eula don't ride bikes, I didn't mean anything by it. I think it's great that you ride a bike. Really. I think your whole life here is great."

"Thank you," Randy said.

Now Wanda felt as if the block had been removed and her breath was free. They finished their dinner and sat for a while talking before empty plates. Then Melissa brought out bowls of ice cream sprinkled with warmed berries.

"These are from Melissa's garden," Randy said, picking up a

blueberry with his fingertips and tossing it into his mouth. "She freezes them so we can have them year-round."

"Yummy," Wanda said.

"It's a shame you're leaving tomorrow," Melissa said. "We could have shown you the area. Oh, but I forget, you've been to Portland before."

"Yeah, well, barely," Wanda said.

"What do you mean?"

"I was here with some friends for a weekend. All I saw of Portland was the inside of a few bars."

"You didn't go to the Cascades?" Randy said.

"Nope."

"Have you been to Seattle?" Melissa asked. "Have you seen Puget Sound?"

"Portland's as far as I got."

"You didn't even go to the beach? It's just over an hour away!" Randy said.

"No. I've never seen the ocean. Isn't that stupid?"

Melissa and Randy were dumbstruck. Then they glanced at each other as if to confirm something.

"What time is your bus tomorrow?" Randy asked.

"Noon."

"You can't go back to Eula without seeing the ocean."

"Wanda," Melissa said, "would you like to stay here tonight, in the guest room, and go to the ocean in the morning? We can have you back at your hotel in time to make a noon bus."

"Don't you guys have to work?" Wanda asked.

"The shop doesn't open till ten," Randy said.

"And I can be late," Melissa said.

"You guys are so nice," Wanda said, humbled yet again.

"DID YOU MAKE them?" Enrique asked Gene when they met that night to paint the diorama.

Gene handed over not several large, colorful posters but a flimsy chart made from taped-together sheets of lined notebook paper. Small cross-sections of lakes drawn in pencil were accompanied by mathematical calculations marred with eraser marks. "Crater Lake in Oregon is the deepest lake in America," Gene said in his computer-voice. "It's two thousand feet deep. Three times as deep as Lake Nyos, and five times the volume. If this happened there, everyone in the towns of Kirk, Fort Klamath, and Union would die. Thirty thousand people."

"That's neat, Gene, but it's not our project. Our project is to list the possible causes of what happened, and show what it would be like if it happened here. Remember what Abby said? *Narrow the focus.*"

Gene pointed farther down the chart. "Pend Oreille Lake. Twelve hundred feet deep, three times the surface area, five times the volume. Everyone in Sandpoint and Coeur d'Alene could die—half the population of northern Idaho."

"Gene," whimpered Enrique, flapping the sheet, "we're doing Lake Overlook, not Pend Oreille! You didn't make them, did you?"

Gene ducked his head.

Enrique had been forced to give Gene assignments to keep him from following tangents such as this one. Gene was supposed to have made posters listing the gases that could have poisoned the people, demonstrating how the weight of the water could have held down the gas and showing the volume of Lake Nyos versus Lake Overlook.

"Will you make them, tomorrow, *please*?"

Gene's face churned.

"Let's paint," Enrique said.

As they covered the papier-mâché surface with green tempera, Gene repeatedly ran to the kitchen to wash smudges from his hands. Then Jay came home and Gene's attention was lost. He sat poised over the project, a paintbrush ready in his hand, and watched Jay watching TV. "Go home, Gene," Enrique said finally. There was no formality between the two boys as far as bidding each other good-bye. Often Gene slipped away soundlessly without Enrique noticing; other times he stayed late watching TV after Enrique had put on his pajamas and brushed his teeth. Enrique or Lina would tell him to go home without risking offense.

"Your friend's a retard," said Jay once Gene was gone, and this time Enrique didn't spring to his defense. He couldn't deny it: Gene stared at Jay like a retard.

Before heading off to bed, Enrique looked over the diorama. It didn't live up to his vision. At four feet square, it took up an entire corner of the living room. Lake Overlook was a round metal bowl in the corner. They had made the papier-mâché slope leading to the lake as gentle as they could, but it still looked a little like a volcano. Headlines showed through the green paint. Mr. Hall's trees and houses would save the project. It might not be identifiable as Eula, as Enrique had hoped, but it would at least resemble a lakeside village. When dry ice was placed in the metal bowl on the day of the science fair, the effect of carbon dioxide fumes swirling among the tiny trees would be dramatic.

WHILE RANDY TOOK the dogs on their night walk, Melissa showed Wanda the guest room. "This wing of the house can get a little chilly, so if you need an extra blanket, there's one in the closet. There should be a new toothbrush under the sink and a bathrobe and towel on the back of the door. Is there anything else you need?"

"No."

"We're just down the hallway if you need us." Then Melissa hesitated, apparently wondering if there was something more she should do or say. She looked around the room, shrugged, and said, "Sleep tight, then. I'll be getting you up pretty early."

Wanda brushed her teeth, undressed, and slid into bed. She lay for a few minutes with the lights on, feeling restless. Having always slept in a big T-shirt, she didn't know if she could sleep like this, in her bra. And more than this, although she didn't articulate it to herself, she wanted to see Melissa again before bed, maybe to stay up for a while, talking.

I'll ask for a T-shirt to sleep in, Wanda said to herself. She put on the bathrobe and went down the hall. A door was ajar at the end, allowing a great bar of light to shine on the wood floor of the hallway. Wanda heard a tiny sound. *Tick . . . tick . . . tick . . .* Maybe the faucet was dripping. She tapped on the door and it swung open a little, revealing Melissa in plaid pajamas with her foot on the rim of the toilet, clipping her toenails.

"Oops, sorry," Wanda said.

"That's all right," Melissa said. "Do you need something?"

"I was wondering if I could borrow a T-shirt to sleep in."

"Of course. Come in. I'm almost done."

Wanda perched herself on the side of the big tile bathtub, which had steps leading down into it, like a swimming pool. She watched Melissa lift one toe away from the others and . . . *tick* . . . *tick* . . .

"You know," Wanda said, "Hank was the first person I ever saw cut his nails inside."

"What do you mean?"

Wanda felt like telling her stories, as if she could again make the magic she had at dinner by telling the truth. "Growing up, it was just something you'd do outside, off the edge of the porch. The boys would pee off the porch if the bathroom was full."

Melissa laughed.

"When I caught Hank cutting his nails over the kitchen trash I asked him, 'Don't you wanna go outside to do that?' He called me a shit-kicker."

"A what?"

"A hillbilly."

"Do you miss him?" Melissa asked.

"No. He's not as good as I made him out to be." She stopped herself from admitting he hadn't moved to Washington, DC, but to Chandler, fifteen miles away.

Melissa folded the nail clippers closed and set them on the counter. "Let's get you a shirt."

They walked around the corner—there was no door—into the bedroom. Melissa opened a drawer. "Will this one do?"

The dogs rushed in, grazing Wanda's leg with their wet fur. Then Randy appeared in the doorway.

"Mind if I loan Wanda one of your shirts?" Melissa asked.

"Not at all."

Wanda took the shirt. "Thanks for everything, you guys. I'll leave you alone. Good night."

Wanda closed the door behind her and walked down the hallway. Beyond her door, the hallway curved, then ended in a window that reached from the floor to the ceiling. Wanda stood looking out on the pine trees, hairy with moss and lit pale by the moon.

. . . .

Liz arrived home and went into the darkened kitchen for a snack. No sooner had she opened the refrigerator, though, than a voice made her jump: "Good news, sis."

"Winston, what are you doing here in the dark?"

From the window seat he tossed an envelope toward her, and it slid across the tile floor. "You got in." Winston held a beer can, and there were two more crushed on the windowsill.

"Why are you opening my mail?"

Winston shrugged and looked out over the lights of the back walk, haloed by the steamy window. "Figured you wouldn't mind. Congratulations."

With a thrill, Liz picked up the envelope and thumbed through its contents. Since Abby had gotten her acceptance letter, Liz had dreaded the humiliation of not getting in, too. They had made a promise, *Both of us, or neither*, but it was still a relief.

"Are you gonna go?"

"Of course. That's been the plan all along."

"Yeah? All along?" There was a tremor in his voice that surprised her.

"What's wrong?"

Winston shrugged, tipped his head back, and emptied the can into his mouth. "I always kinda figured you and me would stick close, that's all."

"Why?"

"*Why?*" Winston mimicked her with a sneer. "It's not like we're brother and sister or anything."

Liz shook her head in confusion, and returned to the refrigerator. "Don't go telling everyone at school, okay?" she said. "I don't want all the talk yet."

"Like anyone gives a fuck, Liz. Jesus." He crushed the can and slid away.

For the rest of the evening, Connie thought about nothing but what had taken place between Bill and her. Even in her hour of prayer at the end of the day, she continued to wrestle with her mistake. But now she told herself to put it behind her. They would go to Marsing on Wednesday; she would continue this important work, careful not to overstep her bounds again. She tried to banish these thoughts from her mind and concentrate on that day's scripture, but they would not leave her alone. She prayed to the Lord to deliver her from them. Then she closed her Bible and prepared for bed.

As she lay waiting for sleep she realized why she could not get over it. She was angry at Bill—nearly as angry at him as she was at herself. "Showmanship," he had called it. It wasn't showmanship, thought Connie. It was a lie, and a lie was a sin. A great sadness came over Connie with the knowledge that Bill, like so many others, wanted to stretch and test God's law.

She thanked Jesus for showing her this, Jesus, who had overturned the tables at the temple because of just this, "showmanship"—lies.

"Lord Almighty, help Bill. Be with him, and guide him in the one true way."

This put Connie at ease and allowed her to sleep.

In the middle of the night, Wanda's door creaked open. She woke with a start and lay with her eyes wide open, afraid to move. She wasn't in her own bed. Where was she? In the foster home? Of course not. They had talked about it at dinner, was all. She was at Melissa and Randy's. "Hello?" she said.

The click of a dog's claws against floorboards put her at ease. She turned on the light and saw Simon gazing up at her and wagging his L-shaped tail. "Do you want up?" Wanda lifted the dog onto the bed and looked into his black, soulful eyes. He had a long nose for a small dog. He must have been part dachshund. "You're one of those special dogs, aren't you?" When she was little, before her mother had married Alan and stopped going to church, Wanda had had a Sunday school teacher, Mrs. Kray, whose lessons always ended up being about dogs—maybe not *every* lesson, but that's what she remembered: parables about Mrs. Kray's own dogs (it seemed she had dozens); reports she had seen on the news about dogs saving their owners; and articles she had read in *Guideposts* or *Reader's Digest* about angels in dog form who inspired their owners to be born again, or give up drinking, or become a better parent. Although these stories didn't bring Wanda into any closer communion with the Lord, they did instill in her a belief in the mystical powers of dogs.

"You know Melissa and Randy," she said to Simon. "Should I do this?"

The dog wagged his tail.

Wanda nodded.

Simon went to the bottom of the bed and lay between Wanda's feet, facing the door. Wanda turned out the light and went to sleep.

In the morning, Randy insisted on sitting in the backseat as Melissa, elevated on her little pillow, drove. Wanda understood now: Randy didn't drive.

The day was bright. Wanda put down her visor and, through the makeup mirror, saw Randy loosen the strap and take off his glasses. His eyes suddenly appeared huge. He pinched the bridge of his nose and gave the morning a few big blinks. Wanda could now see that Randy had been handsome before he lost his hair. He still was handsome, in fact. He had a strong brow and big, rich, brown eyes. Now it made sense that Melissa, who was so pretty, was with him. Also now, Wanda felt less squeamish about having Randy's stuff inside her. This childish concern, which Wanda had been too ashamed even to think through, was put to rest.

When they reached the beach, there was a bright fog over the ocean. "Low tide," said Randy. He and Melissa sat in the dry sand near the car while Wanda took off her shoes, rolled up her jeans, and walked down toward the water, which was washing far up the beach, then receding back into the mist, leaving tangles of seaweed like knotted hair. Wanda could hear waves crashing off in the distance. She walked onto the shell-littered sand, and the water returned to flow over her feet, numbingly cold. She hopped from foot to foot, giggled, and turned to look back at Melissa and Randy, who waved. A little frightened of stepping on a crab or lobster, Wanda walked gingerly toward the sound. It was the biggest sound she had ever heard, not loud, but all-consuming. She walked and walked and still the water, when it washed in, only reached her ankles. She knew so little about how the ocean worked; could a huge wave come and take her away? She turned back to Melissa and Randy, but they were lost in the whiteness.

In the years since Louis's suicide, Wanda had never been able to wade in water without thinking of him. Such a weird way to go, giving yourself to the river when there was a shotgun in nearly every house. Maybe he had been in a rush to leave this world, and the river had been there. It was just a five-minute walk from the psychiatric hospital. Wanda knew this because she had met a man who had once worked as a porter there. He had been trying to pick her up at a bar. Wanda had grilled him about how patients spent their time, if the doctors were kind or cruel, and, especially, the distance of the hospital from the river. Then she had fallen into silent rumination and the man, surely thinking her a nut who belonged in Blackfoot, had scooted out of the booth.

Wanda imagined that Louis checked out of the psychiatric hospital and walked to the river quickly, as if late for an appointment. (She had heard that people became exhilarated after they made the decision to commit suicide.) But when he got there, did he sit on the bank for a while, wishing for a friend to talk to? Did he stand there, shin-deep, as Wanda stood now, and cry? Or did he trudge in, battling the water that impeded his walk toward death?

Wanda was about to go back to Melissa and Randy, when she saw a man, both his figure and his figure's sliced-and-restacked reflection, many yards ahead of her, walking toward the waves. Seeing that he too was only up to his shins, and that he walked easily with his hands in his pockets, gave Wanda courage, and she went forward. Finally the surf came into view, and she turned away from the man. This is what she had expected the ocean to look like: a great swell that crested, then thundered down, sending spray high into the air.

Her feet ached with cold. She ran back up the beach, arrived at where Melissa and Randy huddled together against the wind which whipped at their hair and clothing, and stood breathless, hugging herself and stepping from foot to foot.

Shielding her eyes, Melissa said, "We bring you to the ocean, and you can't even see it!"

"I did see it, though!" Wanda insisted.

"I mean, the *ocean*," Melissa said, with a sweep of the arm to indicate a horizon.

"I *did*!"

CHAPTER 11

It was a week later now, the night before the District Science Fair. Enrique had been forced to make the posters himself, since Gene, on their evenings together, had insisted on exploring several fat chemistry textbooks he had checked out from the library. "It's essential to the project," he had said when Enrique complained. That was so like Gene, to choose a one-sentence response and repeat it again and again, unaware that it sounded weirder and less powerful with every iteration. All the research that Enrique had been counting on Gene to do, he had done himself—shoddily. He had failed to find out how deep Lake Overlook was. On every zoning map in the library, it was just a wide, flat blob that wasn't even labeled Lake Overlook, only RESERVOIR. Finally, at a loss, Enrique had called the City of Eula Water Department. "Welp, it's purdy deep," was the answer he got.

So the completion of the diorama was delayed until now, Friday night. Enrique begged Gene, "Please, just for tonight, work on the project we *have*. The science fair is tomorrow. Don't you want to win?"

Gene said nothing.

"Here," Enrique said, handing over the posters. "I did them myself. I'm sure the calculations are all wrong. Could you at *least* color in the drawings? You're good at that."

Gene took them and returned home.

Enrique was glad to have the house to himself. Jay was playing in a football game, certainly one of the season's last, since Eula never made it into the finals, and Lina had gone to watch, as she had nearly every game, although she and Jay went and returned home separately.

Enrique took the bag containing the trees and houses from the closet and brought it into the living room. Each piece was twist-tied in position inside a box, which featured a miniature backdrop: green hills and a distant silo for a house, an orchard for an apple tree. Even though Enrique was rushed to finish the model in order to have time to practice the presentation a few times before bed, he removed each piece with the greatest care. He enjoyed observing all the tiny details, but more important, he intended, after this and any subsequent science fairs, to put the pieces back in their boxes and return them to Mr. Hall. At the bottom of the bag he found two pieces he hadn't yet seen, as before tonight he had only let himself dig halfway down: a schoolhouse and a church. The tiny schoolhouse bell actually rang, and the church had stained-glass windows with panes of colored cellophane separated by black wire. He set these pieces down with the rest, carefully stacked the boxes back into the bag, and returned it to the closet. Then he looked down at his jumbled little village. What would it be like, he wondered, to live in a cottage with a pine tree blocking your front door and the church doors right outside your window? Slowly, using only the tiniest blobs from the glue gun, he put the pieces into the model.

At nine o'clock, before it got too late, he took a break. As he dialed the number, a queasy feeling stirred in his belly. What would he say if Mr. Hall answered the phone? But it was Abby who answered.

"Hi, Abby. It's Enrique."

"Hey!" she said.

"Um, I wanted to make sure you knew that the science fair is tomorrow, in Chandler."

"Oh, Enrique, I'm sorry. I can't go. I'm leaving for Salt Lake really early."

Enrique was so disappointed that he couldn't speak.

"I'm really sorry, Enrique. Maybe you can show it to me afterward."

He didn't want to say it, but he couldn't help it: "Didn't you know it was tomorrow?" He felt silly, of course—why would a high school girl base her schedule on him?—but in all his science-fair fantasies, Abby stood solemnly at the back of the crowd in rapt attention as Enrique spoke, then gave him one of her funny thumbs-ups at the end.

"I have to go see my mom, Enrique," Abby said gently. "It's not something I can really put off."

"Okay." In his selfishness, Enrique let the wounded tone of his brief answer hang in the air.

"Enrique, my mom is sick. Like, *really* sick. She's probably never going to come back home. So . . . I have to go there."

"Oh!"

"So," Abby ventured, "maybe you can show it to me afterward?"

"Of course," Enrique said in a kind of cough. His face was burning. He was an idiot.

"I really hope you win, Enrique. You deserve it."

"Thanks."

"Well, have a good night."

"Good night, Abby. And I'm really sorry . . . about your mom."

"Thanks."

Enrique hung up and, flushed to the tips of his ears, went back to gluing. He was careful now, not only with the delicate trees, but with himself. He felt as if a sudden movement would shake something loose, and tears would fly from his eyes. When he finished, he tied a string across the entrance to the living room, and hung a sign from it: DO NOT ENTER!! He didn't want Jay to come in and kick his basketball into the corner, as was his habit, and ruin the model.

Gene burst in the front door. "Guess what," he said.

"You colored them in?"

"I solved the mystery."

"Where are the posters, Gene?"

"It wasn't a poison gas that killed the people at Lake Nyos," Gene said.

"It has to be. That's our project."

"It was carbon dioxide."

"Carbon dioxide is already in the air, Gene. It doesn't kill you."

"It does," Gene said, "if it's the *only* thing in the air. The lake, down deep, was carbonated like soda pop. Then it turned over. All the carbon dioxide escaped at once, and since it's heavier than air, it ran along the ground. Everything that breathed oxygen suffocated. That's why there was no evidence. It didn't smell like rotten eggs. It didn't get gunk on everything. The plants weren't affected. They like carbon dioxide."

Enrique gave himself a moment. Such a long, sputtering string of words was rare and embarrassing from Gene, as if he had vomited. This new information was exciting, but Enrique wouldn't admit it. It was far too late for changes and additions. He inhaled, then, realizing that what was about to come out was a whimper, checked himself, stood up straight, and deepened his voice. "You didn't color the posters, did you?"

Gene bunched up his face and looked at his feet.

"We were supposed to be a team, Gene. I let you decide the project, when we could have done something a whole lot easier, and you know what you've done since then? Nothing but waste my time."

"I made a poster," Gene said.

"And you did a crappy job. Do you even *want* to be in the science fair, Gene? Do you even *want* to go there tomorrow?"

Gene now looked up at Enrique and said, with complete innocence, as if his answer might be of help, "No."

Enrique stomped his foot. "*Good*, then! I don't want you there either! This is *my* project! You can just stay home for all I care!"

Gene turned and quickly walked out.

Enrique followed him. "Give me my posters!" he yelled.

Gene stomped up the stairs and into his trailer and, a second later, returned with the posters, which he threw into the grass.

"My brother's right," Enrique said. "You *are* retarded!"

"I am *not* retarded," Gene said.

Enrique picked up the posters and went back to his house, leaving Gene on that tiny aluminum box they called a porch breathing loudly, his arms folded tight.

Far too upset to color the posters, let alone practice his

presentation, Enrique went straight to bed. He would rise early, finish, then go get Mr. and Mrs. Smiley, who lived at the far end of Robin Lane. They had a pickup truck with a shell and had promised to take Enrique and his project to and from the science fair if he fed their cats while they were in Wyoming over Thanksgiving. But then Enrique lay awake for a long time, thinking what an awful night this was, and how very wronged he had been.

For Lina, on the other hand, it had been a good night. She had sat with a group of mothers from church eating popcorn and gossiping, and Jay, who usually spent most of the game on the sidelines—basketball was his sport—had prevented a touchdown with a good tackle, at which point Lina had stood up and cheered and called his name. Still, Eula High had lost.

Now Lina walked into the house and saw the little sign. It seemed Enrique had gone to bed, so she untied one end of the string, turned on a light, and looked the model over. All of a sudden, it looked really good.

Her next thoughts came in rapid succession. How had Enrique afforded those little houses? They were Chuck's train accessories. Had Enrique stolen them? No, of course not, Chuck had given them to him.

What was Chuck up to?

Fearful, suddenly, that Enrique would find her snooping, Lina turned out the light and retied the string. She slipped down the hallway quietly, like a thief in her own house. It was only when she was safe in her room that the rage took over. Chuck had crossed a line now. This was it. No more.

Connie came home too and sat at the kitchen table for a few minutes, allowing the wonderful mood of the evening to wash over her. "You are a blessing to me, Connie," Bill had said when she dropped him off at the parsonage. He had paused, as if there was more he wanted to say. Connie couldn't meet his eyes, so her gaze fell to his neck and then rested in the little notch of his sternum, which was framed by the collar of his oxford shirt, which, in turn, was framed by the V of his sweater. She could see by the dim interior car light that this notch was covered by a light coat of short blond hairs and traversed by a thin gold chain.

"You're a blessing to me, too, Bill," she had said, then, shocked by the intimacy of her own words, added, "You've touched many lives in these churches we've visited." She wished now she hadn't panicked, but let her initial response stand. She felt the business with the upside-down slide was now over.

Enrique heard his mother come home, he heard Mrs. Anderson's car pull up, and then, much later, he heard Jay go through the house to his room—and felt it, too, as Jay's heavy steps caused the house to shudder on its stilts. He thought of ways that his mother and Jay had wronged him. The house fell silent, and still Enrique seethed.

I've got to go to sleep, he thought, *or else I'll do bad tomorrow morning.* So he curled up and imagined, as he often did when he was too upset to sleep, that he was sealed up in an egg made of a strong, transparent material that protected him completely from the surroundings. He could go anywhere in this egg. Sometimes he floated through the night sky into outer space, other times he settled onto the cold ocean floor. This time, though, he glided through the warm surface water of the Indian Ocean while great whales rose from the depths. One nudged him aside with its massive, blunt nose, sending him spinning away until his egg rolled up the side of another, great and flat as the wall of a barn. He reached the whale's tail, which gently flicked him up and away toward the moon, jiggling at the water's surface.

SOME PEOPLE TRIED to describe Eula's relationship with Chandler, which lay fifteen miles away in the direction opposite Boise, as familial: Chandler was Eula's big brother or little sister or lazy cousin or wicked stepmother. But none of those worked, as Eulans couldn't quite assign a human character to Chandler. Going there felt like being sent to the office. Although smaller than Eula, Chandler was the county seat, so all the buildings to which Eulans were beckoned for unpleasant business—to renew their licenses, to argue tickets, to bail out brothers—were there. While going to Boise meant glamour, going to McCall meant leisure, going to Blackfoot meant insanity, going to Salt Lake meant matrimony, and going to Portland meant abortion, going to Chandler meant many things—drudgery at best, incarceration at worst. So the road to Chandler still bore the residue of those bothersome visits, even when one was going there for something more pleasant, say, to visit one of Chandler's two attractions: the Oregon Trail Museum (located in Chandler although a seldom and, some said, only mistakenly used branch of the Oregon Trail had passed through), and the rodeo grounds. Chandler's rodeo, the River Valley Round-up, was on the national circuit and drew crowds every July, their pickup trucks, livestock trailers, and RVs filling campgrounds and motel parking lots as far away as Boise. It was Chandler's true claim to fame and the only thing Eula envied it.

The rodeo grounds, which were also used for the county fair every August, were vast and well-maintained, featuring lawns, stables, an outdoor stadium, and a field house. In the fall and winter this field house was used by the City of Chandler for its own events and rented out for functions—car shows, swap meets, and a Mexican dance every Saturday night.

The day before the Snake River District Science Fair, the field house had been used for the Rabbit Show, where breeders from around the state met to buy and sell rabbits and trade tips and recipes. The scent of rabbit—a musty combination of sawdust, mold, and urine—still hung in the air when Enrique arrived on Saturday morning. Anyone allergic to cats was doubly allergic to rabbits, or so claimed the Chandler High science teacher, who guided Enrique and Mr. Smiley to the assigned space. "Just set it down on the table, hon, it's yours to use," she said. Then she blew her nose with a honk. Her watery eyes were as red as a rabbit's. Enrique and Mr. Smiley carefully eased the model onto the table. "I'll be outside if you have any questions," the teacher said.

"Well, I'll see you at two, Enrique. Best of luck to ya," said Mr. Smiley. And Enrique was alone, apparently the first student to arrive. A couple of men were setting up tables, and a woman in a white apron and hairnet was putting out coffee and doughnuts. A quick look around his row revealed Miriam's name written on a card taped to a neighboring table, and a pile of rabbit droppings, small and spherical as peas, under his. He scooped these up into a piece of newspaper and considered switching Miriam to a table farther away. Then he thought better of it; there might be some confusion when

Miriam arrived, she'd find out what he had done, and he'd seem the fool or, worse, the coward.

Enrique and Miriam hadn't spoken since the day he called her fish project stupid. They still sat next to each other in Miss Holly's English class, but in stony silence. Miss Holly was their favorite. Once, after Enrique and Miriam collaborated on a dramatic reading of Maya Angelou, she had called them her "dynamic duo." Still in her late twenties, she was the only teacher who made attempts at fashion, by crimping her hair on some days and putting it up with plastic clips on others. Her efforts to add emphasis to her broad, blank face resembled punctuation marks: blue bars over the eyes, an oversized beauty mark. She had a funny way of folding her hands when someone said something stupid that made the class laugh. A few days ago, Enrique had caught Miss Holly giving her dynamic duo a sad sigh from the back of the room. This affected him more than anything else, because Miss Holly's versions of things seemed grander than reality, like the novels she taught. The alliance between him and Miriam had been more powerful and the current rift wider and more permanent than their real versions. He liked Miss Holly's better.

As Enrique set up his display, other kids began to arrive and do the same, and parents and teachers began to congregate around the doughnut table. When he finished, he went on a little tour up and down the rows, checking out his competition. Most of the kids were from the smaller outlying towns, and most of their projects seemed to have been adapted from 4-H presentations—"The Life of the Sugar Beet" and "Pasteurization: What Is It?"—while a few were retellings of current events: "Can Chernobyl's Radiation Reach Us?"

He returned to his project to explain it to visitors and wait for the judging to begin. A few parents meandered past with doughnuts cupped in napkins and gave him friendly nods, but none asked him questions.

Lina arrived, carrying a bucket. "The man was so nice," she said. "He lent us tongs. He says you gotta use them, so you don' get burned. It's so cold that it burns your skin!"

"Wow!" Enrique said. He hid the bucket behind the table—he

didn't want anyone to know about the dry ice until the moment he put it in the bowl—and went to take off the lid.

"Careful, *mijo*, use these." Lina held out a pair of thick, white rubber gloves. They looked like Mickey Mouse hands.

"Neat!" Enrique said. He put on the gloves, removed the lid, and gazed down through the steam at a cube wrapped in newspaper. With the tongs, he peeled the newspaper away.

An hour later, the rows were crowded with projects. The judges began going from table to table at the opposite end of the field house, which led Enrique to believe he would be near the last. This might be an advantage. And still, Miriam hadn't arrived. He hoped she had decided to drop out.

Lina ate doughnuts and asked question after question but, Enrique noticed, didn't ask about Mr. Hall's gifts. "This is so exciting, baby. What is this newspaper stuff called again?"

"Papier-mâché. Same as a piñata."

"Of course."

"Ma, don't get crumbs in the model." Her presence was making him nervous just when he needed to relax. "Do me a favor," he said. "Go follow the judges and see the other projects. I can't do it myself. Then you can tell me how they are."

"Good idea."

Finally, Miriam arrived, carrying three large planks under her arm. She wore a homemade dress with belled sleeves like those of a choir robe. She dumped the planks on the table, then lifted her arm to brush sawdust from the satiny fabric.

To ignore her would be too weird, so Enrique gave her a quick "Hi."

"Hello," Miriam snapped. She gave herself a final brush-off and began to bustle around her area. The planks turned out to be a hinged wooden triptych, which she opened enough to stand on the table but not so much as to reveal its contents. Enrique filled the metal bowl in his model with water and removed some cobwebby strands the glue gun had left in the trees. Miriam's space looked very empty next to Enrique's; he would have felt sorry for her and might have even said something nice if she hadn't been acting all secretive.

Then there were no more preparations to make. Enrique knew the presentation by heart. He sat down, straightened his clip-on tie, smoothed his greased-down hair, and waited.

After what seemed like ages, the judges rounded the corner at the end of the row, holding clipboards like shields over their hearts. Enrique stood.

There were three judges: the mayor of Chandler, who, during his twenty-eight-year tenure, had judged countless science fairs, fiddling competitions, and rodeo-queen pageants; a female veterinarian from the Chandler Large Animal Hospital, whose muscular forearms made one picture her holding down a sheep to administer a vaccine or twisting the tangled limbs of a colt from the womb; and a chemistry professor from Boise State University, who, perhaps ironically, had worn his lab coat, and who wheezed and sneezed and padded his flushed face with a handkerchief. Between tables, the veterinarian asked the professor if he wanted to step outside to clear his lungs, but he had thanked her and forged ahead. A few minutes later, they arrived at the table where a Mexican boy with shiny cheeks and shiny hair stood before what seemed to be a Swiss village threatened by a salad bowl.

Like the presenters who preceded him, Enrique took no notice of the professor's condition. In a voice that had only a touch of a tremor, he began:

"I'm Enrique Cortez, and my project is entitled 'What If It Happened Here?' On August 21 of this year over seventeen hundred people died in the middle of the night. They were villagers in the mountains of Cameroon, a country in Africa. Not only did humans die, but hundreds of cows and untold numbers of wild animals. If you direct your eyes to Poster A, you will see some newspaper headlines and photos that were published right after this tragic event. Why care what happened in a country on the other side of the world? Well, as long as this mystery goes unsolved, how do we know it won't happen at other locations around the globe, say, at our own Lake Overlook? Many scientists believe that poisonous gases from inside the earth could have seeped into Lake Nyos through fissures—that means cracks—in the lake floor. Since the lake is very deep—seven hundred feet—the heavy layers of water could have kept the gases trapped under the lake like the lid of a bottle keeps the bubbles in soda pop."

From under the table, Enrique pulled a liter-sized bottle of club soda and gave it a vigorous shake. He had decided to add this part of the presentation at six o'clock this morning.

"Something may have happened at Lake Nyos—a rock slide or even just a strong wind—that caused the layers to shift, allowing the gases underneath to escape." Enrique twisted the bottle open, and it hissed and sputtered. "A bottle of pop overflows when you open it because carbon dioxide is being suddenly released. The morning after the tragedy at Lake Nyos, the lake was suddenly red and muddy and its surface level had dropped by six feet. Maybe it was gases from under the lake that came up and killed all those people. This is a theory scientists call 'lake overturn.'"

A scraping noise came from Miriam's area. She was opening the triptych.

"But could lake overturn happen at Lake Overlook? There is no reason to think it couldn't. Lake Overlook is roughly the same depth as Lake Nyos, and about three times the surface area." Enrique, who really had no idea how deep Lake Overlook was, quickly scanned the judges' faces for signs of disbelief. He found none. "The phenomenon of lake overturn is not yet understood, but if the amount of gas trapped under a lake is proportional to the weight of the water keeping it down, we could be in big trouble."

Enrique put down the soda bottle and pulled on the gloves. He uncovered the bucket holding the dry ice and, using tongs, lifted out the steaming block.

"The lake in this model represents Lake Overlook, and the town represents Eula. At Lake Nyos, almost every oxygen-breathing organism in a fifteen-mile radius was killed. Given the size of Lake Overlook and its closeness to Eula . . . well, I'll let the model explain."

Enrique had come up with softened wording after the science club had called the project "creepy."

He put the dry ice into the steel bowl, and the water began to bubble. A rich gray mist poured down the slope, braiding among the houses and trees, then gathering against the Plexiglas wall. The other kids began to leave their projects and gather around.

The mist overflowed the box and cascaded down in tendrils to lick the floor. This was even better than Enrique had imagined.

Now came another part Enrique had added this morning: "If you direct your eyes to Poster C, you'll see a list of poisonous gases that could be to blame. But add to this list one more: the very gas being released by the dry ice in my model, the very gas released from that soda bottle earlier, carbon dioxide. But, you might argue, carbon dioxide isn't poisonous—it's in every breath we breathe. Plants need it to survive. True, but, as you can see, carbon dioxide is heavier than air. If carbon dioxide escaped from Lake Nyos in a great enough volume, it would have blanketed the ground and suffocated all oxygen-breathing organisms. And, since there was no trace left afterward and the plants in the area weren't damaged, this is what we believe happened. This *harmless* gas might have killed over seventeen hundred people in a matter of minutes."

Enrique felt a twinge of guilt, but he *had* to use Gene's discovery. It made the project complete. The same gas released by the dry ice could have killed all those people, and this fact tied everything into one neat, terrifying box. Gene would never find out. He himself had admitted he didn't care about the science fair.

"In conclusion, lake overturn is a serious threat to lakeside communities. We should not rest until scientists have solved its riddles and figured out a way to prevent it from happening again. Until then, how can we be sure that lake overturn cannot happen at Lake Overlook?"

The group that had gathered broke out in applause. No one had applauded the other projects; the judges had simply thanked the students and moved on.

"Enrique," said the veterinarian, "has this *lake overturn* ever happened before?"

"Yes. Two years ago, at another lake in Cameroon, the same thing appears to have taken place. Forty people were killed. But what caused it remains a mystery. We haven't found any other recorded incidents, but, as I said, this phenomenon leaves no trace, so, who knows?"

"You said 'we,' Enrique," said the mayor. "Who is your partner?"

Enrique had a lie prepared: "Gene Anderson, but he's at home with a sore throat."

"What is that stuff?" a little kid asked.

"Dry ice. It's carbon dioxide in solid form. The fumes you see are actually carbon dioxide gas mixed with steam from the water. At Lake Nyos, it would have flowed in exactly the same way, but would have been invisible."

The child stepped away from the model, blindly holding a hand out behind him for his mother's leg.

"Thank you, young man," said the professor. "Very impressive." He gave the other judges a nod heavy with perseverance, and they obediently followed him to the next project.

Lina rushed forward and embraced Enrique. "My little genius," she said. "You did so good."

"Thanks, Ma."

"I think you're going to win, don' you?"

"I hope so."

Her voice became a whisper. "I didn't see anyone could beat you, *mi vida*."

April Martinez and Tommy Hess came through the crowd. They were both dressed in tight black clothes and black stocking caps. If it wasn't for the hand-sewn stuffed-animal bacteria that hung from Tommy and bounced with his every step, they would have looked like a pair of cat burglars.

"Good job, Enrique," said April.

"That was awesome," Tommy added.

"Thanks, you guys," Enrique said.

"What happens now?" Lina asked.

"Hold on, Ma. I want to see this."

Miriam stood in front of her opened triptych which, in big letters in the center, said EULA RESERVOIR: OUR MISUNDERSTOOD LAKE.

"Who here has ever water-skied in Eula Reservoir?" Miriam said loudly. "All right, then, who has ever taken a swim in Eula Reservoir? Really? I sure have. Okay, here's an easy one: Who has ever *seen* Eula Reservoir? No one? Well, you're all liars, because you have. In fact, many of you standing here can see Eula Reservoir from your front lawns. You just call it by its nickname, Lake Overlook.

"In 1880, what we now call Lake Overlook—Eula Reservoir—was merely an empty field in a large cattle ranch owned by Robert Dewey, one of Eula's founders. It was determined that, in order to make the area around Eula suitable for farming, Walker's Creek should be dammed about eight miles before it flowed into the Snake River. Robert Dewey sold the land to the city, and the dam was built. This photo shows the dam under construction. It's really just a fifteen-foot dirt levee. And this photo shows the field that would become Eula Reservoir. You can see that, at its deepest, the reservoir would only be twenty-five feet deep, not even as high as the roof of this field house. Not deep enough for much gas to collect under it."

A couple of observers glanced at Enrique, but most missed the reference to his project. Their gazes had already wandered—to wristwatches, to the tables where the lunch ladies were putting out Styrofoam boxes, even back to Enrique's project. Several of the smaller kids had returned to cautiously put their fingers in the mist that still fell from the diorama. Enrique was enraged and, in spite of himself, intrigued. Where had Miriam found those photos? The landscape looked as old-fashioned as the handlebar mustaches of the men who stood before it with their shovels and picks. Even the sagebrush looked antique, the way it polka-dotted the hillsides.

"The name Lake Overlook seems to have come about in the thirties, when the city put out a road sign directing drivers to a hill, now part of Overlook Park, where they could enjoy a view of the lake and surrounding countryside. People mistakenly thought the sign was directing them to the lake itself, not the lake *overlook*. Hence, Eula Reservoir became Lake Overlook. Silly, isn't it?

"Now that we have a bit of history, let's turn our attention to the uses Eulans have put their reservoir to, and to how it affects the environment."

The eyes of the judges dimmed in boredom, but Enrique couldn't savor the sight. He was too angry. The whole purpose of Miriam's project was to refute his. She obviously didn't even want to win.

Eventually, nearly everyone had wandered off. The mayor had his eye on the food table, the professor covered his mouth with his handkerchief, and the veterinarian occasionally shot curious glances toward Enrique.

"In conclusion, this project is a celebration of the Eula Reservoir. Without it, Eula would have stayed a tiny railroad town and died with the railroads, rather than becoming the vibrant agricultural center it is. Eula couldn't survive without its life-giving reservoir."

The veterinarian picked up a handout from the pile and studied it quietly. It seemed that, after the attention the judges had showered on Enrique's project, they couldn't move on without asking a question.

Enrique broke the silence. "Miriam, how long have you been working on this project?"

"About two weeks," she responded in the same chipper voice with which she had delivered her presentation.

"Interesting," Enrique said. "So you started *after* you saw me present mine to the science club."

"That's right."

"Thank you, that was my only question."

The judges exchanged glances. "Thank you, young lady," said the mayor, and they moved on.

Enrique took off his gloves and folded his arms as Miriam, avoiding his eyes, put away her notes and restacked the handouts. "Where's Cam Pierce?" he asked.

"Where's Abby Hall?" Miriam asked. She adjusted the triptych to stand straighter.

"She had to go to Salt Lake."

"Cam and I decided we needed to spend some time apart."

"Are you trying to tell me you and Cam are, like, *going* together?"

"No, I'm trying to tell you we're *not*."

Enrique allowed Miriam to continue organizing, but her display was too small for the act to be convincing. Again, she restacked the handouts.

"Well, I think it's pretty pathetic that the whole purpose of your project is to prove mine wrong," Enrique said.

"Yeah? Well, that's how science works. If your hypothesis can't pass the test, then tough—you shouldn't win."

"But I *will* win, Miriam. I think it's pretty much in the bag."

"You'll win because you've got dry ice and little houses, and because this is just a stupid junior high science fair where no one cares about what's right."

Enrique saw in Miriam's eyes that Gene had been correct: his project scared her.

"*Right*, Miriam? Is it *right* to base your project on meanness, just to get me back for choosing Gene and not you?"

"At least mine is scientifically sound, unlike yours. If this were a *real* science fair, you'd lose."

"I've got news for you, Miriam—this *is* a real science fair and I'm going to *win* and *you're* going to lose."

Miriam took a big breath. It appeared she was trying to draw everything in—the tears in her eyes and the words on her tongue. She turned and folded closed her triptych. "Last summer," she said, "I thought we could be friends. Like, really good friends. But now I can see you're just a stupid boy like all the rest. You want to play with your little cars and your little houses and smash them all up. Well, go ahead. See if I care." She unzipped her backpack and threw in the pile of handouts.

"What are you doing?" Enrique asked.

"I'm going home."

"You can't go home. It's not over."

"You said it yourself, Enrique—you're going to win. Why should I stick around?"

"Jeez, Miriam, you're such a spoilsport!"

Miriam said nothing but put on her backpack and struggled to balance the folded triptych under one arm.

"Quitter!" Enrique said.

"Don't be immature, Enrique," Miriam said. "You want me to stay and cry when you win? Give me a break." She marched away toward the exit.

Enrique *did* want her to stay. But he didn't want her to cry, he wanted her to apologize. He wanted to win and for everyone to apologize—Gene, his mother, Jay, Pete Randolph—he wanted everyone to take back everything they had ever done to him and say they were sorry.

"Go home, then, little girl," said Enrique, at a loss. "If you can't stand the heat, get out of the kitchen!"

"Screw you, Enrique!" Miriam called over her shoulder.

Enrique noticed that a few adults had been standing and watching and, maybe, deciding whether to intervene. Lina came up and put her arm around him. "You okay, baby?"

"Yeah."

"I can't believe her!"

"Let's not talk about it, Ma."

"Okay."

They went over to the eating area, where a line had formed. $1 LUNCHES PROVIDED BY CHANDLER BAPTIST, a sign on the table read, and two women in aprons exchanged Styrofoam boxes for $1 bills with exaggerated nods and bright thank-yous. Lina and Enrique took their lunches and sat at one of the long tables. They cracked open the boxes like oysters, slowly, as if they would hold pearls. Instead they found Tater Tots, boiled carrots, and a vivid pink disk of ham.

When the judges reached the last table, the boy there seemed tired, hungry, and resigned to the fact that his project would be rushed over. He eyed the lunch line as he spoke, as if worried there would be no box left for him. Then, at last, the judges were finished. A teacher led them into a side office where they could eat and deliberate in private.

"If you don't mind," said the professor, once they were alone, "I'll put my two cents in, then get going."

"Of course," said the veterinarian.

"Looks like your head is about to pop off," chuckled the mayor.

The professor ignored this comment and addressed the veterinarian. "I think we know who the winner is."

"Lake overturn," she said.

"Little fella is darn bright," the mayor said in a pleasantly surprised tone.

"Well, then," the professor said, "there you have it. I'm going to pass on lunch and go find an antihistamine."

He wriggled out of his lab coat as he charged down the center aisle past all the projects, then burst out the front door and breathed fresh air into the whistling, rattling depths of his lungs. Nearby, a group of similarly afflicted parents and children used a communal paper-towel roll to blow their noses and wipe their eyes. And down at the curb Miriam stood, in her strange dress, with her folded display, waiting for her ride.

THAT NIGHT LINA took Enrique to their favorite restaurant, El Charro, to celebrate. She ordered herself a margarita, which came in a huge, frosty goblet encrusted with salt. "My little genius," she said, raising her glass.

She let Enrique have a sip. "Yuck," he said, and made a face, mostly just to see his mother laugh.

In the dimly lit dining room, fake vines and colored lights lined stucco arches, and a dusty stuffed parrot hung above the bar. There were paintings on black velvet of bullfighters, guitar players, and large-breasted women carrying water jugs.

When the waitress, a young woman whom Enrique recognized from church, came to take their order, Lina said, in Spanish, "Enrique won the science fair today."

"*Ma*," said Enrique.

"*Felicitaciones*," the waitress said.

"Show her your ribbon," Lina said.

"I didn't bring it," Enrique said.

"You got a ribbon?" the waitress said.

"Yes."

"The mayor of Chandler presented it to him—and twenty-five dollars, and he gets to go to State!" Lina said.

"So, are you using the money to take your ma out for dinner?" the waitress asked.

"Oh, no," Lina said. "That money goes toward college."

"Are you going to be a mad scientist, Enrique?" the waitress asked.

Enrique refused to look up as he whispered, "No."

"Are you going to be a doctor, then?" she asked.

"I don't know. Maybe."

Enrique heard his mother gasp, and when he looked up, her eyes were full of tears.

"I'll come back in a minute," the waitress said. "Congratulations, Enrique. You're a good kid."

"Don't cry, Mama," said Enrique.

Lina swallowed, lifted her head, and said, "How about those other projects! Bo-ring!"

They compared notes on the different projects that Enrique had beaten. The waitress took their order, and soon they were laughing and eating off each other's plates tamales, carne asada, and cheesy, sauce-soaked enchiladas.

"April Martinez did a good job with her bacteria," Lina said.

"Yeah, I liked that project."

"It's so gross to think about bugs living in your eyelashes." Lina's focus seemed to swim a little around Enrique's face. That margarita had made her tipsy. "*Ay*, but that Miriam! Can you believe her?"

"Forget about Miriam, Ma."

"Oh, Enrique, you know I don' like this word, but that girl is a *bitch*."

"Mama!"

"I can't help it, Enrique. That's what she is."

"She's still my friend."

"No, she's not. That girl is not your friend, *mijo*. Friends don' do that stuff to each other."

"Still . . ." Enrique let his voice trail off. An unexpected tenderness toward Miriam had risen in him after he won, and now he could see that a few of the things she had said were right. Lina was quiet and flushed, and Enrique wondered if she was ashamed of having used a dirty word. Then she asked the question he had been expecting all day: "Enrique, where did you get those little trees and houses?"

Trying to mask the scrutiny with which he watched for her response, he said, "Abby Hall gave them to me."

"Yeah?"

"Yeah. They're her dad's. He gave them to her to give to me."

"Wow. That's pretty nice. Do you have to give them back?"

"No, it's a gift."

Lina nodded and chewed.

"Yeah," said Enrique, "Abby wanted to come today, but she had to go down to Salt Lake City, since her mom is, like, dying."

"What?"

"Oh, I thought you knew, since you clean their house. Mrs. Hall is super-sick. Abby made it sound like she's going to die."

"I didn't know."

"Yeah. Isn't that sad?"

For a moment Lina doubted the truth of what Enrique had said, but then she remembered the last time she had seen Sandra Hall, how worn-down she had looked, how she couldn't take the noise of the vacuum cleaner. And her makeup! Now Lina realized that Sandra's eyebrows had been drawn on. She had no eyebrows. All those trips to Salt Lake City made sense now, a different sense than they had before. What was Hall up to? Lina sat in quiet rumination as Enrique finished his dinner.

"Can we get dessert, Ma?"

"Of course, baby."

"You seem sad."

"I *am* sad."

"I'm sorry. I didn't think it would bother you so much."

"Of course it bothers me! Why wouldn't it bother me?"

"Because, she's sort of your boss. She's not, like, your friend."

"Enrique! What's gotten into you? She's my boss *and* she's my friend. Of *course* I'm going to be sad to know she's sick!"

"Sorry," Enrique said angrily. "Let's go, I don't want dessert."

"Oh, don' you pout now. We're getting dessert."

Lina ordered a flan, and the waitress went to the glass-doored refrigerator behind the bar, lifted a tray from where it rested atop the beer bottles, and cut a large piece. "Here, Enrique," she said, setting it down, "on the house."

"Thanks," muttered Enrique.

"Now, Enrique, stop it!" Lina said once the waitress had left the table. "No more pouting. We're here to celebrate."

"I'm sorry," he said, unable to look up from the quivering brick of custard before him. Now he was quiet, not out of anger, but because if he spoke, he would cry. He had said those things to provoke and observe a response, but when his mother called Mrs. Hall her friend, it had conjured, for him, an image of a lovely woman in a forest of well-wishers' bouquets, her voluminous bob a tasteful shade between blond and gray, her emaciated body neatly pinned down under a satin sheet. There was a pale film over her eyes, and she saw not the beautiful room, the flowers, or Abby, who sat at her bedside, but soft-focus scenes from her life: riding horses back at school, climbing the stairs to the cathedral with her twenty-foot train on her wedding day, lifting a silk handkerchief to her eye at the news that she only had a year to live. Enrique wasn't thick-skinned enough for this type of experiment; his own fantasy overwhelmed him.

After dinner, they drove home. Lina parked, but kept the motor running. "You go on in, Enrique. I'm going to Saturday night Mass."

"I'll go with you," he said.

"I want to go alone tonight, baby."

"Okay."

"To pray for Mrs. Hall."

Enrique nodded.

Lina kissed his forehead. "I'm proud of you, *mi vida*."

Enrique went inside and stood for a while in the empty living room. He had won, but now he didn't quite know what to do with himself, alone at the end of such a day.

Lina drove straight to the Halls'. She glanced at the neighbors' houses to see if anyone was looking, took the garage-door opener from where she kept it hidden in the springs under the car seat, and pressed the button. The garage door jumped as if it had been jolted out of sleep, then slowly opened, panel following panel into the ceiling. A floodlight under the eave automatically turned on, casting a circular shadow of the netless basketball hoop down onto the pavement. Lina drove into the dark garage. She had never been here at night before.

The door to the kitchen opened, and Chuck Hall appeared in silhouette against the yellow light. Only when the garage door was completely closed did Lina get out of the car. Now she could see a surprised smile on Chuck's face. He went to embrace her, but she stopped him. "Do you have anything you want to tell me?" she asked.

"There are many things I want to tell you," he said.

"Don' be cute."

His smile trailed away and his expression became that of a schoolboy who's been told to stop daydreaming and study. "Is it the train accessories?"

"We can start there."

"I don't need them anymore."

"Did you think I wouldn't recognize them? I've dusted them a million times."

"No, Lina, I thought you *would*."

"So," Lina faltered, "you thought I'd be *grateful*? I'm poor, Chuck, but not that poor. I don' need your handouts, and I *sure* don' need you messing with my kids."

"It's not like that," Chuck said.

"Oh, no? Then explain it to me."

"Lina, I can't walk down the street holding your hand. I can't phone you whenever I want, and I can't write you love letters. But I can give you a garage-door opener, and I can give Enrique some old toys that I don't need. I'm sorry if it offended you. That certainly wasn't my intent. My intent was for it to be a kind of love letter."

Lina laughed in spite of herself. "You idiot," she said. "You do everything wrong."

He smiled and reached for her.

"No, Chuck. Can we go inside?"

"Of course."

They went into the kitchen and sat at the same bar where, two months before, when the sun was shining through the skylight, he had given her that glass of wine.

"Chuck," said Lina, "why has Sandra been going to Salt Lake City?"

Again, his faraway look was reined in. "Well, she's having chemotherapy treatments."

"I thought she was going down there to stay with her parents because you two were splitting up."

"I never said that."

"I know, but you let me believe it."

"No," he said, seemingly surprised, "I didn't."

"Then what did you *think* I thought?"

"Honestly, Lina, it never crossed my mind."

"What's wrong with you? Don' you think things through?" As had happened before, the things Lina had planned to say to him were defused before she could lob them. *What, am I some replacement for Sandra?* she had wondered in the car. *Aren't you ashamed of yourself, taking advantage of your wife's illness to fool around?* But now, given the sorrow evident in the lines etched around Chuck's eyes, to say such things would have seemed crass, jarring, as false as a line stolen from a movie.

Then Chuck himself reminded her of yet another accusation she had planned to make, by owning up to it: "Lina, you are my escape. *You* are my *escape*." He said this in a hushed voice, like he was telling her his one secret. "You are my— This is why I don't feel bad about what we've been doing—because you're my *wife* now, Lina. That's how I see it, and I think that's how God sees it as well."

"You're like a little kid, you know? Thinking that you can say things and they'll happen like magic. There are laws we have to live by."

"I suppose you're right, Lina. I mean, I *know* you must be. But what I *feel* is that your husband isn't your husband anymore, and Sandra's not my wife. She hasn't been since you and I started this."

Lina inhaled, then her voice caught and she released a frustrated sigh. "*I* should talk!" she said, and then in answer to Chuck's inquisitive expression: "I was dishonest, too. Jorge and I, we were never married in the church. When I had Jesús, then Enrique, I said on all the forms that Jorge was my husband, and I pretended that made it so. But it didn't make it so. We weren't married in the church, and that's what counts. He said he hated priests. He called them devils. I should have known then that he was crazy." She took a paper napkin from the holder and blotted at a shiny smudge on the counter. "Even my kids don' know."

They sat quiet for a while, then Chuck said, "Lina, if you're not legally married, that's all the more reason we can be together."

"I can't, Chuck. Not with Sandra down there, sick. You know that—that I can't see you now."

"I know it. I do. But then I think, why? What is there, really, to keep us?"

"Everything right."

He nodded in a way that made Lina see that he had expected that answer, she had confirmed something for him, and he was now trying to understand how it was true, to learn its logic and integrate it. Something—Sandra's illness or something before—had obliterated everything for this man and left him like an amnesiac who has to relearn the world. She loved him for it.

Chuck looked at Lina. "Stay with me tonight, Lina. Then I'll leave you alone, until . . . until after."

Lina winced. How could a man who was so kind think in such ruthless terms?

But Lina didn't realize the difference between Sandra's impending death and the only death to which she could compare it, her mother's. Her mother had died of "old age," which meant that she died of many things, few of them named. Lina hadn't wanted them named and hadn't listened when they were, in order to more easily hold out hope to the end that her mother would recover. Chuck, on the other hand, had been to many of his wife's appointments, seen all those X-rays, and knew the shapes of gray masses in his wife's liver, lungs, and, most recently, kidney.

A week ago, the day before her flight, Chuck had helped Sandra from the bedroom down the stairs to her little office off the kitchen, where she had shown him the bills: how to pay them and where to file them. "In May," she had said, "call Sammy to schedule him for mowing. Don't wait until late in the month, or he'll be all booked."

She's telling me this because in May she'll be gone, Chuck had thought. *Why aren't we crying?*

Now Lina and Chuck sat still and mute. It seemed everything had been lain bare between them, and what had been complex was now simple. Lina loved him, and she would stay with him tonight. She felt what she had as a child when she watched her mother unwrap and marvel at the pair of rhinestone earrings that she had swiped from the rack at the drugstore: the awful pleasure of giving something stolen.

Finally she said, "Can I use the phone?"

Chuck nodded and left the room.

"Hello?"

"Enrique, baby, I'm with Nita Rodriguez from church. Her mom's real sick, and I'm going to help her out a little. Is Jay home yet?"

"No."

"Are you okay there by yourself?"

"Uh-huh."

"What are you doing?"

"Watching TV."

"Arright, baby. Don' wait up for me. I'll probably be home real late. I might spend the night if Nita needs the help. Will you be okay?"

"Uh-huh."

"Good night, *cariño*."

"Good night."

Enrique sat for a while thinking about the scientific method, which said that there were ways to test a hypothesis and prove it right or wrong. He went to the kitchen and from the drawer that contained all the pens and pads of paper took a little booklet labeled *St. Paul's Parrish Directory*. He looked up Nita Rodriguez's number and called it.

"Mrs. Rodriguez?"

"Yes."

"Sorry to be calling so late. This is Enrique Cortez."

"Hi, Enrique."

"I was wondering, is my mom there?"

"No."

"Oh, I thought she said she was going to your house, but I must have heard her wrong. Sorry to bother you."

"That's okay. Tell her hello for me when you find her."

"I will. Good night."

Enrique wandered slowly back into the living room. He stood for a long time looking down at his little village, thinking a *real* boy would smash it all to pieces.

CHAPTER 12

It was nearing Thanksgiving, and the fall sugar-beet harvest, which had been piled outside the factory in three hills as tall as houses and as long as football fields, now dwindled to a few scattered beets on the ground, like brown stones the size of softballs. Kids would sneak under the fence and grab an armful while their mothers waited in the car; a sugar beet kept for months and made a good midwinter treat for a horse. Eula gave a sigh of relief this time of year. The smelliest part of sugar processing, when the factory produced a plume of burned-molasses-smelling smoke that made its way into everyone's clothes and hair, was over. Kids in Eula subconsciously linked the smell of clean, cold air with the coming of Christmas. But the end of the smelly season also meant the end of many Eula residents' jobs.

One crisp morning, Liz Padgett arrived at school and opened her locker, hoping in spite of herself to find another tightly folded note atop her wad of gym clothes. Her heart leaped, then dropped. What she had thought was a note was merely a card that had fallen out of one of the books from the school library. But, on closer examination, it proved to be not a due-date card, but one taken from the card catalog, showing an author's name, a Dewey decimal number, and the word *Renaissance*. Puzzled, she slipped the card into her back pocket and went to class.

Liz realized that the thrill she felt when she got notes from her secret admirer was a vain thrill, as there was no one at Eula High she would ever date. There were a few boys, though, she wanted to *want* to date *her*—three, to be exact. Two were handsome jocks, Eddy Nissen and Caleb Stone, and the third was the student-body president, Cordy Phillips. She wouldn't date Eddy because he was a friend of Winston's, and she felt a blanket distaste for all of Winston's friends; Caleb because he was dumb as dirt; and Cordy because Sarah Fagan, his longtime girlfriend and likely future wife, was a friend. There were some juniors and even sophomores who were cute enough, but Liz wouldn't date anyone younger than she, not so soon before graduation and not after having dated Matthew, the Boise State University student. She had gone steady with Matthew for nearly a year. He was smart and cute and only really had one fault: he had insisted on calling his massive stereo system, which included the first CD player Liz had ever seen, "the Tower of Power." Liz had had sex with Matthew, liked it well enough, and figured high school boys could do no better.

All of these were minor, momentary thoughts, however, since the mental space that most seventeen-year-old girls devoted to boys Liz devoted to Abby—the only person in Eula whom she truly loved—and the Big Plan.

Some, if they had observed the gradual development of the Big Plan, would say that Liz had led Abby into it, that she had drawn out Abby's frustration with Eula and cultured it into hate; but this mattered little—less and less as graduation approached—because the end result would be the same: Liz would be far from Eula, and so would Abby, and Abby would be happier. Abby had a beauty the boys in Eula would never recognize, but maybe the boys at Stanford would. Her face was made for sadness. Liz missed her on the weekends when she was down caring for her mother.

So, while her secret admirer's notes flattered Liz, they fell outside the Big Plan and were therefore worthless. This did not stop her, however, from going to the library during lunch and looking up the book whose catalog card had been slipped into her locker. It was a big, heavy book called *The Art of the Italian Renaissance*, and Liz took it to one of the carrels that lined the long, windowless wall behind the bookshelves. She saw the rim of a paper that had been inserted between the pages. She opened the book to this page and removed the note, and, so doing, uncovered a detail from a painting—a woman with small, red, parted lips and great round globes of eyes. The note said:

> You have the most beautiful eyes in the world. They are not green. They are blue with a ring of yellow. What does your driver's license say?
> There's only one Liz Padgett.
> YOU ARE BEAUTIFUL!!!

Liz smiled, slipped the note into her backpack, and took out a fresh sheet. *You have a way with words*, she wrote. *Who are you?* She put the sheet between the pages where she had found the note and returned the book to the shelf.

When she returned the next day, her note was gone and in its place was another card from the card catalog. She took it and went to the section indicated by the number, a section, which contained college catalogs and SAT preparation guides. It did not contain, however, the book listed on the card, *Pierson's Guide*. Liz took some books off the shelf and fanned their pages, but found nothing. She double-checked the card and scanned the neighboring sections for the title in vain. It occurred to her then just how long she had been at this. What if the boy had sent her on a wild-goose chase just so he could watch? She made a quick walk through the aisles, but there was no one else in the library; nobody studied during lunch. Maybe, she then thought, the boy had put the note in the book, and someone else had checked it out.

Liz went to the librarian's desk. "Hello, Miss Trask," she said.

Miss Trask looked up from her book. Her tiny nose hardly seemed up to the task of supporting her large glasses, and together they gave her the appearance of a barn owl. She blinked. "Liz! How nice to see you!"

"I was wondering, has someone checked this book out? It's not on the shelf."

"Where did you get this card?" Miss Trask held it close under her eye and gave a subtle nod to get it into the correct lens of her trifocals.

"From the card catalog."

"Funny," said Miss Trask, taking another card from the countertop to show the difference in size, "it's from another library."

Connie went to the trouble of driving out of town to buy her eggs from Sue Deal both from a sense of loyalty, as Sue was a Dorcas, and compassion, as Sue's husband was one of the sugar-factory workers who got laid off this time every year. A flat of Sue's eggs was fifty cents cheaper than Albertson's anyway, and who cared if sometimes there was a little crust on the shell?

"You wanna come in for some coffee?" Sue asked after Connie had paid for her eggs.

"Oh, Gene's getting home about now," Connie said.

"Gene's a big enough boy now. You just go on and put those eggs in your car, and I'll put on some decaf."

Connie took the two flats out and set them carefully in the backseat. When she returned, Sue had set out some sugar cookies, and the coffee maker was popping and sighing in the next room.

"So, you been takin' Reverend Howard around?" Sue asked.

"Yes."

"How's that been for ya?"

"Such a delight, Sue. Such a blessing. He's a good man, very well spoken—you saw—and very kind."

"And very handsome," Sue whispered, leaning forward.

"Sue, it's not like that."

"I'm not sayin' it *is* like that. All's I'm sayin' is that the man's handsome," Sue chirped, thrusting her elbows back like a sassy bird.

"Sue, if I thought for one minute that you and the other ladies thought I was up to something other than the Lord's work . . . well, I'd be fit to be tied."

"Relax, Connie. No one thinks anything of the kind. But we all got eyes. And we all use 'em, even old married ladies like me."

"Well, I don't."

"Got 'em or use 'em?"

"Honestly, Sue, if you don't stop this talk right now, I'll get up and leave."

"Connie, I'm just playin'." With that Sue got up to get the coffee. Sue's shoulders were petite, but her hips were massive. Her top half rode atop her bottom like a child on a horse.

In the minute she had to herself, Connie listed the churches she had visited with Bill. One was in Arco, a town whose claim to fame was that it was the first in the world to be lit by nuclear power; another was deep in Owyhee County, a neat, humble building surrounded by saplings and situated on a square of green in the blue sagebrush expanse. This desolate site had been chosen because of its location, in-between the two towns it served. Then there was the one in Horseshoe Bend, a picturesque town in the crease between two gentle slopes. Walking at Bill's side toward the church, she had heard the voice of a creek and felt nothing but happiness.

There was a new ease to their conversations during the long drives. Bill told Connie stories from his mission that he didn't tell in the presentation.

A child tricked his mother into being baptized by telling her that afterward she could eat for free in the hospital kitchen. When she found out this wasn't true, she threatened to put a curse on Bill if he didn't reverse the baptism and give her back her soul. After arguing with her for several minutes, Bill, exasperated, said, "Abracadabra," and did a waving motion over her head. The woman left satisfied.

(Bill's laughter allowed Connie to laugh. None of the other Dorcases, perhaps no one else in Idaho, had seen this: how, when Bill laughed, his eyes pinched at the outer edges, making them appear to be looking outward in separate directions—wild, in such a tame face.)

Earlier in his mission, Bill had contracted dysentery, and, delirious, wandered out of the hospital and into a stranger's house, where he fell asleep on the sofa. In the morning, the stranger asked him if he wanted breakfast.

(*Dysentery*, Connie marveled. It was a disease from novels, not from life.)

Privately, Connie used these stories to assemble a landscape of Bill's Africa, where a brown river meandered across a savannah, and colorful birds studded the rushes. A warm breeze made the grass bow and rise in waves, as if it were being stroked by the hands of an invisible giant. She visited Bill's Africa every night before she drifted off to sleep.

Was Connie in love, as Sue had suggested? If she was, she didn't know it, or, at least, would never allow herself to use the word. There was a dramatic change in her feelings, though, even at a physical level, as if she were breathing more deeply, as if she had climbed one of the walls she had built around herself and was now gulping fresh air and taking in the view. She asked herself questions, just as she had after Reverend Raleigh's sermon—different questions but in the same dizzy manner: Where was her husband? Was he still alive? Had he tricked another girl into marrying him?

On the latest church visits, while Bill gave his presentation, Connie busied herself: if there had been a meal before, she would wash dishes; if there were children, she would watch them. She told herself this was to make herself more useful, but really it was because only when she heard a group break out in laughter when they saw the upside-down slide did she feel the fact of Bill's dishonesty painfully lodged in her, like a burr.

Once, a woman picking up her baby from the nursery said, "You and your husband are doing great work, Mrs. Howard." Connie didn't correct her. To do so might have embarrassed the woman.

"Milk, hon?" Sue called from the kitchen.

"A little," said Connie.

Sue returned holding the handles of two mugs in one hand and a box of sugar in the other. Spoons rang the mugs like bells when she set them down.

"All right, change of subject," Sue said. "Did you hear Marlene Bailey got engaged?"

"No. To who?"

"Angie Wilder's boy. He's been livin' in Boise the past few years. Good kid. Quite a bit younger than Marlene, though."

"Well, I hope she won't be leaving us," Connie said. Marlene was the church organist whom Connie revered.

"No, Angie said Jeff's gonna move back to Eula."

"It's Jeff?" Connie remembered this boy, and he *was* young for Marlene. In fact, he had sung in the youth choir—Connie remembered his strong baritone voice. Marlene would have led him in youth choir when he was in high school.

"Yep, Jeff," said Sue. "Connie, are you all right?"

"That makes me so sad, for some reason," Connie said, forgetting herself.

"Because he's so young?" Sue asked.

"No. I don't know why."

With effort, Sue scooted toward Connie. She took the mug from Connie, set it on the table, and held both Connie's hands in her own. "I know why, hon." Connie gave her a dazed look as if Sue really could tell her. "It'd be good for you to find a fella," Sue whispered.

"Oh," said Connie.

Sue nodded.

"Sue, I thought you knew. I'm still married," Connie said, pulling her hand away from Sue to show her her ring. "I never divorced."

Sue, who could cry at the mention of a pet's illness (Connie had witnessed this at the Dorcas Circle), released Connie's hands to grab a tissue. She inhaled to say something, thought better of it, and lifted her glasses to wipe her eyes.

That evening at dinner, Gene surprised Connie by breaking the silence with his loud, high-pitched voice. It made her jump. "Don't be sad, Mom," he said.

"Thank you, Gene," Connie said. "I am a little down. It'll pass."

Gene finished his meal and went to his room to work, Connie assumed, on his charts and drawings, but Connie stayed at the table staring down into the crinkled aluminum shell that had held her potpie. Marlene Bailey was, to her, an inspiration, a model Christian—talented, bright, and exceedingly humble. Sunday mornings she would sway crazily over the organ, her long, frizzy hair falling over her face, unselfconscious, in an ecstasy, playing for the Lord. Music and the church were the whole of her life. Now the church would lose her to this boy. Connie didn't want Marlene to get married, because it would taint her and make her less holy. But Connie checked herself. These thoughts seemed Catholic and, therefore, wrong. Didn't the Bible say, "to avoid fornication, let every man have his own wife, and let every woman have her own husband"? Devout Protestants were encouraged to marry.

It dawned on her: while Marlene was single, Connie could hope that her own abandoned state would make her holier. Now she would just be alone.

Walking into the Eula Public Library, one might wonder for a moment if one had mistakenly entered a daycare. Tattered picture books were crowded into short bookshelves, which were arranged in a ring around a center area filled with bean-bag chairs and child-sized tables. The walls were covered with children's drawings, and there was even a terrarium containing two despondent tortoises. One had to pass through this children's area to find the circulation desk and, beyond it, a small reference section. Books of fiction were shelved on a narrow mezzanine, and everything else was in the low-ceilinged, fluorescent-lit basement.

It was here that Liz found the book that corresponded to the card, *Pierson's Guide to American Universities*. It was thick and paper-bound, like a phone book. She took it to a table and, yes, there was a note between the pages. When she opened the book, though, she started. The pages between which the note had been hidden contained a profile of Stanford University.

The note said:

> You have the thickest eyelashes of anyone I've ever seen.
> YOU ARE BEAUTIFUL!!!
> WHO AM I???
> You've always known me. I've always watched you. Maybe I'm like your eyelashes, too close to see.

Liz had been curled over the catalog, but now she straightened with a chill. Who knew she had been accepted to Stanford? Only her closest friends, all girls. But Winston knew, and he could have told anyone. Feeling a bit miffed and invaded, she tore a strip from the bottom of the note. She wrote, "You could be anyone," fit the strip between the pages like a bookmark, and put the book back on the shelf.

The creepy idea of being "too close to see" and the suspicion that her secret admirer was a friend of Winston's kept Liz from returning to the Eula Public Library right away. Of course, it could have been Eddy Nissen, the cutest and least annoying of Winston's friends. It would be a little thrill to find him out, tease him, promise she wouldn't tell, then spend the rest of the year trading good-natured, flirtatious smiles with him in the hallway. But then again, Eddy had arrived at Eula High sophomore year. He couldn't really say to her, "You've always known me."

So it was curiosity much more than hope that brought Liz back to the Eula Public Library. She again found the college guide, and when she took it from the shelf, something dropped onto the floor. A key had been placed on top of the book. She picked it up by the plastic card that was attached to it by a ring. The number 21 was printed on the card. The key itself wasn't flat like a house key, it had a plastic grip, the type you twist in order to free the key after you've inserted your quarter. This was a key to a rental locker. Where did they have lockers like that, the Greyhound station? Locker 21, she thought. She quickly thumbed through the college guide and, finding no note, returned it to the shelf. Then she examined the key more closely and turned over the little plastic card. There was a logo on the other side: a top hat on a roller skate. A troubling new possibility occurred to Liz: could a junior high kid be sending her on this treasure hunt? This was the logo of the Rollerdrome, a place where high school seniors never went.

IN THE MIDDLE of the night, Adele Burnham had a tiny stroke. A blood clot stopped the blood flow to her brain, and the dream that she was having, dim and indistinguishable from waking life as it was, flickered out. A minute later, the clot dislodged and the blood flowed again. Adele didn't die—her lungs continued to pull air into her body and push it out—*but she did die.* In the morning she woke up, *but she didn't.*

At breakfast, the aide, who sat at the center of the semicircular table feeding Adele and three other clients, noticed Adele was more lethargic than usual. She chewed, but her tongue misbehaved, pushing the food out rather than swallowing it. Finally the aide gave up and wiped Adele's face. Maybe she would wake up a little by lunchtime.

Adele spent the morning dozing in the hall. This was what she always did. But, inside, her life was gone.

Connie had rituals with some of her charges. When Mr. Ellis was in a stupor and couldn't get up, she'd give him a piece of chocolate. Within a few minutes his confusion would lift and he'd go on his shuffling rounds. When Mrs. Horn got cranky, Connie would get her started on gardening. "You know, my marigolds are wilting," Connie would say, even in the dead of winter.

"Are ya soakin' 'em?"

"Not for the past few days."

"Marigolds, you gotta soak!" Mrs. Horn would say, her bad mood forgotten. "Put sugar in the water. That'll perk 'em up."

And, of course, Adele Burnham liked to be placed in the sunlight.

But when Connie, who still had a residue of sadness on her heart from learning yesterday that Marlene Bailey was engaged, rolled Adele through the craft room and placed her into the great square of light before the sliding glass door, Adele didn't respond. She didn't tilt her head so the sun would strike her eye, and she didn't warble happily. Thinking that, with the chill that radiated from the glass door, Adele might not yet feel the light, Connie gave her a moment. She adjusted the wheelchair so the light hit her eye more directly. Then she knelt and tucked the blanket in more firmly around Adele's tiny, curled feet. "Mrs. Burnham, we're here. You're in the sun," she said. But the woman's eyelids hung low, the light didn't reach her pupils, and the whites of her eyes were a milky blue.

Connie took Adele's long, powder-dry hands. "Lord," she said, "please take her soon."

Connie never would have said this in front of Adele before, not aloud, but after years of work in the nursing home, she knew how a life could be snuffed out in an instant, even if the heart continued to beat away like a soldier who hadn't gotten word that the war had been lost. She thought of that day of the power outage, when she looked up and the world was dark, just like that. Adele was gone.

Connie went to the nurses' station and called the church office. Sissy, the church secretary, answered.

"Well, hello there, Connie. How *are* ya?"

"Fine, Sissy. How are the boys?"

"Well, Reverend Keane is out sick today, but Reverend McNally is in eatin' his lunch."

Connie had meant Sissy's sons. She would never have referred to the pastors, both grown, married men, as "the boys," but she let it go. "I was hoping to make an appointment to see Reverend McNally," she said. "Should I call back after lunch?"

"Oh, he don't mind. Hold on half a sec."

The church did not have a fancy phone system where calls could be patched through; Sissy just walked back and forth to the pastors' offices. Reverend McNally sat turned away from his desk, staring out the diamond-paned window. An open book and a bag of Cheetos lay on the desk. "Ed?" Sissy half-whispered.

He turned a smile on her.

"Connie Anderson's on the phone. She'd like to make an appointment."

"Have her come in this afternoon."

Ed McNally enjoyed meeting with Connie. She was one of the few members of the congregation who made appointments rather than simply dropping by the church offices. It was Ed's job as junior minister to answer the ethical and theological questions of the congregation, but, aside from children, Connie was the only one who ever asked such questions.

"Thank you for seeing me so quickly, reverend," said Connie when she arrived. In her ugly, flat-fronted dress and white loafers Connie looked, as always, like a puritan nurse. Her bun had loosened over the course of the day, though, and Ed could see the luster of her dark hair, which he couldn't on Sunday mornings when it was as hard and glossy as polished wood. "Please sit, Connie. It's nice to see you."

Connie sat and stared at her hands, which she sandwiched between her knees as if to warm them. Ed allowed her some time to gather her thoughts.

"Is it wrong, reverend, to believe the words of Jesus over other parts of the Bible?"

After a moment's thought, Ed answered, "We are to consider

the Bible, the whole Bible, the word of God. However, as you know, Christ released us from many of the laws of the Old Testament."

"And gave us some new laws. He made some of the laws stricter."

"Yes," said Ed. This was, he guessed, about divorce. He clearly remembered Connie's speech to the board of deacons regarding the formation of the divorcées', support group. He had found it almost comical to watch the group confronted by the harsh realities of the scriptures. Of course, it was against God's law to divorce, and of course, in this day and age, the church allowed it, as every modern Protestant church did. The only other option was to become a conservative relic of the past with few members.

Connie said, "A woman I take care of at the nursing home became unresponsive today. Maybe it'll pass, but I don't think so. I've seen it before. Her eyes were open, but she's no longer conscious." Her voice changed for a moment: "She couldn't have gone to heaven already, even though her body is still here?"

"Not yet, Connie."

Her eyes fell again and she returned to her previous line. "When I was sitting with her this afternoon, I thought, *This will be me, if I'm lucky. I'll be lucky to have someone notice when I go.* I'm being self-pitying, I know."

"You have your son."

"I don't think he'll be able to care for me, reverend. He doesn't . . . support me in many ways."

They were quiet for what seemed a long time. Ed wondered if Connie was waiting for a reaction from him, but by the way her eyes searched the floor, she seemed to be formulating a question.

"Moses allowed for divorce," she said at last. "Men could give their wives a certificate of divorcement and leave them. But Jesus said that divorce was not allowed."

"Moses," said Ed, "had incorrectly interpreted God's law in order to appease the Israelites."

"Jesus said that to divorce was forbidden, and to marry a divorced person was to commit adultery."

"That's right," Ed said cautiously. It was an interesting theoretical discussion when it led to the point he had assumed Connie would make—that the church was wrong to bless second marriages—but by the look of extreme pain on Connie's face, Ed knew that she was not merely looking to put down the other women in the church, she was talking about her own situation.

"He was correcting a mistake in the Bible," said Connie.

"Well," said Ed, tipping his head from side to side in a gesture of balance, "I wouldn't use the term *mistake*. But he was clarifying an interpretation, and giving his followers the true meaning of God's law in Genesis: 'What God hath joined together, let no man put asunder.' "

"To remarry is to live in sin," said Connie with finality.

"Connie, Christ himself said that adultery dissolves the marriage bond. And in First Corinthians an allowance is made for those who are abandoned."

Connie shook her head in a way that made clear that she had already considered this. "Only if you are abandoned by an unbeliever."

Ed gently asked, "Was your husband a Christian man?"

"He had been saved, but he wasn't . . . devout."

"You're free to marry again, Connie."

"No, I'm not. Not if he's still alive and single and living a Christian life."

"Do you believe that he is?"

"I don't know. I have no idea."

"You're free to marry again," Ed repeated.

Connie smiled ruefully. "Aren't you just trying to make it easier for me, reverend, the way Moses did?"

Ed smiled also, a smile of submission. He didn't have an answer. Connie was one tough customer.

Connie said, "The goal of my life, reverend, is joy. I want to claim the joy that God has for me in this life. I've lived most of my life without it. It's right to want joy, isn't it? I used to think my sadness would get me into heaven, but that was wrong. So I've asked and asked for joy, and the answer God has given me is that to claim it, I must live by His laws. Following the laws in the Bible is the way both to eternal life and to joy in this world, right? But following those laws seems at odds with happiness. Tell me I'm wrong, reverend!"

Ed shook his head.

"Well, it's simple, then. It's so simple," Connie said in resignation.

Ed leaned forward on the desk. "Connie, can I tell you something I absolutely *know*? I know that God wants you to be happy, and happiness is achieved by following His law *and* by taking our own steps. The two are not mutually exclusive, Connie, especially in your case. You have been abandoned, and you have no idea if your husband has remarried, or if he's still a Christian, or, for that matter, if he ever was. You are allowed to remarry by the *spirit* of what Paul wrote in Corinthians, if not the word."

"Don't Paul's writings seem less . . . authentic . . . to you than Christ's words?"

"Not in the least," said Ed. "God was speaking through Paul."

"The way He spoke through Moses?"

"Connie." Ed laughed incredulously. "Do you realize, in your rigidity, you're approaching blasphemy?"

Both words seemed to hit Connie harder than Ed had meant them to. "*Rigidity*," she said. "*Rigidity*, in interpreting God's word, can't be wrong. We're encouraged again and again all through the Bible to be rigid. I'm rigid because I want that joy."

There was a long silence. "Connie," said Ed finally, "you are an inspiration to me, do you know that? There are times when I hold my actions up to yours, because you are an example of Christian living."

Connie blushed and, again, wedged her hands between her knees.

"Read First Corinthians again, and ask God to show you how to understand it. He wants you to be free, Connie, and so do I."

Connie's mood recovered a bit over the next few days. Having spoken that way to Reverend McNally made her feel insulated from the world around her. When she drove, the steering wheel seemed far away; at work, the voices of the aides gossiping at the nurses' station were muffled; even the sight of Adele sitting in her chair doing nothing gripped her more weakly than it had that first day. At least she wasn't in pain, Adele.

On Saturday afternoon, Connie knocked on Gene's bedroom door. "Come in," he said.

Gene sat at his desk with his calculator, making a chart. "I was thinking, Gene, I can't afford to buy you magazines this week." He stopped writing but didn't put down his pencil or look up. "Instead, we could go to the library, the big one in Boise, and you can look at magazines there. Would you like that?"

"Yes," he said.

"Should we go?"

"Yes."

So they went to the Boise Public Library. While Gene set up camp in the periodicals section, Connie went to the reference section where they kept the phone books from around the country. Eugene, her husband, had originally come from Kansas City, Missouri. Connie wrote down the phone numbers of all twenty-seven Andersons in Kansas City. Eugene's brother, the only of his relatives who had come to the wedding, had lived in California. What was it, Bakersfield or Fresno? She wrote down the phone numbers of all Andersons in both.

That night, Gene and Connie sat down to their separate projects. For the first time Connie wished that she had a touch-tone phone. Everyone was getting them. Somehow, to dial each number and wait as the disc made its rattling return seemed more than she could bear. Should she go to K-mart and buy a touch-tone phone? Now she was being silly.

She dialed the first number. A woman answered, "Hullo?"

Connie's throat was suddenly dry. She coughed. "Is this the Anderson residence?"

The woman said yes the way Eugene had: "Yayes."

"I'm looking for Eugene Anderson. Is this his residence?"

"No."

"I'm sorry to bother you, but do you happen to know a Eugene Anderson?"

"Sawry. No."

"Have a good evening," Connie said. She hung up and dialed the next number.

One by one, the Andersons of Kansas City answered their

phones and told Connie that, no, there was no Eugene there, and, no, they didn't know any Eugene Anderson. They all had Eugene's twang. Thirteen years ago it had seemed exotic, big-city, but now it sounded hickish and—Connie thought the word before she could stop herself—stupid. Why had she feared calling these people?

It took less time than she had expected, so she had Gene put himself to bed, and she called the Bakersfield and Fresno Andersons, as they were in an earlier time zone. One of them knew a Eugene, and Connie's heart raced in a moment of fear—not hope, fear—but this Eugene was the man's eighty-year-old uncle who lived in San Diego.

Connie sat at the table long after she had finished her calls and Gene had gone to sleep, wondering if she had really wanted to find him.

With no schoolwork to do this Tuesday night, since Thanksgiving break started the next day, Liz finally had time to go to the Rollerdrome. A sign taped to the Plexiglas window said, ENTRANCE: $2.50. NO EXCEPTIONS. Would she really have to pay for what might be a fruitless visit that lasted only a minute? She bent to speak into the vent, which was situated low to be within reach of little children. "I'm picking up my little brother. Do I have to pay?"

The woman waved her cigarette and said, "Pull hard." With her other hand she unbolted the door.

Liz entered, then stood for a moment to let her eyes adjust. Fragments of light cast by the disco ball raced along one wall, then jumped the gap to race along the next. The floor was blackened at each entrance to the rink, and the walls, where they met the floor, were riddled with colored marks left by the rubber stoppers of roller-skates. There were only a few kids skating in the rink. Their shouts echoed, and their skates hissed. Liz wondered why the place seemed so forlorn, then realized there was no music.

A boy whizzed by her and disappeared into the deejay booth. A moment later, a song began. The boy emerged and whizzed back behind the snack bar. His face was marred with zits and freckles as if to match the walls. A bank of lockers, Liz noticed, stood near the snack bar. She went to it and found locker 21 in the top row. She took from her pocket the key that she had been carrying for the last two days, inserted it into the lock, and twisted. Machinery shifted, locking the key into place. She opened the door, peered in, and saw something near the back. She reached in and took out a plastic Ziploc bag, half-full of water. She looked at it for a moment, then opened it an inch and sniffed. Just water. She tossed it into a nearby trash can. Then she rose to her tiptoes and again looked into the locker. There was a wet sheet of paper stuck to the bottom. She carefully peeled it up and read the blurred, typewritten message:

YOU'RE THE ONLY ONE I LIKE.

Was that it? Were these clues or some sort of booby trap? Was the water meant to pour out on her head? Maybe it *was* some junior high brat.

"Hey!" yelled the boy behind the snack bar.

Liz crumpled the note and turned toward him.

"You want a Red Hot?" he asked. He rested an elbow on the lid of a giant jar in which pickles swam in a cloudy liquid, and held toward Liz a bright red ball in a plastic wrapper.

Liz smiled and shook her head.

"For free?"

"No, thanks," Liz said. She dropped the wet wad into the trash and left.

Jay, who had watched the whole thing from the game room, huddled into the black booth of the Frogger game until Liz was gone. To allow her time to leave the parking lot, he finished his game. This took quite a while; he had gotten quite good at Frogger over the past two nights. Then he strolled over to the lockers. He took a few deep breaths, as if her scent would still hang here, or anything of her—the dust of her skin in the air or a wet finger-smudge on the key.

Step Four:
Experimentation

CHAPTER 13

At the end of Thanksgiving dinner, when the Nelsons, Chuck's big, hearty in-laws, began to clear the table, Sandra, who had been quiet during dinner, put her hand on his wrist to stop him from rising to help. "Take me for a walk, Chuck," she said.

"Should I?" Chuck asked. The reason they had spent Thanksgiving crammed into Sandra's parents' little shoebox house in one of the older neighborhoods of Salt Lake City instead of having it at her brother's ranch in Ogden was because of Sandra's condition. Sandra was too weak to be jostled into cars and up stairs, and, moreover, she was to use her oxygen as much as possible to ease the burden of her low lung capacity on her heart, the doctor had explained. The tank stood like a green sentry in the corner of the living room; its twenty-foot tube reached the kitchen and the bedroom Sandra's parents had given over to her, having themselves moved upstairs to Sandra's old room.

"Yes," Sandra said. "The doctors say it's good for me to walk, when I have the capacity." The day before, they had drained the fluid from her lungs with a needle. They did this once a week; Sandra had told Chuck that she looked forward to it, because she breathed easier after. "Abby?" said Sandra, unhooking the tubes from her ears. "Could you—?"

Abby appeared over her shoulder and took the tube to the living room, coiling it as she went, then returned with Sandra's coat. Abby, it seemed, knew the details of her mother's treatments, the dosages and the drug names, better than Sandra herself. She kept track of her mother's appointments from Eula and called reminders in to her grandparents. Chuck helped Sandra up, and all those big, nice Nelsons turned and assaulted them with questions: "Where are you going?" "Do ya need a hand?" "Are you sure you should go out, Gully?" They had called her Gully since childhood, because Sandra, who had never had the square face of a Nelson, looked like a seagull.

"I'm fine, I'm fine," Sandra said, and the children, who had seemed to forget about her during dinner, parted with frightened expressions.

Sandra held Chuck's arm as they walked. There had been no snow yet, but the grass was silver at the tip, as the overnight frosts no longer melted in the sun. They passed little houses with two-dimensional windmills, milkmaids, and welcome signs standing in their yellowed gardens. Almost all the mailboxes had something childish painted on them, ladybugs or flowers with faces.

Sandra hadn't let the illness take any of her stature; she was still as tall as Chuck. All the Nelson women had wide shoulders, but Sandra held hers high while her sisters allowed them to fall into the general thickness of their bodies. Sandra had been stout too, but now her body hung from her shoulders like a curtain from a rod. Slowly Chuck led her down the shadowy block and around the corner into the light of the setting sun.

"Pretty," Chuck said.

"Mm," Sandra replied. "Can we sit?" She indicated a wrought-iron bench on someone's lawn.

"Is it all right?" Chuck asked.

"The Jacobsons. They brought over a casserole."

The frosty grass crunched with every step as they crossed the lawn, but gave underneath like a cushion. *No one's sat on this bench for years*, Chuck mused as he eased Sandra down, *not even the Jacobsons.*

"Chuck," Sandra said presently, "I have a favor to ask."

"Yes?"

"It might be difficult for you. I want you . . . *not* to continue coming down here, after a certain point." She let this hang for a minute, perhaps to let Chuck accept it before she explained it. "I don't think I can bear to have you see me, how I might come to be, near the end. I've thought this through, and it has nothing to do with malice or hard feelings between us, it just has to do with my own comfort. I'm prepared for the pain, but I need to be comfortable. Do you see the difference?"

"Yes," Chuck said. "You might need me, though."

"I'm sorry. I won't. I'll need Abby. She's proven, without even trying, to be the one. Mom and Dad are helpless without her."

"It's a lot for her to carry," Chuck said.

Sandra inhaled quickly, then stopped herself—from telling him, he was sure, that she *knew* it was a lot for Abby to carry. Instead, she said, "We don't always have a choice about these things. Abby knows she's the one, and I don't think she'd have it any other way. She's strong. I only hope it doesn't make her bitter."

The way I made you bitter, Chuck thought. *I didn't mean to.*

They sat for a while, gazing at the jagged peaks visible through the black, leafless branches of the willows that crowded the house across the street, touching it here and there at the corners and under the eaves, as if to keep it standing. The snowy mountains were made rosy by the sun that, in setting, no longer struck this low-lying neighborhood.

"We were never everything to each other," Chuck said. This was something he had only realized as Lina had, more and more, showed herself to be someone who could be everything to him.

"No," Sandra said.

"Would you . . . like to talk about why we weren't?"

Sandra shook her head and looked down at her hands, folded in her lap.

"Sometimes," Chuck said, "I look back, and I can't remember what I was thinking. Like I was in a fog all those years, and it took the fog getting really, really thick for me to come out of it. In the meantime, I didn't give you what you needed."

"You did, though," Sandra said. "You gave me Abby."

They watched the line of darkness climb the mountains, until only the tips were lit.

"When is it, that you want me to stop coming?"

"When it's too late for me to tell you so. That's why I thought we should talk now."

"That's pretty hard."

"It's all hard, Chuck."

"I'll look like a bastard."

"I'll explain to Mom and Dad, and to Abby, sometime between now and then."

The most inappropriate thoughts occurred to Chuck all the time. Jokes popped to mind in the middle of meetings at City Hall, and he'd have to suppress a laugh. He had read that this was the way the minds of people with Tourette's syndrome worked, and sometimes Chuck wondered if it was a side effect of the antidepressant. All through this conversation, Lina had been springing to mind, as if to mention her would make Sandra happy. He thought of how Lina, who was clearly ashamed of her widely spaced teeth, would keep them covered with a tight-lipped smile, until it grew too big and her lips parted. Then she'd cover her mouth with her hand. Chuck had taken to holding her hands down when she did this, which made her laugh and whip her head from side to side. Nothing made Chuck happier than this toothy, uncivilized smile, but to call it to mind now was absurd.

Now that Chuck had found his happiness, he wondered where Sandra had kept hers all those years, or if she had never had it, and that made it easier for her now to die. Or, by the same token, if she had had that happiness all along, would it have inoculated her against this illness?

"We'll see how this next round goes," Sandra said. "Maybe I'll have another . . ." (In her pause, Chuck feared that she would say "reprieve.") ". . . good spell."

"Let's hope," Chuck said.

"Hope and pray."

"You're shivering, Sandra. We should go back."

It was Chuck's turn, that night, to sleep in the living room. Weeks before, Sandra had tripped on the way to the bathroom and bruised her elbow. Abby had made her promise to let someone help her out of bed from then on. So Sandra slept with the door ajar and the others took turns sleeping on the couch. She took more pain medication at bedtime, which made her forget whose turn it was, so, in the middle of the night, she didn't call Chuck's name, only, "Hello? Hello?"

Chuck started, then leaped off the couch. "Sandra, I'm here. Are you all right?"

"Oh, Chuck, I'm okay. I just need to use the bathroom."

Chuck turned on the bathroom light, then took Sandra's arm and led her in. He went back and sat on her bed and waited. He heard a flush, then Sandra opened the door. She held a small bottle in her hand. "Could you help me with my morphine?"

Chuck took the bottle from her, unscrewed it, and fed her a dropperful of the red liquid. "What hurts?" he asked.

"My back and my leg."

Chuck took her hand and eased her back into bed. She didn't immediately let go of his hand, so he sat down beside her.

"Sometimes, when I wake up in the dark," she said, "I think it's already happened."

The thought horrified Chuck and made him feel small and quiet. He decided to let it pass without comment, and Sandra seemed to fall asleep. Rather than waking her by removing his hand from hers, Chuck lay down beside her.

"I think about Yellowstone sometimes," Sandra said dreamily.

Chuck gave a little laugh of assent, then said, "We should have kept going."

"One thing Elder Robinson said . . . in our meeting . . . after the diagnosis . . ." It was harder for Sandra to speak lying down. Her sentences were punctuated by deep breaths. "Don't regret."

"He was right," Chuck said. "What I meant is, I'm glad that we went to Yellowstone those times."

Sandra was quiet for so long that Chuck, again, thought she had drifted off, but then she said, "You're lonely, Chuck."

"I'm all right."

"Still, I wouldn't fault you . . ." She didn't finish.

Grateful, both for her saying it and for her not finishing, Chuck fell asleep like that, holding her hand.

. . . .

BACK IN EULA, winter was announced, not by a blanket of white snow but by an old man who lived on the boulevard, rising after his Thanksgiving dinner, walking outside, flipping open the rusted metal cover that guarded the outlet under the front porch, and plugging in the cord that dangled nearby. The multicolored lights that he had left up all year turned on, then off . . . on, then off . . . all in unison. He had used a staple gun to put them up, and feared that, given the chewed-up state of the boards, if he pulled the lights down, the gutter would come with them.

By the next morning, Santa's Village had sprung up at the crossroads of the mall, with its glitter frost and quilt-batting snow, and the great stable that would contain a larger-than-life Mary mechanically rocking the baby Jesus was under construction on the lawn of First Church. Soon the stores downtown had colorful scenes of candy canes, holly leaves, and red bows painted in their front windows by artists from Boise who had been trained in the art of how to make a painting on the inside of the glass look right from the outside; and soon after that, kids scratched dirty words backward into the paint.

It snowed in Eula about as seldom as it rained. The ground hardened in early December and, by Christmas, Lake Overlook was frozen solid enough for hooky-bobbing, a kind of late-night wintertime waterskiing, using a car with a rope tied to the back bumper leading to a kid on snow skis, or an inner tube, or merely a pair of old boots. The disadvantage of hooky-bobbing was that one had to do it late at night, and, even then, only in half-hour bursts, to avoid being interrupted by the sober strobes of a patrol car catching the shiny tire trails in the otherwise-dusty lake top. The temperature would drop so low on these nights that mothers set the faucets to dripping before bed to keep the pipes from bursting, and fathers, in the morning, went out early in slippers and parkas to warm up the cars and scrape off the ice, which had grown thick in fantastic starburst and snail-shell patterns on the windshields. When the children got into these cars after breakfast, they touched their curls, still wet from the shower, and found them frozen.

December would often end without the arrival of snow. When it finally fell, people would remember why they had been hoping for it all that time: their yellow, broken gardens were buried and the trees were full again, only this time full of jewels. Snow was like a good sermon that made everything simple and clear: there was the snow and the sky, with Eula wedged cozily in-between. It only stayed that way for a day, two days at most. The snow didn't melt, it just got pushed around, changed colors, and became tiresome.

And some years it didn't snow at all.

So, in this snow-poor town, they looked for other signs of winter: the lifting of the sugar factory's odor, a line of colored lights marking a house lost among the dark fields, or the announcement of the first basketball game and wrestling match in crooked capitals on Eula High's sign.

The gap between the end of football season and the beginning of both basketball and wrestling season—a gap that was due to Eula's never making the football playoffs—gave Coop a break. For a couple of weeks he didn't have to take a team to another town, and all his nights were free. He took the glider from the porch to the basement. Then began the season when Coop worked hardest and, with all the overtime, caught up on bills and maybe bought something nice for Maria. In the fall there was only one team each for high school and junior high, football, with one away game per week between them. In winter there was both basketball and wrestling, so nearly every weeknight he was driving some team somewhere. Occasionally a basketball game and a wrestling match were scheduled for the same night, and he had to call in Dwayne Shelby, who had been the bus driver before Coop, and who, now in his seventies, still liked to pick up a few extra bucks from time to time. True, he drove the bus down the middle of the road, but everyone saw him coming. Coop preferred to pass the wrestling team on to Dwayne, as it was the rowdier bunch, and Dwayne, being nearly deaf, was less likely to be distracted by the noise. Coop kept the basketball team for himself. It was made up mostly of tall Mormon boys who sometimes sang hymns on the way to and from games. This too was an annoyance to Coop, one jarringly unnatural to teenage boys compared to the wrestlers' fighting and hollering, but it made for an easy drive; and Coop liked watching basketball better than wrestling anyway.

One night in December, Coop drove the team out to Homedale, and Maria joined him at the top of the bleachers. She carried with her a bag of books and papers, which she proceeded to spread around her. "Translating," she answered to Coop's raised eyebrows. Part of her job as Owyhee County's one and only social worker was to translate forms into Spanish. Coop's attention remained primarily on the game, and Maria's primarily on her work as they traded bits of conversation:

"Might snow this weekend. You gonna come out?"

"Never stopped me before, did it?"

"Maybe come out Friday rather than Saturday, in case we get snowed in."

"Unlikely."

"Still."

"It's a deal, then."

Then, a minute later:

"A dog, if it licks your wound, might heal it. Saw it on TV."

"You don't say."

"Something antibiotic in the slobber."

This was how Coop and Maria talked even at her home, offering subjects like stones picked up from the path. They neither praised the pretty ones nor disdained the duds, as to do either would too much interrupt the walk.

Maria said something in Spanish, which meant she was returning to her work for a minute. She repeated the phrase, sounding it against an imaginary tuning fork to see if it was right. It seemed to be; she hunched over and wrote it down, and the only sound for a while was the shrill music of the game, made of sneakers' squeaks, referee's whistle, and shouts from the audience.

Maria was a block of a woman with a face like a dinner plate. Her black eyes, set in deep creases that rode atop her broad cheeks, were chinks in the plate that admitted light. It was these eyes that alerted the Mexicans with whom she worked that she was part Indian and, therefore, probably a drunken thief. It was her short stature that told the Indians from Duck Valley Reservation that she was part Mexican and, therefore, lazy and apt to tell half-truths. And it was her brown skin that made the white welfare recipients she visited far out in the country look over her shoulder back to her car, wondering, where's the person from the state? To hear Maria tell it, her job was a comedy of errors, like *The Jeffersons*, where every day she walked into a room and was met with a look of surprise. Coop had met her at a school board meeting where a group of migrant workers petitioned that the bus come out to the camps. The board hadn't changed the route, but Coop asked the feisty little translator out for coffee afterward.

"How's Uncle Frank?" she asked now.

"They say he has diabetes. I'm supposed to watch what he eats."

"You can get more aid than you do, you know."

This was enough to turn Coop's face from the game. "If that means I can have a busy lady like you come over and try to get him to stand up and walk around, I'll pass."

Maria didn't put down her pen or rise from her work. "Of course, if Frank lived with two people rather than one, he might do a little better."

Coop smiled. "As I've told you before, dear, I don't think you'd like living with us. He says stuff all day long that'd ruffle your feathers."

" 'Drunken spics need to learn how to drive?' " Maria guessed.

"Pretty much."

Maria nodded.

What Coop didn't mention was how he laughed along, all day, as Frank said these things. The two men had no way of interacting other than smiling and nodding and commenting to the tune of the television set, and in a way Coop liked it.

"Traveling," Coop said, in reference to the game. "Ref didn't ketch it."

"Still," said Maria, "with a little help he might get better."

"Why this sudden interest in Frank?" Coop asked.

Maria didn't answer.

"He shot his own brother and watched him die. You don't go on after that."

"What, then? You die?"

Coop breathed deeply. "You die."

A few minutes later, Coop said, "You know, we've never gone fishing. Why is that?"

"We don't have time to fish," Maria said.

Coop squinted at that one, critically. "I'd like to go fishing with you."

Down on the court, Jay swished a three-pointer. *Yes!* He gave his hands one sharp clap as he turned to run back down the court. When a cheer rose from the small group of Eula parents, Jay imagined Liz leaping up and calling out his name with a happy laugh. When Liz laughed, her face lost its composed beauty. Her delicate nostrils flared almost inside-out, and her overbite showed. But Liz was neither the type to study herself in photos to find this out nor the type who would hesitate to laugh once she did. And, of course, she wasn't there. She never came to games in Eula, let alone this distant town, but Jay imagined her cheer whenever he made a basket.

Jay had replayed the moment innumerable times in the weeks since it had passed: Liz had thrown away the Baggie, then read the note in which Jay had given the final, self-revealing clue, YOU'RE THE ONLY ONE I LIKE. She crumpled it. There was no mistaking her disappointment. She had hoped it was someone else.

When they were ten or eleven, Winston, Jay, and the boys had gone to the Rollerdrome Friday nights, more to play foosball and eat nachos than to roller-skate. There was a deejay, a teenage girl, who, every half-hour or so, would break from the disco and play one for the boys—Styx or Rush or Queen. Then they'd all fly out into the rink until the song was over. Liz didn't usually join them, and Jay didn't remember why she had on that particular Friday. She hadn't brought any friends with her; maybe the Padgetts had had a party to go to, so they dumped her off with the boys. In any case, Jay watched her all night from the game room as she struggled along the railing that encircled the rink, stepping heavily in her oversized skates like a lamb learning to walk. At one point she tripped, dangled from the railing, and fell. Jay darted from the foosball table, cut straight across the rink, and helped her up. "Ow," she said, "I twisted my wrist."

Jay took the wrist in his hand to keep it straight and put his other hand around Liz's shoulder. He guided her slowly out of the rink to a seat near the snack bar. "Are you all right?" he asked.

She held her wrist between her thumb and forefinger and tentatively flapped her hand. "It hurts," she said.

"I'll get you some ice," Jay said.

"Don't," Liz protested, but Jay was already whizzing over to the snack bar. He returned with a bag of ice. He took her wrist again and pressed the ice to it. She might have had a cold, because her voice caught on some phlegm when she whispered, "That helps." They stayed like that for some minutes, unable to look each other in the face. Then she said it: "You're the only one I like."

Jay must have returned to the boys; the rest of the night was lost to memory. But over the years, as he watched Liz develop her hatred of Eula (which she thought she kept so well-hidden), her words, *You're the only one I like*, stayed with him. They had given him the courage to drop that first note through the slot in her locker door.

He had stupidly thought she would come to the Rollerdrome right away after finding the key, but two days passed and the icepack melted in the locker. Even if the bag of water confused her, though, there was no mistaking the words in the note. She knew it was Jay. And she had never meant that he was the only one in her stupid life in this stupid town that she loved; she had meant, simply, that on that night six years ago he was the only one of Winston's friends she could stand.

Jay had learned early that the people south of town would tolerate a Mexican among them, especially if he was tall and athletic, but only to a point, and that point usually had to do with sex. He could live at the Van Bekes' as a son until their daughters came home on vacation from college, then he was sent to Lina's for a few days. He'd had sex with plenty of girls—all of them white—and those from the neighborhood had sworn him to secrecy while the poor girls at school had bragged to their friends and begged to be his girlfriend. The Padgetts could accept him as Winston's best friend, but never as Liz's boyfriend. The line lay between the two. Jay had imagined that Liz, in mapping out her rebellious new mindset, had erased the line. Clearly she hadn't: since the Rollerdrome, she hadn't even met his eye in the hall.

When the game was over, Maria gathered her things, and she

and Coop walked slowly down the bleachers and out under the star-encrusted sky. There was a thick halo around the moon, as if it were being viewed through a frosty window. "Till Friday?" Coop said, placing his hands on Maria's shoulders. Maria shuddered with cold, leaned in, and rested her cheek against his sternum. They were both shaped like barrels, but Maria was a couple of heads shorter than Coop. It was luck, he had told her once, that he had never gotten her pregnant, because any baby they made would roll around like a bowling ball. Maria had laughed at that, but then sadness had come over her, causing Coop to wonder which she regretted: being short and round, or having reached forty without a child. He hadn't asked. But he made sure to never again say anything to Maria that approached an insult, even in good humor. She was too precious to him.

"Maria," he said, "you and I have never had an argument. Do you know that?"

Maria said, "We don't have time to argue." She gave him a peck and left, just as the steaming crowd charged from around the end of the bus with their gym bags and basketballs, laughing and congratulating each other on good plays. They had won.

"Looks like Chicken Coop's got himself a hen," Jay said under his breath as he mounted the steps into the bus. He couldn't help but sneer at anyone happy in love.

Coop chuckled in response. Jay was one of Coop's favorites. He often made those three-point shots and wasn't a goody-goody. "Looks like he does," Coop said, mostly to himself, since Jay was out of earshot.

ONE DAY IN science class, Mr. Peterson said, "Enrique, could you give us some of the differences between deciduous and coniferous trees from last night's reading?"

"Sorry, Mr. Peterson," Enrique said, "I skipped it."

This was a lie. Enrique always did the reading, and, even if he hadn't, he could have answered the question. He had known the difference between deciduous and coniferous trees since he was six years old. But his little test worked: the look on Mr. Peterson's face was less one of anger or disappointment than of wonder. What had happened to his star student to make him so different? Enrique wanted to seem like someone who had been jarred loose from his moorings by a few hard waves—because he had been—and although it would have ruined the experiment to peek down the row at Miriam, he could imagine she wore the same expression of wonderment.

Enrique had never been more alone, estranged as he was from those closest to him. Yet he was no longer sad. His newly imagined role in junior high was the lone wolf, cruising the halls quietly, broodingly. Pete Randolph had steered clear of him since the day over a month ago when Jay punched him. Enrique naturally gave Pete a wide berth as well, but even from a distance perceived, or imagined to perceive, Pete's diminished standing in his circle of friends. The circle itself seemed to be loosening, and its members no longer made fun of Enrique. This could have been out of fear of Jay. It could also have been because Enrique no longer raised his hand gloatingly in class, or stole the big-handled plastic combs from girls' back pockets, then ran down the hall laughing loudly and holding them high out of reach, or toured the lunchroom with Miriam taking silly surveys ("Do you believe in Bigfoot?"), or wore cat-eyed glasses cut from construction paper, then made a pair for anyone who wanted one, setting off a daylong craze. He no longer gave his taunters any material.

But Enrique didn't miss being that happy, frivolous boy. In fact, he looked back on things he had done six months before with a clarity that felt new and masculine. Cat's cradle? He had sat on a bench in the middle of the mall last summer with a loop of string and done cat's cradle with Miriam. (Pinch the Xs and lift them through: tram lines! Hook the pinkies to make diamonds, dip and lift: the manager!) How many people had walked by and seen him? He hadn't deserved the boys' abuse, but he had been asking for it.

After the science fair, it seemed that Enrique's mother had slipped into a depression that mirrored his own changed mood. Enrique imagined that somehow she sensed that he had found her out and was ashamed, but whatever the reason, she rarely visited him at bedtime anymore. In her absence, his sexual fantasies became more powerful and elaborate and lasted deeper into the night. The pro-wrestling matches he could hear Jay watching in the living room became, in his mind, gut-slugging, ear-biting orgies, and Enrique masturbated wildly into a gym sock. He was tired of feeling guilty. Of course, in some future chapter of his life he would come back around to God and family and his story would have a wise and cozy *Cosby Show* ending, but in the meantime he gave himself over to fantasies of bullies ripping the gym shorts off sissies and burly teachers keeping bad boys in detention so long that they wet their pants: grounds for further punishment.

Enrique ate lunch alone or at a table with his more distant friends, saying little. These tended to be Miriam's friends too, and if she joined them, she would sit at the opposite end of the table. Gene's claim that he didn't care about the science fair now seemed true—he had never asked how it went. In fact, the boys hadn't exchanged one word since their fight on the porch. Enrique felt a jab of guilt when he saw Gene eating alone, but, by the looks of it, Gene hardly noticed. The same war was going on among the features of his face; the conversation with himself continued whether or not Enrique was sitting across the table. It was nice, for a while, to be disassociated from the weirdest kid in junior high, and Enrique knew that, when he needed to, he could pick up where they had left off and Gene would neither offer nor seek apologies. He didn't understand their point.

Not long after Thanksgiving break, Enrique invited Abby over to see the model. He was proud of it and wanted to show it off, and, more than that, the event would be a kind of three-pronged experiment: How would Abby react to being in a trailer park? What would Jay say when he saw a peer hanging out with his little brother? And what look would cross Lina's face when she found her lover's daughter in the living room?

But when Abby arrived, her hooded eyes showed neither disgust nor pity. Enrique recited his presentation, interrupting himself to give parenthetical visual descriptions: "The steam from the dry ice flowed down like this, all through the houses. It stayed really low, just like it was supposed to."

Kneeling next to him on the floor, Abby said, "Enrique, that's so cool. No wonder you won."

Now his affection for Abby and for his project overcame his desire to be a detached observer. "Here's the posters," he said, taking them from behind the couch to the kitchen, where he laid them out on the table. "They turned out pretty good. I'm going to color them all in before State." Abby studied the posters and nodded. "I have to change this one," Enrique said. "It turns out Lake Overlook isn't that deep."

"Was Gene excited to win?" Abby asked.

Enrique put the posters back in a pile. "He dropped out before the science fair."

"He dropped out?"

At the sound of a basketball being dribbled up the walk, Enrique positioned himself so he could see the front door. "Yeah," he said absently, "Gene was being kind of a pain. He kept wanting to change directions, like, change the project to be about how lake overturn could happen at all the different lakes all over the world. And when I didn't let him, he dropped out."

Jay threw open the door, then stood there with the ball propped between his hip and arm. He wore his letterman's jacket over his basketball uniform, and his hair was still wet. At the sight of the visitor, his eyebrows leaped and his face opened. "Hey, Abby," he said. "Hey, little brother."

"Hey, Jay," said Abby.

"You're letting in the cold," Enrique said.

Jay went to his room, then emerged carrying a towel, went into the bathroom, and closed the door. A minute later the hiss of the shower started. Jay had never called Enrique "little brother" before; this was one result to be filed away and analyzed later.

"Well," Abby said, "you might want to get Gene back on board. The State Science Fair is pretty big and goes all day long. You need someone to man the ship if you want to walk around or go to the bathroom."

An idea occurred to Enrique. "Do you think . . . Would you want to be my partner?" he asked shyly.

Abby laughed. "First of all, I can't. I'm in high school, so I'm not allowed. Second of all, I'm too busy. And third, this was partly Gene's idea, and he should be your partner. But," she said, pinching his shoulder, "if it weren't for those reasons, I'd have loved to be your partner."

Enrique smiled. Anyone else would have called his offer "sweet," but not Abby. Of all the girls he had ever been friends with, she was his favorite.

When Enrique walked Abby out, Lina pulled up. "Hello, Abby," she said as she climbed out of her car. She seemed relaxed and genuinely happy to see the girl.

"Hi, Mrs. Cortez."

"Thanks so much for helping my Enrique with his project." She ruffled Enrique's hair and pulled him, by the top of his head, toward her.

"It was my pleasure," Abby said. "He just showed it to me. It's the best ever. He could really win State."

Abby and Lina both smiled down at Enrique in a moment of uncomfortable silence. Abby seemed to like his mom. Would she still, if she knew? Enrique hypothesized no. The situation offered Enrique one final and definitive experiment. But did he have the nerve?

"Well," Lina said, "I'm going to get dinner on. Good night."

"Abby," Enrique said when they were alone again, "could you give me a ride to the Circle-K?"

"Sure. Is it all right with your mom?"

"Yeah. I can walk home and be back before dinner's ready."

They got into Abby's car and drove through the bad part of the trailer park, then out past the used-car dealership where strings of plastic pennants hung limply in the cold air.

Jay, toweling off after his shower, wished that he had brought in fresh clothes, for now he was stuck walking back out into the living room in a towel or in his sweat-soaked uniform. He opted for the uniform. How could he show Abby he was more than just a dumb jock? Although he had given up on Liz, it wouldn't hurt to somehow convey something positive to her through Abby. For Jay to pretend interest in Enrique's project at this late hour would be too transparent. Maybe he could ask politely after Abby's parents, or Liz herself.

But when he opened the door to the chilly living room, it was Lina who sat at the table, sorting through mail. Enrique and Abby were gone.

Abby parked at the Circle-K and turned her gentle smile on Enrique. The oddness of having asked her for such a short ride, in effect, trapped Enrique; he didn't want to seem too lazy to walk or too clingy to let her go. So he spat it out: "There's something going on between my mom and your dad."

Abby's smile didn't falter, but her eyes deepened in compassion. Enrique was sure she thought he was crazy, or childishly inventing things.

But what she said was, "I was wondering if you knew yet."

Had he known? He thought he had. He had reached that conclusion. But the force of the fact now hit him in a different way. His experiment bubbled over a little.

"How did you find out?" Abby asked gently.

Enrique shrugged. "I just added up the evidence. How did *you*?"

"I came home early one day and . . . heard them."

Enrique winced. It was too real. "When?" he coughed.

"Couple weeks ago. Before Thanksgiving. It bothers you, doesn't it, Enrique?"

"Of course it does!"

Abby nodded and looked down.

"Doesn't it bother you?" Enrique asked.

Abby grimaced and wrinkled her nose, as if she were admitting to a nasty habit. She shook her head no.

"Really?"

"Yeah, really. Maybe what they're doing is wrong, but it makes my dad happy. And it's really important for my dad to be happy. He needs it more than other people do. Not just because of my mom's illness. It's almost like his life depends on it—on staying happy. It's been that way for a few years. So I guess I give him more leeway—I make more allowances for him than other kids do their parents. It's hard to explain. I'm sure it doesn't make sense to you."

"They're not supposed to." In saying this, Enrique heard how it sounded like something whimpered in the school yard: *No fair! I'll tell!*

Again, Abby gave him a smile that united embarrassment and compassion. "I know," she said. "It probably should bother me. It just doesn't."

"Does your dad know you know?" Enrique asked.

"No. Does your mom know *you* know?"

"No."

Enrique couldn't think of anything else to say, but he didn't want to leave Abby's car. He felt safe here.

After a minute, Abby said, "How about, when you need to talk about this stuff, you call me, and when I need to talk about it, I'll call you. Okay? We'll be partners after all."

Enrique smiled.

CHAPTER 14

Across the table from Connie and Bill, Kaye Horton chattered away as her husband, Cal, turned over lettuce leaves with his fork and piled peas and carrot shreds into a reject pile. Like most farmers, including Connie's father, he appeared to distrust raw vegetables. "Theresa has an allergy to penicillin, I guess, and when she got that shot she puffed up just like a puffer fish." Kaye paused to puff up her cheeks, laughed, then continued: "And that was the least of her worries. Few days later her son got sent home from school for refusin' to stand for the Pledge of Allegiance. They said it was for arguin' with the teacher, but that's what they were arguin' about, so take yer pick. Kyle—that's her boy—said that he couldn't salute a country that allowed the murder of the unborn and he couldn't stand, because it would be to stand on the bodies of all those babies. Well, Theresa sure was mad, but I told her to stand up for him. He's doin' what he believes. I would never refuse to give the Pledge, but I see his point. He's real adamant about it. Says he wants to take up the cause and go on the clinic circuit, soon as he's old enough. What do you think, reverend?"

Her yarn had so quickly come to a point that it appeared to catch Bill off-guard, and he stammered, "Well, I suppose the boy should follow the rules of the school, and find another way to protest."

"Well, you're on Cal's side then," Kaye said with a disappointed air, turning to her salad. "When Cal heard the whole thing he says, 'If that kid don't want to salute our flag, then he can just go to Helsinki.' "

Connie winced with embarrassment, and Cal seemed to awaken. "I said that!" Cal said.

" 'Course you did!" Kaye swatted him. "I said so, if you were listenin'! He gits so mad if someone steals one of his jokes."

Connie offered a sniff of laughter—to refuse to give Kaye anything would have been rude—while Bill drew his lips tight into an apologetic expression, the same one he wore when he entered a room to speak—apologizing, it seemed, for having the gall to believe himself worth listening to. His head ducked, his eyes flicked around, ready, if they should be caught by someone, to trigger a shy smile. Kaye's prattle seemed to Connie such a waste of Bill's time, when he was used to eating dinner with the other missionaries and planning their work. Why had they invited him to this event? And who? Connie suspected Sue Deal.

The Dorcases, their husbands, and a few of their children who were of that special age of having outgrown babysitters and having not yet outgrown their parents were gathered at the home of Pamela Hendrick for the salad course of their annual progressive dinner. The point of the progressive dinner was food, fellowship, and the enjoyment of each other's homes, decorated for the holidays. It was also a chance to thank the church staff for their work. Although Reverend Keane, the head minister, hadn't come, Reverend McNally and his wife had, and Sissy, the church secretary. It had been a surprise to Connie that Bill had been invited.

The group had started at Bess Morgan's for appetizers composed of tiny piles of meat and cheese melted onto crackers. Bess, who always tried to do something striking and unusual with her decorations, had dressed her tree only in red lights and red bows, put red lightbulbs in the plastic candelabra in the window, then refused to turn on the lights in her living room, which resulted in an atmosphere like that of a sleazy bar lit by neon beer signs. But Connie tried not to judge, since she, as the resident of a trailer, could not host a course of the progressive dinner, and instead contributed to the main course that was served at one of the larger houses. Pamela's decorations, on the other hand, were modest and tasteful. Her tree was covered in decorations she had bought over the years at the Mennonite store, where volunteers sold crafts made by the poor people of their missions around the world: angels woven from dried banana leaves and the like.

At every turn this evening, Bill had been gently nudged toward Connie—embarrassing, especially when she caught Reverend McNally looking. Here, for example, Pamela had put out place cards and seated Connie and Bill together, as she had the married couples.

"What language do they speak in the Ivory Coast?" Cal asked Bill.

"French is the official language, although there are dozens of tribal languages."

"Do you speak French?"

"Yes."

"Do you know what French women use as antiperspirant?"

Kaye interrupted: "Don't you dare, Cal!"

Connie looked around for an escape. In the kitchen, a girl was forcing the family's dog, a beautiful greyhound, to dance with her. The poor thing took big, tapping steps with its hind feet and ducked its head in shame. Connie could help Pamela, who had risen to clear dishes, but that would abandon Bill to the Hortons. Then she spotted Maxine Sedgwick attempting to simultaneously tend to her daughter Janice and eat from the salad plate she held in one hand. Maxine only attended meetings of the Dorcas Circle occasionally, when her husband could stay at home with Janice, who was perhaps twenty now but had Down's syndrome. Janice's eyes, under their puffy lids, seemed to overproduce tears, and Maxine wiped them away with a handkerchief she kept tucked into her watchband. On the Sunday morning years ago when the family first appeared at church, Connie had thought that this mother was comforting her daughter, who was weeping through the sermon. Janice proved to be a sweet girl, bright in her way, affectionate, and unaware, as far as Connie could tell, of her condition. Connie always made a point of chatting with her, not only out of kindness but because it was a relief to Connie, who usually measured what she said so carefully, to spend ten minutes discussing whose dog had recently had puppies, or the advantages of laced versus slip-on shoes, or how having a birthday in January didn't necessarily make one older than someone whose birthday was in February.

"Maxine, sit down, please," Connie said. "I'm done with my salad. Here—have you met Bill Howard?"

"No," said Maxine, "but I've seen his presentation. It's a pleasure, reverend."

Now Bill and Maxine could talk—the Hortons had turned to bicker with each other anyway—while Connie watched Janice.

"What a pretty sweater!" Connie said.

"Thanks, Mrs. Anderson," Janice replied, giving Connie a little hug.

Connie allowed her arm to remain around the girl's shoulder. "I think that you're old enough to call me Connie."

"Really?" Janice said, brightening, as if Connie had given her a big, bow-wrapped box.

"Do you want some salad?" Connie asked.

"I ate my mom's radishes."

"Oh? I don't really like radishes."

"No one does," Janice said, "but they're my favorite."

Some minutes later, Pamela called from the head of the table, "Folks? Folks? No rush, of course, but if you don't know how to get to the Russells' house out on Orchard, you might want to join the caravan, which will leave in about five minutes. It's our main course, so you don't want to get lost!"

There was a murmur both of intrigue and approval, and Cal Horton, apparently ready for some real food, hoorayed. Connie, though, felt suddenly uneasy. Bill had ridden with her thus far, but now she had to go home and pick up the ham before proceeding to the Russells'. It was vain, she knew—Bill would never judge her—yet she didn't want him to see her trailer.

"Janice," said Connie, "would you like to ride with me? I have to pick up a ham at my house, and I could use your help."

"Really?" Janice said.

"Sure, just let me ask your mom." Connie went to the table and placed her hand on Maxine's shoulder. Bill stopped mid-sentence and smiled up at Connie. "Maxine, I'll trade you. You can take Bill in your car and continue your conversation, and I'll take Janice in mine."

"All right," said Maxine.

Bill nodded. The whole thing seemed perfectly natural.

"Does it move?" This was Janice's reaction when Connie pulled into her parking spot.

It took her a second to realize what Janice meant. "I suppose it would, if you put wheels on it and dragged it behind a truck. But it hasn't moved since I've lived here, and that's been a very long time."

"My grandpa has a motor home," Janice said.

They entered the trailer, where Gene sat slumped in the easy chair. He didn't move until he saw Connie had someone with her, then he hunched his shoulders, bristling like a cat. Janice, on the other hand, gazed at Gene, blinking shyly, her pink tongue filling her gaping jaw to the lip, the way a powder puff fills a compact. Her stocking cap had been pulled down past her eyebrows, and her puffy ski jacket rode up a little, exposing a strip of her belly, which looked like white marble striated with blue veins. Patches of wetness glistened under her eyes and nose.

"Gene, you know Janice Sedgwick."

"Hi," Janice said in a horn-like toot.

Gene glanced at Janice, then turned a raised shoulder toward her, as if to shield his eyes from the interruption as he continued watching TV. "Gene, say hello," Connie hissed. It was rare for Connie to bring home a guest, but that was certainly no excuse for Gene's rudeness.

"Hello."

Connie went into the tiny kitchen and, using pot holders, removed the roasting pan from the oven.

"What are you watching?" Janice asked.

Gene didn't answer.

Connie put the pan down on the stove with a bang. "Gene, the young lady asked you a question!" she said. In the seconds that followed, Connie watched Janice. She continued to blink at Gene, but took a couple of shuffling steps backward and groped unconsciously with one hand—was it for her mother?

"*Cosmos*," Gene answered. "It's a show about outer space."

Connie searched his face. The fuzz of his sideburns had grown into wisps, which threatened to cross his cheeks and make contact with his mustache. Each feature seemed to struggle to shut out everything except the TV screen—the lips gathered into a purple bunch, the eyebrows drew low, like awnings. Why was he so angry? Of course, it was Gene, and the answer was simple: he was angry that his show had been interrupted, that was all. Then Connie looked to Janice, whose features, grouped together like an island in her chinless expanse of a face, were similar to Gene's except each was a picture of openness—her mouth, her nostrils, and those beady eyes struggling toward comprehension. Connie couldn't help it. She thought the awful thought: *I would trade.*

"Janice," she said, "hold the door open for me, please."

Connie took the roasting pan and left without another word to Gene.

"If you go down Tenth Street," said Janice, "we can see the lights."

"Oh?" Connie said, feigning ignorance. The residents of Tenth Street had, for as long as Connie could remember, tried to outdo each other with their Christmas decorations.

"I'll show you," said Janice.

So they took this detour and Janice pointed out plastic reindeer and trees encrusted with twinkling lights, and Connie gasped and said, "Isn't that pretty!" while the thought haunted her. *I would trade.* She felt less shameful than sad, for Gene and for herself. It was an injustice both of them had suffered, that Gene had been born to her. It was certainly part of God's plan, and she accepted it, but it wasn't fair. This was a heavy, heavy thought, and it helped to know that she would soon walk into a warm room that contained, among others, Bill.

He would be leaving before Christmas, and she would no longer have that next drive to look forward to. She would no longer pull up to the parsonage and wait those wonderful seconds before he emerged, waving, with an awkward smile, as he pulled on his jacket. What would she do then?

The windows of the Russells' house had steamed up by the time Connie and Janice arrived. Choral music thick with sleigh bells played in the background, candlelight warmed every corner, and the smell of gravy was heavy in the air. All eyes were on Mr. Russell, who braced a turkey with a great fork, and gently guided an electric knife through the flesh, letting slices fold down onto a pile. This was the nice thing about the progressive dinner—each course had its own color, mood, and aroma.

Connie went to the kitchen and handed off the roasting pan to Binnie Russell, then went to the dining room and saw that a seat had been saved for her, again, next to Bill. This time she didn't mind. The Dorcases were her friends—she tended to forget that—and they saw the road she had traveled. They saw that it had been unfair, and they were trying to hand her a little happiness. They were clumsy about it, but it was well-intended.

Connie had not yet made it to her seat, though, when Binnie burst from the kitchen carrying the roasting pan, and shouted, "Folks! I hate to interrupt, but I cannot cut into this until you've all seen it. Just *look* what Connie Anderson brought!"

Connie admitted to herself that the ham, which she hadn't bothered to uncover before, was glorious. Dotted lines made of cloves snaked between pineapple-ring-and-maraschino-cherry bull's-eyes, creating a crazy pattern like the sixties wallpaper her mother had hung in the bathroom when Connie was a child. Behind this pattern, the meat glowed a honeyed pink like sweaty, sunburned skin. The scent, which reached her a second later, was heavenly. Connie had overspent. It would be buttered noodles for her and Gene until Friday's paycheck, but the applause the group now gave her justified the expense. Connie laughed and covered her face with one hand as she slipped into her chair.

Sue Deal, at the far end of the table, managed to say to her husband, "Look at her!" before she was choked by a noose of happiness, and tears sprang to her eyes. She had never seen Connie laugh with her mouth open and her short, regular teeth showing like that. She was pretty. "Thank you, Lord," Sue whispered. Connie had been at the top of her prayer list since that day they had had coffee.

The group fell to eating, and Connie, feeling a bit overcome by the attention, sat back and listened to Bill answer the questions of those seated across the table. These questions were the same she had heard asked many times: what religion were the Africans, were they responsive to Bill's mission, and that silly one, were there any dangerous animals there? Connie paid less attention to Bill's answers than to the interplay between him and his listeners. Dale Russell, the man of the house, was so insistent in his affirmations as Bill spoke, "Yep, uh-huh, right, right . . . ," that at one point Bill paused, apparently assuming Dale had something to say. But Dale paused, too, so Bill went on, having learned that that's just how Eulans listened, nudging the speaker along like a border collie herding sheep. Bill wasn't like that. When he listened it was with a steady, wordless gaze that sometimes caused the speaker to seek affirmation: "Do ya see what I mean?" Then Bill would answer in a way that assured the speaker that he had not only been listening, but considering what had been said more closely and intelligently than anyone else present.

Connie remembered that the French exchange student in high school—what was her name?—had listened this way, and it made people think she was stuck-up. It didn't help—the fact that she often wrinkled her nose and said of Eula, "Eet is *so* small!" This, from someone who thought nothing of wearing the same blouse three days in a row. But the manner of Bill's listening made Connie remember something else, something farther back, and she gave a little start when she named it: the picture of Jesus that had hung on the wall in her bedroom.

For a time, when Connie was nine or ten, she had talked to her Jesus portrait at length when no one else was around. It was one of those paintings that had been reproduced a thousand times; in fact, one hung in the Sunday school room the Dorcas Circle used for its meetings. The reproduction that hung on Connie's bedroom wall had been shellacked to a board, which made Jesus's eyes deeper and browner. Connie wasn't praying when she talked to the picture—she prayed on her knees with her eyes shut—rather, she was giving long, rambling, diary-entry monologues: "So then the teacher sent him to the office and everyone was afraid that he was going to get swats, but Mr. Miller just chewed him out and called his mother." Jesus's compassionate eyes gave her courage, and she told him of her frustrations with her parents, fights with friends, and crushes on boys.

Maybe this was what had allowed Connie to tell her rambling stories to Bill on their long drives—he listened like Jesus.

At a point near the end of the meal, Dale Russell rose to help Binnie in the kitchen, another of Bill's listeners went to the bathroom, and the remaining two went to say hello to people down the table. "Well," Bill said, turning to Connie, "it looks like I scared everyone off."

Connie just shook her head and blinked. Then they sat for a while in the comfortable silence that was the reward of their many hours together.

The group caravanned to the Hortons' house for the fellowship portion of the evening. Kaye played piano, they sang a few Christmas carols, and Reverend McNally led them in prayer. Then they all piled back into their cars and drove to the Deals' for dessert. Sue had made a massive Christmas cake: two layers of white cake—one that had been soaked in red Jell-O mix, the other in green—covered in white frosting and stacked. The vivid red and green, framed by white, showed only when Sue sliced and plated the cake, to the oohs and aahs of the group. The cake, when they cut into it with plastic forks, was moist bordering on soggy, and the cherry and lime flavors sweet bordering on cloying; still, everybody begged to know how she had done it.

The evening had gone longer than planned. The late hour and the smothering heat that radiated from the wood stove sent some of the younger children to curl up on couches and fall asleep, while adults moved in small groups to the farther reaches of the house, where it was cooler. Connie, after finishing her cake, strolled out into the yard to look at the stars, which shone brilliantly here, away from the lights of Eula. The chill felt good against her skin, and she hoped, without admitting it to herself, that Bill would follow her. If he did, it would prove something—something she didn't dare name so as not to feel even lonelier when the minutes passed and he didn't come.

She walked down the slope of the lawn and rested her hands on the top board of the fence. The night was moonless and very dark, and the lights that glowed here and there across the expanse of fields, each marking a farmhouse or barn, were distinguishable from the stars only because they were lower, less plentiful, and emitted a poorer, steadier light.

The sound of footsteps on the grass caused Connie's heart to race. But when she turned, it was Reverend McNally, not Bill, who walked down the lawn toward her. His arms were folded across his chest, and from one hand swung Connie's coat.

"I saw you leave, and then when you didn't come back, I figured you'd need this," he said.

"You were right," Connie said.

Ed held open the coat, and Connie put her arms through the sleeves, then turned toward him and folded her arms just like his.

Without admitting it, Connie had been avoiding Ed tonight. She was worried that he would think their last conversation, when she met with him at his office, had been about Bill—that she wanted to know if she was free to marry him if he asked, which hadn't been her intent at all. It had been about her freedom in general. Or at least that was Connie's position in the argument she was constantly having with herself.

"You seem happy tonight, Connie," said Ed.

"Oh . . . the holidays, you know," she said.

"You and Reverend Howard—you seem to be getting along well."

"Reverend Howard is a good man," Connie answered. "I'm very interested in his mission."

"Yes, Pamela was telling me that you've been driving him to meetings. I hadn't known that."

"It's my offering, Ed."

"That's wonderful," he said, but his expression was one of unspeakable sadness.

He's jealous. The thought horrified her and gave her a profane thrill. To mention Ed's wife seemed an escape. "Jenny looks lovely tonight," Connie said. "She has the cutest earrings."

"Snowmen," Ed said miserably.

An awful silence fell over them. "Well, I'm just about frozen to death," said Connie. She walked up the lawn toward the house, and Ed followed at a distance.

UNLIKE JUNIOR HIGH kids, students at Eula High School had to pay for their lunch, and therefore were allowed, the school board had decided a few years before, to eat off-campus if they so chose. Some students paid the three dollars and got the same slop the junior high kids ate an hour earlier for free. The lucky kids with money and cars left school and went to McDonald's on the boulevard, often arriving late to fifth period slurping pop from sweaty, waxed-paper cups. Others, whose parents had demonstrated financial need, got "red-ticket lunches," which meant they paid five dollars every Monday and got five red tickets, which they then traded, one a day, for their lunches. Red tickets were badges of shame, the high school equivalent of food stamps.

On Mondays and Thursdays, there was another option: to go to church for lunch. The Eula Assembly of God, an evangelical church just down the road, offered a free lunch that was usually better than that served in the school cafeteria—free, that is, unless one considered conversation with one of the youth ministers who wandered the room a price.

For Jay, there was yet another option. On days when he didn't have any money (he refused red tickets, though Lina qualified, and never asked for more than the $20 she left on his bureau every Saturday morning) he would skip lunch entirely, go to the gym, and shoot hoops for an hour. By the end of the day he would be dizzy with hunger, but this extra hour of practice improved his game, and, this year more than ever, all he cared about was his game.

It was time to shake off the sadness of having been rejected, though, so one frosty day, when Winston proposed that they go to church for lunch—and do it stoned—Jay accepted. They jogged out to Winston's car, shared half a joint from the ashtray drawer, then made the short walk along the fence of the field that separated the school from the church. Everything was suddenly vivid and crisp—the prostrate weeds and the frozen mud puddles crunching under their feet. The cows had huddled for warmth in the center of the field. When the boys passed, they lifted their heavy heads to watch, steam shooting from their gaping black nostrils rimmed by white scales.

The boys descended the staircase into the church basement, stood in line with all the goody-goodies (all the while stifling laughter and nudging each other), and were served big plates of farm fry—a casserole made from layers of potatoes, bacon, and American cheese. This proved to be fantastically delicious. They huddled at the end of one of the long rows of folding tables and gorged themselves, making approving sounds, until Jay caught Winston's eye and they both burst out laughing, coughing, nearly choking.

"Hey, guys, enjoying the food?" said a young man with puffy orange hair as he slid into the seat next to Jay.

"Yeah," said the boys, suddenly sullen.

"My name's Chris. I'm visiting with Campus Crusaders. My friend Sarah and I go to Boise State." Chris nodded toward a girl who hung over a group at another table. Chris wore a black cardigan sweater over a paisley-print shirt, which was buttoned up all the way to the top, New Wave style. No one in Eula dressed New Wave. "What are your names, guys?"

They mumbled their answers.

"Well, I was wondering if I could sit here with you for a minute and share something that happened to me a few years ago, probably when I was around your age."

Jay sat up and cocked his head. "Eeh, sorry, main, but we no speaka *inglés*."

"Yeah, yeah, yeah," Winston said, nodding and slumping his shoulders as if he could drift off to sleep. "Jus' Spanish."

Winston had been watching Cheech and Chong videos on the Padgetts' new VCR and working up an impression. Cheech and Chong were, for Jay and Winston, a cool alternative to the lame humor served up on network TV—the lighthearted life lessons of *The Cosby Show*, the sisterly high jinks of *The Golden Girls*, the cheeky social commentary of *Family Ties*: shit, all of it. The boys had been doing Cheech and Chong at school, too, as a way of weeding out the squares: if you didn't know whom they were impersonating, you were a square. And for Jay, putting on a Mexican accent somehow made him less Mexican.

"That's pretty funny, guys," said Chris. "Is that, like, Speedy Gonzalez?"

"Speedy Gonzalez?" Winston said, squinting his eyes. "Who's that?"

"Come on, main," said Jay. "He's that *cholo* with the auto body shop out in Homedale."

"Aw, right, Speedy. That dude does a lot of speed, man. Freaks me out."

"Pretty funny, guys. Well, do you mind if I tell you my story?"

"Shore, main," Jay said. "But you might wanna keep an eye on your *puta*. She's sitting with some other guy."

"Yeah," Winston added. "If I were you I'd go over there. She's a fine piece of ass."

"Well," Chris said, rising, "it looks like you guys just came here for a meal and a laugh. I'll leave you to it."

"Bueno," Jay said. *"Hasta mañana."*

"Have fun and stuff," Winston added.

Close to noon that day, Wanda awoke. The first things she saw were the undersides of the tiny, painted shoes of the clowns hanging from the mobile above her bed. She smiled and, without so much as lifting her head from the pillow, reached for the thermometer.

Even though Wanda hadn't yet signed a contract with Melissa and Randy (it was being prepared for her next visit), Helen had told her to go ahead and start an ovulation-predictor chart. It was *imperative*, she had said, that Wanda remember to take her temperature before rising every morning; even getting up out of bed could elevate it enough to invalidate that day's entry on the chart. But Wanda could never remember. She'd roll out of bed and be halfway through a good long pee before she'd stiffen and curse. So, on a Saturday afternoon trip to Empire Mall in Boise with Coop and Maria, she spent $20 on this mobile to hang over her bed. It was handmade and imported from Germany: a red-striped circus canopy with tasseled trim from which cords of different lengths led to wooden clowns with block bodies and stick limbs jointed with tiny metal rings at the hip, shoulder, knee, and elbow. If you pulled down a wooden ball that hung at the canopy's center, the mobile began to rotate and the clowns danced, arms and legs swinging, hands and feet jiggling, joints working backward and forward. Each clown had been painted with a different costume. Now when Wanda woke and saw those tiny shoe-soles, she remembered to take her temperature.

The mobile would be her gift to the baby. It was nice enough to hang in the Weston-Sloanes' house.

Now she sat up in bed, picked up the clipboard that held the chart, and wrote in the box: 98.9. The phone rang, and she went to the kitchen to answer it.

"Wanda? Helen."

"Hi, Helen."

"Tell me, Wanda, what is your last name?"

Wanda's heart plunged. She became very still, as if that would allow the moment to pass without sticking, without becoming real.

"Answer me, Wanda."

"Cooper."

"Yes, Cooper, not *Coper.*"

"Did I write Coper?"

"Wanda, it doesn't matter what you wrote. All I had to say was your first name, and the woman at the Chandler Police Department gave me an earful."

Wanda swallowed, then said, "I have to go."

"Did you think I wouldn't be *thorough*, Wanda? Sure, it took a while, it took a few calls, but did you honestly think you could *trick* me? It's my job to protect my clients from people like you, and I'm good at my job."

Wanda hung up. She had to get to Melissa before Helen did. She scrambled through a pile of papers for the number, then dialed it quickly.

"Melissa," she said, once the secretary had patched her through, "listen to me. There's something I have to tell you."

"Wanda? Hold on, I'm getting another call."

"Don't answer it!" Wanda shrieked.

There was a stunned pause on Melissa's end.

"Please, give me a minute to explain before you talk to Helen. There's some things I didn't tell you."

Melissa's voice dropped in pitch. "What things?"

"I've gotten in trouble, but it's all over. You've got to believe me. It's all ancient history."

"What kind of trouble, Wanda?"

Wanda took a deep breath. "Drugs. I was arrested for drug possession. Twice."

"What drugs?"

"Pot once, then speed."

"Wanda, I don't—"

"Wait, there's more. I drove a car when Hank and his friend stole some things out of this guy's garage. But I didn't know they were going to do it; I thought they knew the guy. And it was Hank that got me into speed. God, I wish I never met him! But that's it! That's the truth! There's nothing more! I swear, all of that's over. It's like I'm a different person now."

Melissa said nothing.

"No," said Wanda, bowing her head, then pushing back her hair. "That isn't everything. I *did* know what Hank was up to. I did."

The words of Melissa's response were clipped and businesslike: "I don't believe anything you say, Wanda." She hung up.

WHEN FRED CAMPBELL, the principal, got the call from the Eula Assembly of God, he didn't recognize by description the boys who had caused a disturbance—a tall Mexican boy and a shorter white boy, both athletic-looking, both "big boys," juniors or seniors—so he went to the school secretary, Francine, who, having worked in the office for nearly twenty years, had an encyclopedic knowledge of the student body.

"Sounds like Winston Padgett and Jay Cortez," Francine said.

"Who are they?" Fred asked, folding his arms and perching at the edge of Francine's desk.

"Winston's a wrestler, Liz Padgett's twin brother; dad owns a trucking business. And Jay's a basketball player. He used to live with Carl and Janet Van Beke, but this year he's gone to live with his mom on the north side."

Fred nodded. "Call them in, one at a time," he said, returning to his office. "And pull their files. Thank you, Francine."

So, in sixth-period English, just when Jay's high was beginning to settle into a comfortable sleepiness, a loud crackle came from the loudspeaker on the wall, followed by Francine's slowly and clearly annunciated words: "'Scuse me, Mr. Barton, Jay Cortez to the office, please."

The class gave a knowing, approving laugh, and Jay, allowing an increased swing in his movements to express something between exhaustion and insolence, got up and gathered his things. "Godspeed, sire," Mr. Barton said, bowing low as Jay passed, which caused the class's laughter, not to be hijacked by a teacher's joke, to die.

When Francine led Jay into Mr. Campbell's office, the principal's feet were propped on the radiator, and his fingers, spread thoughtfully, rested together on their tips. By the hot hiss of the radiator, Jay knew that Mr. Campbell couldn't have had his feet there as long as his pensive air suggested. Without turning from the window, Mr. Campbell waved Jay into a chair, then put his fingertips back together and returned to his reverie. Jay sat quietly for what seemed minutes. There were pens neatly lined up on Mr. Campbell's desk. Back when Jay took driver's ed., Mr. Campbell had been one of the instructors who took kids out on practice drives. Jay had been assigned to a different instructor, but he remembered Campbell as peevish and jittery; his kids drove recklessly just to scare him, and he passed them anyway.

Finally Jay shifted in his seat and cleared his throat to remind Mr. Campbell he was there. Campbell swiveled toward him. "Sorry," he said. "I've been trying to work through some problems with the budget. Must have lost track of time, there. I don't believe we've ever met. I'm Fred Campbell."

"Hi," Jay said.

"Jesus Cortez." Mr. Campbell pronounced *Jesus* in the English way, the son-of-God way.

"Jay."

"Sorry. Jay. Looks like you're one of our basketball stars. Now, remind me, Jay, when is tournament?"

"Couple weeks."

"Yes," Mr. Campbell said. "A couple of weeks. Basketball tournament is in a couple of weeks." He seemed to lose himself again, and Jay shifted in his seat. "Sorry, am I taking up too much of your time, Jay?"

Jay shook his head.

"I am, I can tell. You need to get back to class. So then, let's get down to business. Ginger Wallace from the Assembly of God called and told me you and Winston Padgett caused some trouble over there at lunch. Is that true?"

"We were just playing around," Jay said.

"That's what I thought," Campbell said, quick to agree, "playing around, pretending not to speak English. Those Jesus freaks they got over there at lunchtime are pretty nerdy, I'll bet. Real dweebs."

"Kinda," Jay said.

Campbell sat quietly for several seconds. Then he took a deep breath. "*Hogwash!*" he shouted, slamming his fist down on the desk and making all the pens jump. Jay was so taken aback that he half-stood. "Sit your butt back down, young fella! You just sit until I tell you to stand. The Assembly of God is a house of worship, and you were a guest there. I ought to suspend you right now. That's what I feel like doing, suspending you. You've made a mockery of Eula schools. Do you think I like getting calls like this, from churches? You think you're real funny. Well, listen to this, Bozo: if I see your face again, if I hear that you've caused trouble, even the littlest bit, cutting class or passing notes, you will be off that basketball team *pronto*. No second chances. Do you hear me?"

"Yes."

"Do you understand me?"

"Yes."

"Looks like your English has improved. Now get the heck out of my office!"

Jay grabbed his backpack and left. On the way out he couldn't help but give the secretary an incredulous shake of the head. Francine didn't respond, just gazed at Jay emptily. The innumerable times Jay had seen this woman since he entered junior high she had always been cheerful, but today she was different—hollow in the eye, shell-shocked. *I have no pity to give you*, her expression seemed to say. *I have to spend the whole day with him.*

In his office, Campbell again propped his feet on the radiator and tented his fingers, assuming the position for when Winston arrived. This ambush method of dealing with problem students had come to Campbell in a revelation—had been *given* to him, he felt—earlier in the semester when he was dealing with a boy who wouldn't confess to having spray-painted an upside-down cross on the back of the gym. It had worked like a charm several times since.

When Jay got home that night, Enrique was watching TV and

Lina was cleaning the kitchen. Without a word, Jay sat down at the table. Lina took a plate from the oven and peeled off the aluminum foil with pincer-like, oven-mitted hands. "It's hot," she said as she placed the plate before him. Then she returned to cleaning as Jay waited for the food to cool.

"They called me," Lina said.

"Who?"

"The office. School."

"Jesus Christ," Jay said. "If they want to involve everybody in Eula, why don't they just announce it on TV?"

"Is this something you want to tell me about?" Lina asked.

He turned in his seat to square himself to his mother. "No, it is not something I want to tell you about." He let his gaze linger with disgust on her for a few seconds, then he turned and began to eat. It was her fault, after all, that Liz didn't love him. Why would someone so pure love the son of a wetback, a washerwoman?

A few summers earlier, when Mary Lou Retton won her gold medals in the Olympics, Liz and Abby took to wearing their leotards all day long. They cartwheeled around the lawn and assisted each other with backflips while Jay watched from his place hidden in the living-room window curtain. Liz raised her arms in a V, then bent backward slowly until her hands reached the ground. Nothing on earth could be more beautiful than the arch of her body with its crown, its prize—the pubic mound at the crest. She was more exposed than if she had been naked. And then her knees buckled and she folded onto the grass.

There and then Jay decided to keep this image safe. He could jerk off to dirty pictures and to images of other girls at school, but never to the memory of Liz's mons. To this day, he never had.

He had ruined his treasure by sending those notes. What made him think he could touch her? It was the nature of his love that it would be spoiled by exposure, just as it was the nature of her beauty that it would be marred by his touch. Anything he would get from her, he would have to steal; yet he would kill anyone who stole from Liz. These were the facts that trapped him.

Lina interrupted his thoughts. "You won't even give me a chance to be on your side, will you?"

"Nope."

She wiped her hands on a towel and went to the living room.

"Watch this, Ma," said Enrique, who hadn't heard her exchange with Jay. "Pamela has gone crazy 'cause she can't get pregnant. She's gonna jump off a building."

"Enrique, you know I don't like you watching this *Dynasty*," she said.

"It's *Dallas*."

"Garbage," Lina said. But she sat down anyway and watched the rest of the show.

CHAPTER 15

Lina had rushed through Mrs. Hood's house on several occasions in order to meet Chuck. Now, on an afternoon in mid-December, she gave it her full, punishing attention. She emptied and scrubbed the refrigerator, then restuffed it with the old and rotten food in front so it would be noticed and tossed. She picked up and dusted every piece of Mrs. Hood's nativity set, even though it had so recently been put out that it hardly needed it. She got down on her hands and knees to work pine needles out of the shag carpet. She stood all the dining-room chairs upside down to scrub their feet, then dragged them to the living room to dry as she took a soapy rag to the molding.

Lina had missed confession the last few weeks. She had gone to Mass several times, though, and arrived early to pray the rosary. That, and cleaning, were her penance.

One of the many unjust differences between her and Chuck, Lina had noted, was that Chuck, during his workday as a lawyer, met with people, made calls, wrote briefs (whatever those were; he had mentioned it once), while Lina had long stretches of solitude in which to remember their last meeting, to look forward to their next, or, now, to miss him. She would allow herself no hope. Perhaps Chuck could consider what might happen "after," but she couldn't; it would be like plotting Sandra's death. So she shut off parts of herself, the way poor people in farmhouses shut off rooms for the winter, to save on heat. She consigned her thoughts to her past or fixed them on the object in front of her, but, like errant children, they'd always wander back to Chuck.

Now she stood before Mrs. Hood's mahogany sidebar full of dusty plates. She would prove herself before God by cleaning every one in ten minutes flat without thinking of Chuck once.

Here was a memory to occupy her mind: when Lina was a teenager, she liked to go to the Saturday night dances at the field house in Chandler. Back then, girls would still wear their mothers' embroidered circle skirts and put calla lilies in their hair when they wanted to look pretty. Lina's sister Ana, married already to a stern man who wouldn't take her to the dances, would spend an hour ironing Lina's hair and making her up to look like Cher, then send her off with their cousins, tears of longing and regret in her eyes. When Jorge bought Lina a Coke the night she met him, he took off his gray felt cowboy hat and removed a $20 bill from the lining to pay. He had come from Texas, a friend had told her. He was a citizen and his father was white. This was apparent in that he was the tallest man there—Lina's mother would come to call him *el espantapájaros*, the scarecrow—and his skin was so light it showed freckles at the cheek. He was so shy that he never met her eye. He started the few sentences he spoke softly, as if he were speaking to himself; then his voice would rise as he decided the thought worth giving her; then he'd turn away at the end—it wasn't, after all. Again and again, she put her hand to his plaid sleeve, not to flirt but to encourage him to turn toward her so she could hear.

"Do you want to see my truck?" he asked.

"Sure."

He took her outside, paused to light a cigarette, then led her to his big blue Chevy pickup with white fenders and running boards. Moths the color of ash fluttered about as Lina and Jorge stood under the streetlamp in silent respect, as they would in the presence of a prize bull. Then they returned to the dance.

That summer they would throw blankets into the bed of that truck and drive out by Lake Overlook. They had no choice but to do it in the truck, having nowhere else to go. Jorge made love the way he spoke, turning his face away from her, folding into himself, as if the experience was, in the end, only his. And now she saw it *had* been only his. Chuck had made her realize this. Chuck never turned away, but, rather, pierced her with his eyes more and more deeply as he went on, daring her to stay with him.

"I love you."

Chuck had whispered this after they were done on that last night together. She had always wondered what she would say when he said it, and when it happened, she had pretended to be asleep.

There. She failed the challenge she had set for herself. She had thought of Chuck, and only half of Mrs. Hood's plates were clean.

The doorbell rang, and Lina retreated a few steps from the sideboard to look down the hallway, expecting to see Mrs. Hood, who liked to come home while Lina was there, show her pictures of her grandchildren and ask her to get things off high shelves, since her medication made her unstable on the stepladder. It wasn't Mrs. Hood's voice, though, that called, "Lina? Are you here?"

"Come in," Lina said.

Janet Van Beke stepped into the hall and looked around with a curious smile. "I saw your car here, and I know you clean Marilyn's house."

"Hello, Janet. Come in."

"I haven't been in here in years. Carl and Jerry Hood were good friends." She nodded approvingly at the dinner table, which Mrs. Hood always kept set, as if awaiting guests. "I was going to call you tonight," Janet said. "Then I saw your car outside, and figured you wouldn't mind a break."

"It's fine."

Janet disentangled her reading glasses, which she wore on a chain, from her brooch, and when she stepped into the light, Lina made out what the brooch was: mistletoe leaves made of green glass, with a trio of berries—pearls, real ones probably—dangling below. She wore dark slacks and white walking shoes. Once, when Lina had been driving through the neighborhood early in the morning, she had seen Janet, in a gray sweat suit, her arms folded up like little chicken wings, "jogging," although it was little more than walking, quickly, bouncingly. Still, Lina had been surprised; Janet was nearly seventy.

"How are you, Lina?" she asked.

"Good. Everything's going good. How are you?"

"I'm well."

"And Carl?"

"He's very well. He loves this time of year." They sat down at the dinner table, and Janet folded her hands, which, bony as a bundle of sticks, seemed older than the rest of her. "I wanted to tell you, Lina, that Jay was at the house the other day. He asked if he could spend Christmas with us. Has he talked to you about this?"

"No."

As if she could lessen the discomfort of the subject by rushing through it, Janet rattled off, "Well, I told him no, of course, you know, in accordance with our talk last summer. It really should be clear that his home is with you now. We never discussed the holidays, did we? I don't remember it occurring to me. We always sent him over to your house on Christmas, and now Jay's saying that's why he should come over to *our* house this year—a kind of reverse of years past. But for the sake of continuity, I said no, and in any case I felt I should check with you. Now, I wouldn't mind, of course, having him, even though all the kids will be home." She steadied her gaze on Lina.

"I think he better have it with us," Lina said.

"For the sake of clarity," Janet said, nodding. Then, after a moment, she added, "Well, I'm glad I did the right thing. Now, I better run before Marilyn comes home and thinks we're having a tea party."

"At times," Lina said, "I'm ready to give up on him."

Janet sat back down and refolded her hands.

"And that's what he wants, for me to turn on him, and hate him."

"Jay is a stubborn, stubborn boy," Janet said. "Over the years, I spared you some of the problems. Carl's gotten after me about that. He says I should have kept you better informed of the bad as well as the good, and he may be right."

"Did Jay talk at dinner?" Lina asked.

"Talk!" laughed Janet. "We had to tell him to quiet down and listen."

"At my house," Lina said, "Jay never talks at dinner."

Janet inhaled—to express her surprise, it seemed—then thought better of it and shut her mouth, her thin lips fitting together so tightly that tiny creases showed above and below. Lina could tell by her expression that Janet was angry with Jay. It was a motherly anger.

"Thanks for listening," Lina said, moving to rise. "I guess that's all I wanted, was to tell someone."

"If Jay brings this up again," Janet said, "I'll be firm. But if you change your mind, Lina, about Christmas or anything, give me a call."

AT THE PARSONAGE on Wednesday night, after their last church visit, Connie remained stiffly at the wheel as Bill gathered the boxes of slides from the trunk. She didn't even get out of the car. "I'll see you Sunday!" Bill called as he walked up to the house.

She lifted her hand and held it there.

Sunday morning either before or after the service, she would say good-bye to Bill, perhaps forever. He would go spend Christmas with his family in California, then return to Africa. Why hadn't she gotten out of the car?

She picked up Gene from school on Thursday, and took him to the library in Boise. Seeing Gene from the corner of her eye studying his magazines made Connie feel less like a madwoman as she wrote down the number of every nursing home in Kansas City. Mavis, Eugene's mother, her mother-in-law, would be in her eighties now, if she wasn't dead.

Friday morning Connie rose at six. The time difference was on her side. She dialed every number, and when her fingertip got sore, she used the eraser-end of a pencil. The receptionists were hesitant to tell her if there was a Mavis Anderson living there. Some of them refused, even when Connie told them she was her daughter-in-law calling with urgent business. She could have predicted this; she herself instructed new aides never to give out information over the phone at the nursing home, as many con artists targeted the elderly. She completed the last call, then froze. It was at these ending points that silence buzzed like something ready to burst.

She got into her car and drove, not to work but to church. She felt uncomfortable about what had happened at the progressive dinner, but Reverend McNally was the only one she could talk to. And only by talking could she sort this out. She climbed the stairs and entered the office, where Sissy was just raising the blinds.

"Hello, Sissy," Connie said. "Is Reverend McNally in?"

"Connie! Ya scared me! He's not in yet, but he should be soon. You can sit down if ya like."

"Thank you, I will."

Connie chatted with Sissy, who switched off the answering machine, then closed her purse into a drawer, then turned up the thermostat, causing an electric heater that ran along one wall near the floor to tick and ping. Chatting seemed to allow Connie's mind to grind into motion again. Only in the silence did it freeze. What she thought, now, was this: *All right. You win.* (*You* being the world, which had consigned her to a corner and withheld joy from her as punishment for seeking it so long.) *I will be less "exacting," less "rigid." But I won't fool myself like the women in the divorcées' support group. I'll do it with open eyes, and maybe God will forgive me.*

"Here he is!" Sissy sang.

"Good morning, Sissy," said Ed, taking off his hat and hanging it on the rack. He eyed Connie, almost as if he had expected her to be there, and said, simply, as if it were a question, "Connie?"

"I hope you don't mind, reverend. I didn't make an appointment."

"Not at all," he said, and he made a gentle motion with his hand, indicating that he would follow her down the hallway.

Now that Connie's mind was working properly, she realized that not only should she have called for an appointment, but she should have called in late to the nursing home. But unlike the other aides, Connie was never late. They could cover her for an hour.

Connie sat for a while before speaking, just as she had the last time. But now Ed didn't watch her with an open expression, attempting to draw her out. He gravely gazed at his own folded hands.

Finally Connie laughed and said, "Do you want to hear one of my self-pitying thoughts?"

Ed gave a wry smile and a barely perceptible nod.

Connie gathered herself up, almost like a little girl about to recite a poem. "I look forward to helping my clients onto the toilet. Isn't that strange? I was wondering the other day, why do I look forward to this, when it's one of the nastiest parts of my job? Then I realized, part of helping them—" Connie breathed. "The old people embrace me."

Ed closed his eyes.

"I've spent many hours thinking about our last meeting," Connie continued. "Days, really. And what I've decided, just now, in your waiting room, is that I give up. I'm willing to remarry, even if God sees me as an adulterer."

"Connie," said Ed in a voice just above a whisper, "does this have anything to do with Bill Howard?"

"No!" Connie barked. But she didn't hide the panic in her face. She let it betray her.

"Because I realized, in talking to Pamela Hendrick the night of the progressive dinner, that Bill hadn't said, in his presentation, that he's engaged to be married. He is."

These electric heaters had made the air so dry it was hardly breathable. Connie's nostrils felt sunburned. She couldn't speak for a moment, too busy folding herself down into a little square so tight as to be impervious.

"I wanted to tell you that night, on the lawn," Ed continued carefully. "Janey Tanner is one of Bill's fellow missionaries. She's in California, speaking to churches there. Bill's going to meet her there for Christmas. They're going to marry before returning to Africa."

Now Connie was in control again, albeit from deep, deep inside, and able to say, "But Ed, really, this has nothing to do with Bill Howard."

Ed nodded.

"I just wanted to tell you my decision," she said.

"Okay."

"Thanks for taking me without an appointment. I'll see you Sunday."

Connie rose and left, knowing already that she wouldn't be in church on Sunday.

. . . .

THAT AFTERNOON, WHEN the final period let out and the other boys ran through the halls, banging locker doors, shooting rubber bands, titty-twisting each other in celebration of the weekend, and the girls congregated under the stairs and by the drinking fountain, hugging their books like teddy bears as they gossiped about the boys, Enrique spotted Miriam walking through the fray alone and approached quickly and directly, just as he had planned. "Hey, Miriam," he said.

Having not seen him approach, she jumped. "Hey," she said.

"I need a partner for the State Science Fair. Do you want to be my partner?"

"Are you insane?" she asked.

He said nothing, but continued to look at her intently. He hadn't fully worked out the effect he wanted to achieve, but *insane* was good.

"We haven't spoken a word to each other in, like, weeks," Miriam said.

"I know," Enrique said. "I'm tired of not being friends."

Miriam gave him a hard look, then dropped her shoulders. "Me, too."

"So, friends?"

"Yeah." They shook on it, but still Miriam didn't smile. They strolled together toward the stairway that led up to the school entrance. Seventh-graders had their lockers in this subterranean hallway. Pale light flooded in through the building's glass front and shone in rippled reflection on the painted concrete floor like a pool of water. "Still," Miriam said, "I don't know why you'd want me to be your partner."

"Well, it's like, at the science fair, you presented evidence on the other side. It was the scientific method. You proved my project wrong. So I was thinking you could help me fix it." Enrique knew that he would have to change his presentation, given that Lake Overlook was only twenty-five feet deep, so the idea had occurred to him to see how an appeal to Miriam's vanity worked, to ambush her with the surrender and the spoils all at once. He was getting lonely anyway, and, as Abby had pointed out, he needed a partner. "That is," he added when Miriam was slow to respond, "unless you hate my project so much you can't even stand to look at it."

"Actually, Enrique, I think your project is really neat. I just think you did the wrong thing by telling people they could all be killed, when it totally couldn't happen here."

"I know. That was Gene's idea anyway."

"I figured," Miriam said. Then she laughed suddenly. "I had been feeling pretty stupid about my project. But it looks like you actually listened."

"Totally." Then Enrique told the lie that he had planned to use only if Miriam was resistant and required hardcore convincing: "I wish you would have stayed for the award presentation. I was going to invite you up with me and share the prize with you."

Miriam gave him an incredulous look.

"Like, I hadn't decided *one hundred percent* to do it, but if you stayed I think I would have."

"If I help you, Enrique, you're going to have to change it. It can't be the same project all over again."

"I know."

"Well, should I come over and look at it?"

"How about Monday?"

"Neat."

"I'm glad we're friends again, Miriam. I think you're my best friend."

Miriam smiled and nudged Enrique with the wrist that held her textbooks. Then she ran up the stairs and outside.

Sometimes, in order to avoid riding the bus with Gene, Enrique stayed and did his homework in the high school library until Jay had finished basketball practice. There was a tacit agreement that if Enrique waited by the car and didn't bother him with attempts at conversation, Jay would drive him home. Often he dropped Enrique off, then headed to some other, unnamed destination. Today, though, Enrique was excited again about his model and wanted to spend some time with it before dinner. So he boarded the bus and went to the back, far from where Gene would sit when he boarded. Sitting back here over the past weeks had afforded Enrique a view of how the grade-school kids scrunched up their faces in an imitation of Gene as they walked down the aisle, sometimes putting a finger to their foreheads to indicate the tuft of hair between his eyebrows.

Coop had noticed the rift between the boys. On one hand, he was saddened. Who would pick up Gene now that Enrique had dropped him? Gene seemed one of those kids who could drown in himself, unnoticed. Louis, Coop's youngest brother, had been that way, although Louis had splashed around and groped for wreckage before he went down.

On the other hand, Enrique, a well-behaved seventh-grader, unintentionally served as a kind of hall monitor in the back of the bus; the rowdy kids had quieted down significantly since Enrique and Gene had parted ways.

Enrique and Gene both got off at the same stop, but now Enrique used the main entrance to the trailer park while Gene went through the hole in the fence.

Dinner that night was Wednesday's chili, reheated, with some scrambled eggs thrown in to liven it up. It had gotten spicier in the intervening days, an effect Enrique liked—he enjoyed the sweat on his scalp and the burn on his tongue that he smothered with a soft, cool, folded piece of white bread.

"I don' see how you could want her to be your partner, *cariño,* after what she did," Lina said.

The two hunched over their bowls and didn't look up as they spoke. "I need a partner, Ma, and Miriam's one of the smartest kids at school. It's not a big deal, what she did. She made a mistake. She's my friend. You're supposed to forgive and forget, right?"

"There's plenty of other nice kids for you to be friends with."

"There aren't, Ma. That's not how it works."

Lina was quiet. Of course that wasn't how it worked—she remembered—but she wanted it to work that way for him. After a moment, she said, "Is Miriam, kind of, your girlfriend?"

"Ma!"

"Just asking, baby. You can talk to me about that stuff, you know."

Enrique returned to eating. Lina watched the muscles of his jaw lurch as a blush rose from his neck to his face like the red of a thermometer. It was the first time she had raised the possibility that Enrique should have a girlfriend. And it was the arrival of a doubt with which she would wrestle for years before calling a truce: the doubt that he ever would. She turned quickly away from it now. There was another explanation for Enrique's loneliness, his inability to fit like a puzzle piece into the world the way other kids seemed to. It was Jay's fault. Enrique had been happy before Jay came.

As if summoned, there was the rev of the Maverick outside, and headlights illuminated the curtain. Lina went to the cupboard, got a bowl, and ladled in some chili.

Jay burst through the door and marched straight into his bedroom.

"Jay? Are you going to eat?"

He came to the table and, without sitting, took a spoonful of chili. Lina knew by his eyes, black with rage, that he had spoken to Janet Van Beke. Jay put the spoon down and said, "Tastes like shit."

"Jay? Jay?" said Lina, her voice elevating as he went back into his room. "Excuse me, Jesús!"

"What!" he yelled.

"If you're not going to eat, could you please clear your bowl?"

He marched back in, took his bowl, and threw it into the sink, where it crashed against the other dishes and sent a spray of chili across the wall.

Lina sprang to her feet. "How dare you!" she cried. "Who tol' you you can act like that?"

"Fuck off," he said.

She turned him by his shoulder. "Don' you walk away from me, Jesús. Apologize. Apologize and clean that up."

"Or else?"

"Or else you can just get the hell out of here."

Jay laughed in her face. He dropped to his knees and pressed his palms together in prayer. "Please, please, kick me out. I want you to. *Por favor, Madre*. Save me! Save my soul!"

Lina pushed him, and he caught himself from falling. "*Desgraciado*," she cried. "Stop that! You want to go to hell? Get up."

He rose to tower over his mother. He took the flesh of her upper arm just under the shoulder, and squeezed until she whimpered. "You pushed me," he said through his teeth.

"Don't you touch her!" Enrique screamed, shoving himself between them. "I'll kill you!"

"Faggot." With a move so quick and effortless it was hardly visible, Jay pushed Enrique, sending him stumbling across the room to hit the wall. The dishes jumped on the table, and a pan fell from a peg in the kitchen. Then Jay turned and stormed out of the house.

"Enrique!" said Lina, and ran to him.

Jay stormed back in, grabbed his basketball, which was wedged under a chair in the corner, then left again.

Lina held Enrique. "Are you all right, baby?"

Enrique sobbed and held his arm where he had hit the wall. "I hate him so much!" he cried.

Jay returned yet again and went into his room. He cared so little what Lina and Enrique thought of him that he didn't mind diminishing the drama of his exit through repetition. He threw some clothes into his gym bag, took his school books from his desk, and left the room, drawers agape and papers littering the floor.

"You've ruined my home!" yelled Lina. "You don' belong here!"

"That's right, I don't," Jay said emotionlessly. This time he sped off in his car.

Enrique suddenly saw that the last thing Jay had seen was Lina cradling him like a baby. He pushed her away and sat up. She gasped. For a moment their eyes locked, and Enrique teetered on the verge of apologizing, kissing her, and helping her to her feet. He had a choice, to melt or to freeze. He froze.

Lina heaved herself up and began cleaning and muttering Spanish words to herself.

There came a voice from the porch. "Lina?"

Lina threw down her rag and went to the door.

"Is everything all right?" Connie half-whispered.

The ruckus had roused her from that spot deep inside herself from which she had been operating, turning her head and seeing out of her eyes like a periscope, since her meeting with Reverend

McNally that morning. "Should I go over?" she had asked Gene, who had considered, then answered: "Yes."

Lina's face remained fixed in its stony scowl. "Yes, everything's all right."

"I just . . . I'm sorry . . ."

Connie began to turn away, and Lina reached out and squeezed her arm with a hand still wet from cleaning. Connie said nothing, but expressed her solidarity with a nod. When Lina went back inside, Enrique had disappeared into his room.

CHAPTER 16

The following Monday, in distant Portland, Wanda sat against the sticker-festooned bumper of Melissa's jeep, waiting. Five-thirty; Melissa would have to come out soon. Unless she worked late, that was. Wanda drew her coat more snugly around her and tightened the cross of her legs. The cold here was different than in Eula—wetter and more invasive—and Wanda's clothes weren't up to the task of fending it off. Every so often the mottled gray sky released a few fat snowflakes, which caught in her hair and melted.

"Ma'am?"

Wanda looked up. It was the guard from the booth of the parking lot. His beige uniform with its official-looking patches on the breast and shoulder was a little tight around the middle.

"Is that your car?" he asked.

"My friend's. I'm supposed to meet her here."

"When?"

"Um, now."

"You've been here over an hour. Nearly two, actually."

"Well, she's late."

"I'm going to have to ask you to move along."

Wanda paused. For the first time in over a month, she wanted a cigarette, only because this moment required one—to be flicked away angrily before she rose. The guard followed her to the lot entrance, then returned to his little booth. Wanda walked slowly up the sidewalk to Melissa's office building. She pushed through the heavy revolving door and sat down on a vinyl-upholstered bench behind a planter. She watched the bank of elevators, scanning each group of businessmen that filed out for Melissa's glazed curls. Before long, however, another guard, this one wearing a gray suit and red tie, approached. "Ma'am?"

Wanda went and waited outside on the street. The sun fell behind the buildings and she was chilled to the bone by the time Melissa emerged from the building. She wore a black coat with shoulder pads, a fluffy pink scarf and matching beret, and held a folded newspaper under her arm. She looked up at the sky. Wanda gently approached. Melissa looked at her and froze.

"Melissa," Wanda said.

Melissa turned and walked down the street.

"Just let me walk you to your car. I just need a minute. I came all the way here on my own money, from babysitting."

Wanda said this not only to prove to Melissa that she had earned a moment of her time, but also to fully disclose everything. No more lies. She didn't have a job at K-mart. Before, she hadn't had a job at all. Now, for the first time since she was a teenager, she was babysitting.

It seemed to work; Melissa slowed a little.

"Remember when you first saw me? When you cried? That was *real*, Melissa, for me, too. I never believed in this stuff, but I was *meant* to have your baby. If there's a God, He wants it. I really, really mean it, Melissa, and I think you know it's true. Maybe there's no reason for me to be here, in the world, you know? But if there is, this is it. This is my job. I know I should act all calm and cool about this and try to convince you with some smart argument, but I can't. It's about this feeling, Melissa. It's not about reasons, and it's not about the money."

Melissa still walked ahead; Wanda could not see her face. "I know it's not about the money," Melissa said.

"I lied to you and that was wrong. But no more lies. No more surprises. I swear on everything—on my mom and dad's graves. Just forgive me, and we can pick up where we left off. We can have this baby."

They had reached the parking lot entrance. Melissa turned to face Wanda. With her fuzzy pink-gloved hand she pointed to her face, which was wet with tears. "I never cry," she said with a desperate hiccup of laughter.

Wanda moved to touch Melissa's shoulder, but Melissa stopped her with a severe look. They stood for several seconds, Melissa searching Wanda's face skeptically. Then her shoulders dropped and she turned slightly. "I'll talk to Randy," she said. She walked away a few steps, then turned to Wanda again. "I'll talk to Randy," she said with a trace of humor, "and he'll agree."

THAT NIGHT, AS planned, Miriam came over to Enrique's house. "Why don't you give me the presentation how you did at the science fair," she said, "just so we have it fresh in our minds." She sat on the sofa's armrest and folded her arms.

Enrique propped the posters against the wall behind the model in the order they had been hung on the wall. "Well, how I started out was—" It felt awkward to give the presentation standing with the model at his feet, let alone give it to the very person who had shot it down. Enrique knelt, to be at the same level he had been, relative to the model, at the fair, and began: "On August 21 of this year over seventeen hundred people died in the middle of the night."

Miriam nodded slowly as Enrique gave the presentation. The crease between her eyebrows grew though—a little valley of trouble—which made Enrique wonder, was she finding new faults with the project, or reliving the pain she had experienced at the science fair? When he came to the part (which had been his favorite) when he said, "*But* could lake overturn happen at Lake Overlook?" his voice lowered in pitch and increased in speed, and his gaze left Miriam to wander about the corners of the room.

When he finished, Miriam stood and chewed on a pen as she paced back and forth before the model. "So, the idea is we make it *just* about Lake Nyos, about what happened there. It's like a mystery the scientists are trying to solve, and by suggesting that it might have been carbon dioxide and not some poison gas, we're offering one possible answer."

"Sure," Enrique said. He stood up and rubbed his knees.

Miriam stopped pacing, removed the pen from her mouth, and held it in the air like a conductor poised to begin a symphony. "The trees have to go," she said.

"What?"

"And the houses."

"That's the best part!"

"I know," she said, shaking her head with a pity that seemed more for the trees than for Enrique.

"Why?"

"Enrique, it's Africa. This is going to be a model of a lake in Africa. That village is cute, but it looks like—I don't know—Hansel and Gretel."

"What are we going to replace it with?"

"Palm trees. Huts."

"And where do we get those?"

"Where'd you get this stuff?"

"Abby Hall gave it to me. It was her dad's."

Miriam nodded gravely. "We'll have to construct them ourselves, then. Do you have scissors?"

They went to the kitchen table and Miriam tore a few sheets from the notebook in her backpack. She folded one into a square, then into a smaller square, then into a triangle. Enrique wondered if she was making an airplane. Then she took the scissors and wrestled a lightning bolt–shaped cut into the folded paper. A snowflake? "What're you doing?" Enrique asked. Miriam ignored him. This is how she got when she was scrutinizing a blouse at the mall that she wanted to copy. She unfolded the paper and revealed an eight-sided star with tiny tufts of pulp showing at the jags in its spokes. She rolled another sheet into a tight cylinder, then balanced the hub of the star on top. "Palm tree," she said before the star teetered and fell.

Enrique's shoulders collapsed and an ugly look of resignation took over his face.

"I mean, this looks crappy. We'll use construction paper and cardboard, even fabric if you want. It'll be fun. The judges will like it better because we made it. *Oh my gosh!*" she said, looking at the kitchen clock. "I have to go. My mom's picking me up at the Circle-K!" She quickly gathered her things. "You're not worried, are you?"

"No."

"Trust me, Enrique, it'll be even better than before."

Miriam left, and Enrique stayed at the table, leaning crookedly on his elbows, like an old barn on the verge of collapse. The only sound was the rustling of the blinds when the wind sucked at the window. Enrique felt a draft and assumed it was entering the house through the seam down its middle where the men had stuck it together last summer. A month ago Lina had set the thermostat's dial at sixty-five, then covered it with an X of masking tape to keep Enrique and Jay from turning it up. So Enrique wore his hooded sweatshirt inside. He rolled the sheet of paper back into a cylinder, removed some of the chewed tabs of paper that hung from the snowflake-star, and balanced it on top again. A palm tree twice as tall as the church's steeple? But, he supposed, they could make them a quarter this size. And for huts, they could cut toilet-paper rolls in half, coat them with glue, and obscure the cardboard behind rows of toothpicks, then make roofs out of dried grass.

The refrigerator ticked, then hummed. Enrique was about to get up and turn on the radio, when he heard his mother pull up.

It had been awfully quiet like this all weekend. Saturday night they went to the house at the edge of town—the spooky house with a crumbling chimney and dormers that looked like eyes—where every year they bought their Christmas tree. The floodlit forest had lost its magic for Enrique, and he had encouraged Lina to buy a modest, inexpensive tree. She had nodded sadly. In previous years, he had always pushed for the biggest one she could afford.

Jay had hurt them both, but it was the moment after he left that haunted them as they hung tinsel on the tree's sparse branches. *I should take better care of her*, Enrique thought. He remembered Abby saying, of her father, "He needs happiness more than other people."

Despite the Christmas music, the house seemed quiet. The crackling possibility of Jay's arrival had been removed, and Enrique didn't miss it, really, but he missed its power. It was Jay's crashing about the house and the noise of his voice that had jarred Enrique into changing from a boy who played cat's cradle at the mall to one who observed the workings of junior high from a comfortable distance, like a crow in the rafters. Jay's long legs lying crossed on the coffee table, the stupid sports he watched on TV, his stinky shorts hanging in the shower—Enrique would no longer have these around to hate.

Little brother, Jay had called him once.

Now Enrique waited for his mother to come in the front door and break the silence. When she didn't, he went to the window and lifted the blind. It was not Lina who had pulled up to the house, but Jay. He was unfastening a strap on the trunk of his Maverick and lifting something out. Enrique went out onto the porch.

"It's my old bike," Jay said, keeping his eyes on the handlebars as he guided the dirt bike up the walkway to the foot of the stairs. "It was at the Van Bekes'. You can have it if you want."

Jay had spent the weekend doing chores—he had insisted on it. The Van Bekes' children and grandchildren were about to descend for Christmas, so there was plenty to do. He had spent Saturday gathering all the sticks that had fallen from the globe willows onto the frosty lawn. Those bothersome trees seemed to grow by splitting in half, then recovering, and they shed more branches than they kept. The gardening gloves Jay wore had stiffened with cold, and his ears came to ache as if they had been boxed. "Jay! Put these on!" Janet had called from the front door, tossing him a hat and earmuffs. Sunday Jay had gone to church for the first time since moving to Lina's. The members of Eula Lutheran had ruffled his hair and asked about basketball.

Underneath, Jay felt an ache of remorse. He tried to remember how hard he had squeezed Lina's arm and pushed Enrique. He hoped he hadn't really hurt them. It wasn't their fault, really. They were poor, downtrodden; Liz would judge him harshly for being so cruel. Even now, it was only for Liz that he wanted to do good. What message could Jay send to Lina and Enrique to say he was sorry? Should he call? If he ended up staying here at the Van Bekes' permanently, it would be nice to show there were no hard feelings.

Sunday afternoon Jay added a line of colored lights to the Van Bekes' front fence, thinking it would be a nice sight for their kids to see when they turned onto the lane after the long drive from the Boise Airport. Then he cracked the sticks he had gathered the day before into kindling and put them in the garage to dry. There, under a tarp, he found his old bike.

Enrique swallowed an expression of excitement that would have sounded girlish and descended the stairs. His pocketed hands formed balls with knobbed ridges at the knuckle like little spines. Jay put down the kickstand and stepped back. Enrique ran his fingers over the handlebars. He squeezed the grip and saw that this caused two rubber pads to clamp onto the wheel. Brakes. On the bikes Enrique had ridden, you worked the pedals backward to brake. He indicated a pair of levers and asked, "Are those the gears?"

"Yeah."

"How do they work?"

Jay shrugged. "Figure it out. It's not hard."

Enrique was grateful, and aware that he should thank Jay. But what would happen if Enrique said nothing, if he stood impassive and froze inside?

"Merry Christmas," Jay said, with an unfamiliar, inquisitive look. Then he walked back to his car and said, "Tell Lina I'm sorry."

Lina—was that what Jay called her? Enrique had never heard Jay call her anything.

"There's a man here to see you," one of the other aides said near the end of the day.

"At the desk?"

The aide smiled.

Connie finished dressing the bed. She tucked in the blanket with trembling hands, then walked down the hall past old folks dozing in wheelchairs, to the reception desk. Bill stood when he saw her. His brows were drawn low over his eyes, almost obscuring them.

"You weren't in church yesterday," he said.

"I wasn't feeling well."

"Sorry to hear that. I leave tomorrow. Just thought I'd come by and thank you. Here, I brought you something." From a pocket inside his jacket he took a small wooden cross attached to a key ring. People in a village near his mission carved these. Connie had seen him give the same gift to pastors in the churches they visited.

"Thank you."

"Well . . ." said Bill, shifting his weight from one foot to the other.

"Bill, in your presentation, why don't you mention that one of your fellow missionaries is also your fiancée?"

Bill swallowed. "Because I don't see how our romantic life is relevant to our work."

"Why don't you include pictures of her in the slide show? There's pictures of all the other missionaries."

"I . . . She is in the pictures."

"Yes, one, the group photo, in the back row."

"Connie—"

"Because when I was thinking about it the other day, when I was told you were engaged, I figured, either you didn't mention it because you've lied to her, and you're not going to marry her"—Connie paused to allow Bill to weakly shake his head—"or because you thought the women in the groups we visited would be more likely to give money to a handsome single man."

Bill took a deep breath. "In my prep meetings with the missions board, before I came to Idaho, they suggested that might be the case."

"I find it difficult to believe that the missions board would have you lie—"

"I don't like that word, Connie."

"I don't like it either," she hissed, aware that if she spoke as loudly as she wanted to, the other aides would hear. "A Christian *shouldn't* like it. A Christian shouldn't *do* it. I find it difficult to believe that the missions board would have you *lie* to women's groups in order to make a few extra dollars."

Bill lifted his chin. "A few dollars, in my line of work, can save a life."

Connie raised the back of her left hand to face Bill, and pressed her wedding ring with her thumb. "I still wear it, Bill, twelve years later. When I take it off to do dishes, my fingers don't fit together anymore. Why? Because I follow the Bible *to the letter*. God says to follow it to the letter, or not at all. You know the verses. You teach them!"

"Everything I do," Bill said with an angry tremor, "is for my mission. Everything. It is the whole of my life. I live for those disadvantaged, uneducated people, Connie."

"And for Janey Tanner. Don't forget her." Connie couldn't help it—tears were rising. "Well, I'll pray for you, Bill. And for those disadvantaged, uneducated people, and for Janey Tanner." Connie walked around the counter, sat down at the desk, and sheltered her eyes. When she looked up again, Bill was gone. She took his gift and dropped it into the wastebasket.

That night, Enrique plucked the trees from the model one by one, quietly and without much fuss, so his mother, who was in the kitchen talking on the phone, wouldn't ask what he was doing. Bits of green-painted newspaper came away with the trees like clumps of grass; these he tore off and rolled into balls. Then he peeled the glue from the trees' flat bases. He did the same for all the houses, the school, and the church. The rubbery blobs of glue came off clean, sometimes showing reversed impressions of the tiny words that were printed on the bottom of the pieces—the name of the manufacturer and an identifying number. Then Enrique took all the trees and buildings to his bedroom and lined them up on top of his bookshelf. After Christmas vacation he would return them to their boxes, which he had kept in the closet, and give them back to Mr. Hall. At last he would see what this man looked like—how his eyebrows would lift upon finding his mistress's son here, not to challenge him but to return his gift. A chagrined shadow would pass over the man's handsome, weathered face before he threw back his shoulders and straightened his tie and said, "Thank you, young man," accepting the handles of the shopping bag. Then Enrique would jump on his bike and jet off before Mr. Hall could say another word. Mr. Hall would turn, walk down the echoing hall, and open a large, ornately carved door to reveal his special room: a wonderland of cities and forests, clock towers, Ferris wheels, all ticking and whirring mechanically as trains dashed in and out of mountains riddled with tunnels like Swiss cheese.

Returning the gift would be an experiment, just as this submission to Miriam's new vision of the model was an experiment. With a little scientific distance, things that would otherwise hurt became, simply, interesting.

CHAPTER 17

"Oh my *God*," said Penny, Miriam's cousin who was visiting from Stockton, California, for Christmas, and who apparently didn't mind taking the Lord's name in vain. "You'll never guess what I found over there." She had just returned from the dark, cobwebby recesses of the cellar to the lighted corner where Enrique and Miriam had set up a pile of bean bags and old, mildew-smelling sofa cushions.

"What?" Miriam asked.

Enrique barely looked up from the little papier-mâché palm tree he was painting.

"Babies' brains!" From behind her back, Penny presented a Mason jar in which peaches, halved and brownish, swam in syrup.

Miriam practically screamed with laughter. "Gross!"

Penny threatened Miriam with the jar and spoke in a wicked-witch voice: "Mmm! Babies' brains."

"Get those away from me!"

"They're nutritious."

"Gross!"

"You guys are so immature," Enrique said. "They're peaches."

Penny's smile dropped and her head cocked. "No shit, Enrique," she said.

Miriam and Enrique both looked down shyly. Bad words still stung them a little.

Penny wore a miniature bowler hat on the back of her head, but you would never know looking at her face-on. Her bangs, which were bleached white, had been teased into a rat's nest that sprang up several inches before plunging over one eye. From under the chaos of her hair dangled an earring that resembled a checkerboard from a dollhouse. She turned and disappeared again into the dark part of the cellar.

"She's not helping," Enrique said. The whole reason they had gotten Miriam's brother to bring the model over here in the bed of his truck was because she had promised a comfortable place to work, and a helpful cousin.

"She's entertaining us," Miriam replied.

"She's entertaining *you*."

Miriam just shrugged. She tied a knot around a small bundle of straw. She cut the string, then chewed with the scissors into the straw about three inches under the knot. Then she dug a knuckle into the bunch, forming it into a cone: the roof of a grass hut. "Looks good, huh?" she said, holding it up for Enrique.

"Oh my *God*!" Penny cried. She came around the corner and blew the dust off another Mason jar, this one containing stewed tomatoes. "Monkey hearts!"

"Ew!" Miriam cried.

"The tape's over," Enrique said.

Penny put down the jar and squatted before the pink portable cassette player she had brought down.

"Put on Cyndi Lauper," Miriam said.

"That *poser*?"

In the short time Enrique had spent with Penny, she had used this word countless times. It seemed an odd favorite for the girl who posed more than anyone he had ever met. Only yesterday, in the record store in the mall, she had made a game of picking up albums by the bands she liked, and mimicking the dramatic expressions of the weirdos on the covers—a look of shock, all teeth bared: the Human League; a Satanic scowl, chin tucked, eyes menacing: Siouxsie & the Banshees. Miriam had eaten this up, of course.

"I thought she was your favorite," Miriam said.

"She was never my favorite. She dressed Wave but she didn't *sing* Wave." Apparently New Wave was so entrenched in Penny's psyche that it was no longer "New." What a poser!

Penny's rebuke silenced Miriam, who returned to her grass hut. Enrique, too, returned to his work, until, suddenly, the lights went out. Miriam emitted a little shriek. Then the music started, and a flashlight illuminated Penny's face from underneath. "Let me take your hand, I'm shaking like milk . . ." she lip-synched as she lurked across the cellar's empty space and tossed her head, "turning, turning blue all over the windows and the floors." She draped herself across the furnace, snarled, rolled her eyes in their sockets. Her eyelids, which caught the light from her flashlight-microphone, fluttered like moth wings. The effect was more that of a silent-movie Dracula than a rock singer. Miriam cheered. Penny picked up her jar of monkey hearts, cupped it like a lover's head, and sang to it. "The two of us together again. It's just the same, a stupid game." Then, during an interlude of synthesizers and bass, Penny lit the jar from below and swirled the water, creating a homemade lava lamp that cast blobby shadows across the puffy insulation that bulged between the ceiling beams like pink tissue between bones.

When the song ended, Enrique himself rose and turned on the light, worried that Penny would continue to lip-synch the entire record.

"That was totally awesome!" Miriam cried. "Who was that?"

"The Cure."

"Rad!"

"Did *you* like that song, Enrique?" Penny asked, overly solicitous.

Enrique shrugged, as if the Cure were old hat to him. If Miriam could be ridiculous enough to use one of Penny's words, he could use Jay's: "Pretty cool."

When they had finished their afternoon's work, one of the farm hands, who was heading into town anyway, gave Enrique a ride to the Circle-K. As he walked through the trailer park and up Robin Lane, Enrique didn't notice the dusty old Plymouth, so the first indication that something was amiss was the warmth and the cigarette smell that met him when he opened the door. He stepped in and glanced at the thermostat. The X of tape was gone. His first thought was, Jay turned it up. But, of course, Jay was gone. Lina was in the kitchen, seesawing a large knife back and forth on its blade using the heel of her hand, which was covered in a plastic bag. This was how she diced chilies, and she usually only diced chilies on the weekend.

"Mom—" said Enrique, then stopped himself from pointing out that it was warm in here, lest she turn it back down.

Lina looked up from her task, her lips pursed. She nodded toward the living room. "Say hello," she said.

Of course. Cigarette smell.

The old man—*his* old man—had been so still, bent in places like a rolled-up rug propped in the corner of the sofa, that Enrique hadn't noticed him. The man leaned forward to park his cigarette in the ashtray (the one Lina kept in the top of the cupboard only for him) and beckoned Enrique by lifting his chin, which bristled with white and black slivers.

Enrique shot a glance at his mother, but she had returned to her dicing and didn't look up.

"Hi," Enrique said.

The old man's long, leathery arms lifted like those of a marionette. Enrique sat down on the couch at a couple feet's distance, and the man draped his arms around his shoulders and kissed the top of his head. "You been good?" he asked.

"Yeah."

The man picked up his cigarette. "I been in Nevada, countin' cattle. They got me countin' and drivin' the truck as they throw out hay. And overseein' the migrants. And I do some of the things they used to have a vet out to do. Hornin' calves." The man's eyes, set like chips of coal deep in his head, turned from Enrique back to the television as he spoke. They were like Jay's eyes. "One day they had me in the house answerin' the phone, 'cause their daughter had to drive to Winnemucca to help her aunt or somethin'. Felt weird gittin' paid for sittin', but I s'pose that's what some folks do all their lives. Sit and move papers from one pile to another and git paid for it."

Enrique was stunned. This was the longest string of words he had ever heard his father speak. Something had shaken loose in him.

And he wasn't done. "Fella named Warren, he's the owner, sits on the county commission. You start to see how things work. He gits to own the land and make the rules that he'll have to follow. He ran for the legislature a few years ago, and probably will again. Then his son'll run the ranch, and run it by the rules his father and the other owners make. Be able to divert the water and graze the cows wherever they want. Been good to me, though. I don't fault them for makin' the rules, just wish I coulda known how things worked earlier, so I coulda had a part, given more to you all."

As far as Enrique knew, his father had never sent them a dime. "Um, I'm gonna help my mom," he said.

The lines in the man's face all tilted up into an inquisitive, perhaps hurt, expression, but he didn't stop Enrique from leaving.

"He's talking," Lina said simply.

"How long is he going to stay?"

"Not long, I'm sure."

"Why don't you ask him?"

"You used to like it when he came."

"Yeah, back when I was a kid and he brought presents."

From the firm set of her jaw, Enrique could tell Lina was going to give him nothing, say nothing against her husband.

But inside, Lina had buffered herself with memories of Chuck. The only way to endure the presence of that ghost sitting in her living room was to pick up the love she had been denying herself in the past weeks and pull it around her shoulders like a blanket.

Over dinner the man told about the different ways of horning cattle. He spoke without lifting his eyes, almost as if he were speaking into a microphone hidden in his collar, recording everything he knew and remembered so it would survive him, a condemned man determined to leave a record. In the past, he told them, they swabbed the calves' heads with acid, which burned into the bone and prevented horns from growing. But it was hard to keep the acid from dripping into the calves' eyes, blinding them. Now they waited until nubs appeared on the calves' heads and gouged them out with specially designed clippers. Jorge had learned to use them. His eyes flicked up in pride with this revelation: they no longer had to call out a vet to horn the calves—he could do it.

Enrique had been determined not to ask his father any questions. But now the sweet young calf he had conjured blinked his Bambi-eyes in fright as he was zapped with a cattle prod into the chute with the other calves. Up the ramp he was driven, toward Enrique's father, who worked handles that led, through madly scissoring machinery, to chomping stainless-steel jaws. "Why do you have to horn them at all?" Enrique asked. "Why don't you just leave them alone?"

"Imagine you're one of three hunnerd head of cattle in a field, all jabbin' each other. You ain't even fightin', just stabbin' your neighbor in the flank when you lift your head. We'd have to patch up a cow every day."

Enrique's father talked like any cowboy, not a trace of Spanish in his mouth pushing vowels up into his nose and consonants toward his teeth. Why was it that his mother had her faint accent when she, like his father, had been raised in the United States? Because they spoke Spanish at the Hacienda. But also, Enrique now suspected, she *chose* her accent, just as she chose to speak Spanish to him when he was growing up. She had instilled it in him as his language of comfort and happy bedtime thoughts, the language he loved in. She had hobbled him with it. Only now was he ridding himself of this version of baby-talk by pushing words back on his tongue. No wonder he had felt so lonely since he had stopped speaking Spanish. It was her fault. She should have been speaking English to him from the start.

After dinner, Enrique's father called him from the kitchen back to the sofa. "Do you know who you're named after?" he asked.

"Your brother."

Enrique's father nodded. Nothing in the man's face prepared Enrique for what followed. The voice of another man came out of him, a man speaking from the back of a church—singing, even, in vibrato: "He's dead." His face froze again, then he opened his mouth and inhaled.

He's crying, Enrique realized. The dried-up old man didn't make tears. A flash of pity in Enrique was quickly overwhelmed by embarrassment. He wanted to get up and leave. And why shouldn't he? He didn't owe this man anything. Enrique boldly rose and went to his room.

Tomorrow, the last school day before Christmas break, there would be cookies and gift exchanges. Teachers hadn't bothered to assign any homework, so Enrique had nothing to do once confined in his room. He took the trees and houses off the bookshelf and arranged them into a little village on the bed. Then he rearranged them into a ring, so the villagers shared a circular park. Downtown, which consisted of the church and the school, stood apart, atop the knoll of his pillow. He noticed the long, late-afternoon shadows his reading lamp cast across his bedspread. He unclipped the lamp and moved it in an arc over his bed, changing the shadows from morning to noon to night. *How's that, Mrs. Cuddlebone?*

Try again, Enrique. He clipped the lamp to a drawer, to be suspended at sunset, shoved some clothes under the bedspread, and reerected the village so it now occupied the slope of a valley.

Lina, too, went to her room early and sat in bed with a *Reader's Digest.* Then, when she was just about to turn out the light, the door handle turned, and the door opened to reveal Jorge's long frame. He bowed his head—was it a gesture of polite submission or one of a man used to running into door frames?

"No," Lina said, sitting up in bed.

"No?"

"You're sleeping in the other bedroom, Jorge. Go on."

"Man should sleep with his wife."

She shook her head. "You had your chance."

Jorge stepped in and sat at the edge of the bed. He lay one long hand on the ridge at Lina's ankle. "I'm sorry about that, Lina. It's one of the things I been wanting to tell you, that I'm sorry."

Lina pulled her leg away, swiveled in bed, and stood. She took Jorge by the shoulders and steered him out. "Tomorrow," she said as she closed the door. He stood there a long time—she could feel him through the door, radiating like heat—before he moved away and she heard the *flick-flick-flick* of the lighter. Not so long ago, she had dreamed of an apology from Jorge, and wished for him to share her bed every night. How far she had come!

The next afternoon Enrique again shut himself in his room with his little village, attempting to make it feel more like a model and less like a toy, more like homework and less like playtime. He was missing his favorite shows because the old man was out there. He and his little village had fallen under siege by an evil troll outside the city wall. How had this come to pass? The answer he came up with followed the loosened logic of the make-believe village: Enrique had unintentionally brought on the arrival not only of his father but of Penny, by opening his borders, by calling a truce with Miriam. The lone wolf must balance the cost of loneliness against the threat of encroachment.

There was a knock on his door.

Enrique threw a blanket over the village. “Yeah?” he said.

The old man’s head entered. “Come with me,” he said.

“I really have a lot to do for school,” Enrique said.

Again, all the lines of the face tilted up, and it withdrew.

The last time he was here, three years ago, Enrique’s father had said, “Come with me,” and Enrique had gone. It had been a few days after Christmas, and there was some old snow on the ground. They had parked by Lake Overlook, and the man had gone to the trunk of the car, taken a few shells out of a small paper bag, and dropped them into his pocket. He took out a shotgun and slammed the trunk closed.

They walked across an empty field toward a grove of maples whose trunks were a jumble of black bars imprisoning the white lake. The snow on the field had frozen hard on the surface, then settled underneath, creating a glazed crust that crunched when you stepped through it, then banged your ankle when you went to move on. The only way you could walk across it was to lift your leg high between steps, like a cat crossing a puddle. At least that was how Enrique crossed the field. Unaware of their destination, he had worn sneakers. His father trudged along, invulnerable in big boots.

They stopped when they reached the trees. Enrique’s father flipped a switch and bent the gun like an arm at the elbow. “Shells in here.” He plugged the two holes with shells. Then he dropped the limbs back together so they again made a shotgun. Without a word, he cocked the gun, then positioned the butt against Enrique’s shoulder. He put his hand on Enrique’s to steady the barrel, and put his finger around Enrique’s on the trigger. He squeezed. The gun jumped and popped and sprayed tiny holes across the tree trunk. Some birds, black beads studding the naked lacework of a nearby tree, rose and scattered.

“Ow,” said Enrique.

"Hurts, don't it?"

Was that the lesson? That guns hurt? Back then, Enrique still wanted a father so badly that he reconfigured the three grammatically misgrouped words into something like wisdom. Shooting a gun hurt you, the shooter.

But it didn't hurt, really, not the recoil, which was what his father had meant. It would ache later, and the hollow of Enrique's collarbone cultured a yellow, marbleized bruise, but it didn't hurt then, out in the cold. Enrique had said "Ow" because his father had pinched the flesh of his finger against the trigger.

Enrique hadn't thought of that pointless trip to Lake Overlook once since it had taken place. That's how far back he had filed his father away in the past three years.

Now it was Lina's voice at the door: "Enrique?"

"Come in."

She entered and pressed her back against the door. Relief at having a wall between her and the man for a moment passed across her face. Then she opened her eyes, looked with pity on Enrique, and steeled herself. "Go with him," she said.

"*Ma!*"

"Go with him, and I'll tell him he has to leave tomorrow."

So Enrique went. His father stopped at the Circle-K for two cans of beer, then drove him, again, to Lake Overlook. There was a gray haze along the horizon that dissipated halfway up the sky. Above it, the moon was faintly visible, like a floury print left by a baker's finger on the steel of the sky. They pulled into the park that, according to Miriam, had given the lake its name. The evidence of hookybobbers, shiny figure-eights on the matte surface of the lake, shone like Scotch tape on paper.

"Your Uncle Enrique and me used to sneak beer outta the cooler at picnics, go hide in a dry ditch and drink 'em. He always had some trick he wanted to pull. Mean kid. He'd pull a sock over the cat's head just to see it run around crazy. Put a frog in the breadbox to scare our ma. Got beat up good for that one." With his thick, black-bordered fingernail he lifted the tab on his beer, twisted it off, and dropped it back into the hole. Then he traded cans with Enrique, did the same again, and took a long drink, which caused his Adam's apple, prickled as a bud on a cactus, to bob. "Grew outta that, though. He worked for our daddy most his life. Wish I'da done the same."

Stories of Uncle Enrique marched steadily out of the man's mouth like exhausted troops. He wanted to memorialize his brother to his brother's namesake. He wanted a warm body next to him to absorb some of his grief. But Enrique had never met his uncle and didn't care. In the past his father's silence had seemed evidence of hard experience, or secret wisdom, or manliness. Now Enrique saw that it had been evidence only of emptiness.

Why don't you just keep quiet? Enrique said in his mind.

Why don't you die?

He immediately recoiled from the words in horror, but then dared himself to face them, the way boys dared each other to hold their eyelids open with their fingertips and look at the sun—a thrill only in that it so directly disobeyed their parents and teachers. Enrique became fascinated. *Why don't you die? Maybe then we'll get some money.*

His father paused and raised the car lighter's glowing coil to the tip of a cigarette. He opened the window a crack, sent out a stream of smoke, and tapped the lighter against the rim. A couple of ashes fell off, and he plugged the lighter back into its hole. He tipped back his head and finished his beer, ashed into the can, then grunted and exhaled through his nose—a belch. "Like it?"

Enrique shook his head and offered the can. His father took it with the three fingers that were not occupied by the cigarette. "It tastes like pee," Enrique said.

Success—that pathetic expression again. If he had to endure the old man's presence, he could at least play with him a little.

Lina didn't keep her word. Jorge stayed. On Christmas Eve he gave Enrique a present, a plastic boat. "Thanks," Enrique said, as flatly as possible. Where would he play with such a thing, even if he wanted to? They had a shower, not a bathtub, and the lake was frozen.

Lina went to church Christmas afternoon. Enrique, tired of being confined to his room, came and sat at the far end of the sofa to watch TV.

"Your mother's got herself a nice place here," the old man said, nodding and looking up, as if to check the ceiling for holes. "I think it might be time."

Having barely sat down, Enrique rose, put on his hat and jacket, and took off on the bike Jay had given him.

IT SEEMED TO Jay that hours had passed since they finished Christmas dinner and sent the children to play with their new toys in the den, but still the adult Van Bekes sat around the table, talking. "I fell out of love with Reagan the moment he gave control of the Interior Department to a businessman!" Emily Van Beke said. "Reagan let snowmobilers into Yellowstone and loggers into the Boise National Forest, and you, Mom, still defend him."

Janet's eyes sparkled with delight at being so challenged. "So, are you saying, Emily, that you voted for Mondale?"

"I voted for Bergland."

"So you're a Libertarian," Emily's brother said.

"No, independent."

Janet shook her head and beamed at her husband. "Are you listening to your children? Next they'll be telling us they're Socialists!"

"Can't believe my ears," said Carl.

"Marx had some good ideas," Emily's husband said.

"Tell me," Janet said, leaning forward on her elbows, suddenly free of irony.

This was how it had been for days—endless talk. Radiation was spreading from Chernobyl; Idaho was selling water to California; Jim Bakker was making a mockery of Christianity. Every so often, someone remembered Jay and tossed him a question about the basketball season. The grandchildren, as bored as Jay, climbed their fathers like jungle gyms. Why didn't anyone propose a game of touch football or a caravan to the movie theater? Even after all his years at the Van Bekes', Jay was too shy and out of place to speak up. He would go play with the Walkman they had bought him, but he had left all his tapes at Lina's and was stuck with the faggy Bon Jovi one he had borrowed from a Van Beke grandchild.

After a lengthy discussion of Marxism, one of the sons began to complain of a neighbor down the road: "The Cransons' place is an eyesore, Dad, worse than last year. They use car engines as lawn ornaments. You should sue them."

"For what?" Carl asked.

"Anything. Inbreeding. Cruelty to guinea hens."

"That's quite enough of that talk," Janet said with a wide-eyed laugh.

It seemed that Janet and Carl had had children expressly to be given cause to widen their eyes, again and again. So why had they taken Jay? Over the years, Mrs. Van Beke sat with Jay at the kitchen table night after night, bargaining with him. "You can go outside once we've finished your times tables." Only now did he see that he was supposed to take it from there, become interested in things, and bring ideas home to Janet, the way some children brought home money. How could he ever have thought he belonged in this world when he didn't understand its most basic rules?

The doorbell rang.

Janet looked to Carl quizzically. "On Christmas?"

Carl rose and disappeared into the hallway. Everyone was quiet. Then he returned and said, "Jay, it's your brother."

"Invite him in, Carl," said Janet.

"I did. He seems a little shy."

Jay rose and went to the door. Enrique was breathing hard, each exhale a jet of steam like one from a teakettle. His face was mottled and his spherical nose-tip and round cheeks shone as if they were frozen solid. The elastic cuffs of his dirty, rainbow-striped ski jacket were pulled over his hands. The bike lay on its side on the lawn. Had Enrique ridden all the way here?

"Dad's at the house." With a boxer's hook, Enrique wiped his nose. "Mom said she would make him leave, but she didn't. He's driving me crazy."

Jay dug in his pocket. "Put your bike in the trunk. I'll be out in a minute."

Enrique's hand emerged from the sleeve to take the keys. Was it that easy?

Enrique didn't know that, after a stifling week, Jay was ready for a fight. "I'm going to spend some time at Lina's," Jay announced to the group. They all gave kind nods and sighs of approval, and Jay knew with utter certainty that he would not be missed.

The boys sped home, and Jay jogged up the walkway and entered the house the way he did the basketball court from the bench. The old man looked up from the sofa and started. "Jesús," he said, and began to lift his marionette-arms for a hug. Lina, who had returned from church, stood frozen in the kitchen holding a vibrant green head of lettuce.

"Can I have your keys?" Jay said to his father.

The man gave Jay a confused look and didn't move.

Jay picked up the ashtray. "You can't smoke here," he said. He kicked open the screen door and tossed the ashtray out onto the ground. "Keys?" He held out his hand.

Jorge bowed his head and rocked to his side. He reached into his back pocket and took out the keys. Jay snatched them from him, went outside, and started the car. Then he gathered from his room what he could find of the man's things—flannel shirts and long underwear, all of which gave off a spicy smell like smoked ham. He tossed it all onto the front seat of the Plymouth.

"You're all packed and ready," he said. "Your car's warmed up. It's time to go."

The old man did what he had that first day. The features of his face, which was bowed a little toward the coffee table, froze. He opened his mouth and gasped. Only Enrique knew that he was crying. Jay came and crouched next to him. Lina, still in the kitchen holding the lettuce, couldn't hear what Jay said, but Enrique could: "Listen, you old fuck. I will hurt you if you don't leave. Understand?"

The old man breathed again. Slowly he extended his arm and dropped his hand over the cigarette pack the way the crane at the arcade clutched stuffed animals. He rose and limped out the door. Jay closed it behind him.

"He might have a shotgun in his trunk!" Enrique said suddenly.

A jolt of laughter shook Jay's body.

"What!"

"The look on your face," Jay said.

Lina came and sat in the recliner. She no longer trusted the knife in her shaking hand.

The Plymouth slowly crawled past the doublewide toward the entrance of the trailer park.

When Lina finally built up the nerve to look at Jay, she saw that he had been watching her with something like warmth in his eyes. He looked away before he spoke: "I told Enrique"—he cleared his throat—"to say sorry. I'm sorry."

"He tol' me."

The three sat gazing at different spots on the floor. Then Lina sat up and said, "Do they deliver pizza on Christmas?"

Before bed that night, Jay found, in the corners of his room, a half-full carton of cigarettes, a balled-up pair of socks, and a tar-stained pair of coveralls. He took them all outside and dropped them into a pile next to the porch. Days later, the pile was still there, frozen to the ground, except for the cigarettes. A neighbor had taken those.

CHAPTER 18

The day before the Idaho State Science Fair, Lina insisted that Enrique come to confession. "We haven't been to church in two weeks," she said shrilly.

Enrique was slumped in front of the TV. "Who cares, Ma? We'll go on Sunday."

"Who cares? God cares!" Lina barked, half-playfully. She turned off the TV. "Let's go. We'll pray you win the science fair."

Enrique released a frustrated groan. "I don't care about the science fair," he said, rising.

"Of course you do!"

Enrique let Lina's answer stand, but, as they drove to church, he was surprised to conclude that, no, he didn't really care. In the redesign of the project, all the danger and intrigue had bled out. Now it was kids' stuff. The experiments Enrique had done on his teachers, his father, Abby, and Lina were far more fascinating. The dullest situation could become a thrill with the addition of just a little lie.

While Lina entered confession, Enrique pretended to pray, but really he was hatching a plan. A year ago, when Enrique had resigned as first altar boy, Father Moore had told Lina to watch him closely, in case he started having "adolescent difficulties." (Lina had let this slip during one of their bedtime talks, and they had both chuckled guiltily about it.) What could Father Moore have meant?

Lina tapped Enrique's shoulder. It was his turn.

"Bless me, father, for I have sinned," Enrique said, once situated in the dark confessional, which smelled vaguely of wet wool. "It's been a couple months since my last confession."

"Yes, my child," came Father Moore's weary voice. "It is good that you have come."

Enrique let a few seconds pass, then he said, "I let some of the older boys at school touch me."

After a stunned pause, Father Moore cleared his throat and said, "Touch you?"

"Yes, in the locker room. They wanted to touch me . . . down there . . . and I let them."

"Did they force you, or intimidate you?"

"No, I let them."

"This is a very serious sin, my child. You must never do it again."

That someone believed this fantasy had taken place doubled its potency, and Enrique began to be aroused, there, in the confessional. "I'll try not to."

"There'll be no trying. We are told that this behavior is an abomination to God. You must never, ever do it again."

Enrique had never heard Father Moore so flustered. "Okay."

"Do you know the Act of Contrition?"

"Yes."

"Recite it for me now."

"O my God, I am sorry and beg pardon for all my sins," Enrique began. He had always disliked the Act of Contrition. He didn't understand how *his sins* had crucified Jesus. Hadn't the Roman soldiers dressed in leather skirts done that?

When he finished, Father Moore said, "Now, I want you to repeat that when impure thoughts occur to you, my child, until they go away. And if these boys approach you again, go tell an adult. Do you understand?"

"Yes."

Father Moore hesitated and took a frustrated sigh before he said, "You are absolved."

Enrique left the confessional with his heart pounding in his ears. He adjusted his pants to hide his erection. How would Father Moore look at him from now on?

The next morning, while Enrique rode to Boise with Miriam

and Penny, Lina went to the Sheltons'. As usual, most of her employers had rescheduled over the holidays, so she would have to work a few Saturdays in January to catch up. She would work fast, though, and make it to Boise before the judging started.

Lina sprayed a shimmering blue coat of Windex onto the Sheltons' sliding glass door and, before it had a chance to collect and drip onto the carpet, wiped great frothy circles into it. Beyond the glass lay the icy planks of the deck, and the swimming pool, covered for the winter. This house was a great accordion of additions upon additions wrapped around this deck. It was hard to find the light switches, and when you did, they usually turned on a light in the next room that you didn't need.

It had been summer, Lina recalled, the first time she had cleaned the Sheltons'. After showing her the house, Mrs. Shelton had opened this sliding glass door and led her outside. ". . . And this is the pool. You can use the net to fish out the junk."

Lina stopped her. "Sorry, Mrs. Shelton, I only clean inside."

"Oh!" Mrs. Shelton said. She stiffened her spine and led Lina back in.

Cleaning swimming pools! Lina had to draw the line somewhere, or else they'd have her feeding the sheep and burning leaves.

Grains of ice, too small to call snowflakes, fell through the air, collected on the swimming-pool cover, then blew off into the yellow lawn. It hadn't yet snowed this winter, and this was no real indication that it would.

Lina remembered taking Enrique to the public pool when he was little. She enjoyed carrying him around, taking those long underwater steps, pushing off and floating before landing again, like an astronaut on the moon. She tried to convince Enrique to put his face in the water, as she had heard this was the first step toward learning how to swim. Again and again, he gasped, held his breath in puffed-out cheeks for some seconds, then exhaled through his nose. "That's right, *mijo*. Now do it in the water." But he wouldn't. "You can do it, *mi vida*! You're brave!" The expression on his sun-browned face—excitement, pride, fear, a hundred emotions at once, all while his cheeks remained inflated—made Lina laugh. Enrique responded by changing the task at hand. His goal now was to keep her laughing by making funny faces. She must have done something right for God to have given her such a boy.

He hadn't put his face in the water, not that day.

A thought struck Lina with such force that she had to sit down on the armrest of the Sheltons' sofa. *She* had never put her face in the water! When they had gone swimming in the irrigation canal near the Hacienda, she had dog-paddled with her chin so insistently thrust up that she got a kink in her neck. Of course, she hadn't told Enrique this. She let him believe that she had dunked her head, that every adult had, that it was part of growing up, and that he should, too. A flash of remorse at never having admitted this to Enrique was followed with relief: now she could. He wouldn't feel deceived, he would laugh. Again, she felt lucky, but for a different reason: her funny boy was now her friend. She would tell him tonight. It had been a while since their last bedtime talk.

In Boise, Enrique, Miriam, and Penny toured the State Science Fair.

Two boys from Pocatello had invented a machine—a robot, they called it, although it looked like a car battery on wheels—to run along train tracks, searching for cracks in the rail. When it came across one, it both marked the spot with a blob of fluorescent paint and emitted a radio blip. To demonstrate, they made room in the crowd that had gathered, lay a twelve-foot rail in the aisle, and set the robot on top. One boy flipped a switch, and the machine zipped down the rail, paused halfway down to deposit a pink spot, then zipped off the end and on down the aisle. While one boy chased it down, the other pointed to a green spot on a radar screen. "Railroad officials can now easily find and patch the break."

A team of three girls from Sandpoint—twin sisters and a cousin—had cured an algal bloom in the family pond by inventing solar-powered electrodes that floated on Styrofoam blocks. The before-and-after photos showed that the surface of the pond had turned from sickly-green foam to pristine glass mirroring the pine trees that encircled it. An accompanying video proved that the electrodes didn't harm the fish. A school of ghostly white, mustached carp placidly nibbled on bread crumbs that floated near the electrodes.

A boy-girl team from Bonner's Ferry proved with a colorful array of charts that their hens had produced more and bigger eggs after a noisy rooster, who cock-a-doodle-doo'ed every morning, was butchered. Egg production went up again after the team began playing classical music in the henhouse every afternoon. Their presentation, titled "Pity Not the Single Mother," was laced with wry double entendres, and their area, which had conveniently been placed at the end of a row near the corner of the gymnasium, became a kind of lounge where people enjoyed Chopin and snacked on deviled eggs.

Enrique, Miriam, and Penny dejectedly returned to their project to wait for the judges. Penny, who had not returned to Stockton because of unnamed family problems, had contributed a large, semicircular display—a collage of newspaper headlines ("Hundreds Mysteriously Poisoned in Cameroon"), interspersed checkerboards, and paint splatters. "What Happened?" the project's new title, was spelled in dagger-shaped letters cut from silver Mylar. This collage, Enrique now admitted sadly to himself, was the project's strong point. The model itself looked so flimsy and childish they might as well have added Fisher-Price people and a smiling paper-plate sun.

What happened?

The judges rounded the corner, and the team quickly pulled on their lab coats, each of which had their name and a paint splatter stenciled on the pocket, and took their places: Miriam in front, Enrique behind the model with tongs poised in his gloved hand, and Penny concealed behind the collage.

"Names?" said one judge, a short man with a pointed, fox-like face, reading glasses riding low on his muzzle. ANGUS PHILLIPS, PH.D., his nametag read.

Miriam gave their names.

"Project number?"

Again, Miriam answered.

Angus Phillips folded his reading glasses and tucked them in his pocket, and he and the other judges lifted their chins with smiles of forbearance.

Penny pushed PLAY, and the sound of buzzing insects and hooting monkeys emanated from behind the collage: *Sounds of the Rainforest*, a cassette they had found at the record store in the mall. Miriam began, "On August 21 seventeen hundred people died in the middle of the night . . ."

Enrique's mind wandered. Despite the Tarzan soundtrack, the project had been tamed. Without the suggestion that it could happen anywhere but Lake Nyos, lake overturn had turned from a real threat into a ghost story from across the world, conceptual and colorless as the *Twilight Zone* reruns they played Saturday mornings after cartoons.

"We suggest that the gas in question was not volcanic poison but carbon dioxide," Miriam said.

Enrique shook the soda bottle without heart and opened it at arm's length. He let his movements convey boredom—he wanted Miriam to lose. When it came time for the dry ice, the *Sounds of the Rainforest* ceased with a loud click, and the haunting minor chords of the Cure began. Enrique lowered the steaming block into the bowl. When the cascade of mist ran through the village, the palm leaves curled and their paper stalks wilted.

Angus Phillips thanked them with a quick nod, then led the judges to the next table. There were no questions.

"How are we supposed to compete," Miriam demanded over lunch, "when half of these kids are, like, millionaires?"

"I'm sure their dads built that railroad robot," Penny said.

Enrique stayed quiet.

Three acne-faced boys in cowboy shirts approached, carrying their lunch trays.

"These seats taken?" one asked.

Miriam and Penny shook their heads.

"We stayed in a hotel last night," one of the boys bragged as he stepped over the bench to sit.

"So?" Penny said.

"My mom was in a separate room. They showed rated-R movies on cable after midnight."

"*Porky's Revenge*!" said one of the others.

At this, Penny turned fully toward Miriam, as if to say something, but remained silent. Enrique quietly ate his lunch.

The boys' conversation was a loosely connected series of claims, barked over each other, undaunted by Miriam and Penny's refusal to respond:

"I'm gonna get a retainer in April. I'm only gonna wear it at night, though."

"My sister has to have rubber bands."

"I almost had to have headgear."

"You know who my uncle's best friend is, and I'm not even lying? Merle Haggard."

At this, Penny rolled her eyes at Miriam, who smiled as she dipped a fry in ketchup. As annoyed as they pretended to be with the boys' presence, they didn't tell them to get lost, or shut them out by starting a conversation with Enrique.

"You look like Cyndi Lauper," said one boy to Penny.

"You look like Howdy Doody," she replied.

The boy wouldn't be deterred. "I shot a wild boar once with a cross-bow. Killed it, too."

"You want a trophy or something?"

Enrique glanced up and saw, with relief, Lina wandering between the lunch tables, looking for him. "Ma!" he called.

Lina waved and rushed over. "Did I miss it?"

"Yeah."

Tears sprang to her eyes. "Enrique . . ." she began.

"It's no big deal."

"I got stuck at the Sheltons'."

"Really, Mom, it's okay."

"Will you show it to me?"

Enrique quickly weighed the idea of returning to the scene of his humiliation against remaining here with these boys. "Sure, let's go," he said.

When they reached the project, Lina strolled around it. Neither she nor Enrique could think of anything to say.

"What is all that?" Lina finally asked, indicating Penny's collage.

Enrique shrugged. "It's, like, artwork."

Lina couldn't help herself. "I liked it better before."

"Can we go?" Enrique said.

"Go home?"

"Yeah."

"But you don' know who won!"

"My stomach hurts. Really bad."

"Are you okay? Are you going to throw up?"

"No. I just want to go home, okay?"

"Okay, *mijo*."

They returned to the table, where one of the boys had taken Enrique's space. The girls were now surrounded.

"Miriam," Enrique said, "I'm not feeling well. My mom's gonna take me home. Do you mind just taking the project back to your house?"

"Okay," she said blankly. If there was more she wanted to say, she couldn't under the gaze of these boys.

"Thanks," Enrique said.

Enrique would next see the model months later, in Miriam's basement, littered with her little brother's toy cars.

CONNIE DROVE HOME from the nursing home under a blinding white sky, the kind of sky that could fall suddenly in big flakes that spiraled and hesitated, moving every which way in their paths to the ground—even up, as if they had second thoughts. She would have liked that, for everything to be muffled in white and frozen for later.

At home, she slipped off her white nurse's shoes and sat on the couch. Allowing her mouth to hang open, she began to massage her jaw muscles with the tips of her fingers. She tried to remember to unclench her jaw during the day, but the moment her mind strayed, it buckled back into its habitual state. On the coffee table lay the massive book she had given Gene for Christmas, *The National Geographic Society Book of the Galaxy*. It had cost $25, the most she had ever paid for a book or, for that matter, any gift. She had thought Gene would like it, and he had seemed to, on Christmas day at his grandparents' house. He had laid it open on the rag rug before the fire and studied it for hours. But as soon as they returned home, he had gone back to his drawings, maps, and charts. What was he doing?

She had never asked him. Why not? She was his mother, and she should check up on him. Aside from Christmas day, she had barely spoken to him in weeks. They ate their dinners in silence before going their separate ways. Enrique hadn't been coming over. For all Connie knew, Gene could be completely alone in the world—as alone as she.

Connie got up and tapped on one panel of the accordion door. "Can I come in?"

"Yes."

Gene sat at his desk surrounded by books. There were papers spread over his bed.

"Are you doing homework?" Connie asked.

"No, my project."

"Your science-fair project?"

"The science fair is over."

"Oh. Well, then, what project is it?"

Gene, who still hadn't fully turned toward her, gave an exasperated sigh.

"Can you show it to me? I'd like to see it."

The feet of his chair groaned as he pushed himself from the desk. The chair only went so far before it hit the bed, and Gene had to lift out his legs from under the desk. He carefully piled the papers on the bed, then set them aside. Then, from under the bed, he took a large sheet, which, unrolled, covered the bed. Connie wondered for a moment where he had gotten such a large sheet, then she saw that it was made of dozens of sheets of lined notebook paper taped together neatly. On it Gene had drawn a map of the world in black marker. Here and there across the world were circles of different sizes in red-, yellow-, and orange-colored pencil. The circles were perfect, as were the squiggling lines that separated countries. "Gene, this is very good!" Connie said.

Gene pointed to the largest, reddest circle, which covered the eastern part of Russia. "Lake Baikal is over a mile deep. It holds one-fifth of all the fresh water in the world. Its surface is twelve thousand square miles. It could hold under it enough carbon dioxide to suffocate every living thing in a five-hundred-mile radius, which would include Ulan Bator, the capital of Mongolia, population one million." He moved to another large red circle, a foot to the left. "The Caspian Sea is half as deep as Baikal, but thirteen times the surface area. It could hold enough to suffocate everyone in Tehran, definitely, possibly Kiev and Moscow, since they sit in this low-lying plane. Moscow could get it from these arctic lakes just as well. Lake Kivu"—he pointed to Africa—"is two thousand times larger than Lake Nyos. Two million people live on its shore, double that in a fifty-mile radius. It's on a fault line, and the geological record shows there's a massive biological extinction around it about every thousand years." Gene's reedy voice still showed no signs of changing. Seeming to love consonants, it parked at *k*s and spat out *t*s. "Ocean trenches don't get stirred by the currents. If they stored carbon dioxide, they could kill everyone in the world. The Mariana Trench is six miles deep. It could suffocate everyone in the Caribbean. I haven't worked out how many people that is. But if it overturned, there would be a tsunami that would wash over the islands and drown everyone anyway."

"Gene, stop it!" Connie hissed.

Gene obeyed immediately and completely, putting his arms to his sides like a tin soldier. In his face, though, there was an embattled protest.

"Do you realize what you're describing here?"

"It's my project," he said.

"You're talking about the end of the world, the Rapture. That will be decided by the Lord God, and not by lakes and gases. The end of the world is Judgment Day, Gene. That's the day we're waiting for, the day we're called home."

"The world will still exist," Gene said, "after the human race is extinct."

"Hush!" Connie said. "Who's been teaching you that? Your teachers?"

Gene was silent.

Connie's attention cast around the room, as if in search of a culprit. "All these magazines and newspapers and books I've spent my hard-earned money on—I should have known they'd give you ideas. These are wrong, sinful thoughts, Gene. Do you understand that? This is like evolution or the Big Bang theory. This is what we Christians are fighting *against*."

"The Big Bang theory will be proved by the year 2000," Gene said.

"Stop it!" Connie cried. Her eyes finally rested on Gene, and she shook her head. "Where did you come from?" she asked him.

JUST AS SHE had planned, Lina went into Enrique's room before bed that night and lay on top of the covers.

"Mom?" Enrique said after a moment.

"Yes, *mi vida*?" There was a smile in her voice, because, in gathering the words to tell him she had never dunked her head in the water, she had again remembered the funny faces he had made at the swimming pool.

"I was thinking . . . I might be getting too old for this."

"For what?"

"For you to come into my room at night."

Lina swallowed.

"We can't do it forever. Don't be sad."

Lina sat up and faced the doorway so Enrique wouldn't see the tears. She steadied her voice and said, "You're right, Enrique. You're too old." She stood and left the room.

Jay, who was watching the end of a basketball game on TV, saw that Lina's face was wet and shining as she walked through the living room to the kitchen, where she began vigorously scraping spots of food off the stovetop. A few minutes later, he saw Enrique duck into the bathroom, wiping tears from his eyes.

"*Jesus Christ*," Jay muttered to himself. He had had enough. Very loudly, he announced, "YOU BOTH CRY LIKE LITTLE GIRLS."

From opposite ends of the house came similar-sounding cries of protest: "Shut up, Jay!"

This made him laugh. As far as he could remember, it was the first good laugh he had had in this house.

Enrique and Lina both heard this laughter—a high-pitched squawk, free of any note of cruelty. As wronged as they felt at the moment, this sound would lodge in their minds. They would remember it—as would Jay—as an announcement of a new era of equilibrium in the house. It was their Armistice Day, but it would pass without celebration.

Step Five:

Analysis

CHAPTER 19

Abby sat in the Temple waiting room with a large textbook in her lap, doing a set of calculus problems, which was part of the packet of assignments she had picked up during her last trip home. Planted twenty feet apart in the gold-and-scarlet patterned carpet were two brilliant white columns, which rose high and divided into four angels whose wings lay flush against the vaulted ceiling. Clusters of impossibly green plants stood here and there among the seats. For a break between problems Abby looked up to gaze through the window, past a lawn, to the gift shop entrance in the visitors' center. Here, she mused, sturdy Mormons from around the globe wasted their money on cards printed with the Temple's famous spires, tiny burlap bags of salt from the Great Salt Lake, CDs of the Tabernacle Choir, and pocket-sized, leather-bound Books of Mormon.

A woman gently approached and tapped Abby on the shoulder. Abby took off the Walkman headphones she had been wearing to drown out the inspirational video they were playing on TV.

"I thought you might be able to use this." It was the grandmotherly woman with thick arms who sat behind the desk, and she offered a folded TV table. She wore white loafers—nursing shoes, which seemed appropriate, because Abby had classified her with all those other secretaries and nurses, the annoyingly kind women with whom she dealt at her mother's various appointments.

"Thank you," said Abby. She slid her homework onto the next seat and stood.

"Oh, you sit back down. I'll set you up." The woman popped the table open and placed it squarely in front of Abby. It wobbled, so she kicked gently at one of the legs. "I've noticed you doing your homework here every time you come. Then yesterday I came across this in the staff room and I thought, 'That young lady could use this.' That's a little better," she said, pushing the table's feet deep into the carpet.

"That's a big help. Thanks."

"You know, your mother is doing sacred work of the Lord that will bring her many blessings."

"Uh-huh," Abby said.

The shortness of the answer seemed to jar the woman. "I mean, some work for the dead—marriage by proxy, for instance—can only be done by members of the priesthood. And most of them don't have time to come to the Temple regularly. We appreciate it."

"Thank you."

"Is your mom . . . all right? It looks like she might be going through some kind of treatment."

"Yes. She's in chemotherapy. And radiation."

The woman nodded. "Well, I sure hope she gets better."

Abby nodded. Then a voice inside said, *Why coddle this woman?* Was it Liz's voice? Not really. Liz might have said the woman should mind her own business. Not to her face, but once she went back behind the counter. It was more Abby herself, the side of her that had grown weary of well-wishers, that prodded her to say, "Actually, she won't. She won't get better." When the woman's eyes widened, Abby added, "Sorry, I just don't see the point in pretending."

The woman nodded and heaved a great sigh, which, at its crest, caught a little in a sob. "I didn't mean to be nosy," she said, and she turned to go. Then she stopped and said, "I lost my husband . . ." She let a few nods of the head complete the story, because she couldn't speak.

Abby softened. "Thanks for the table." She lifted her books and papers onto it. "It helps."

"What's your name?" the woman asked.

"Abby."

"I'm Sister Weller. I'll be praying for you and your mother, Abby."

Abby finished her calculus and moved on to *Crime and Punishment*, which she was reading for advanced-placement English. She made a point of resting the book on the TV table, in case Sister Weller happened to see, all the while chiding herself for being so Mormon, so ingratiating, about it. Then she heard her mother approach—heard her before she saw her: the wheels of the dolly on which she kept the miniature oxygen tank, then the hiss of the air.

"All done?" Abby asked.

"All done."

Her mother's wig was too low over the brow, as it always was when she put it on herself. Abby would fix it once they got to the car. Sandra steadied herself against the back of a chair while Abby put her books into her backpack. When they approached the desk, Sister Weller smiled bashfully and looked down to the appointment book, as if what she and Abby had discussed was secret. "Would you like to come again next Wednesday?" she asked.

Abby spread her own appointment book on the counter. "No, she has an appointment that morning. How about Monday?"

"We're all full on Monday," Sister Weller said. "Tuesday?"

"Another appointment."

"Thursday?"

"No. She's not usually able to come here . . . the day after."

"Maybe I won't come next week," Sandra said. Her voice had a wheezy groan to it, like a badly played clarinet.

"Nope," said Sister Weller with finality. "Monday it is."

"Are you sure?" Abby asked.

"If Monday's the day you *can* come, Monday's the day you *will* come. Ten a.m. okay?" Sister Weller's tone said there would be no more talking about it, and hinted at the strings she'd have to pull, but the tilt of her head and the set of her lips asked for no thanks.

JAY WAS NO good at baseball and didn't like it, but he joined the team anyway, only to avoid a season of empty afternoons. The dreariness of the sport and the way games seemed to drag was given perfect expression by Mr. Shepherd, the sixty-something-year-old coach, when he nodded off in the dugout, arms folded over his belly, chin nestled into the roll of fat that insulated his neck. If a boy tickled the old man's nostril with a straw, he'd snuffle and brush it away without opening his eyes. Jay would have joined Winston and their gang, who had enlisted in a boxing league in Chandler, but he couldn't afford the fee.

He had done what he could to banish Liz from his mind after that afternoon at the Rollerdrome. Being the hero of basketball season had helped. But now, as he stood in the outfield with nothing to contemplate but the white scuffmarks on the cobalt sky, she sneaked back in.

At a pep rally last year, they and several other classmates had been called down to take part in a silly race which consisted of lying in a row on the gym floor and passing a stuffed animal—lion, Eula's mascot—down the line using only their bare feet. Liz had been placed next to Jay. He remembered the U-shaped gap between her big toe and the next, her laughter, her shoulder pressed against his. When he passed the stuffed animal to her, a braided friendship bracelet fell from the place on her ankle where it usually lay, exposing a line of raw white in her golden skin. This was the color she must be under her clothes. She dropped the lion, and he jabbed her playfully. She jabbed him back.

To lie on his back next to Liz—in the grass under the stars, on the carpet before her TV, in bed . . . He had to stop imagining it, the longing was so painful.

Jay now insisted to himself that if she had smiled when she read his note at the Rollerdrome, if a dreamy look of reminiscence had come to her eye and she had held the note to her heart, then he would have left the Frogger game and taken her into his arms. He would have been that bold. Maybe they needed no words after the ones in the note. Things in life could be just that simple and easy—in fact, they *had* to be, when two people felt the same way. But she had crumpled the note. Jay had found excuses not to go to Winston's after school so many times that the claim he made to Liz on the day he gave her a ride home—that he and Winston were "growing apart"—had come true.

The only way to combat this terrible longing was to do it again. Jay skipped lunch to strut casually into the library and down one of the aisles back to the wobbly old aluminum table that kept its wings at its sides, leaving only enough room on its top for the typewriter. His typewriter. Jay was sure he was the only one who used it. Beyond the small, circular keys, through the machine's innards, he could see the surface of the table.

He took a sheet from his bag, fed it behind the roller, and cranked. Then he typed only one word: "Disappointed?"

WANDA LAY ON the metal table, naked from the waist down and covered with a paper sheet. As a nurse helped her get her feet into the stirrups, Dr. Edwards squatted onto a stool and rolled out of view behind the skirt. "This is the only bad part," he said as he eased in the speculum's cold, metal bill. Wanda bristled with goose bumps. Then, with a few rapid clicks, Dr. Edwards pried her open.

"Too fast!" Wanda gasped. This machine could rip her.

"I know, I'm sorry," Dr. Edwards said.

Wanda knew that minutes before, in another room, Randy had collected his sample and now Dr. Edwards had it there behind the skirt, in a plastic cup on a tray, most likely.

Both *collect* and *sample* seemed the wrong words. The former called to mind a boy collecting stamps or a girl collecting flowers; the latter made Wanda think of toothpicks standing in bright orange cubes at the supermarket: *Sharp Cheddar.* "I'd prefer it if *you* collected my sample, Mel," Randy had joked at the dinner table the night before. He had removed his glasses for emphasis, O'ed his lips, and exhaled a coat of steam onto one lens. Then the glasses disappeared under the table, and his hand worked invisibly with a shirttail to clean the lens.

"I will if they let me," Melissa had replied, never one to be cowed by a dirty joke. "Should I bring the Tiger Balm?"

"The what?" Wanda had said.

"Nothing," Randy had said, blushing.

Now there was a brief tinkle of instruments behind the sheet and, with a snap that again made Wanda gasp, the speculum was released. Dr. Edwards pushed a cloth against her privates. "Try to keep this in place as you take your feet down now," he said.

"Did you do it?"

"Yes, all done."

"That was quick."

Still on his stool, Dr. Edwards whizzed to her side. His head hung low between his hunched shoulders, not, it seemed, from poor posture as much as from an attempt to shrink into himself and seem benign. He wore sandals with socks, and his dimly lit office down the hall was decorated with ragged South American tapestries. "Women always say that. I suppose we're all used to a little more fireworks surrounding conception, but if you think about it, fertilization itself is a very simple occurrence." Dr. Edwards emphasized important words with a smile of wonderment, as if reproduction still made him marvel after decades in the business. "Two cells coming together." He held up two fists and folded them into one. "Very small, very quiet. Let's hope it worked."

"Would you like Mrs. Weston-Sloane to come in?" the nurse asked.

"Oh, yes." Wanda tucked the paper skirt around her legs.

"I'd like you to stay on your back for a few minutes, if you don't mind," Dr. Edwards went on. "There's no proof it helps to let it sink in, but it certainly can't hurt."

He left the room, and Melissa came in. "How do you feel?" she asked, taking Wanda's hand.

"Fine. It was nothing."

"Randy had to go back to the shop, so it's just you and me. Ready to be lazy?"

Melissa waited on Wanda for the rest of the day, allowing her to rise only to go to the bathroom. It was fun, like a grade-school sick day, but without having to endure (or feign) illness. Wanda watched movies on the videocassette player with Simon, the L-tailed dog, wedged beside her. She didn't have a VCR of her own, and still could hardly believe she could watch anything she wanted without having to wait for it to come on the Sunday Night Movie. When Randy came home, he teased Melissa, saying that she was subjecting Wanda to the "rest-cure" (whatever that was) and that she should allow her to take a twilight walk in the woods. To this, Melissa dryly responded: "It's half-medical—she has a better chance of getting pregnant if she sits still—and half-superstition. Oh, and half just for the fun of it."

"Yeah!" Wanda agreed.

"That's three halves," Randy said, winking at Wanda. There was a little bit of effort behind this joking; it was the tiniest bit forced. But Wanda knew they were trying to let her know that they really did forgive her, and like her, and trust her. She appreciated it.

Randy and Melissa went to get dinner on, leaving Wanda in complete comfort. She rested her hands on her belly, closed her eyes, and visualized those two cells uniting in her.

THAT NIGHT, ABBY told Liz over the phone, "I draw out my homework. I take longer than I need to because I'm afraid to run out."

"Because then you'll be bored?" Liz guessed.

"I'll be bored, and I'll be *all theirs*. No escape. They all tell me I work too hard."

"Shit."

"And when I think of the people, other than you, who I wish were here with me, I think of my mom—my *old* mom, before she got all churchy, back when she was mean and funny."

"I liked her that way, too," Liz said.

"Sure you did. Who wants a Mormon mom who hesitates to take pain pills because of the caffeine? She feels guilty about *all* her medications! And I can't help but feel like, if she stayed the old mom, she wouldn't be dying. But she became this way because she *is* dying. My thinking is all backward, but I can't help it."

As often happened on these phone calls when Abby inadvertently crossed a boundary, there was a rustling on the other end, Liz fiddling with the things around her bed—the tarot cards she had bought at a yard sale, perhaps, or the matryoshka dolls, egg women within egg women. It wasn't selfishness, it was fear, so Abby didn't mind.

"Anyway," Abby said. "What's new in Idaho?"

Liz gave a derisive snort of laughter. "Nothing, naturally. My secret admirer is back."

"The one from months ago?"

"Yep."

Abby's grandfather called from downstairs.

"*God*," Abby said, "they're so helpless. I can't have an hour to myself. *What is it, Grandpa?*"

"Could you come down? Yer ma's askin' for ya."

"*Coming!* Well, I guess I have to go."

"All right, Abby. Don't let them get you down. Come home soon. I love you."

This was something new: Liz ended every call since Abby had been coming down to Salt Lake by telling her that she loved her. It embarrassed Abby a little, even as it overwhelmed her with gratitude. "Love you, too. Talk tomorrow?"

"Sure."

Abby ran down the narrow staircase.

"I gave her two doses of morphine," said Grandpa Nelson, "one an hour ago and one just now, but she's still in pain."

Sandra sat in the easy chair. One arm supported her curled body against the armrest, the hand clutching her brow.

Abby knelt in front of her. "What hurts, Mom?"

It seemed to take a great effort to release her clamped lips. "My leg. All the way up."

"Did I give you your afternoon codeine? Did I forget?" Abby leaped up and went to the bureau where she kept the box that divided her mother's medication into doses by the hour. When she looked at today's, Thursday's, she saw both the ten a.m. and two p.m. codeine pills wobbling in their compartments like tiny yellow eggs. "Oh my God!" Abby cried. She picked one up and rushed to her mother. "I didn't give you this morning's either. You haven't had any today. No wonder you're in pain."

Abby's grandmother handed Sandra a glass of water and steadied it as Sandra swallowed the pill with a wince.

"Mom, I'm so sorry." Abby buried her face in her mother's lap.

"Hush, Abby. It's all right. I'm fine."

"It's so much, for a girl," Grandma Nelson said, laying her hand on Abby's shoulder.

". . . and all that homework," Grandpa Nelson added.

Abby stayed there for a while, letting her grandparents believe she was crying. In her mother's lap, Abby smelled baby powder, the smell of her old mother, her hard-jawed, bloodshot mother who was so stingy with hugs but whom Abby loved. When Abby sat up, her grandparents were gone.

"See?" Sandra said with a wan smile. "It's already kicking in. I feel better."

"Do you?" Abby reached up and gently hooked the hose, which had come loose, back over her mother's ear.

Sandra nodded slowly. "Don't be hard on yourself, Abby. You'll need . . . yourself—"

Abby smiled teasingly, and her mother responded with a faint roll of her eyes. Despite the circumstances, it was funny to see her mother, who all her life had been so precise with words, muddled by painkillers.

"Who's sleeping in the living room tonight?" Sandra asked.

"It's Grandma's turn."

"Oh." Her mother asked this question every evening and was disappointed if it was anyone but Abby. "Have you done your homework?"

"Yes."

"Would you read to me?"

"Sure." Abby went through the pile beside the chair and held up the copy of *Vogue* she had brought from home. Sandra had always kept up her subscription to the magazine, whisking it from the mail pile up to her bedroom, where she could read it in private. She had done her mission in New York City and, Abby suspected, *Vogue* was her way of keeping an eye on that frivolous, far-off, beautiful world. Abby offered it now half in jest, half hoping her mother would break down and let her read some bit of fluff that didn't have to do with the Fruits of the Spirit or the Word of Wisdom.

But Sandra shook her head and said, "The Bible, please."

The next morning, Connie went to her parents' house a few miles out of town to clean. She did this every spring. She used a stiff dead sunflower to clear the spiderwebs from the porch and the arbor and the garden shed. She didn't want to kill the spiders or muss the dust broom. She threw the old flower, now bound and cocoonish, over the fence into the field that had once been theirs. The breeze carried away some strands, up to the white sky, where they disappeared. About half the sky was covered in clouds, or not clouds, really, but a shroud that reduced the sun to a glow. Mid-sky, this cover was rent, leaving some fibrous trails, then the sky was blue to the horizon, and populated by bright, bulbous clouds, the kind Gene called "cauliflower clouds"—or had until the day when Connie pointed and said, "Look, Genie, a cauliflower cloud," and he had answered, flatly: "Cumulus."

She mended a broken plank in the fence with some wire and swept the walkways. All these chores she did mechanically, just as she had mechanically gone to work and made dinner in the past months. Her spine was stiff and resolute, the contents of her chest scooped up and underpinned with her shoulder blades. She hadn't taken a deep breath since Bill's departure.

She went inside for lunch. Connie's father was nearly deaf and answered any attempt at conversation with an annoyed "Whuh?" as he raised his arm to a right angle and twisted the dial of his hearing aid with his blunt fingertip—a gesture paradoxically close to that of plugging his ear. *This better be worth it*, his sneer seemed to say. Rather than sit at the table, where her father examined the spread-out newspaper with a magnifying glass, Connie stood at the sink, where her mother was polishing silver and talking about something from the news, and ate some chicken salad straight from the Tupperware container.

"I think that Jessica Hahn is a demon sent from the Devil to destroy a wonderful ministry."

"Who?" Connie asked.

"Jessica Hahn, that woman that's saying all those awful lies about Jim Bakker. I don't know if someone's paying her to do it, or if it's just out of pure evil. I'm just praying she'll take it all back and they'll put Jim back on the air."

"Oh, Mother, I wish you wouldn't watch all that."

"Why shouldn't I? It's Christian programming."

"You don't send them money, do you?"

"I tell her not to," grumbled Connie's father.

Connie's mother said nothing, but fiercely polished a spoon.

"He rides in a Rolls-Royce, you know," Connie said. "It's vanity."

"He speaks the word of God," her mother said with finality.

Connie was quiet for a while, raking gently through the salad, looking for pieces of white meat. Then she said, "I was wondering, Mom . . . I might need to go away. Could you maybe take Gene for a few days?" She said this as if it were something reasonable to ask, as if her mother took care of Gene all the time. Connie had been planning it all morning.

"Oh," her mother said, and waited, it seemed, for Connie to qualify the request or take it back. After a few seconds she said, "No, sweetheart, I don't think we could."

"Why?" Connie asked.

"We're too old. It would drive your father crazy to have a little one running around."

"Gene's not little anymore, Mom. He doesn't run around, he keeps to himself. He's very little trouble."

Her mother sighed. "I'm sure you could get someone at the church to help you."

In the silence that followed, Connie wondered if all children taught their parents how to treat them, as Gene had her. If so, then Connie had taught this woman to act always in her own best interest, as if there were no other option. She had allowed her mother to drop neat little gates between them, plotting out her own comfortable space, never considering how it might confine Connie and make her less free.

"Wind's picked up," her mother said.

"Yes," Connie said, looking up from the salad. "Good thing I did all the outside chores this morning."

"My eyesight is so bad, sometimes I think I see men in those trees."

Connie looked where her mother was looking and saw that the trees around the ditch were thick, their trunks barely visible in the darkened gaps in the canopy. The wind caused man-sized shadows to shift and sway. "We should get your eyes looked at," Connie said. This response seemed inadequate next to the frightening idea of backyard phantoms.

Her mother took off her glasses and gave them an exasperated look, as if they should just clean up their act and work right.

Connie went upstairs and dusted the high shelves her mother could no longer reach, cleaned under the sink in the bathroom, and hung a couple of plaques her mother had bought at a craft fair.

Where was Eugene? Where had her husband gone? She had asked herself that again and again in the time after Bill left, until the question became a mental tic. Where was he? She'd never be free unless she knew. The fact that she had started her search, she had gone to the library and looked up all those Kansas City Andersons because she had imagined she could marry Bill and work with him in Africa . . . this fact was something she chose to forget. Now the simple question was, where had her husband gone?

This naturally led to imagined scenarios of finding him. She would find his brother in Fresno, who would lead her to the sunny hillside cemetery where he was buried. Or she would find Gene himself confined in the psychiatric ward of a Kansas City hospital, rocking in a chair and muttering. *Eugene?* He would regard her with fearful, unrecognizing eyes, and she would lift him, as she did her charges at the nursing home, and take him out for a walk around the grounds. Or she would find him, overweight and alone in the bleak glow of a television, smelling of whiskey and neglected laundry.

Or she would find him in a blue suit, a little wider at the middle and grayer at the crown, selling insurance from an office in a tall building. She would ride up in an elevator. He would be speechless.

Goodness, Connie, I— I don't know what to say. Well, let me start with this: I'm awfully sorry. How is little Gene? Connie, would you consider coming over for dinner tonight? I mean, only if you're comfortable. I'd like you to meet my children. My other *children.*

And though this scenario caused a pang or two—how could he be kind and respectable and still the same man who had abandoned her?—it had an advantage over the other scenarios. After dinner, when the children had been sent off to do their homework, Connie would linger at the table with Eugene and his wife, a solemn woman who might have a lame arm or one leg shorter than the other, and Eugene would say, *Connie, I wonder if . . . No, it's crazy. You'd never . . .*

I'd never what, Eugene?

I wonder if you might let Gene come down here, for a visit, or perhaps an extended period, the summer maybe, so we could get acquainted. I know I'm probably overstepping a boundary, but if there was any way that I could prove myself a father, and make up for all those years . . .

Connie would refuse, of course. *Eugene, you can't just pick up with a boy after . . . You're a stranger to him . . . What makes you think . . .*

But then it would happen. A summer.

Without even meaning to, really, Connie had set a plan in motion. She responded to the Christmas card sent by Tess of Kansas City, a member of the prayer-chain letter, "I've been thinking of coming through Kansas City in the spring. I'd love to meet you face-to-face after all these years." It was only an offhanded remark, a friendly gesture really. But then Tess's response had been immediate: she would be delighted to meet Connie; in fact, Connie mustn't *think* of staying anywhere but with Tess, who had a little apartment above the garage, where Connie could stay as short or long as she wished, and Kansas City was beautiful in the spring, and Connie should just let Tess know when she was on her way.

After such a deluge of benevolence, Connie would feel bad *not* going.

Connie went to her old bedroom and sat on her bed. A child's bed, it was low to the ground and as comfortable to sit on as a couch. After Connie married and moved out, her mother had made this her sewing room, and then, with the first touches of Parkinson's years later, her hands had become too shaky to sew. So, now this room was a little graveyard of her parents' hobbies—the sewing machine, the lathe, the loom; all under dust cloths. The house responded to a wind gust with a few creaks and taps. When Connie was about eight, there had been a windstorm so strong that she had hidden under the covers waiting for the house to be picked up and spun around like Dorothy's in *The Wizard of Oz*. The house hadn't been picked up, but it had shifted, and across the room a gap had opened up between the ceiling and the wall, and some black dirt had rained down on Connie's desk and bureau. Close examination the morning after showed the dirt to be made mostly of the broken bodies of dead bugs. The thought still gave her the shivers.

Connie glanced at the Jesus portrait, whose eyes she had been avoiding, and felt that spark of emotion that she sometimes allowed herself, a split-second flash of something huge, like a glint of sun through the trees. The bond she had felt with Bill was more than she felt with Gene or with Christ. It was the strongest thing she had ever felt, and it wasn't real. He was a false prophet. She only allowed herself a peek through squinted eyes, and even that was dangerous.

Driving home that evening, she wished she could have an appointment with Reverend McNally and discuss some theological point with him, just to ground herself—to reason something out with him to prove that she was still reasonable. But she couldn't, not after what had happened last winter. She felt a deep cringe in the center of her belly, she was so ashamed of what had happened on the Deals' lawn the night of the progressive dinner. Ed had wanted to tell her that Bill was getting married, and Connie, vain and stupid as she was, had thought Ed was jealous. A married man, a minister, jealous. Thank God Connie had had no confidante. As it was, she could still look everyone in the eye as if the whole thing had never happened.

WHEN COOP PICKED Wanda up at the Greyhound station that evening, Wanda said, "I'm starved. Do you want to drop by Denny's on the way home? My treat."

Coop turned slowly to her with a brow full of wrinkles. The usual stretch of his smile slackened into something more natural: surprise. He inhaled to say something—something teasing, Wanda could tell by the twinkle in his eye—then stopped himself. "Sure," he said simply.

A hot blast greeted them when they hauled open the heavy glass-paned door of the restaurant. The hostess, a hefty woman whom Coop knew well, seemed to get the idea that this was a special night.

She deposited Coop and Wanda in a booth and left them alone. Gina, too busy to flirt, marked them as special customers only by dropping her voice an octave when taking their order, from the syrupy soprano she used with other tables to her regular smoker's rasp. Maybe she would tease Coop tomorrow about being taken out by his little sister, but Wanda didn't mind. Time spent with Randy and Melissa made Wanda realize that Coop was the one person in her life worth loving. When Melissa had said, on that beautiful evening on the mountainside, "It's forever," she had made Wanda yearn to say that about someone, even if it was her brother, or a friend, or them, the Weston-Sloanes.

"Order surf and turf if you want," Wanda told Coop. "I want to thank you for helping me out."

The line of Coop's smile lengthened with sincere emotion, his lips disappearing into his mouth.

Sunday night, Sandra was so racked by waves of pain that she was up twice, vomiting, and in the morning her breath was so shallow that Abby called to push up the appointment to have her lungs tapped. Every Tuesday for months now they had inserted a needle through Sandra's back and drained a week's worth of fluid. To ask for a Monday appointment seemed to Abby a failing, not on the part of her mother but herself.

She had given her mother a bedtime-size dose of morphine in the morning (another failure), so she assumed her mother wouldn't be fully aware of what she discussed with her grandfather: "I'm going to call the Temple and cancel her appointment. Then I'll take her to the hospital to get her lungs tapped."

"I'll come along, keep you company," said Grandpa Nelson.

But then Abby glanced down at her mother and saw that she was shaking her head miserably, squeezing her mouth and eyes. It often happened that when they least suspected she was aware, she was listening, and when she seemed alert, she was really far away.

"Mom," said Abby, crouching down beside her, "you're in no shape to go to the Temple. I'm sorry. Maybe next week."

Sandra's eyes looked away and filled with tears, and her hand fluttered up to tug for solace at the garment of the holy priesthood, which showed from under her nightgown. Abby could see that, for her mother, to miss an appointment at the Temple was to give in to death.

"I'm sorry, Mom, but we don't have much choice. Maybe I could go in. Maybe they'd let me take your place."

"Would they?" Sandra asked.

"I'll see. Would that make you feel better, Mom?"

Sandra nodded.

"What will I have to do? Look up the names of dead people?"

"No, no, they've done that already. They have lists."

"Do I have to wear anything special?"

"They have the robes there."

"Well, I'll see if they let me, okay, Mom? You go to the hospital."

Again, Sandra nodded.

Grandpa Nelson followed Abby to the kitchen, where she picked up the keys to the second car. "Abby, sweetheart," he said, "I'm afraid they're not gonna let you do this. She's been endowed. She is a member of the priesthood. It takes work."

"Well, it won't hurt to try, will it?"

"And I don't know where I'm supposed to take her."

"To radiology, at the hospital. The same as always."

"Could ya help me get her out to the car?"

"I have to go or I'll be late. Where is Grandma? She can help you. You both should go anyway." Abby's grandfather kicked at the floor, a childish gesture of fear and shame at being afraid. For only the third time, Abby allowed herself to snap at him. (She had to limit herself; both he and Grandma Nelson were so inept and apologetic it could easily become a habit.) "*God*, Grandpa," she said. "You're not going to *break* her."

Abby knew that, to become endowed, Sandra had had to get a Temple recommend from the bishop of their home ward, and to get this, she and the church had to be "reconciled." This was accomplished through a couple of meetings and a large offering on the part of Abby's dad—to catch up on many years of missed tithes. Then followed hours of secret meetings at the Temple, while Abby sat in the waiting room doing homework. Now elders dropped by the house now and then, to "lay hands" on Sandra. Abby retreated to her bedroom during these visits.

It was a dazzling afternoon, and Temple Square was alive with tour groups, teenagers with their bag lunches, lawns bordered by banks of tulips. Once inside the Temple, Abby was glad to see that same woman, Sister Weller, behind the desk.

"Hello, Abby. Is everything all right?"

"Well, no. Not really. My mom's not doing so well, and she was really upset to miss her appointment. So I told her—I'd like to take her place, if that's allowed."

Sister Weller took off her glasses and let them hang from a cord around her neck that was decorated with bobbles. Her hair was a perfectly symmetrical, perfectly white arrangement of ripples and curls, like one tier of a wedding cake. "Your mother's been doing very holy work for the dead. Do you have a Temple recommend?"

"No."

"Well, Abby, under normal circumstances I'd have to turn you down. But these aren't normal circumstances, are they? I'll try to track down the bishop and have a chat with him."

"Thank you."

"In the meantime, I'll have you wait inside. Follow me."

Sister Weller led Abby through a glass door into a second, smaller waiting room. "I'll be just a minute," Sister Weller said, and Abby was alone. In the corner of the room stood two shoe racks. One was neatly lined with white slippers, the other covered in a jumble of street shoes. A video was playing from a monitor suspended from the ceiling.

". . . but what if the Bible is only *half* the story? Evidence exists that Christ reappeared in South America *after* his resurrection to minister to Indian tribes. You can read about these teachings in the Book of Mormon . . ." The video showed a depiction of Christ surrounded by brown people in robes and loincloths, which faded to Christ holding a little boy in his lap. The boy had stripes of red paint on his face. She had seen this before, either as a TV commercial or on the film strips they showed in Sunday school when she was little.

A glass door at the far end of the room swung open, and a large man wearing a white suit and white slippers entered. He was not only wide but tall—a mountain of a man, whose little glasses with round, black rims seemed a small attempt at combating the blinding largeness of his form, his wide lapels, and his fat white tie. "Are you Abby Hall?" he asked.

"Yes."

"I'm Bishop Helman. I've met your mother several times. Sister Weller tells me she's not feeling well today."

"That's right. She was very upset that she couldn't make her appointment."

"I'm sorry to hear that. Do you think she'll be able to return next week?"

"I hope so."

The bishop sat down in the chair next to Abby's, causing it to squeak and groan. "Your mother has been doing different types of work for the dead. Some of it is very sensitive, things we don't let teenagers do, even if they're in good standing with the church. But she's also been in several times for baptisms. Your friend Sister Weller seems to think that this is a ceremony where you could stand in for your mother. Is that your wish?"

"Yes."

"It is church law that, to enter the sacred precincts of the Temple, you must have a Temple recommend from home. I understand that you don't."

Abby nodded.

The bishop folded his hands on one broad thigh and nodded for a while. "This is very unusual, Abby, so, first of all, I need you to assure me that you'll keep all of this secret."

"Of course—"

"Not just in the normal way. I'm sure you've noticed your mother never talks about what goes on inside the Temple. But more than that. I have the power to issue you a Temple recommend. However, it's highly unusual that I would do so after a short chat. I'd rather not be called upon to defend my actions. Do you understand?"

"Yes."

"Abby, have you accepted Christ as your Lord and Savior, and do you have a firm testimony of the restored gospel?"

"Yes." Abby had accepted Jesus one night at Camp Gabriel with the warmth of the campfire on her back, sparks in the air, all the children's eyes aglow.

"Have you been baptized?"

"Yes." This she had done at the Ward House in Eula when she was eleven, shortly before her family stopped attending regularly. She had worn a tight, itchy jumpsuit, and Elder Robinson had shown her how to plug her nose as he supported her head before dunking her swiftly in the lukewarm water.

"Do you live the law of chastity?"

"Yes."

"Are you right with the church?"

"What do you mean?"

"Do you attend your church back in Idaho, and do you tithe?"

Abby lied—here in the Temple, to a bishop: "Yes."

The bishop gave her a hard look.

"Well, I don't tithe, really, because I don't make any money. But my dad gave a big offering not long ago, for my mom to get her Temple recommend." She would tell Liz tonight, and Liz would give a big, whooping laugh ("You're going to hell for sure now!"), and then Abby wouldn't feel so bad about it.

The bishop sat back in his chair to another chorus of squeaks. "Sister Weller is much more than a secretary or a receptionist. She is a member of the priesthood herself, a faithful member of the Relief Society, and has worked in the church far longer than I have. She's been my conscience on several occasions over the years, and sometimes I think she is an angel. Through her, I feel God calling me to do this for you and for your mother. So . . ." The bishop leaned forward again, took a breath, and smiled. "Bow your head," he said. He laid his hand on the part of Abby's hair and murmured a blessing.

Abby closed her eyes and folded her hands the way she had seen her mother do on that day a few weeks ago. Abby's hunger had overcome her desire to stay hidden, and she had darted through the parlor to the kitchen, keeping her eyes low to avoid the church elders' bleary, inviting smiles.

Then the bishop took his hand away. "Well, young lady, that is the quickest sanctification I've ever performed." From a pocket inside his suit, he took a pen and what looked like a business card.

"Abby Hall, is it?" he said, filling in lines on the card. "Your Temple recommend. Keep it safe. It's good for a year. And please don't go flashing it around your home ward. Now, if you'll put on a pair of temple shoes, we can get started."

Abby stepped out of her sneakers and found a pair of slippers marked 6 inside the heel. She followed the bishop down a long, white hallway, hung with paintings of scenes from the Bible.

This trip to the Temple had, at first, seemed a convenient escape from her grandparents and from spending another long morning at the hospital. Then, when she got here, it had turned into a chore. She had hoped they wouldn't let her in. But now Abby felt a thrill of fear and mystery. She passed a group of people wearing slippers and formal suits and dresses with white, shimmering togas draped over one shoulder, then cinched at the waist. They nodded respectfully to the bishop as they passed. The men wore hats made of white paper, like short-order cooks, and the women wore miniature bridal veils, thrown back. Abby bit her lip to keep from laughing. The people looked so silly, and she was so nervous.

"Here is your dressing room," said the bishop. He opened a door, flipped a switch, and a fluorescent light flickered, then bleakly glowed, revealing a couch, a mirror, a stack of fluffy white towels, and a row of robes covered in dry-cleaner's cellophane hanging on a rack. "Most people bring a change of clothes. The robes are designed to keep you dry underneath, but I'm afraid they don't always work. Go ahead and put one on, and I'll meet you on the other side." He nodded at a door on the opposite side of the room.

When she was alone, Abby took a robe off the rack and tore off the cellophane. She couldn't walk through Temple Square, then drive home in wet clothes. She hadn't even brought a bag to put her underwear in if it got wet. So, with another profane thrill, she slipped out of all of her clothes and pulled the cold, stiff plastic robe up over her naked body. It was a jumpsuit, really, with Velcro at the wrists, ankles, and collar. She cinched and fastened each cuff hard, but she could see that this would never keep her completely dry.

When Abby was a girl, she had had a farmer-girl doll who wore overalls and a gingham shirt. You weren't supposed to undress her, but Abby had anyway, ripping apart the stitches of the doll's clothing. She wanted to see the doll's private parts, but was disappointed to see that the body revealed was made of soft cotton up to the neck and down to the wrists and ankles. Only her head, hands, and feet were pink porcelain. This was just how Abby now appeared to herself in the mirror.

She opened the door and entered the baptistry.

She was surprised at the size of the room. It was nearly as big as a gymnasium, with white tiles covering the floor and walls, and one vast domed skylight lighting the room from above. It smelled of chlorine with a hint of mildew underneath. To Abby's right was a long marble bench, which held six teenage boys, sitting on their hands, whispering to each other and curling their bare feet against the cold tile floor. Smiling demurely, Abby took an empty spot at the end of the bench. Most of the room was taken up by a huge baptismal font. Its base was made of stiff-legged life-sized oxen with bored looks on their faces, made from the same white stone as the goblet-shaped pool. Two great, sweeping staircases led to a catwalk from which a teenage boy was just now descending into the pool. A white-haired man helped the boy down the last steps, then said some words, which Abby couldn't make out for all the echoes. The man put one hand to the back of the boy's head, and one to the wrist of the hand with which the boy plugged his nose. The man said some more words, and swiftly dunked the boy. The room was suddenly filled with the tinkling, questioning notes of water—the cozy music of indoor swimming in the winter. The boy wiped his eyes and blinked. Then the man said some more words and dunked the boy again.

Abby's guts hardened, and she shuddered. There was something so violent about this, so calculated and cruel, like an execution. She didn't pity the boy or fear for herself, she was angry: Had they been doing this week after week to her mother? How had she been able to handle it? Abby had once gone in while her mother had her lungs tapped, and the doctor had shown her, on a blurred sonogram screen, how full her lungs were, how she was breathing only with that iceberg-tip of lung space—how she was drowning.

The bishop, who was suddenly beside her, must have seen the horror in her face. "With your mother," he said, "we go very slowly."

Abby nodded.

The bishop addressed the boys: "I hope you all will understand if I take this young lady in before you. She's got to get back to her mother, who isn't well."

The boys shrugged and nodded.

"Follow me."

The bishop wore the same jumpsuit Abby did, but huge. He looked like a star-shaped Mylar birthday balloon, partly deflated, as he crinklingly led Abby up the staircase. The boy was just climbing up the stairs out of the font. His bottom eyelids were red and there was spit on his chin. "Elder Lowell," the bishop said to the white-haired man in the pool, "would you like to get some lunch?"

"Don't mind if I do."

The man climbed the stairs out of the pool, and the bishop, then Abby, slowly descended into the water, allowing the air to be squeezed from the jumpsuits and out of the collars. Abby felt a deep shiver behind her sternum, despite the warmth of the water.

"It's just like when you were baptized at home," the bishop said. "When you're ready, plug your nose. I'll bear your weight as I submerge you. I won't let you fall. Are you cold?"

"No," said Abby through chattering teeth.

The bishop gave her a worried nod. He turned to a tile podium built into the side of the pool. There was a matching one on the opposite side. *They can do two baptisms at once*, Abby thought; *an assembly line*. A stack of papers that had been individually slipped into plastic sleeves lay on the podium. The white-haired man, who had not yet followed the boy down from the catwalk, knelt and pointed to a name on a long list. "Start there, Joe."

Even Abby, so unfamiliar with the ways of the Temple, knew that the man had slipped up by using the bishop's first name. Joe. A small name for such a big man. Your average Joe.

The bishop, Joe, put his hand to Abby's shoulder. She plugged her nose. "Having authority given me of Jesus Christ, I baptize you for and on behalf of Hannah Shuck, who is dead, in the name of the Father, and of the Son, and of the Holy Ghost. Amen." The bishop's large hand covered Abby's and took her down into the water. Even though she was expecting it, she still gasped a little, and inhaled water. She came up coughing.

"Are you all right?" he asked.

"Yes."

"Shut your mouth this time. Having authority given me of Jesus Christ, I baptize you for and on behalf of Hans Shuck, who is dead . . ."

The bishop baptized Abby for one after another member of the family Shuck, strangers whose names might have been lost to the great vacuum of the past if a Mormon volunteer hadn't looked them up in the records of some hospital, coroner's office, or church.

Bridget Shuck.

Rudolph Shuck.

Abby was glad for the water streaming down her face when she came up, and the fact that she could sputter and gasp, because that way the bishop—Joe, her mother's gentle murderer—couldn't see her cry.

CHAPTER 20

Enrique was no longer a lone wolf, he was a spy plane flying above the town. This sensation that arose from riding his bike. On Christmas day, when Enrique had raced across town to retrieve Jay from the Van Bekes', he had been impressed by how quickly he had gotten there. Now, as the weather warmed and the soil softened and began to give off a loamy aroma, Enrique realized he could zip to and from school on his bike and avoid having to walk past Gene, who still sat alone at the front of the bus. The bicycle afforded him new views of his hometown, ones that could only be caught by someone at a certain altitude, who was moving at a certain speed. When in a car, he was too confined and moved too fast; when he was on foot, he was too exposed, worried too much for his safety. But on his bike he could swoop in, check things out, and still be home in time for dinner. And it was exhilarating, freeing, to fly about town using his own strength and balance—his own wings, if you will.

He especially loved to cruise the back alleys downtown. Most of these were tidy lanes populated by delivery trucks and employees on smoke break milling among the aluminum trash barrels. There was one exception. The stretch of alleyway behind the Greyhound station was by far the most colorful in Eula. The area was always littered with bottles and was very rarely deserted. Enrique was guaranteed a glimpse of life, whether it be sleeping, drinking, playing, or fighting. Hobos sat on milk crates and played dominos on a makeshift table; once a woman in a leather jacket with tassels hanging from the sleeves like bat wings screamed at a man who cowered against the blue cement wall, demanding he give her the money he owed her. It was a one-block stretch of a big, faraway city in the heart of Eula.

A few times a day a bus would come through, and people on their way from Seattle to Salt Lake City would spend five minutes in Eula. They were bowlegged cowboys in their tight Wranglers, women in tube tops with jagged teeth and big hair, and black people. They got off the bus, blinking, dazzled by bright bits of cottonwood fluff that hung in the air, stretched, and walked stiffly into the bathroom, whose graffiti-covered metal doors opened directly onto the parking lot. Or they went into the station, used the pay phone, and bought a Twinkie from the vending machine. Some of them stayed sleeping on the bus, their hair forming flattened blossoms against the windows, like pressed flowers. They were people who were going somewhere but didn't own a car. Enrique had never known an adult who didn't own a car—even those who didn't have a house to live in—and he had never met a black person.

There was a different type of person at the bus station, too, men who weren't getting on or off a bus. Enrique knew, because he saw them again and again. (An old man in sunglasses and a white *Miami Vice* blazer was there nearly every day.) These men would sit in the station pretending to wait for a bus, or browse the businesses along the street. But again and again, they'd return to the bathroom off the parking lot. Enrique sat on the curb under a tree late into the afternoon, daring himself to go in and see what they were up to.

"Disappointed?" the note said.

No, Liz wasn't disappointed. She couldn't care less. She had put the entire affair behind her, figuring only a junior high prankster would have sent her to the Rollerdrome to find a Baggie full of water and a soggy note. *YOU'RE THE ONLY ONE I LIKE*. It had creeped her out, and this new one was nearly as creepy. In a few months she would graduate and never again have to deal with any of these stupid boys, or these stunted, depressed teachers, or these ammonia-smelling halls, or that bleak landscape visible through these grated, prison-like windows.

But an unsolved mystery was an unsolved mystery, and with little else to stimulate her, as her schoolwork was easy and Abby had been in Salt Lake City since February, Liz couldn't help taking it up again and looking it over. How would any junior high boy know that she had applied to Stanford? Of course, now it had gotten around, but back in November, when her secret admirer had placed the note in the Stanford section of the college catalog, only Liz's and Abby's families had known. Had Winston told one of his friends? Liz had given Eddy Nissen plenty of opportunities to confess and had at last, shortly after the Rollerdrome incident, teasingly prodded him, "Come on, Eddy, tell me who you like." Eddy blushed and looked away, causing her heart to race—it *was* Eddy! She could tease him now! What a thrill, to keep him at arm's distance! But then his blue eyes swam shyly back up to meet hers, and he said, "Trisha Morton. But don't tell anyone, Liz. Her parents don't know." Liz swallowed, and her throat had made an embarrassing click. So Eddy was secretly seeing Trisha. It made sense. Trisha's father was a Methodist pastor who would never let her date Eddy, a Mormon.

Liz turned haughtily from the memory. Which other of Winston's friends could it be? Did she care? How she longed to ask Abby that question face-to-face, not during their hour-long phone conversations, and receive the disdainful answer: *Of course you don't care, Liz. Some Eula boy? Please.*

So, with indignation, Liz decided that she must solve the mystery once and for all. She couldn't let some stupid Eula boy waste any more of her time. She had to root him out and turn him down in the hall at school in front of his friends.

This note—"Disappointed?"—did not lead her to any sort of mailbox; there was no key sending her to a locker or card directing her to a library book. Even so, it didn't take long for Liz to figure out another way to answer.

The *Eula High Gazette*, of which Liz was assistant editor, featured a classifieds section on its back page. Here, for a dollar donation, students could post anything they liked, as long as it was free of profanity and under twenty words. "Ten-speed for sale. $20. Call 467-4531." "Binky loves Carlos, 4-EVA." The paper was distributed in homeroom every Friday, but—and this was what made it perfect—only to high school students. A junior high boy could get a hold of a copy easily enough, Liz supposed, but he would have no reason to, as the paper covered only high school events and sports. It was a good, if not foolproof, way to shake a junior high pursuer.

So she placed a notice, centered neatly in a box, among notes of encouragement to the baseball team and birthday greetings, to appear in that Friday's *Gazette*:

Disappointed?
How could I be when I don't know who you are?
Be a man. Declare yourself.

The response came that afternoon, in the form of another typewritten note dropped into Liz's locker.

DECLARE MYSELF?
I thought I had. But I'm glad I didn't.
When I thought you were disappointed, I couldn't sleep.
When I couldn't sleep, I couldn't dream of you.
YOU ARE BEAUTIFUL!!!

Liz couldn't suppress the thrill. Someone had lost sleep over her.

That first insemination didn't take; after a week, Wanda did the stick test and a tiny pink minus-sign appeared. Good thing she had kept up the ovulation chart in the meantime.

Despite this disappointment, Wanda enjoyed leading a quiet life, her days beginning and ending under her little clowns.

The advance the Weston-Sloanes had given her had dwindled, despite the babysitting jobs she had. She needed another, and she found it advertised on the bulletin board at the grocery store. Wednesday and Sunday nights she began to babysit the five Jarrett children while their parents attended church meetings. They lived a ten-minute walk from Wanda's in a big ranch house where all the surfaces were sticky. In the backyard stood a trampoline covered in pine needles next to a sandbox in which several dolls were partially interred. The younger children seemed unimpressed with Wanda—only obeying her the third time she said something—while the oldest girl, an eighth-grader named Lucy, stayed in her room. "She's pretty grown up," Mrs. Jarrett told Wanda the first night. "Best to leave her alone." Lucy's wavy red hair, cut in a bob, formed two curtains through which a narrow triangle of her freckled face was visible. Wanda caught glimpses of her walking swiftly through the side rooms of the house on bare feet, a notebook covered with drawings braced under her arm, her chubby legs jiggling under a long skirt.

After Wanda put the younger ones to bed on her third time babysitting, Lucy came to the living room and curled up into the far corner of the sofa. They watched TV in silence until Lucy said, without turning toward Wanda, "The last babysitter got eight dollars an hour." Her sneer appeared to be unintended; she had to clear her lips from her braces in order to speak.

Wanda, who only got five dollars an hour, nodded.

Lucy opened her notebook and began to draw. "She threatened to quit, and they offered it, just like that. I was there."

"Thanks," Wanda said.

"You're welcome," Lucy replied.

IN THE WEEK she had to wait before she could post a response in the *Gazette*, Liz decided that simple demands wouldn't work with this boy. He obviously enjoyed their cat-and-mouse correspondence too much. Perhaps he clung to it out of fear he would never touch her. She would have to play his game and gently draw him out.

To my sleepless friend:
I'll be in Chandler tonight. Will you?

This was a tactical move. Maybe it wasn't as subtle as he had been, but it was the best she could do. There was a boxing match in Chandler that night and, as much as she despised the sport, she would go watch Winston compete. Any of Winston's friends who were on the boxing team would be in Chandler, as would, coincidentally, many of the brains, since there was a debate competition that night at Chandler High. The baseball players, on the other hand, would be stuck at a home game in Eula. Anyone who fell in-between these teams could certainly drive the fifteen miles to meet her in Chandler, so long as he had a car. In short, Liz could learn much from the response.

The note arrived in her locker between fifth and sixth periods that afternoon. Perhaps not having had time to make it to the typewriter, he had hand-written this note in small, straight letters:

I won't.

The population of boys had been effectively reduced by half, so long as her secret admirer was telling the truth. And she sensed he was. There were rules to this game.

These same rules required that Liz go to the boxing match, as she said she would. So, that night at the Chandler Field House she spread her things onto a few folding chairs to keep anyone from sitting beside her and glanced up from her work only occasionally to gauge which Eula boys were here and, hence, out of the running. After several matches, Winston jogged over in shorts and padded mask with towel hanging from around his neck. "I'm up next. Afraid you picked a bad night, though. It's like spic city here."

"What did you say?"

"It's all beaners. I don't know how we're supposed to compete against dropouts with nothing to do but train all day every day. And half of them have full beards by the time they're twelve. Just don't expect me to score a knockout tonight."

Liz studied Winston's face. Blows had blunted its delicate angles, and the training had drawn its dimples into creases. Meanwhile, his shoulders had become as round and hard as veined stones. "When did you start talking about Hispanics that way?"

"I dunno, sis. Maybe around the time you became a boring, self-righteous bitch." He squinted a smug smile at her, then inserted his mouth guard and headed for the ring.

She gathered her things, hoping her brother would see her leave before his match.

A new possibility occurred to Liz over the following days. Cordy Phillips, the student body president, and one of the only boys she would actually consider dating, was a member of the baseball team. He wouldn't have been able to go to Chandler on Friday. It began to come together. Cordy would have had every reason to keep a crush secret. He had been dating Sarah Fagan—a friend of Liz's—since junior high. There was talk that the two would marry that summer before Cordy left on his mission. This might be his desperate last lunge at the girl he had always secretly loved, before settling for Sarah, who, despite having thick, honey-colored hair and being bright and well-spoken, tended, in class, to hunch her shoulders and twiddle her fingers like an old woman knitting a scarf. It all fit. Before putting his future at risk, Cordy wanted to slowly test the waters, see if Liz was open to his advances. It was sweet.

Liz planned her next posting carefully.

To my sleepless friend:
Why not meet me for Lunch at Church on Monday?

There would be a meeting of the student body council during lunch that Monday. Cordy would have to tell her, again, that he couldn't meet her and, wittingly or not, declare himself. The friendly, offhanded tone was meant to put Cordy at ease. They were friends, after all. She would never ridicule him or tell Sarah. She might even give him a little consoling hug in some private recess, which would turn into a clinging, groping make-out session before she pushed him off. *What are we* doing, *Cordy? I can't do this to Sarah. I'm sorry.* Liz would tell only Abby, and they would share a sigh of pity for poor Sarah. Cordy would tell no one, but treasure the memory forever. He would call it up when he made love to Sarah, when they conceived their children.

No answer came that Friday, but this wasn't a surprise. Cordy realized he was cornered and was taking the weekend to consider how much he was willing to risk. But when there was no answer Monday morning, Liz began to wonder if he would now drop out of their little game and return to the script of his life that his parents and Sarah had written. It took a lot to turn your back on everyone, to have a Big Plan.

Or might she go to Lunch at Church that afternoon and find him there, sitting alone, his eyes fluttering up to her, then back down, his face glowing with shame and desire and surprise at having found himself willing to skip the student council meeting—and the rest of his life—to be with her?

But then, when Liz opened her locker to drop off her books before heading to lunch, there it was. She unfolded the paper.

I can't. I'm not allowed.

Sarah hasn't allowed him, Liz thought. *Life hasn't allowed him.*

But then, as if Liz had been shut in a closet and her eyes were only now becoming accustomed to the dark, the note's true meaning became apparent. Only two people at Eula High weren't *allowed* to go to Lunch at Church: her brother and Jay.

Jay.

It all fit. It couldn't have been anyone else. "I'm like your eyelashes," he had said, "too close to see." And he had been right.

If she had looked up at that moment, she might have spotted Jay himself, half-hidden in the phone booth under the stairwell.

This time Liz didn't wad up the paper, but folded it carefully up and held it for a moment, as if it were a card she was about to play, to end in victory or defeat a high-stakes poker game. A faint depression appeared along her jaw, then her pale cheek was smooth again, and she hooked the silk drape of her hair behind her ear and set the note delicately on the shelf in the locker. It was maddening how, at a moment like this, a face could reveal only the depth and not the nature of an emotion. She was moved, but how? And then, still frozen before her open locker, Liz moved her lips. She said something to herself, and her eyes became glassy with sadness, or fear, or love. What had she said?

Liz had realized that she needn't go to church for lunch now. She had no plans, no one to eat with, and what she had whispered was, "Abby, come back."

. . . .

MAYBE IT WAS the blood that was at last coursing with some speed through Enrique's veins, as his biking time cut into his reading and television-viewing time, that set off the growth spurt. That spring he shot up a full inch in height and became longer in the face. Enrique certainly didn't look athletic, but neither did he look teddy-bearish anymore. His jeans were too short now, but this was easily disguised. The more daring kids at school were "pegging" their jeans by folding them over at the cuff and rolling them up, so Enrique joined them. His wrists, with bony knobs now, appeared from the cuffs of his shirts, and his cheeks, having lost their fullness, no longer reflected a sharp point of sunlight when he smiled. At last, Jay and Enrique were recognizable as brothers.

Mr. Dodd, who taught history and coached track, seemed to notice. While he had always appreciated Enrique as a good student, now he began to tease him in the familiar way he did the more athletic kids. Enrique encouraged this by smiling wryly and ignoring it, the way he had seen the older boys do when Mr. Dodd harassed them in the hallway. In addition to being the coolest junior high teacher, Mr. Dodd was also the easiest. His class was final period, and he seemed to enjoy easing his students into the leisure of the afternoon. While other teachers got after kids for slumping in their seats—Mrs. Neeley liked to creep up and swat a nearby desk with her grade book, causing the offender to jump—Mr. Dodd encouraged it. He dragged his own chair from behind his desk and reclined in the corner, balancing on the back two legs. One day Mr. Dodd conducted an ungraded, verbal pop quiz on the Civil War. He spat out questions to his students, who were supposed to either answer quickly or say "Pass."

"Angie, who led the march to the sea?"

"Sherman."

"Wally, the Battle of the Merrimack and the what?"

"Pass."

"Cindy?"

"Monitor."

"Good."

This "test" bore a clear resemblance to tennis, which Mr. Dodd coached for the city league over the summer.

"Enrique," he said, "how fast can you run the 440?"

"Pass," Enrique responded without missing a beat. The class laughed.

Mr. Dodd didn't relent, but served again, still in his quiz-voice: "Enrique, are you going out for track-and-field this year?"

"No," he said.

On his bike ride home, Enrique revisited this little exchange. Mr. Dodd had, by joshing Enrique, shown the class that Enrique was *in* with him. While in previous years this would have so excited Enrique that he would have spazzed and missed the ball, now, after a good six months' practice being a man of few words, Enrique was steady enough to volley back and had made the class laugh. On top of this, Mr. Dodd was inviting Enrique to be on his track team. Enrique would never join, of course. Despite progress in some areas, Enrique was still secure in the knowledge that he was not athletic. He could see himself running around the track, heavy in the foot and light in the hand, swishing over the finish line long after everyone else, causing Pete Randolph and his gang to laugh from their perch high in the bleachers.

One day Enrique lingered after history class, chatting with Tommy Hess. Over the year, Tommy had become well-liked among their classmates, verging on popular. He was an expert at the well-timed caustic aside, which teachers never punished him for because of his goony good nature. Mr. Dodd came up and said, "Tommy's going out, aren't you?"

"For track? Sure," Tommy said.

Mr. Dodd spread one hand, and used the extended thumb and pinkie to pull the two curtains of his hair out of his face. They promptly fell back exactly where they had lain before. "So, how about it, Enrique?"

"I'm not the most athletic guy, Mr. Dodd," Enrique said.

"Track-and-field is perfect, then. You can sign up for as many or as few events as you like. I see you in the 440. I'll bet you have good lung capacity. Just sign up for the one event, if you want. You can spend the rest of the track meets just hanging out on the grass."

"My brother told me it's pretty fun," Tommy added.

"Do it as a trial membership," Mr. Dodd said. "Come to practice for the first week or two. Train a little, and if you like it, you can compete; if not, you can quit."

Enrique opened his mouth, and was a little surprised by the word that came out: "Okay."

The population that comprised junior high track-and-field couldn't have been more perfectly assembled for Enrique's comfort. The jocks, including Pete Randolph and his crew, had all gone out for baseball, which meant they were practicing in a nearby city park. The male members of the track team were generally the smart boys who disliked team sports but knew athletics would be an important part of their college application. There was no alternative sport for girls, except for dance team (cheerleading, but without a sport for which to cheer), so all the truly athletic girls were here. Most of them were already Enrique's friends.

Mrs. Wheeler, the girls' coach, was a stocky woman with a voice like a whistle. She didn't walk, she charged, her torso and hips twisting in opposite directions back and forth like a pepper grinder. And although she and Mr. Dodd seemed to get along—their brief interactions in passing were full of elbow-jabs and muttered jokes—their coaching styles couldn't have been more different. Mr. Dodd gently prodded his boys to raise the bar or decrease their time, but only when he wasn't reclined in the bleachers with his ankles crossed, chatting. Mrs. Wheeler sorted out the real athletes and proceeded to ride them hard and ignore the other girls. That she never grew hoarse seemed due to the fact that she sang, rather than hollered, her refrain: "Faster, Jenny, faster! Faster! C'mon! Faster!" No sound could have been more out of place over the lovely buzz of locusts from the field and warbling birds in the sumacs by the road.

And so practice was very nearly what Mr. Dodd had promised. After Enrique changed into his sweat suit, he, Tommy, and the other long-distance boys ran for a while on the track (Mr. Dodd's only requirement was they run farther than the day before), then he'd relax until his event was called. He'd race three other boys one lap around the track and, shockingly—maybe it was because of the energy he conserved, or maybe Mr. Dodd was right and he was a natural—he won about half the time. He spent the rest of track practice at the center of the field, where the kids laid their jackets out in a colorful patchwork on the grass. They gossiped and joked, wrote on each other's arms with dandelion heads, shared answers for homework, and generally enjoyed each other's company in the absence of the more grating elements of junior high—abusive jocks, squealing cheerleaders, grumbling dirtbags, and strutting cowboys. In the middle of telling a funny story one afternoon, Enrique looked around at the amused expressions and realized that he was breaking a rule he had made the previous fall, *Don't talk to groups.* He went further. His laugh loosened a bit. He allowed himself to tease his new friends and be teased by them. He became an expert at undoing girls' bra straps, quickly, through their shirts, with a quick pinch. Some of the old, giggling Enrique showed himself in the new Enrique, and it was all right.

There was also the advantage that Enrique got to spend his afternoons looking at athletic boys in sweat suits. His bedtime fantasies began to change yet again. The various scenes of intimidation and punishment gave way to one quiet, even romantic, fantasy: in the dark, Enrique was embracing a boy, feeling the boy's hair against his cheek, his breath in his ear. Enrique couldn't see the boy's face—that would have made it shamefully intimate—but he did let his hands move down the boy's back and rest on his buttocks, which felt like two volleyballs—hard, in comparison to the boy's soft mouth, which searched Enrique's face and found his mouth and mashed against it.

MELISSA CALLED WANDA late in the month with an offer. "I don't know how it seemed to you," she said in her business voice, "but to me the insemination procedure seemed pretty simple. I was thinking, if you feel comfortable with it, maybe we can do it here at home."

"With what?" Wanda asked.

"Well, use your imagination," Melissa said, then she paused. "These seven-hour bus rides can't be very fun for you, Wanda, and the appointments at the clinics are pretty pricey. With the money we save by doing it at home, we could fly you here."

"On an airplane?"

"No, on an albatross. Of course on an airplane!"

Wanda giggled. "I've never been on one."

"All the more reason."

"What do you wear?"

"Oh, Wanda." Melissa laughed. "You're too much."

So, a week later, Wanda, her face pressed against the window, watched Boise drop beneath her and the Interstate become a thread and the pale brown patchwork landscape pass behind her as she moved over the treeless Owyhee Mountains, where the wrinkled-leather earth was veined with dry rivers. They passed a squiggled border, where the leather seemed to have been bleached. Snow. The stewardess came by and served Wanda a Coke, and before she could finish it, the descent began. Wanda pulled at her earlobes and yawned to ease the pain in her head, disappointed that the flight had gone so quickly.

They did it every morning for a week, in order to better their chances: Melissa timidly woke Wanda in the early morning and handed her a little plastic syringe full of milky liquid on a neatly folded towel, then left her alone. Wanda slipped off her underwear, elevated her feet on some pillows, and emptied the syringe into herself. Then she dozed off for a while with Simon at her feet. By the time she went downstairs, Melissa and Randy were gone, having left breakfast for her on the bar. Wanda spent the day watching TV and taking the dogs for walks through the woods. At night, they had conversation over dinner, like a family.

"Catherine and I went to see this band we like," Melissa said the last night. "Catherine's a lawyer for Legal Aid. And this big tattooed guy offered to buy me a drink . . ." The story went on; but the idea of two wealthy, successful women, still young enough to go to rock shows and attract men, one with a husband at home, so gentle and adoring that he could hear the story with a cocked head and amused smile . . . the idea had so overwhelmed Wanda that she missed the rest.

In the car the next morning, Melissa slipped a wad of bills into Wanda's hand and kissed her cheek. "I realize you missed a lot of work this week. Keep this. It's not an advance, it's reimbursement."

Wanda thanked her, then ran across the rain-glazed lot into the airport.

This time the plane passed through a bank of gray clouds on its way up. Water beaded and flew away, leaving horizontal streaks on the window. Wanda worried that the pilot would get lost and crash into a mountainside. Then they burst out into sunlight. Above the clouds the weather was fine! As soon as Wanda realized this, she wondered if it was something she had always known.

"I FIGURED OUT who my secret admirer is," Liz told Abby over the phone.

"*Real*ly," Abby said, allowing herself a teasing tone. Liz hadn't mentioned to Abby anything other than the fact that he was back. "Well, who is it?"

"It's not good."

"Who?"

Liz whimpered, "Jay Cortez."

"Wow."

"I know. Wow."

But Abby's *Wow* was different from Liz's. Her impression of Jay had been based on the day years ago when he and Winston offered her a Hershey's Kiss and she had opened the bag to find a dead mouse among the silver-wrapped chocolates. This and a hundred other incidents had driven her and Liz gradually to change their after-school hangout from the Padgetts' to the Halls'. Jay was Winston's sarcastic crony with toothpick legs in basketball shorts, and Abby would have left him to his meager Idaho fate, had it not been for the afternoon she came over to see Enrique's diorama. "Hey, Abby. Hey, little brother," he had said. Jay was this sweet boy's brother, and he had become very, very handsome.

In this small way, Jay had accomplished his goal that afternoon.

"Well, Liz," Abby said, "he's pretty cute."

"Abby!" Liz whined. It was clearly not what she wanted to hear, but only, Abby suspected, because it was true.

"What do you want me to say?"

Liz, sitting on her bed among an array of tarot cards, which she had put out not to read but just to be surrounded by pictures that were simple even if their meanings were mysterious—swords, cups, moons—wondered quietly, what *did* she want Abby to say? She wanted Abby to tell her to forget about Jay Cortez and Eula, Idaho, because they would be together at Stanford soon. And Abby *would* have told her this, Liz felt, if they were face-to-face, if they didn't have to talk over the phone, if all this were done already.

If Abby's mother were dead.

"I guess it's not a big deal," Liz said. "I'll let him down easy. He's not a bad guy."

"You haven't talked about it?"

"Not yet."

AT THE JARRETTS', Lucy began to appear regularly after Wanda put other children to bed. Apparently, Mrs. Jarrett didn't mind if Lucy stayed up late watching TV, and Wanda liked the company.

"Have you ever ridden a plane?" Wanda asked her one night.

"Yeah. We flew to Phoenix to see my grandma."

"I just flew to Portland."

"For what?"

"To visit my best friend. She's an architect."

"Neat."

They fell into silence for several minutes, then Lucy scooted down the long couch toward Wanda. "Look," she said, turning her notebook to reveal what she had been drawing.

It was Wanda, rendered in colored pencil. The likeness in the face astounded her—Lucy was good!—but that's where the accuracy ended. Wanda's hair was a flaming yellow mass, and she rode a winged unicorn with a pink mane. Their eyes, both Wanda's and the unicorn's, were huge and mournful, fringed by thick lashes that licked up at the tips. Wanda was naked, and though her lower body was obscured behind the unicorn's wing, her breasts were round as softballs and pink-nippled. A rainbow-trail marked the unicorn's flight across a sky full of multicolored stars.

"Wow, that's really pretty," Wanda said. "Thanks for the boobs."

Lucy released an embarrassed laugh, then wiped from her chin the spittle she had blown from her braces.

"Can I look at the rest?"

"If you want."

As Wanda slowly turned the pages, she learned that this dorky girl lived in an incredible world full of sailboats, elves with pointed ears, jewels the size of houses, mountaintop castles, crashing oceans, human-headed birds, and bird-headed humans. There was no gravity; everything floated in a wreath of pastel-colored mist or flew on butterfly wings. Lucy herself appeared, not as a chubby girl but a graceful, redheaded sorceress who was always accompanied by a floating crystal ball. There were many women with orb-like breasts and buttocks, but only one man—or boy, really—a brown-skinned, sweet-faced boy, who sometimes rode behind Lucy on her steed, encircling her with lithe arms.

"Who's this?" Wanda asked.

Lucy pulled one curtain of her bob across her face to suck on its tip. "This boy at school, Enrique. He's a year under me."

"What's he like?"

Lucy heaved a great sigh. "He's really quiet and sweet and smart. Like, supersmart, the smartest one in his grade. I see him sitting out on the curb after school sometimes, just by himself, thinking, waiting for his brother. Sometimes I think he's kinda like me. But he's probably got a crush on a popular girl. He doesn't know I exist." She took back the notebook.

"Well," Wanda suggested, "if he is like you, then he doesn't care about the popular girls, right?"

Lucy shook her head. "Boys are different."

"You can say that again."

Lucy pulled her legs up under her. "I bet you were popular in school."

As she considered it, it seemed to Wanda that she had spent her youth spinning: exaggerating the severity of injuries just for the attention, cutting class to give the new girl a tour of the haunted house out on Amity Road, bargaining for rides after school, hopping from this clique to that all across Eula, spreading rumors and forging alliances and breaking promises—all in the hope of finding someone who would like her. "I wasn't popular," she said.

"But you were pretty," Lucy said, beginning to sketch.

"Popular or pretty—that doesn't mean people like you."

"Yeah, it does."

"You know what? That world you have there is worth more than boys and popularity and whatever. Sure, roll your eyes. I would have too, when I was your age. But I wish I had had that—what's in that notebook. It would have saved me from doing a lot of things I didn't like doing." Wanda saw a smile stir in the corners of Lucy's mouth. "You kind of know that, don't you, Lucy? That what you have is worth more?"

Lucy drew for a while, then she shyly said, "That's why I like Enrique. I feel like he knows it, too."

"Can I tell you a secret?" Wanda asked.

Lucy nodded without looking up.

"Seriously, can I tell you a secret that you can't tell anybody?"

"Yes."

"I'm trying to have a baby for these people—my friends in Portland. They can't have kids, so I'm going to get pregnant for them and have their baby. Like Baby M, but I'm not gonna try to keep it. And if I have a girl, I hope she's nice rather than popular. And if it's a boy, I hope I can sit on the curb and just be quiet with him rather than watch him play football. It's opposite from the way parents are supposed to think, but maybe that's why the world's so messed up. You only get one chance in this life, right? Well, when you have a kid, you get two."

Lucy gave a studied nod of profound agreement, although it was doubtful that she knew what Wanda meant when Wanda hardly knew herself. They turned again to the TV. Lucy drew, and eventually Wanda nodded off. At the sound of the Jarretts' car in the drive, she woke up and stretched.

"Here." Lucy tore a sheet from her notebook.

Wanda—Lucy's version, beautiful and fiery-haired—looked down between her breasts to her belly, where a baby boy, visible by a magical cross-section of the circular chamber, gazed lovingly back. The boy had brown skin, elf-ears, and little bat wings folded against his sides. His face was that of the sweet, introspective boy—Lucy's crush.

Wanda hung the drawing in a place of honor at the head of her bed, under the mobile. She started and ended every day with it.

On a Saturday afternoon Liz walked into the living room to find Winston and Jay watching TV with their feet up on the furniture. Shafts of sunlight lit the slow-moving dust in the air, and the boys had sunk so deeply into the soft sofas as to be flat on their backs. Winston, who had a faded yellow bruise on his chin, grunted a hello, while Jay let his head list casually to the side. His eyes took their time meeting hers.

She gave a caring smile—not affectionate really, but tender. He smiled too and lifted one shoulder in a little shrug. Abby was right, of course. He was cute. But to say so aloud had seemed sacrilegious. One mustn't admit to everything. Liz listened to Bananarama, but she didn't talk about it at school.

It made Jay tremble a little, deep in his bones, to look into Liz's long-lashed eyes and watch them close and reopen. They were like the eyes of a deer, but one that lived around McCall, the resort town Jay used to visit with the Van Bekes. There, all the wives and children fed the deer stale bread in the mornings. Those deer didn't run off when you came across them on a trail; they simply gazed at you with large, unthreatened eyes and let you pass.

Liz turned and climbed the stairs to her room.

From the moment she had discovered that it was Jay, Liz had forgotten all about how she was going to expose and humiliate her secret admirer. As someone who considered racial discrimination a blot on the kind face of Eula (that was how she had worded it in an opinion piece for the *Eula High Gazette*), Liz would never admit to herself that the reason she never had suspected Jay and the reason she now felt kind and docile toward him were the same: he was a Mexican.

A half-hour later there was a tap on Liz's open door. She looked up from her book. "Winston fell asleep," Jay said. His hands were stuffed in his back pockets and his gaze remained on the floor. He had cultured his aloof attitude to mask his shyness. Why hadn't Liz seen that before? Because she hadn't cared to look, of course. It was horribly vain, but the singular fact that Jay admired her had made him leap in her estimation, as if it proved his taste if not his intelligence.

"How have you been?" Liz asked.

Jay shrugged. He opened his mouth, and nothing came out but a long, rasping exhale that turned to a laugh as he bowed and shook his head.

"Been sleeping okay?" Liz prodded.

"No, actually," Jay said. Now he nodded. It seemed he needed to encourage himself to speak with these movements of his head. "Not since Monday."

"I never once thought it was you, you know," Liz said.

Jay swiveled side to side for a while, apparently unaware of his elbow knocking the door. "It feels kinda weird talking about it here, don't you think? I feel like your mom's gonna show up and tell me to get downstairs."

Liz quoted the rule from their childhood: "Boys downstairs, girls upstairs."

"Would you like to talk about it . . . somewhere else . . . sometime?"

"Jay," Liz said, "I'm going away."

"I know. Stanford. I was thinking that might be a reason to hang out, rather than a reason not to."

"I've got so much to do before school's out . . ."

She never would have suspected that Jay would so clearly recognize her first false note. But the light in his eyes went out, and she saw that she had called up the old Jay, the one that lived like a hermit in a dark-windowed house.

Jay, though, saw no change in Liz's eyes. They were still steady as those of a McCall deer. "Catch you later," he said as he rolled away into the hall.

MR. DODD'S "TRIAL period" was nearing its end, and Enrique had all but decided he would stay on the team and compete in meets—he had even toyed with the idea of taking on another event, the 880 or the long jump—when he made a terrible mistake.

One of Enrique's new friends was an eighth-grade girl named Annie Schiff. A big girl, taller than any of the boys, she was the best long-jumper and an important leg in the relay race. With only two events she was able to spend a good amount of time lounging at the center of the field before Mrs. Wheeler squealed for her, "Annieeeeee! Long jump!" Mrs. Wheeler was harder on her than she was on the other girls, perhaps because Annie, who braided her red hair into pigtails for practice, was the one who most resembled Mrs. Wheeler. Tommy once said, when Mrs. Wheeler approached with Annie at her side, "Make way for the East German Olympic team."

When Annie was called away, her boobs often became the subject of discussion among the lounging team-members. They were far and away the biggest boobs in junior high and rivaled many of those in high school. Enrique, Tommy, and the other kids were never cruel, merely observant—making dry guesses as to her bra size and speaking with a distanced kind of respect, as if Annie had done something revolutionary in growing them so big so early. By the way Annie carried herself, one could see that she considered her breasts both precious and embarrassing. She always crossed her arms over them when she was standing alone on the field, up until that moment right before she would break out in a run and take flight over the sandpit. She seemed to have resigned herself to letting them go their own way when she was in action. Having obviously confined them in the strongest bra she could find, what more could she do?

Enrique had taken on the role of a needling younger brother with Annie. One afternoon he furtively drew a smiley face on the rubber tip of her sneaker. When she noticed, she seemed irked for only a moment before she twisted her foot around to better see the face and said, "Cute." By the end of practice that day, he had nearly covered the exposed white rubber of her sneakers with different faces.

But on the afternoon in question, Enrique went too far. The girls were practicing the relay race. Annie stood in her spot, halfway around the track, arms folded over her breasts. Once the race was underway, though, she unshielded herself and took her stance: one hand fisted and raised to run, the other open and waiting for the baton. Enrique happened to be standing near the track and, a few seconds before the baton was passed to Annie, saw an opportunity and took it without fully thinking it through. He quickly darted in, undid Annie's bra, and darted out. Annie looked down at herself, and appeared, by the way her eyes receded into her head, to register what had happened the very moment the baton hit her hand. She took a few awkward steps, then lifted her shoulder, nudging one breast up with her arm.

Mrs. Wheeler, who was standing halfway down the track, hadn't seen what happened. "Annie! Go!" she shrieked.

Annie went. Slowly at first, then more quickly she ran, trying to manage her flying breasts, which, unleashed, seemed much bigger. She was like someone who had stolen the contents of a fruit cart, hidden it in her shirt, and was attempting to escape. "What's wrong with you? Hustle!" Mrs. Wheeler cried.

A jolt of unbearable remorse struck Enrique. To watch Annie now was like seeing a horse fall in battle in an old western—heartbreaking, that this gentle thing was subjected to such vain abuse. This remorse, though, was followed almost immediately by anger. *It was just a joke. It isn't my fault her boobs are so big.*

Annie stumbled when she handed off the baton. Then she gathered herself and ran, crying, under the bleachers toward the locker room.

Enrique glanced at the others lounging in the center of the field. They all had seen. Slowly, with a casual air, he took the path Annie had, under the bleachers toward the gym. Maybe he could apologize to her and make it seem like some sort of mistake. But he was glad when he got to the boys' locker room without having encountered her. He changed clothes and rode his bike home.

Between classes the next day, Tommy walked up to Enrique in the hall. With a steadied voice, as if he had been nominated ambassador from the track-and-field kids, he said, "Enrique, what you did to Annie yesterday was really mean."

Enrique's heart pounded and his face burned. "It was a joke."

Tommy squinted. "It wasn't funny. She's still upset about it. You should apologize."

Enrique allowed silent laughter to percolate in him, bouncing shoulders up and down, a gesture he had learned from Jay. Then he said, "C'mon, Tommy. What's the big deal?"

It worked. Tommy hesitated.

"Don't be a priss," continued Enrique. "What? Are you afraid of seeing her boobs? Do they *scare* you?"

A shadow of fear passed over Tommy's face, a fear Enrique understood because he had felt it so many times himself: that what was being implied, if named, would stick.

"You're a jerk," Tommy said. He spun on a heel and walked away.

At least Enrique didn't enjoy it. He hated it, regretted it, was ashamed of it. This difference between himself and Pete Randolph was the only solace Enrique could take as he rode his bike home that afternoon—this, and the fact that the "trial period" had not yet ended, and he needn't go back.

Wanda returned to Portland for a five-day stretch. The awkward giddiness had worn off, and there was a solemn sense of duty to her early-morning ritual. Melissa's parents came for the weekend and, at dinner, politely skirted Wanda's role in the household. Wanda excused herself early, claiming that she needed fresh air. There was the rich smell of moss in the woods, and the spongy soil sucked at Wanda's sneakers. She chastised herself as she walked for not making more of an effort with the grandparents.

But her conscience was eased the next night, when Melissa returned from work, poured herself a whiskey, and made a ringing announcement to her house: "Thank God they're gone!"

This seemed to restore humor and romance to the little family, and before dinner they took the dogs for a long walk. They used the trail, Wanda noticed, that Melissa had taken that first evening, all those months ago. The hues of the forest had deepened since then, and there were birdsongs echoing through the pines. When they reached the open, boulder-strewn slope, Wanda remembered Melissa's command and kept her eyes on the trail. Only when they reached the top of the clearing did she turn.

The gorge had transformed. The forested slopes had changed color from cool granite to glowing emerald. Everywhere, new leaves caught the light, and all along the great corridor—waterfalls. Some dropped from the plateau's edge like strands of silk while others charged, white and frothy, down rocky ravines. Their distant rumble, along with the whistling breeze, made Wanda feel like a speck lodged between the fingers of a living, breathing giant's cupped hand.

Wanda couldn't help but feel that somehow it was the waterfalls that did the trick—the unfreezing of the earth—when, a week later, the plus-sign bloomed on the stick test like a tiny blue flower.

SALT LAKE CITY was Boise's big brother. This thought always struck Chuck when his father-in-law picked him up at the airport and they drove from the white-encrusted banks of the lake into town. It was bigger and busier than Boise, the mountains that rose beyond it were taller and more majestic, and the gothic spires of Temple Square—which seemed to have been plucked from Europe or some other place with history and plopped down in this desert valley—made the Boise Temple look like a fast-food restaurant.

"Thank you for coming, Chuck," Grandpa Nelson said as he turned onto the freeway. "I know that Sandra had asked you not to. But sometimes illness clouds our vision and we don't see what's best for us. I'm sure you'll be a comfort to her."

"When it comes to Sandra," Chuck said curtly, "I do what Abby says." This close to the end, it seemed pointless to pretend.

"Don't be bitter, Chuck," Grandpa Nelson said. "We've had our differences over the years, but it's time to put that behind us."

Grandpa Nelson, and the whole Nelson clan, really, had made little secret of the fact that they found Chuck to be a disappointment again and again. He had taken Sandra away, to live in Idaho. He had given her only one child. He had become what he and Sandra called "ill" but what seemed more like mere laziness. And he had broken with the church. Never mind that this last and most important failing had been Sandra's decision. "Doesn't it all seem *implausible* to you, Chuck?" she had said on the way home from the ward house one Sunday, seven years ago. "Joseph Smith and Moroni. All this money we give, and the little old ladies are still sniffing for coffee on my breath."

"Not in front of Abby, dear," Chuck had whispered.

"Why not? She's old enough to think for herself."

Abby, visible in the rearview mirror, had sat blinking like a dazed little bird. Poor girl. That nose would keep the boys away.

"I'm not saying we should break with the church," Sandra had continued, taking Chuck's hand. "I'm just saying, next Sunday maybe we could catch up on some gardening."

He had admired her then for her independent thinking. She had still been his tall, sleek, urbane wife. When had she turned on him?

"Abby's been such a godsend," Grandpa Nelson said, apparently wishing to return to common ground. "She's the type who sees what's in front of her and does what needs to be done."

"Always has been," Chuck offered.

Grandpa Nelson gave a great sigh. "Gets that from you," he said.

They reached the house and Grandpa Nelson stopped Chuck from leaving the car. "Just one second, Chuck. Like I said, we haven't seen eye-to-eye on everything over the years. But you're here now, and for that I'd like to thank you . . . son."

Fuck you, old man. "Thanks for saying that. That means a lot."

When Sandra was gone, there would be no reason ever to see this man again.

Inside, Grandma Nelson made a tamping-down motion with her hands. "She's resting. They had a bad night."

Chuck went to the bedroom door and quietly pushed it open. Abby had her mother's hand in a large plastic bowl and was soaking the fingernails in water. She took the hand out and laid it on a folded towel in her lap. With a Q-Tip she worked delicately and intricately to clean along the cuticle. Here was proof of what her grandfather had just said: who else but Abby would know the perfect act for this moment, something so gentle, soothing, and banal as doing her mother's fingernails? He wanted to rush to Abby, but that would have woken Sandra.

Abby looked up with her wonderful, deep, sad eyes. She drew her lips tight. It wasn't a smile, it was closer to a frown, in fact, but it spoke much more: everything she had gone through, how glad she was to see him, how hard this was going to be.

Lodged in the corner of the easy chair, Sandra looked completely different from the way she had the last time Chuck saw her. Free of makeup, her face was gray and withered. She no longer wore a wig, and in the weeks since they had deemed her "beyond" chemotherapy (as if she had somehow graduated), her hair had grown back, an inch of silver straw, tousled like a young boy's. What a funny little haircut, like a pixie. It made Chuck smile. Maybe he breathed an audible laugh, because Sandra shifted. She opened her eyes and lifted herself in her seat. Then she saw Chuck, and everything in her face twisted into an awful look of dismay. She shook her head, *no . . . no . . .*, and took her dripping hand back from Abby. She covered her eyes and leaned forward as if to bury her face in the mounds of blankets.

Chuck retreated, gently pushed away Grandma Nelson, who tried to embrace him, and went upstairs.

Abby called Grandma Nelson to sit with Sandra. She found her father with one index finger hooked into the crease between his nose and mouth, the other fingers splayed like bars over his lips. His eyes were wide, studying a tree out the window as if they had never seen one before. Abby pulled a chair up beside him and draped her arm over his shoulders.

"I shouldn't have come," he whispered.

"Daddy," Abby said, "she wants you here. No, she does. She asked me to have you come. She'd never admit it, she's too proud, but she changed her mind."

"Really?" Chuck said.

Abby bit her lip and nodded.

This was the first lie in what would become, for Abby, a season of lies:

Yes, she is in a better place now, isn't she?

I feel like she's watching us right now.

Abby would be surprised how, after the first few, they would roll off her tongue fluently, as if she believed them. It would be the only way to take care of the mourners and keep them at arm's length.

She always cherished your friendship.

At least we know we'll see her again one day.

Oh, me? I'm doing all right.

Step Six:

Results

CHAPTER 21

May was a verdant flash in Idaho's yellow year. For a week or two the sagebrush and its big, silver-blue brother the Russian olive flushed green before returning to their metallic hues. The cheat grass did the same, and the hillsides were sprinkled with candy-colored wildflowers. The scraggly wild rosebushes produced some tightly rolled buds among the thorns. In town, the air carried the syrupy smells of lilac, honeysuckle, and wisteria, and the birds, who had all returned, chattered in the trees.

The theme of Eula High's senior prom, chosen after weeks of debate, was *Miami Vice*. The decorating committee borrowed nearly every tropical houseplant and lawn flamingo in Eula and rented several large inflatable palm trees from a party supplier. An announcement in the *Eula High Gazette* showed a cut-out Don Johnson reminding everyone that "Pastels are Mandatory!!" As soon as Ron's Formal Wear on the boulevard ran out of tuxedos in aqua, peach, and lavender, Eula High seniors headed to Boise.

Jay found his periwinkle-blue tux in Chandler. It was a little short in the legs, but otherwise, he thought as he watched himself in the bathroom mirror tug at the lapels and jut out his chin, it looked pretty good. So did his hair, which he had blown from its drooping waves into a fluffy, middle-parted pyramid. He went to the kitchen and from the refrigerator took the plastic box, which looked like it was made to hold a cake but instead held a massive wrist corsage that wobbled as if it were alive. It was a thicket of Madagascan jasmine and curling fronds topped by a single obscenely splayed, speckled-tongued orchid. It had cost $20 at Eula Floral.

Lina walked into the living room and gasped. "Look at you! Let me take your picture."

"Come on, Lina," Jay groaned.

"Just one second," she yelled, running back into her room. "Where's the Polaroid?"

"I'm going to be late," he said. But he wasn't.

"I've got it!" Lina said, returning with the black plastic cube with its red button. She popped it open, squeezed the button, and with an irritated hum the camera spat the picture out. "Another one outside," Lina said, following Jay out toward the car. "Smile this time."

Jay set the box on the roof of the Maverick. He gave his lapels a final tug, then gave Lina the smile he had practiced in the bathroom mirror minutes earlier—practiced it for the portrait that he planned to have taken later tonight, in which he and Liz would stand together like newlyweds.

The smile hit Lina like a fist. She steadied herself and took the picture. Jay had never smiled brightly like that for her before; she hadn't known he could.

Jay came over to watch as the white square slowly began to show a shadow that then became him, in dazzling blue, and his gray car. The lane behind him was lined with trailers, white shoeboxes with colorful trim; above them the pale blue sky showed three vertical wisps of clouds, like brushstrokes. "Looks good. Gotta go." As if doing it quickly would keep it from going on record, Jay tossed an arm around Lina and buried a kiss in her wiry, graying hair. She froze, shocked again but in a different way.

As Jay walked to his car, he caught Gene next door watching him from a window that had been propped open with a soup can. Jay gaped his mouth and bugged his eyes, aping Gene's expression, which sent the little troll back into the darkness.

Lina stood there for a long time listening to the chirrup of crickets and the hum of cars on the boulevard and the occasional hysterical cry of the killdeer that made her nest in the gravel back by the chain-link fence. Then all this was interrupted by the rustle and snap of someone crossing the weeded lot, and Lina wiped her eyes.

"Beautiful evening, isn't it?" Connie said.

"Uh-huh."

"Are you all right, Lina?"

"Yeah. Jay just left to the prom. He looked so handsome and grown-up it made me cry, is all."

Connie smiled. She held her hands solemnly against the front of her skirt, like a member of a choir. "I've been meaning to ask a favor of you. I can't believe I've left it so long."

"What is it?"

"I have to go away for a few days. It's family business in Kansas City. I can't take Gene, of course, because of school. I've talked it over with him, and he seems to think he's old enough to stay in the house by himself. He can get himself breakfast and lunch, but dinner . . . Could I send him over to your house for dinner for the next few nights?"

"When are you leaving?"

"Tomorrow. I know, I've left it too long. But it would be a great help. I could give you some money for groceries . . ."

"Well, sure, I don' know. School's out in a few weeks. You can't wait till then?"

"Unfortunately, no."

"You know"—Lina hesitated—"Enrique and Gene haven't been such close friends lately."

"To be honest, Lina, I'm kind of up a tree. I have no one else to ask."

Lina looked into her face. *What a lonely, lonely woman*, she thought, *lonelier than her son, even*. Connie had always seemed like a crabby aunt, even though she was only a couple years older than Lina. If only she would take her hair out of that bun, she would look so much younger. As it was, her head with its narrow jaw on its skinny neck was the shape of a lightbulb.

"Sure. No problem. Just tell him to come over at six every night. If he doesn't show up, I'll come get him."

Connie broke out in a little laugh of relief. "Thank you, Lina. God bless you."

The sky was growing paler and the wisps were turning blue as if cloud and sky were trading colors. Connie and Lina stood together under this show for a minute more before returning to their homes.

. . . .

JAY WAS RELIEVED to see, as he pulled up to the Padgetts' house, that Winston's car was not in the driveway. He must have gone to pick up Kelly Mills, one of his sluttish on-and-off girlfriends, the one he had decided to take to the prom. Last Monday, Winston had arrived in first-period speech class holding an empty pop can. On days when he and the other boxers weighed in, not only would they fast, but they'd carry containers around and spit into them all day long, dehydrating themselves in hopes of being placed in a lower weight division. Winston sat down heavily at the desk next to Jay's and said, "Look, man, Liz doesn't need you to do her any favors."

"What do you mean?"

"She said you're taking her to the prom."

"Yeah."

"Why?"

"It's no big deal, man. We're just going."

"You think she needs you or something, like no one else will take her?"

"No."

"Then why the fuck did you ask her?"

"I just did. What's the big deal?"

Winston puckered and dropped a dollop of foam into the can. The teacher started to call roll. "It's fucking *weird*, Jay, and I don't like it, understand?"

Jay had crossed Winston's line; they hadn't spoken a word to each other since.

Jay parked and ascended the winding walkway bordered so crisply by vivid green grass it might have been fabric that had been cut and hemmed. He tugged at his pants, trying to get them to completely cover his white gym socks.

Inside, Liz was putting the last touches on her look for the evening. She wore the royal blue dress she had bought to wear to a banquet last year. It was plain and tasteful, with only one flourish—a ruffled strap over one shoulder. She hadn't bought a new dress because she hated pastels and wanted her attendance at the prom to appear as an afterthought, which it was. Last week she had opened her locker to find a folded note atop her gym clothes. She laughed, picked it up, unfolded it, and saw the unevenly typed letters that already inspired a flutter of nostalgia for the days of the treasure hunt.

May I take you to the prom?

It was so sweet. She laughed in the immediate knowledge that she *should* go to the prom with Jay, for old times' sake, in honor of the history that it suddenly seemed they had. At odds all their childhood, they had overcome Jay's crush to emerge as friends. And, more than that, they were alike. Liz had begun to credit Jay with being a quiet rebel like herself; the fact that he found her beautiful was the only proof she had, or needed. So he must consider the prom an inconsequential amusement, high school's ludicrous last act, which—like the end of the rodeo, when the clowns came out and played with the bulls—would acknowledge that the whole contest had been laughable. Jay was, after all, asking her less than two weeks in advance.

Last year, Liz had proved she was above it all by not attending her junior prom. Now it would be fun to make people talk about the mismatch of her and Jay. She could walk into the dance, laughing with Jay and punching his arm like one of the guys, then go off and talk to her friends and dance with whomever she chose. She could even imagine Jay bringing a flask, and she would chide him, then take a slug or two herself.

Liz had done one special thing today to mark the event and to maximize the impression she would make upon entering the gymnasium—she had given in and let her neighbor, Mrs. Warner, do what she had always begged to do: curl her hair. Mrs. Warner had swept it up one side, sprayed and pinned it, then allowed a lacquered tower of curls to cascade into ringlets like overflowing champagne onto Liz's shoulder, the bare one. A little wild, but it was only for one night. The girls would hop up and down in their formal shoes and tell her she looked like a movie star.

For once, Liz was glad Abby—who would have been absolutely merciless—was away.

The doorbell rang. She gave her hair, which had already settled a little, a careful nudge as if it were a sleeping animal she wanted to awaken without angering. She smoothed her dress, stepped into her shoes, and went downstairs. She took a deep breath, opened the door, and there was Jay, handsome, if a little silly, in light blue. Jay's eyes darted up to her hair.

Jay hated it.

Liz could see that he hated it.

Jay saw that Liz saw.

"Hey, Jay."

"Wow. You look great."

"Can you believe my hair?" She prodded it again and rolled her eyes.

"It looks awesome."

Jay couldn't help feeling pleased that she cared what he thought, that her smile had gone stale when she saw his disappointment. He cast his gaze down. "You look beautiful," he said humbly.

With her pointed black shoe she kicked his shin lightly. "Let's not do the whole *prom* thing," she said. "Let's just have fun."

"Okay," he said, offering the corsage. He had wanted to do the whole prom thing.

COOP WORKED A toothpick into his gums and sucked on his false incisor. "Durn good," he said.

"I'm gettin' cold," Wanda said. "You about ready?"

He slurped the last of his coffee and, with a few heaves, scooted out of the booth. He was lighter now. Although surf and turf at Denny's was an important exception, he had been following the diabetic's diet Uncle Frank refused. And Wanda was heavier. She liked this new weight. Everyone said it looked good on her.

"Y'all takin' off?" asked Gina, slipping Wanda the check, as was their custom.

"Yeah, it's been a long day," said Wanda.

"On the bus?" asked Gina.

"Nope," Coop said, putting his arm around his little sister. "On an airplane."

Wanda jabbed him with her elbow.

"Fancy that," Gina said, loading a few rattling dishes into one hand. "I'll see you Monday, Coop."

They walked out the door into the big, sweet-smelling evening. The air felt good against Wanda's skin, which had tightened and goose-pimpled in the air-conditioning. It seemed Denny's was kept frigid in the summer and stiflingly hot in the winter, as if the customers' first grateful expressions upon entering, before they noticed the temperature extreme, were all that mattered.

As they drove across town toward Wanda's, Coop said, "I might go out to Maria's tomorrow."

"Want me to look in on Uncle Frank?"

"You're sure it's not too far to walk? Don't want the little one to jiggle loose." Coop wore the same old smile, but his eyes squinted shyly, as they always did when he mentioned the baby.

Wanda laughed. "I'm supposed to exercise," she said. The doctor had told her that just this morning at her eight-week appointment. Then she and Melissa had picked up Randy and they had gone out for a celebration lunch at a restaurant where they had cloth napkins and the waiters wore bow ties. Melissa had ordered a bottle of wine, and insisted that Wanda have one sip. "Your last, until afterward," she had said.

Coop pulled up to Wanda's apartment and the two bid each other goodnight. Wanda walked into the apartment and was surprised to see the TV on, and more surprised to see a strange girl nestled in the couch with her feet folded under her. "Oh!" the girl said, sitting up. "Oh!"

Wanda looked around the walls, to make sure she hadn't walked into the wrong apartment.

"She's here!" the girl cried. "Hank? You better come out here." The girl sheltered the little bowling ball of her belly in her hands. Wanda could hardly name the wide-eyed expression on the girl's face, so unaccustomed was she to provoking it: fear.

Then the bedroom door opened, and out came Hank wearing brown cords and no shirt. His chest collapsed a little at his sternum—there was a small depression under his ribs and over his belly. His hair was neat at the part, then fell in oily strawberry-blond waves over his ears and down his back. He gave Wanda the skeptical look he gave men with whom he was picking a fight, which Wanda suspected he had borrowed from the kung fu movies he liked to watch Saturday mornings: he jutted his chin forward and narrowed his eyes. His shoulders rode back, and he bounced his weight between his feet. "Where *you* been?" he asked.

"What do you care?" Wanda demanded, leaning to the side to set down her suitcase. "You better get outta here."

"Why should I?"

"Because it's my house, that's why."

Hank put out his hands and spread his fingers like a woman showing off her rings. Then he smiled, sat down on the sofa's lip, and splayed his hands on his knees.

The absurdity of the situation finally sank in. Wanda turned to the girl. "Who are you?" she asked.

"Hank?" whimpered the girl, hitching herself toward him a bit and running her hands nervously over her belly as if it were a crystal ball. Wanda could see that she was a good way into her second trimester.

"Answer her," Hank said. "You don't gotta be afraid."

"I'm Misty."

"What the hell are you doing in my house?" Wanda said.

"Could ask you the same damn thing," Hank said, still smiling.

"What do you mean? This is my house."

"Your name on the lease?"

Wanda allowed her knees to buckle and she sat in the chair. It *was* his lease. Where would she go, to Randy and Melissa's? No. She had sworn to them, no more surprises.

"What do you want, Hank?" she asked. "Money? I don't have any."

"I don't want yer money," he said.

"Then what?"

"Wanda, I don't want nothin' from you. I don't want *you* or nothin' *from* ya."

"*Hank!*" Misty said. Hank continued to smile menacingly at Wanda, so Misty turned to Wanda. "He wants his place back. He needs it. We're gonna have a baby." The girl's head was shaped like a pear, with a black ponytail springing up where the stem would be.

Her bottom lip, painted a shade Wanda had seen labeled "coral" at the drugstore, hung open insolently, in invitation to the fight, although her puffy, dimpled hands still shielded her belly. The gash of her mouth seemed to have been cut into her flesh in a permanent frown.

"I've lived here three years. This is all my stuff. You can't have it." The obvious nature of everything Wanda said allowed her to say it softly.

"We don't *want* your *stuff*," Misty said with a disgusted shake of her head that caused that bottom lip to jiggle. "We want Hank's place back. He's been lettin' you live here—"

"Lettin' me live here? Look, *Misty*, you obviously don't know jack shit about this situation, so you better just stay out of it."

"I'll beat your ass if you keep talkin' to me that way."

"Hank never even moved in here. He went to Chandler, and I moved in. I paid the rent. I got the furniture. This is all just plain crazy."

Hank snuffed a disdainful kind of laughter. "I don't know what you girls're arguin' for. There's nothin' to argue 'bout. I live here. Have for most of the past week. Case closed."

"Where's all your stuff, then, Hank?" demanded Wanda.

"Here and there."

"I thought you had a place in Chandler."

"Didn't work out."

"Well, you can't live here."

"You just don't get it, do you, Wanda? I *do* live here. It's you that *can't live here*." He yanked Misty's hand out of her lap to hold it and leaned back into the couch in a tense display of ease.

"So, I guess I better call the police," Wanda said.

"Exactly," said Hank. "I was hopin' you'd say that. Can't wait to show 'em my copy of the lease."

Wanda felt tears rising. "And what'll you do when I come take away all the furniture?"

"Jump for joy," Hank said, scowling. "It stinks. Like you."

MONA LISA FONDUE was Eula's one and only "nice" restaurant. It occupied a converted nineteenth-century blacksmith's shop, which had, for the last twenty years, housed one after another nice restaurant that failed. The last one had been an Old West–themed restaurant, for which they had done an extensive build-out with fake storefronts on the walls ("Last Ditch Saloon," "General Store") and balconies hanging over "Main Street," the large dining room. Stars and a large crescent moon glowed on the ceiling. These decorations proved so expensive that the restaurant for which they were made had quickly gone broke, and Mona Lisa Fondue, which served fondue and other French specialties, inherited the incongruous interior.

From the balcony, which Jay had reserved specifically when he called over a month ago, long before he worked up the nerve to ask Liz, the two could see dozens of pastel-clad couples. "Oh, look," Liz said. "Joel's wearing a top hat. Oh my gosh! And he has a cane!"

"What a dork," Jay snorted. "Why isn't he with Christine?"

"She's Nazarene," Liz answered.

"Right." Dancing was forbidden in the Nazarene church, so its kids attended "prom alternative," a banquet.

They fell to silence.

"Knock, knock!" Troy Whitehead stood at the balcony's entrance, holding closed the lapel of his butter-yellow tuxedo. One of the members of Winston's and Jay's gang who had joined the boxing league, Troy had a tiny Band-Aid over a scrape on the bridge of his nose. "Am I interrupting anything?"

"No, come in!" Liz said, obviously relieved.

"My date's boring me, so I thought I'd come up and offer you a little . . ." he looked from side to side, though there was clearly no one else on the balcony, and opened his jacket, ". . . *fire water*." A deep inner pocket held a bottle of whiskey.

"Oh, I think we're doing all right," Jay said.

"Well, if you need me, I'm 'round the corner by the hitchin' post."

After going over Liz's plan for the summer (an internship at the *San Francisco Chronicle*) and Jay's ("Oh, I think I'll go somewhere new for a while, maybe Seattle, see what happens"), and briefly discussing Abby's situation ("Her mom's not doing well"), the two found they had little to talk about. Liz cleared her throat, and Jay adjusted the napkin in his lap.

Then Liz let out a nervous, breathy laugh.

"What?" Jay asked.

"You know what I've never been able to figure out? The roller rink. Why the roller rink?"

"Oh," Jay said, sitting up. "It was a clue, to help you figure out it was me."

"But why?"

"Don't you remember?"

"Did we go there when we were little?"

Jay's eyes darkened as clearly as if a blind had been drawn behind them, and Liz knew she had said the wrong thing. She had forgotten something that Jay remembered.

For a moment, and only a moment, Jay considered telling her. But if she didn't remember, she didn't remember. "There was a Baggie full of water," Liz ventured.

"It was ice when I put it in there. I thought you were going to come that day to get it. You didn't, and it melted."

"Ice?" Liz said. "Is it a riddle?"

"Where's our food?" Jay grumbled. "I'm gonna go find the waiter."

"Wait, it's only been—"

Jay skidded down the narrow staircase to Main Street. He went to Troy's table, slipped the bottle into his own jacket, and took it to the men's room.

IT WAS DARK when Enrique got home. Lina was watching TV. "Where you been all day, *mijo*?"

"Riding my bike."

"Should I fix something, or should we go to McDonald's?"

"I don't know. McDonald's?" He rubbed his palms together and gazed absently at the TV. His eyes were bloodshot and his face drained, except for his crimson cheeks. This was how he always looked after hours of riding.

Earlier this afternoon, Enrique had heaved open the heavy metal door and entered the cool, foul-smelling bathroom of the Greyhound station. The first time he had done this, a few weeks ago, he had actually needed to pee. As his eyes became accustomed to the light, he had been disappointed to see that he was alone. The bathroom was shaped like an L, with a trough urinal and a line of sinks in front and a row of doorless stalls around the corner. He peed in the urinal, then rinsed his hands in the sink. So many letters had been scratched onto the thick plastic panels that protected the mirrors that he could barely make out the words, let alone his reflection behind them. The subsequent times Enrique ventured in, it was because he had seen men go in before him. They quickly zipped up and charged out as soon as they saw a kid among them. Enrique himself, with his heart pounding in his ears, returned to his bike and rushed away, standing up to pump the pedals more powerfully, swearing to himself and to God he wouldn't go there again.

Today the men had scattered, all but one. He was a slim man with gray in his hair. He wore a windbreaker and jeans. He remained at the urinal as Enrique took his place at its farthest end and turned to shelter himself from view. Enrique opened his pants but didn't take himself out—he hadn't really needed to pee. Wave after powerful wave of adrenaline surged through his body, shaking him. With effort, he steadied his breath. This was worse than the day he had found *Working Out* at the bookstore. The man stood patiently with his hands at his sides. There was no tinkle of urine. Finally Enrique built up enough courage to cast a furtive glance over his shoulder, and there it was, shocking, even though he had expected it: the man's fully erect penis standing straight out, almost comically, like a cartoon tree limb that would snap off, sending the cat crashing down while the bird flew merrily away. Enrique quickly looked back to himself, down to his own, much smaller penis, which was arcing painfully against the fabric of his underwear. He couldn't help it; he had to look again, and when he did, the man pushed the thing down, causing it to bounce back up, then bob up and down—again, cartoonishly: a dopey nod, *Hello.*

Enrique zipped up and fled.

He played the game he sometimes did, where he was biking on water, splitting it into great sheaves that V-ed behind him like the Red Sea under Moses's staff. If he slowed down, he'd sink. It took hours of hard riding across all the world's ocean to get it out of his system.

And he hadn't even seen the man's face.

Lina said, "Connie asked me to feed Gene dinner the next few nights."

"Huh?"

"She's going somewhere. Kansas."

"Did you say yes?"

"Of course."

"Mom! I don't even *like* him anymore," Enrique said, walking to the kitchen.

"So what? You can eat in your room if you don't want to see him. Connie asked me for a favor, and I'm doing her a favor."

Enrique drank orange juice straight from the carton.

"Stop that! Who do you think you are, Jay? Use a glass."

"Gene's a creep," Enrique said, placing the carton back on the shelf. "Everyone thinks so."

"I'm not thrilled about it either, Enrique, but I tol' her I would do it, and that's that." She leaned forward to pick her keys up off the coffee table. "Let's go. You want Sizzler?"

"Really?" Sizzler was Enrique's favorite.

WANDA CROSSED THE street, wandered through the junk-strewn front yard, and knocked on Darrell's door. The dog ran with a crash through the house and barked and barked, but no Darrell. Whose phone could she use to call Coop?

She hadn't seen Gideon in months. She still avoided walking past his apartment, not because it was a temptation to drop by anymore but because it was a reminder of the pathetic old Wanda who would bum drugs off any loser who had them. But at least he was sure to be home. She crossed the street again and walked down the row of apartments.

Gideon, when he answered the door, looked worse than ever. His V-neck undershirt hung more loosely against his bony, hair-matted chest, his teeth looked browner, and one eye appeared to have grown more alert while the other threatened to fall asleep. "Wanda," he said with a knowing nod. "Well, well, well. Wanda." He opened the door wide and bowed like a butler.

"Mind if I use your phone, Gideon?"

"What, no 'Hello, Gideon'? No 'How are you, Gideon?' No 'Haven't seen you for a while, Gideon'?"

"Sorry, I'm not havin' the best night."

Gideon yanked at the cord and handed over the phone, then shook a cigarette out of a pack, and started moving newspapers and takeout containers around on the coffee table, looking for a light. Wanda called Coop and asked him to pick her up. "I'll explain when you get here. Thanks." She hung up and turned to Gideon, who smiled his old dirty-joke smile.

"What?" Wanda said.

"Is it true?"

"Is what true?"

"What I been hearin'."

"Depends on what you been hearin', but I don't feel much like playin' guessing games."

"Well ain't you all high and mighty all of a sudden! What I heard is that you took up with a couple. A rich couple in Portland."

"What's that supposed to mean?"

"I heard you was their third."

Wanda turned away. Suddenly hungry, desperately hungry to the point of nausea, she reached into her pocket, where she kept a Baggie of crackers for just this kind of situation. She popped one into her mouth, then another. "That's disgusting," she said, chewing, "and you're disgusting for believing it."

Gideon drew his lips over his teeth in a smug smile. As usual, he seemed pleased by Wanda's insults. "Makes sense."

"What?"

"It makes sense. You haven't been around, you show up all high and mighty lookin' rich and taken care of. It all kinda fits with what I heard, that you'd been bought."

"Thanks for letting me use your phone, Gideon," said Wanda, rising.

"Oh, simmer down. I was just joshin'. Come on, Wanda, let's have a chat. Ketch up."

Wanda sat back down, eyeing Gideon as if at any moment he might pounce.

"I got a new hobby," Gideon said. "My own invention. You might like it. I call it Gideon's Bible, for lack of a better name." He reached down between his knees and drew the Monopoly game from under the couch, which was where he had always kept the pot.

Wanda leaped up. "I'm gonna wait outside," she said.

MISS HOLLY HAD been stationed in the "café" on the gym's balcony to keep couples from making out in the dark recesses, but it was still early and the plastic lawn chairs were all empty, so she perched herself against the railing and watched the dance floor slowly fill. The eighties were more than half-over, and finally Eula kids had allowed themselves to enter the decade. Hairstyles and prom dresses were at last asymmetrical, and the sheen of rayon and hair gel caught the light. It was only the odd girl here and there who wore the prairie dress that ruled last year's prom. Miss Holly had grown up in California, where the kids snatched up every new fad and fashion and with dizzy abandon combined them into new ones, and it saddened her that here in Idaho preachers and parents cowed the kids into hiding in the fashions of five years ago.

Jay followed Liz through this crowd. He had just enough of a buzz on that the colored lights suspended from the rafters and the strobe lights stationed on the tall speakers transported him somewhere other than the Eula High gym (which, other than the Van Bekes' and Lina's, was the place where he spent the most time). Around him, girls were doing the dance of the moment, borrowed from the New Wave bands on MTV they claimed to hate. They crouched slightly in their shimmering rayon and organza and taffeta, lifted and poised their hands as if to snap their fingers. But they didn't snap. They touched one toe-tip at a time onto a spot on the floor before them, as if they were crushing a cigarette butt again and again. Their boyfriends watched them, shifting from foot to foot, some venturing to swing their hands a little.

Candy Patton was engaged in her version of the dance, which was a little freer than the other girls in her group—sometimes she threw in a clap over one shoulder—when she saw Liz and screamed.

Liz rolled her eyes and touched her hair, thinking, *At last.* She had made her way through the foyer and half the gym without much reaction beyond Mr. Dodd's raised eyebrows.

"You look beautiful!" cried Candy as the other girls gathered around. Jay waited for a few minutes on the circle's outskirts, then, when Liz began to dance with the girls, he looked around for a boy to talk to, and, finding no one, shoved his hands in his pockets and strolled away.

Liz danced with the girls and took in the gossip of who had shown up with whom until she felt her dress start to dampen and her hair start to fall. Then she danced her way through the crowd and passed the bank of potted palms, which marked the edge of the dance floor. On the bleachers, which were collapsed flush against the wall, hung a fluorescent-paint mural of art deco abstractions—perhaps meant to be building facades—labeled "Copacabana" and "Flamingo" in neon cursive that seemed to vibrate in the black light from the dance floor. A bright flash drew Liz's attention to a flimsy garden gazebo where the photographer had set up shop. Surrounded by inflatable palm trees and pastel-colored balloons, Cordy Phillips stiffly encircled Sarah Fagan with his arms. They wore distressed smiles. At their feet, a large stuffed-animal alligator emerged from the "swamp" of crepe-paper rushes. They looked alike, Cordy having taken on Sarah's daunted expression and her hunch. They were obviously made for each other. How could Liz have ever suspected Cordy was her secret admirer, or, worse, hoped that he was? She decided to put that little fantasy through the paper shredder; she had never entertained it; her conscience was clear. Liz approached a girl in line and asked how much photo packages were. Ten dollars and up. Ridiculous. Jay had already spent at least twenty-five on dinner. She wouldn't ask for this as well. Who needed pictures? She scanned the room quickly for his periwinkle tux.

Jay had found a friend with a flask and the two had lodged themselves in a dark corner of the café behind the punch fountain. Jay was surprised to look up and see Liz pulling up a chair. "Can I have some?" she asked as she sat.

Without smiling, Jay held out the bottle.

Liz glanced around, quickly tossed her head back to take a swig, then wiped her mouth with the back of her hand. "The portraits are, like, superexpensive," she said in a voice suddenly mannish. "You don't want to have one taken, do you?"

"*Fuck*, no!" Jay retorted.

The way Liz retreated in her seat made him wonder if he had spat when he spoke.

COOP AND WANDA sat at the kitchen table. From the living room, a crowd's roars of laughter broke the silence. Johnny Carson was doing his monologue. "Do you want to go to the police?" Coop asked.

Wanda shook her head miserably, and collapsed onto her folded arms on the table. "They told me the next time they saw me or Hank, they'd arrest us both."

"That was ages ago," Coop said gently.

"Less than a year," Wanda sniveled. Then she caught herself, straightened back up, and took a deep breath. Coop's grin took on the aching appearance it did when his ideas ran dry. What would Melissa do in this situation? "Maybe tomorrow," Wanda said, "I'll go in and talk to that lady officer, what's-her-name. Tonight, I just need to rest."

"I'll go pick up Maria in the morning. We'll both come with you. Maria knows all those folks."

Wanda reached over and lay her hand on Coop's forearms, which were thick and hard as firewood stacked atop each other. Coop lay a callused hand on hers.

"Where should I sleep?"

"Frank's room." Wanda's face froze, which made Coop laugh. "The sheets are clean. He hasn't slept in there for years."

They walked through the living room, where Frank sat propped up in his nest of cushions on the floor. His mouth gaped like that of a trout, and his chest rose and fell—just barely and with great effort—from the heap of his body. He opened his rheumy eyes as they passed. "I'm gonna sleep in your room tonight, Uncle Frank," said Wanda.

"'Night," said Frank. But it came out "Nah," his pale tongue only grazing his palate.

Coop opened the door and turned on the light. Wanda had never been in this room before, and she was surprised at the neatly made bed with its gray woolen blanket and the only slightly stale smell of cedar.

Coop put down Wanda's bag and opened the window. A fox pelt hung beside the window, arms splayed as if it were embracing the wall. Pennants hung on the other wall over a small desk, on which stood three big-headed figurines of famous baseball players and a tin can full of pencils. It was a room that parents would keep just so for a long-dead son.

"Can I gitcha anything?"

"No, thanks, Coop."

"Good night."

Wanda sat down on the bed. Someone next door was practicing scales on a piano that badly needed tuning. One note in particular rattled like a dropped fork.

The mobile! Wanda thought. *Lucy's drawing!* What would Hank do to her things? Better not to imagine.

Wanda rose to examine a group of framed family photos atop Frank's dresser: Frank himself, young and a little handsome, making bunny ears over the head of a laughing girl; a soft-focus portrait of Wanda's father; a group photo Wanda had never seen in which she was sucking her thumb and holding Katherine's hand—Katherine, who now lived in Boise and refused to speak to Wanda; Louis, who was now dead; their mother . . .

Wanda turned away and undressed.

"HAVE YOU SEEN Jay?" Liz asked her brother when she found him near the dance floor.

Winston seemed to rein in his focus from far beyond Liz and put it somewhere around her eyes. "Did he ditch you?"

"I'm so sure!"

"'Cause if he did I'll kick his fuckin' ass."

"You're drunk," Liz said, spinning on a heel. Everyone was drunk, it seemed, and that one swig of whiskey had only been enough to give her a headache. The prom was at its height, but Liz was ready to leave. She had seen everyone she wanted to see, and Jay, who she had hoped would stay at her side sniggering at the entire affair, had disappointed her by lurking around its periphery, then disappearing entirely.

She finally spotted him outside in a circle of kids in the twilight of the gym's awning. Liz approached unnoticed. "Don't nigger-lip it," Jay said to a boy Liz didn't know before snatching the cigarette, scrutinizing the filter, and taking a long draw. The cherry, long and pointed as a red Christmas light, glowed in response.

Liz hadn't known Jay smoked cigarettes. She touched his shoulder. "Can we go?" she asked.

Jay nodded, released the smoke in twin streams from his nostrils, and gave the cigarette back to the boy. He followed Liz out into the dark parking lot, past a group of girls walking unsteadily on their heels with their skirts gathered up, to the dew-streaked Maverick. Liz figured Jay would come back after he dropped her off at home. Maybe he had his eye on some girl in that group, some friend's date. This night had proved to her that they weren't similar at all. She had given him way too much credit.

Jay drove slowly—so slowly Liz wondered how much he had had to drink. She wasn't worried, though. His hands were steady on the wheel and the roads were empty. She flattened her palms together and wedged them into the rayon folds between her thighs and gazed out the window, across the dark fields toward the sparkling hills that represented her neighborhood. The lake, out of view beyond, cast a green glow onto the rumpled bellies of some low-hanging clouds.

Jay passed the turnoff for Liz's neighborhood.

"Jay?" Liz said.

He didn't respond.

"You should have turned on Dewey."

Was he angry at her? He certainly had no cause to be. He was the one who had disappeared. Maybe he was ashamed of himself. Maybe he had missed the turn because he was drunk, and he would take the next turn on Locust and come around the back. But the shining sign for Locust approached from the blackness and passed and the car didn't slow. "Where are we going, Jay?"

"*Aiii*," he grunted in a strange voice.

"Is there some party?" Liz asked. "I'd really rather go home."

"Of course there is a party, *chica*. There's always a par-tay." It was the stupid, guttural Cheech-and-Chong voice he and Winston liked to use.

"Well, I don't want to go. I'm tired."

Jay drove quietly on.

"Come on, Jay, we've had fun tonight . . ." she tried.

They skirted the rocky escarpment of the empty hill at whose crest the electric cross shone. Now the subdivisions were behind them and they descended toward the lake.

Liz tried to sound cool. "So, where is this party?"

"Right here, mama. There's a party in my *pantalones*."

Liz made a sniffing, derisive laugh and turned again to stare out the window.

Jay pulled into the boat ramp parking lot. There were no other cars here. This wasn't the traditional make-out spot—that was in the park up the hill.

"Come on, Jay." Liz laughed. "What's going on?"

He killed the motor. "You want to smoke some ganja, baby?"

"You know I don't, Jay."

"Good, 'cause I don' have none."

Liz gave a phony, cheerful laugh. She adjusted herself to face Jay, and behind the folds of her dress her fingers searched out the door handle. "All right, Jay, what are we doing here?"

"We're parking, *mamita*. Don' you want to park?"

"No."

"You never been with a *Chicano* before, baby?"

"Come on, Jay. This isn't funny. We're friends."

He was quiet for a while, and there was no light in his eyes. Liz couldn't tell which part of her he was looking at. Without warning, his hand shot out and grabbed her face. Liz shrieked and pushed him away, but not before his other hand yanked at her hair. She tumbled backward out of the car, scrambled to her feet, and ran away.

Jay sat for a while looking after her, feeling blank. He had thought it would be funny to scare her, but it seemed the joke was over before it began. He would just sit here and wait for her to come back. He left the door open to seem more welcoming. He sat and watched the reflected lights from across the lake flash among the waves.

Then he realized, she wouldn't come back. She didn't get it. He should look for her. He reached for the door handle and saw, with a stir of panic, strands of Liz's hair in his fingers. He carefully twisted them into one cord, which he then curled around one finger and slipped them into his breast pocket. He heaved himself out of the car and walked across the lot down to the picnic tables, but she wasn't there. Should he call out to her? No, she knew where he was. He had actually scared her. Yes, he had meant to, but only to see a new expression on that smug face, before calling it off and taking her home. (That was, unless it didn't scare her; unless she kissed him.) He returned to the car, started the motor, and turned on the radio. It was Van Halen, a song he liked, and this helped keep down a rising, ugly feeling. He stayed there for a few more minutes in the glow of the tiny ceiling light. Then he reached across the seat and pulled Liz's door closed. He drove slowly around the parking lot, allowing the headlights to sweep across the brush. He imagined Liz out there, crouched behind a sage bush when she saw the light coming, her dress full of burrs and her black stockings white with dust. "Fucking *stupid*!" he hissed as he slammed his fist against the steering wheel. What, did she think he was going to rape her? She couldn't be that stupid, could she?

Jay drove the short distance up the hill to the park. He turned on his brights and made his way slowly along the circle drive, but no Liz. Two vehicles stood at a distance from each other in the parking lot overlooking the lake: a long, boatlike Ford and an empty pickup truck with a missing tire. This was Eula's make-out spot, and in the front seat of the Ford Jay could see a couple so engaged. Jay gently rolled up into the spot beside them and was greeted by two fierce, surprised faces. He rolled down his window and, with an apologetic grimace, gestured for them to do the same. The man climbed over the woman to roll the window down. "Fuck off, kid!" he shouted. The woman breathlessly raked her fingers through her hair.

"Sorry, have you seen a girl in a dress walking around?"

"No. Now, git!"

Jay lifted a palm and put the car in reverse.

What could he do? He drove around the lake, far beyond where Liz could have walked. Versions of the same vision flashed before him: Liz crouched down like a frightened animal in this dry ditch or behind that ruined shed. How could she be so stupid? Where had she gone? He made one more drive around the boat ramp and the park, then headed toward Liz's neighborhood, thinking he'd find her walking along the road and convince her to get back in. But he reached the subdivisions without having passed a soul.

A black mood that had settled over him at the prom (it had been almost cozy, the way it muffled his perceptions) began to lift. He no longer felt drunk. Slowly he began to see that he could be in trouble—real trouble.

He drove past Liz's dark house, parked in the cul-de-sac, and crept across the Padgetts' lawn to peer into the garage. Liz's car and that of her parents were there. This meant her parents were at home asleep and Winston was still at the prom.

Jay cruised the streets for a while, looking for Liz. Where was everyone? Even for the late hour, the neighborhood seemed eerily deserted, the big houses dark and cheerless behind their blazing porch lights.

Janet Van Beke was startled out of sleep by the sound of the doorbell. "Carl?" she instinctively said, groping for him across the bed.

"Mmm?"

"The doorbell."

"What time is it?"

She took her glasses from the bedside table and held them, still folded, to her eye to make out the glowing red numbers. "Nearly midnight."

The doorbell sounded again.

"Who on earth?" said Carl, heaving himself up and pawing the floor with his feet for his slippers.

Janet pulled on her bathrobe and followed her husband down the stairs. They both heard Jay before they saw him: "Janet? Carl?"

"Oh. It's Jay," Janet breathed.

Jay peered in from the foyer. "Sorry," he said. "I used my key."

"What's going on, Jay?" said Carl. He spread his knees and lowered himself onto a chair at the foot of the stairs. It was a decorative chair, rarely used, and he couldn't have meant to stay there long.

Jay directed his answer to Janet: "I made a mistake. Can you call the Padgetts for me?"

"What happened, Jay?" said Janet. "Is Winston all right?"

"It's not Winston, it's Liz."

"What happened?"

Jay hesitated. Carl gazed away into the den, apparently content to stand guard while Janet dealt with the boy. Jay had always been more her project than his.

"She ran off."

"What did you do?"

"Nothing. Just— Could you just please call the Padgetts and see if she made it home?"

"I am not going to wake up Carolyn Padgett in the middle of the night unless I know exactly what is going on."

"Liz ran off, out by the lake."

"Did you have a fight?"

"No. I just— She didn't understand."

"Jay, have you been drinking?"

"No. Yes."

Janet didn't abide drinking, not in her own children and certainly not from Jay. She allowed a long silence to follow his admission. Then she said, "Is there anything else I should know before I call?"

"No."

Janet went to the kitchen to make the call. In her absence, Jay and Carl said nothing.

"Liz is at home," Janet said, returning. "She's all right, but she's not very happy."

Jay nodded without lifting his eyes. "Can I stay here tonight?"

"No, Jay."

"Why not?"

"You know why. This is not your home. Lina should have made that call just now, not me."

"She doesn't know them."

"She should."

Jay made a sarcastic noise.

"And what's more, I'm not letting you drive, in the state you're in. I'm going to call Lina and have her pick you up."

"No!" shouted Jay.

This was enough to rouse Carl. "Listen, Jay," he said, "you're the one who screwed up tonight. I think from here on in, we'll make the rules."

"Just let me stay here, please!" This was the voice that had preceded a temper tantrum when Jay was a boy; it had that waver, that seed of hysteria. It was so different from his usual cool key that Jay himself seemed unable to recognize its childish ring. "I'll go home in the morning!"

"We've had this talk before, Jay, and we're not going to have it again. Not in the middle of the night. I'm calling Lina."

No sooner had Janet's back turned, though, than Jay dashed out the front door. Carl and Janet gave each other a look. They walked across the carpet and stood in the open door to see the taillights of Jay's Maverick disappear around the bend.

Then they closed the door—too soon to see a Buick that had been parked under the low-hanging branches of an oak across the street turn on its headlights and follow.

LINA STAYED UP watching TV after Enrique had gone to bed, and eventually fell asleep on the couch, with the dim intent of seeing Jay when he came in. The phone rang, and Lina leaped up to answer it before it awoke Enrique.

"Hello?"

"Lina?"

Lina was so overcome that she had to sit down at the table and gather herself before speaking. It had been an entire season since she had heard Chuck's voice, as he had obeyed her after their night together and left her alone. She had cleaned his house in the meantime, although it hardly needed it, and seen his little traces: his clothes in the hamper and his coffee cup in the sink. With Abby and Sandra away, he must have been eating every meal out.

"Lina, are you there?"

"Yes, Chuck."

Lina heard Chuck take a few deep breaths. Then he cleared his throat and said, "I was thinking I could come by, just for a minute, and you could come out . . ."

So, it had happened. Sandra was dead.

"Yes," said Lina. "When will you be here?"

"Ten minutes."

Lina sat at the table, overwhelmed by thoughts, waiting for the sound of the car. Enrique staggered from his room to the bathroom. He emerged a minute later with concern in his sleepy squint. "You okay?" he asked.

"Yeah, just can't sleep. I'm all right, though."

Enrique nodded and returned to his room.

Lina put on her coat and went outside. She saw Chuck's Cadillac pulling into a spot up the road. With her heart racing, she walked to the car, opened the door, and eased into the velvety, scarlet interior she had until now only seen from the outside. The front seat was broad and soft as any sofa, and the lights of the massive console of the dash glowed orange like the hot coil of an electric range top. Finally, she looked up at Chuck, who seemed pale and fragile.

A woman's voice issued from the dashboard: "Passenger door is ajar."

"Wow," Lina said as she opened and closed her door. "Your car talks."

Chuck smiled wanly.

Lina reached for his hand and squeezed it.

"I have to go to Salt Lake tomorrow," he said. "My flight's at seven. I should be packing. I *was* packing, but then I ran out of strength."

"I'm so sorry, Chuck," said Lina.

"*Thanks*," said Chuck, the word a swing at something he couldn't see. "I don't know. It's sad, isn't it? It's hard for me to tell. Am I sad? I just feel still. Everything's become so simple all of a sudden, and still. She's gone. Sandra no longer lives in this world. What do we do? We bury her." By his facial expression, Lina could see that he was surprised at what lay around the corners in this labyrinth. "I wanted to see you. Not for you to give me hope. I don't want to corner you. But if you wanted to— If you wanted to tell me there was some light at the end of all this . . ."

"Chuck," Lina said, her eyes brimming with tears, "I love you."

His shoulders, which she hadn't noticed were bunched, dropped, and he gave a great sigh of relief. "You love me," he said with feeling. He fell to her, and she held him.

She did love him. Without realizing it, she had been doing the work of loving him for months. She had protected him from his own feelings by only partially revealing hers. This was what she had been doing back on their night together, when she pretended to be asleep. She hadn't told him she loved him because she *did* love him—enough to save him from his own love that would have grown out of control if it was fed.

At least this was the gift Lina now credited herself with having given him.

Chuck turned his head and kissed her with lips wet from her own tears. She clutched him. His tongue darted into her mouth, searching out her own tongue to lift it. His hand moved frantically to grip her thigh. His kisses came harder, they moved from her mouth to her neck. Then they ceased and Chuck went limp. "God, I don't know what I'm doing," he said. "I'm sorry."

She hushed him, and a few minutes later he seemed to doze off in her arms.

Lina felt happy and complete, with Chuck returned to her at last. She looked down the line of trailers toward her own. Stars quaked in a puddle in the gravel road. This place wasn't so bad. A figure caught her eye staggering from the trailer park's bad neighborhood, holding his arm—a drunk, most likely. As he neared the lane on which they were parked, he was obscured behind the row of trailers. Lina hoped his noise didn't wake Enrique.

She closed her eyes for a minute and breathed in time with Chuck. Then the sound of footsteps running on gravel startled her, and she sat up.

Lina would later wonder how Enrique knew just where to find her. "Mom!" he yelled, approaching the car.

Chuck started, and Lina got out. "What is it?"

Hugging himself in his pajamas, Enrique stepped from one bare foot to the other on the wet gravel. "It's Jay," he cried. "He's all beaten up."

CHAPTER 22

The suitcase, whose shiny shell bore no scuffmarks, lay open like a great Bible on her bed, and Connie nervously took articles of clothing from drawers and put them in. Then she took other articles out of the suitcase and put them back in the drawers. How many skirts would she need? She could wear them twice before washing them, three times perhaps, as she wouldn't be working in them. Standing here between her bed and her bureau, she was essentially blocking Gene's exit. His accordion door was open and he sat on his bed swinging his legs and watching her.

"Do you need out, Gene?"

"No?"

"Are you sure you'll be okay until dinnertime?"

"Yes?"

Every answer Gene gave sounded like a question. To Connie it *was* a question, the same one, repeated: *Are you really leaving me alone here?*

"Do you want to go over to Enrique's now?"

"No?"

Connie glanced out the window and saw that Lina's car was still gone. It was Sunday morning. She knew Catholics went to services at odd times during the week. Did they also go on Sunday morning?

Lina was not at church, but at the hospital. She had spent the night there, while Jay's arm was set, his face stitched, and his nose bandaged. When the light of dawn started to show over the steaming fields out the waiting-room window, Lina noticed Chuck across the lobby, waving, trying to get her attention. She had thought she wouldn't see him until his return. She gently rose and left Enrique asleep in his chair.

"They found his car," Chuck said.

"Where?"

"Off Cherry Lane, by the canal."

"How do you know?"

Chuck shrugged. "I called a friend in the department. We can go get it now—you and I—and avoid the fee for having it towed."

Lina looked down. "Aren't you supposed to be going to the airport?"

"I have just enough time."

So Lina awoke Enrique to tell him where she was going, and she rode with Chuck to the spot on the outskirts of town, behind a lot full of irrigation supplies (long stacks of silver pipes studded with sprinklers, chain-link bins full of plastic elbow joints and rolls of black rubber tubing), where those boys or men—whoever they were—had chased Jay down. The Maverick was unlocked, and the keys were in the ignition. Lina quickly scanned the weeds for droplets of blood, ashamed for some reason that Chuck might guess what she was doing. There were none. Maybe Jay's attackers had taken him someplace else. Lina drove the Maverick back to the trailer park, then rode with Chuck back to the hospital. They kissed a dignified, loving, but exhausted kiss—a married kiss—and said good-bye.

"They say he's doing okay," Enrique said when Lina awakened him. "They'll come get us when he's ready for visitors."

"Move over," she said as she nestled in beside him to wait.

Now the suitcase was shut and locked, and Connie stood at the door holding it. "Gene, you're sure you'll be okay?"

"Yes?"

"Try to be home from Enrique's by nine tonight, all right? That's when I'm going to call. Now, give me a kiss."

Gene came over, and she kissed the top of his head and gave him an awkward hug.

"Look at me, Gene." She took his chin, and Gene squinted and squirmed as if the sun could get to him even here, indoors. "Come on. You won't see your mom for a week."

He softened a little. His eyes opened and his fingers reached up and took her earlobe.

Connie released a little laugh. "I love you. Be good," she said.

As she pulled out of her parking space, she noticed Gene watching her leave. It jarred her a bit; she couldn't remember him ever doing that before, looking out after her, his face like that of an anxious little pug dog in the kitchen window. She gave him a little wave and was gone.

By the time she got to the edge of Eula, she no longer felt rattled but, rather, electrified. As she pulled onto the highway, she gasped at her own audacity and laughed. She was going away!

"SHOULD I MAKE some eggs for Frank?" Wanda asked, standing over the sizzling pan. Another wave of nausea and hunger—the two were one for her these days—hit her.

"Nope. Won't eat 'em," said Coop. "I already got him his cereal."

Wanda peered into the living room and saw the man cradling a mixing bowl in the crook of his arm and dipping into it a serving spoon, as if to stir batter. Wanda cast her eyes back to the bacon (better not to look!) and, with tongs, broke off a crisp end of a rippled strip, dabbed it on a paper towel, and ate it.

"I'll call Maria in a bit," Coop said, "see if she can meet us at the station. She's probably up, but I like to let her sleep as long as she needs on a Sunday."

"Uh-huh," Wanda said. She was having second thoughts about going to the police. If only she could call Melissa! But Wanda remembered too well that awful day when Melissa had hung up on her. She couldn't spring this on her just when everything was going right. Coop had scared away Alan, their stepfather, all those years ago. Couldn't he do the same now?

Coop must have sensed her trepidation, because he said, "Best to involve the authorities as early as possible, way I see it. You're in the right. He's in your apartment."

"It's Hank's name on the lease," Wanda replied glumly.

"Your stuff at least. And you can always stay here for a while."

"Thanks, Coop."

They ate their breakfast; then, as they were cleaning up, Frank called from the living room, "Coop? Wander?"

"Whatya need, Uncle?" called Coop.

"Come in here. Somethin' I wanna discuss with ya."

Coop raised his eyebrows at Wanda. He took a beer from the fridge, cracked it open, and followed Wanda into the living room.

"Thank you," said Frank, trading the bowl for the beer can. "Sit down, both of ya."

Coop and Wanda obeyed.

Frank sipped the beer and shifted among his cushions. His eyes didn't leave the television. "They have pills people take nowadays, help 'em not kill themselves. I saw it on TV. They say that, when you got a lot of relations killed themselves, you're apt do it, too. I thought I should tell ya, while I gotcha both here, case you might want to start takin' them pills." Frank ended by nodding in agreement with himself.

Wanda glanced at Coop. If he had looked at her in the right way, she would have burst out laughing. But Coop seemed determined to take Uncle Frank seriously. He said, "Thanks for that, Frank. I'll consider it." And he moved to rise, but Frank stopped him.

"Hold on, now. I ain't finished. I'm sayin' you might want to start takin' them pills, because yer brother Louis killed himself. And . . . and so did yer daddy."

Now Coop shot Wanda a look, but she no longer felt like laughing. Wanda waited for Coop to say something, and when he failed, she said in a generous tone, "Uncle Frank, our daddy didn't kill himself. He died— You—"

"I told you all that I killed him, 'cause that's what he wanted me to tell ya. But I didn't. He shot himself in the night."

"You didn't shoot him?" Coop demanded. He reached out and hit a button on the remote control, turning off the television.

Frank's face dropped in shame, as if he were suddenly naked. "Turn it back on, please."

With an exasperated shake to his head, Coop obeyed. "When did he tell you to lie to us? Before he did it?"

"We had a talk by the fire that night. He didn't want you kids knowin' what he was about to do."

Coop's face was red, the tips of his ears nearly purple. "So he looked at you and said, 'Frank, I'm gonna kill myself, don't tell the kids.'"

"Not in so many words. With Cooper men, kinder gotta read between the lines. You oughta know that."

Wanda cried, "Why didn't you stop him?" It was a belief she held deeply that her father could have fended off all her life's troubles, had he lived.

"Really, Wander, I didn't know clearly what he was goin' to do."

"How come? How could he ask you not to tell us, and you still not know?"

Frank nodded with that awful smile. "I've been askin' myself that, actually."

Wanda rose and walked unsteadily to the door, took her jacket from its hook, and wrestled it on. Coop tried to give her a concerned look, but her eyes swiveled unseeingly and she was gone.

Frank continued to Coop, "I almost spoke up when Louis did what he did. But I made a promise to your daddy, see? The gunshot woke me up, and I found him, and I unnerstood what he'd been tryin' to say at the fire. So I made him a promise not to tell."

Coop's thoughts were in disarray. He pushed the button on the remote with finality to stop the noise, and this time Frank didn't protest. "So all these years I've been takin' care of you, thinkin' you were suffering under the burden of having killed your own brother, you were lyin' to me? I resigned you to die, and resigned myself to help you do it, and for what? Why, Frank? You could have lived a man's life, not . . . *this*," he spat, indicating, with a toss of his hand, his uncle's great form on the floor.

Never had Coop seen such a strain on his uncle's smile; never had it been so ugly. "Thought you kids might forgive me for somethin'," he said, "but it looks like I had it ass-backward."

"Looks *like* it," Coop said, rising. "Don't know if I'll be able to scrape together the money for your food and beer this week, Uncle Frank."

"That's all right," Frank said with a trace of pride. "I'll be movin' along shortly."

"Where you gonna go?" Coop laughed and reached for his keys. "You piss yourself half the time I'm not here to haul your carcass over to the john."

. . . .

THE DOCTORS REASSURED Lina that Jay would be okay, that he needed to be kept under observation for a day or so, and would be required to speak to the police anyway when he awoke; so she took Enrique home and slept. She rose in the early afternoon and ventured into Jay's room. She sifted through magazines by his bed—sports and hot rods—and gently opened drawers to look through stacks of the clothes Jay insisted on laundering himself—at friends' houses or at the Laundromat on the boulevard, she didn't know. What would Jay need in the hospital? A car pulled up outside. Lina quickly closed the drawer and went to the front door.

Janet Van Beke was climbing out of her car. She didn't come up the steps but turned to wait for a second car that approached down the lane. This car parked, and from it a man Lina didn't know emerged. He went to Janet's car, and the two carefully helped Jay out of the backseat. Janet wrapped one of Jay's arms around her shoulders while the man supported the other, which was encased in an L-shaped cast. With their help, Jay hopped toward the house, heavy-footed and dead-eyed.

"What's going on?" Lina demanded, coming out onto the porch.

"He's all right, Lina," said Janet. "Let's get him inside, and I'll explain."

Lina held the door wide, then quickly cleared Enrique's things from the recliner. Janet lowered Jay into it, and the man pulled the lever to elevate the footrest. "Okay?" he said, crouching close to Jay's face.

"Uh-huh," Jay answered through the gauze in his mouth.

"Janet," said Lina in an urgent whisper, "what's he doing here? They said he had to stay at the hospital."

"Lina, this is Dr. Carlisle. Can we sit down?"

Lina nodded.

"Dr. Carlisle is the Padgetts' family doctor—and ours, actually—and he felt it would be okay for Jay to return home."

"Why didn't they call me?" Lina asked. "They said they'd keep him there for observation and to talk to the police."

"That's just it, Lina. The Padgetts think it would be best to keep the police out of this, and so does Jay."

"What do the Padgetts have to do with this?"

"Lina, don't get excited." Janet moved over and patted the cushion beside her. Lina reluctantly sat. "Jay's going to be all right. That's the first thing you need to understand. Dr. Carlisle will visit every day and check on him, and before long Jay will be good as new. And this will all be at no cost to you. Everything will be taken care of. Lina, we don't know all the details . . . but Winston Padgett may have been involved in the attack."

"Winston? He's Jay's best friend."

Janet bit her lip and nodded.

"They could have killed him, Janet."

Again, the woman nodded. She took a great breath and said, "Disgraceful. I know. There was lots of drinking involved, on everyone's part."

"That's no excuse! They should—"

Janet placed her hand on Lina's arm to stop it from gesturing. "On Jay's part too, Lina. Liz Padgett is very upset. It seems that Jay may have tried to . . . hurt her . . . out by the lake."

Lina was speechless, swimming in thoughts.

"You see," Janet said softly, "if Winston Padgett gets in trouble, then so might Jay."

Lina shouldn't have looked to Jay. A real mother would have made this decision for her child, would have said, *No, whoever did this to my child must pay.* But Lina wasn't Jay's real mother, was she? Neither was Janet. The boy was motherless.

"Jay?" Lina said.

The white of one eye was marred with blood, and from its position under the puffy awning of its lid, it labored to follow the other in meeting Lina. The skin visible between the bandages on his face was taut and mottled, the color of different fruits: plums, berries, old bananas. The bandages themselves weren't simply white; they bloomed yellow in the middle and were framed by a bloody crust.

This patchwork face composed itself and nodded.

The sky was clear, there was a cheery breeze, and the sun blazed in the chrome of cars. Wanda charged across Eula in the determined stride she had used six months earlier when she needed to escape her cravings. When she grew tired of men peering up from under the hoods of their cars in their garages, women turning from their gardening to stare at the crazy lady walking, she headed down an alleyway to the canal. As before, it rolled along in swirls and boils, collecting litter in eddies along its walls.

Her father had killed himself. It was something Wanda knew she would never be able to make peace with. When his death had been an accident, Wanda had been permitted a little fantasy in which her father had lived, and so her mother had never drunk, and therefore had also lived, and there hadn't been the rift in the family, and Louis had lived, and they were all healthy and smart and had get-togethers in Sunnyridge Park with all the grandchildren, the way she saw big Mormon families do. Wanda didn't visit this fantasy world often anymore, but it was there when she needed it. Until this morning it had been only a stray bullet that prevented it; the fantasy could have just as easily been reality—more easily, actually. It *should have been.*

But now she saw its awful opposite: her father had killed himself, and so had her mother, although she had taken a longer and less determined route. This was just how Coopers went. Louis had known this when he made his urgent walk to the river. Despair would track down Wanda too in the end.

She should have known. Hank himself had once sniffed and said, "Ain't no such thing as huntin' accidents." He had meant that Uncle Frank had killed her father on purpose. But Hank knew nothing about it. Quietly, she had put that comment in the little treasure chest of things she would never forgive Hank for.

Suddenly Wanda realized that, out of habit, she was heading toward home. But Hank was there. For the first time, she was truly homeless. She had come close before, but this was the real thing. Her heart raced; she was panicking. She changed directions yet again and headed toward Tammy's. Just one pill, to get her through today. It wouldn't hurt the baby. It was just an aspirin, a really strong aspirin. Tammy herself—a nurse—had put it that way.

It took two rings of the doorbell, and when the door finally opened a few inches, it was Tammy's face, not Vincent's, that appeared. "Yes?" Tammy said without her usual smile.

"How are ya, Tammy?"

"Fine."

"Um, sorry I haven't been comin' around."

"That's all right."

Tammy, who had always taken Wanda in with an almost-hungry hospitality, still hadn't opened the door and seemed to look right through her. The same rush of displacement came over Wanda now as last night, when she had walked into her apartment: was this really Tammy? Of course it was, but it really seemed like Wanda had entered the land of opposites, and this was a grim replacement.

"Can I come in for a second?" Wanda asked.

"I'm real busy just now."

"Just for a minute, Tammy? I kinda need to."

"Thanks for droppin' by, Wanda." A square grin appeared on Tammy's face, pushing back her chubby cheeks as though she were trying to show her back teeth to the dentist. Through these clinched teeth she added in a whisper, "Git *outta* here!"

Wanda looked over her shoulder, suddenly aware that someone might be watching. She looked back just in time to see the door close.

AN HOUR INTO her trip, Connie passed the farthest boundary of where she had taken Bill. Within two hours she was in territory she had never seen before. It looked a lot like home, though, the blond hills sometimes giving way to flat expanses of farmland. She went over a pass where sandstone domes showed at the hilltops as if they had been scalped. This was the only point at which she became uneasy, as the only evidence of human life here was the road she drove on and the power lines that dipped and crested endlessly at the periphery of her vision. A dust devil, so dense that it looked like flames where it licked the earth, slowly approached the road. Feeling a little silly, Connie pulled over to let it cross. The fire at its base went out, starved as it was momentarily by the asphalt, then it gathered strength again, the gap ascending the column like a bubble in a straw. The dust devil descended into a dry creek bed, where it scared an animal off up the hill, kicking at the air with white, paddle-like back feet. It was a jackrabbit, so big that Connie would have thought it a fawn if not for its ears, which pointed heavenward, straight as two rulers.

Connie crested a hill and breathed a sigh of relief. Magic Valley opened below her, a quilt of greens. One of the more populated areas of southern Idaho, Magic Valley seemed neither magic nor a valley. It was a wide plain of towns and potato fields along the Snake River, skirted by mountains so distant they were a ragged, purple line barely visible in the dusty haze. At its farthest end, Magic Valley crossed over into Utah; even more than Eula, this was Mormon country.

The air warmed as Connie descended, and she cracked the window open to smell a thinner, cleaner aroma than at home: potting soil, as opposed to manure. The crop here was potatoes alone, none of the smelly dairies or pungent alfalfa fields, and no sugar factory. She pulled down a dirt road between two fields, parked, and ate the spaghetti she had brought in a Tupperware container. Muddy water charged down a ditch, on which semicircular siphon tubes had been arranged at perfect five-foot increments. Each led from the ditch to a furrow. The sun shone on the field, causing the water in the furrows to sparkle like rhinestone necklaces laid out for display. It was pretty here, but as Connie drove on, the redundancy of the landscape began to make her uneasy. Farmland was comfortable to live on, but bleak to drive through. A rattling sound came from her engine when she took her foot off the gas, or was she imagining it? Her car was old. What if it broke down? In a place like this, she would be fine. Some younger version of her father would come by and give her a hand, or at least go call a tow truck for her. But what if she were stuck in a pass like the one she had gone over, or one steeper and more remote, in a place like Colorado? What if she was trapped by a rock slide? That happened all the time in the foothills of the Rockies, beyond Salt Lake. With a chill, Connie realized that she would have to cross a huge mountain range to get to Missouri.

An hour into Utah, the sun set. Connie pulled into a small motel called the Seagull Inn. She had hoped she would reach Salt Lake today, but it wasn't worth the risk of falling asleep.

The motel manager was a little, brown-complexioned, pockmarked man dressed in black. He had an accent Connie couldn't identify. He wasn't Mexican; maybe he was Indian—the kind from India. When he offered to help Connie with her luggage, she let out a shriek of protest. Her overreaction was just nerves, but when she ruminated on it afterward in the room, with the door locked and the curtains drawn, it seemed extreme, offensive even, as if she feared the man because he wasn't white. She would be sure to be sweet and appreciative in the morning, so he'd know she wasn't prejudiced.

Connie lay on the bed fully clothed, hoping to calm herself and quiet the roar of the road that was still in her ears, before cleaning up and calling Gene. Within minutes, she was fast asleep.

Wanda rang Gideon's doorbell. It was dark out. She had walked all day and had nothing to eat. She desperately needed something to put her mind at rest. Gideon had pills—not often, but sometimes—and if not that, one puff of pot wouldn't hurt the baby. Her surrogacy contract said she wouldn't do illegal drugs, but, then, Randy and Melissa had told her they thought marijuana should be legalized.

Maybe Gideon would have some cold pizza to eat.

Gideon opened the door and sneered. "Well, well, well. Wanda. Do I look like Mountain Bell to you? You keep comin' here to use my phone, and I'm gonna start chargin'."

"It's not the phone, Gideon. Can I come in?"

He smiled with relish. "Why should I let you in when alls you do is make fun of me and put me down?"

"I got some money. Not much, but a little."

Gideon glanced around, miffed, and Wanda realized she had violated the correct order of things. The times she had paid, it had always been after the chat and the transaction, in answer to a quietly stated fee—never first thing on the doorstep. "Come on in, then," he grumbled.

"Sorry, it's just, I had a real hard day is all." Wanda resisted the urge to support her belly as she eased herself onto the sofa. She didn't want Gideon to know she was pregnant, as to him it would be nothing but more gossip. "Family stuff," she said.

"I'm sorry to hear that," Gideon said. His voice was frank, and Wanda wondered if she had somehow roused the rarely seen human being inside. As soon as Gideon was seated, his cat leaped into his lap, butted his chest, and ground its head there, back and forth. Gideon ran his hands roughly down the cat's body and released puffs of fur into the air. The cat purred loudly, desperately, like an asthmatic, and with every breath, its pink anus, which was pointed at Wanda, went convex and concave.

"I was wondering if you had some pills lying around. Something to ease my mind."

"Nope," Gideon said.

"Then maybe we could smoke a joint? Like I said, I got money."

Gideon shook his head gravely. "I don't mess with that stuff no more, Wanda—smokin' weed and poppin' pills. I've moved on."

"Moved on?" Wanda said quietly.

"I got somethin' new."

Wanda could see that he wanted her to say it. She acquiesced. "Gideon's Bible?"

He nodded.

"What's in it?"

"Different stuff."

"Like what?"

He eyed her incredulously. "You think if Colonel Sanders was here he'd give you his secret recipe, just like that? Come on."

"I just—"

"There's eleven herbs and spices in there, arright?" Gideon shoved the cat aside, and it darted off. He reached down, pulled out the Monopoly box, and used it to plow a space on the coffee table. When he lifted the lid, Wanda caught a glimpse of miniature Ziploc bags—piles of them. Gideon took one of these out, and a mirror. He pinched the bag open and dumped out a small mound of yellowish powder. With one of the Monopoly game's "Chance" cards, he began to divide the powder into lines.

"I just don't want nothin' that'll keep me up, Gideon," Wanda said. "Nothin' that'll make me *think* more."

Gideon barely acknowledged her. "This stuff'll make everything all right."

"I got lots to do tomorrow," Wanda said.

"The way it works is, first one's free, but I ain't gonna waste my time describin' it. Better to feel it for yerself."

"I need my sleep."

"Ask me no more questions, I'll tell ye no more lies." He held out to Wanda a plastic straw, cut short.

Wanda shook her head.

"Me first, then?" Gideon shrugged, ducked, and quickly snorted a line. He sat up and exhaled. "See? Smooth sailing. Cool as a cucumber. And it's almost bedtime." Again, he offered Wanda the straw.

She took it. She eased herself out of the sofa and knelt on the ground. She plugged her nostril with one hand and snorted the line.

A bleach-scented burn in her nose became a pain in her head, like the headache that comes from eating ice cream too quickly. Wanda pressed the heel of her hand to her forehead. Gideon's mouth hung open and his belly contracted again and again in spasms of laughter, but it took a while for it to become audible. By that time, a surging in Wanda's heart had overcome the headache—a powerful, positive surging. She was purring like that cat, breathing pleasure.

Gideon clapped his hands and whooped like a cowboy. "You kin sleep when yer dead, Wanda. Enjoy the ride!"

FOR A WHILE that afternoon Lina had kept the TV volume down in order not to disturb Jay's sleep. The squares of light from the living room's small windows climbed the opposite wall, lost their sharp corners, and deepened from white to amber, and Lina gradually turned the volume up to a normal level; it was apparent that nothing would wake him. His chest barely rose and fell under the sickly blue hospital robe. More than once, she went over to check for the faint bubbling sound his breath made in his nose. She drank two pots of coffee over the afternoon to stay awake. Despite Dr. Carlisle's assurances, she feared Jay was close to death.

Jay shifted and groaned, and Lina helped him to the bathroom and waited outside while he peed. Then she carefully took the slick, red gauze from his mouth and replaced it with clean white gauze, and in so doing saw that his front tooth was broken in half at a slant. She wondered if he knew.

"I wanna get out of this stuff," Jay said. Lina nodded. She went to her room and got her soft, roomy bathrobe. She undid the hospital robe's paper ties and helped Jay ease it off over the cast. She helped him pull her robe on, then supported him as he shimmied out of his underwear and awkwardly stepped out of his filthy gym socks. Then she helped him back to the recliner and gave him a dose of pain medication. He was out again.

After this she felt reassured, not only that Jay would not die, but that she could be the one to nurse him. Enrique emerged from his room where he had been napping all afternoon. "I didn't sleep a wink last night," Lina said. "Could you sit with him?"

Enrique gave her a worried look.

"He's fine. Those pills knock him out."

Enrique nodded, then stretched. "What's for dinner?" he asked.

"I'll put in some leftovers."

After they ate, Lina went to bed.

Enrique didn't have any homework. He hated Sunday night TV, all boring grown-up stuff like *60 Minutes* and *Murder, She Wrote*, none of the nighttime soaps that he loved. He resented having to sit with Jay, although he wouldn't have had any plans on a Sunday night anyway.

Who had done this to Jay? Probably someone he had picked on. Enrique went over to examine his brother. Bandages covered his forehead, where they had stitched up a cut, and his nose, which was broken. One eye was swollen to a puffy yellow slit from which only the tips of his black lashes emerged. His fingers looked like nicked baby potatoes where they stuck out from the cast. His leg, a hairy strip of which was exposed, brown at the ankle, pale at the thigh, seemed untouched.

Enrique went to the TV, twisted the dial, found a documentary about outer space on PBS, and returned to his seat. With nothing else to occupy his mind, it soon wandered back to what, for the past day, had been its home: the man at the urinal. The man's penis had stuck straight out like a rod. What would it have been like to reach out and hold it?

One afternoon a few years ago, Miriam's older brothers had tricked Enrique into grabbing the electric fence. It was a single charged wire, suspended at what had been his eye-level, above the wire mesh used to keep in the sheep. It hardly worked. The sheep, apparently insulated from the shock by their thick wool, still clambered over the fence into the backyard to eat Miriam's mother's flowers.

"It's not on," one brother said.

"We never keep it on," said another. "It's just to scare the sheep."

Enrique knew this was a lie—the wire buzzed audibly—but he wanted these big boys to like him. And, he realized now, the buzz itself was inviting. He grabbed the wire and the shock traveled up the nerves on the insides of his arms, causing him to grip the wire tighter. The warm buzz shook him to the roots of his hair. It hurt, but in a different way from a spanking or skinned knee or bee sting. It gave a more frightening pain, because it was, at a deep level, moving.

To take that man's penis in his hand would have been something like this. Even though Enrique had already masturbated four times in his room today and he was sore, he again felt a stirring.

What would Jay's penis look like if it grew, right now, under that robe? Enrique watched the spot, but there was no movement.

An animated diagram on the TV screen showed the path of the Viking Lander from Earth to Mars. Then pictures appeared of the desolate red landscape, a desert without end, with no life. Gene was probably watching this show next door.

Enrique jumped. Weren't they supposed to feed Gene dinner? For a moment, Enrique considered letting it pass, but then the guilt won out. Gene would never be able to get a meal on by himself, and, besides, Enrique was bored.

Barefoot, he walked across the empty lot to Gene's trailer. None of the lights were on. He knocked on the screen door and, after a moment, Gene appeared. Behind him in the darkened living room, the TV blared. PBS, just as Enrique had predicted.

"Weren't you supposed to come over for dinner?" Enrique asked. He allowed himself an abusive tone. In the months since they had spoken, he had grown an inch and become independent (Enrique's mom could have left for as long as she wanted, and he'd be fine) while

Gene had stayed the same, except for adding wisps to his beard and pearly-headed pimples to his cheek.

"I ate," said Gene.

"What did you eat?"

"Peanut butter–banana," he said with neither pride nor hesitation. Still, the simple presentation of information.

"That's not dinner. Come on."

"I'm not hungry."

"Fine. I don't care." Enrique turned and hopped off the porch.

"I'm waiting for my mom to call," Gene said.

Enrique turned on him a condescending smile. "Have fun," he said.

Back in front of the TV, Enrique squirmed with boredom. Jay still hadn't moved one muscle. If Gene knew what he was missing—the chance to gaze at Jay uninterrupted—he'd give up waiting for his mom to call. Gene had always had a crush on Jay. Enrique had been too ashamed to articulate this, even to himself, when they were friends. It had been gross, and Enrique had wished Gene would just cut it out. But now he didn't care.

It had been a long time since Enrique had done one of his experiments; bike-riding had overtaken research as his favorite hobby. But stuck here with no entertainment, he became curious.

After a few minutes, Enrique stood and opened the blinds over the couch. This window looked out over the weedy area between their house and the chain-link fence, and its blinds were always kept closed. Then he went next door again.

"Gene," Enrique said when he answered the door, "I know you're waiting for your mom to call, but could you do me a huge favor? Jay got beaten up really bad last night. He's in the living room, and I'm supposed to be watching him. But I gotta go somewhere. Could you watch him for me just for, like, a half-hour?"

"Is he all right?"

"Yeah, he's gonna be fine. They're just keeping him unconscious, you know, for the pain."

Gene twisted his mouth and looked up at Enrique. "Okay," he said, and he followed Enrique back home.

"Thanks a lot, Gene. Like I said, I'll be gone for a while. Just make yourself at home. There's meatballs in the kitchen." But from the moment Gene saw the long body laid out in the recliner, his attention was lost.

WANDA SAT ON the curb, under the night sky where bright stars vibrated in their lodgings. Across the street, the lights still glowed in her windows, her apartment, which was occupied by the enemy. Time seemed to be folding and unfolding since she took the drug; it was hard for her to tell how long she had been sitting here, as every moment that passed brought with it a new reality that required her reaction. With every breath the universe was born anew; every moment splashed against her like water. And she controlled it—the deeper she breathed, the more vivid the world her breath brought about. She giggled, thinking how she would look from the outside, reacting with welcome to the new worlds she encountered.

He felt it, too—her baby. What she felt, he felt. That was being a pregnant mother.

What had Wanda been worried about? She didn't need that apartment. There was only one thing inside it that mattered: the mobile. *His* mobile, her baby's.

She leaped up and started searching Darrell's lawn. She found a rusted metal pipe about two feet long. Attached to its end was a knobby elbow joint, which gave the pipe a satisfying heft and swing, like a baseball bat.

The look that had appeared on that girl Misty's face yesterday—fear—was the opposite of what Wanda felt now. Fear was the encountering of a new world that was awful, not brilliant. Wanda felt especially able to inspire fear in this state. She would throw off worlds that Misty would swallow, like it or not. But she shouldn't become distracted; this mission was not for Wanda but for her baby. She threw a few practice swings. Fantastic. Her breath controlled her arm like a pump, and this pipe was her arm's extension.

Wanda charged across the street and up the walk to the porch. She swung the pipe hard. It met the wall next to the door and left a gray slash. That was disappointing. The impact jarred her shoulder a bit and stopped her from carrying the stroke through, so the cut wasn't deep. She swung at the door. That was better: not only did it punch a round hole and send a splintered crack up the door's center, but it caused a scream to come from inside—the scream of her enemy. Fear was Wanda's best tool. And surprise. If she surprised them, she could rush into the bedroom and seize her prize with no resistance. She swung at the door handle. It popped off and the door swung slowly open.

"Hank!" screamed Misty. She was backing up, climbing the couch backward while holding her belly with one hand. Wanda half-expected her to go on and climb right up the wall like a spider.

Wanda swung blindly and punched a wide, triangular hole in the wall, from which dusty bits of plaster then dangled. She hadn't fully recovered the pipe when a figure flew in from the hallway. Hank tackled her from the side, and they both fell to the floor. Barely shaken, Wanda kept hold of the pipe. She gave Hank a sound kick to the shoulder that sent him rolling away. She sat up enough to gain leverage for another swing. Hank lifted his forearm to shield his head. Wanda met the arm with an ax-chop that made him bellow in pain and curl into a ball.

Misty used this opportunity to dash down the hall. Wanda scrambled after her, fearing she'd blockade the bedroom. But Misty ran into the bathroom instead and slammed the door. Wanda swung at it—an extra blow, just to hear Misty's mule-bray and keep her hiding inside. Wanda pushed the bedroom door open. The floor was covered in clothes, boxes, and scattered papers. Around the bed there was a great mound of belongings. Wanda ran up this bank onto the bed, and took her prize. She didn't want to ruin the ring from which it hung, so she slowed herself and used the pipe to prod it from its hook. This caused all the clowns to dance an epileptic jig, their elbows and knees swinging backward, then they fell into her arms.

"Better git the fuck outta here, you crazy bitch!" Hank hollered from the kitchen. "I called the police!"

What luck! Lucy's drawing still hung in its place. Wanda snatched it from the wall and folded it into her pocket.

Now Wanda had only one hand with which to brandish the pipe; she had to be careful. She crept down the hallway. Hank was cowering in the kitchen, the phone in one hand and a knife in the other. Wanda rushed through the living room and out the door. Hank dropped the phone and pursued.

Out front, some neighbors from the other units had come shyly out onto the lawn, keeping their bathrobes closed with folded arms. They all retreated several steps when they saw Wanda.

"Stop her!" Hank cried. "She wrecked my house!" Wanda turned, and Hank slowed, still brandishing the knife. He took a few careful steps toward her and said, "What's that you got? Whud you steal?"

"It's mine," Wanda said.

"Put it down," Hank said, giving the air a little stab.

"You leave her be!" a neighbor's voice called from behind Wanda.

Taking good aim, Wanda lifted the pipe and pitched it toward Hank's head. It spun marvelously in the air, like a baton, but missed and skidded up the walkway with a surprisingly weak tinkle. Wanda turned and ran.

Gene's calculator-watch told him it was 11:08 p.m. In the ten minutes that he had been observing Jay, neither had moved a muscle.

"*Jay*," Gene whispered. Speaking to him brought on a big bubble—which was the name Gene gave the feeling that started in his belly and rose to his heart and up his throat, shortening his breath. Some bubbles he liked; this one he didn't, but he was moved anyway to speak again, louder. "Jay!" he said. Again, no response.

At 11:13, Gene rose, crossed the room, and tapped Jay's hand. Then he shook Jay by the shoulder, gently. Jay did nothing but breathe a shallow, hissing breath through his nose. Something white showed between Jay's parted lips. Gene bent down to look. Was it fabric? Some sort of gag? At 11:18, Gene put the tip of his index finger, which was trembling, to Jay's bottom lip, pushed, and revealed the white stuff to be a corner of a wad of gauze, which filled one side of Jay's mouth. He must have had an injury—a pulled tooth or a cut on his tongue. They had put gauze in Gene's mouth when he had an extra molar extracted when he was eleven, and he had hated its rough texture, even when it was softened by saliva. Gene released the lip, and it came back up. The lip grew softer, he noticed, as he released it. Now he stroked the lip, out at its rim where it was brown and firm, then inside where it was red and soft and where a slight wetness facilitated his stroking.

It took twelve minutes to build up the required strength of hand and steadiness of heart (these things added up to courage, but that was a name he had learned, rather than a quality he felt), and in that time, Gene stood rigid as a tin soldier. When he had a task to do, he acted like a robot who would conserve energy in one quadrant of its body to use in another. At 11:31, he took the fluffy fabric of the robe from where it opened against Jay's leg, and lifted it. It was dark underneath, but Gene could make out Jay's penis, lying there on its side under a mass of tightly curled pubic hair. Gene knelt to see better. He folded the robe over Jay's leg so the light from the kitchen would shine on what he had found.

Of the millions of minutes Gene would live, the two that followed were the only ones that, he would come to feel, mattered.

Naturally, no one understood Gene. Enrique had come the closest, having become able, over the years, to point out to others the details of Gene's limitations so they wouldn't ask too much of him and to warn them of his quirks so they wouldn't find offense in them. But even Enrique never could see what Gene saw or feel what he felt; the wall was too thick, and what lay behind, too weird. Enrique had, at last, dropped him. Contrary to everyone's belief, Gene perceived beauty, perhaps more than they did. He felt it, and was at certain moments submerged in it, owned by it, unable to feel anything else.

At this moment there was nothing on earth but what he had found. This ash-colored pucker of flesh that he took in his fingers, darker than the rest of Jay's skin (foreskin was its name—he knew from a medical textbook he had read at the library), was the softest thing he had ever felt, softer than any earlobe or flower petal. He held it for ten seconds. Then he pressed it back (he knew, from the textbook, that he could do so without damaging it) and revealed a bulb of flesh whose color was balanced perfectly between brown and pink. It was not like his own; it was wet, and glistened in the light like the stamen of a flower. His memories of every penis he had ever seen—his own, Enrique's, those of the Boy Scouts and the men in the dressing room at the pool—were shuffled and relabeled. He knew them now as the altered, desiccated stamens of the flowers women dried in their Bibles. This was the only living one he had ever seen. When the scent reached him a second later, it made him draw back, then freeze to savor it. It was a dirty smell, like old socks—worse, putrid—but the moment his senses recoiled, the scent was rounded out by something else, something lovely—milk, warmed on the stove, scalded to a skin on the pan's edges.

In the future, when Gene would imagine his life as a *story*, like one told in a science fiction novel or constructed in a role-playing game, it would end here. As far as life is made of moments that stick, be they burrs or diamonds, rather than those innumerable moments that don't, that have no weight and are carried off on the wind, this was it. Gene didn't perceive nuance, but he understood laws. There were express laws in the world that must be obeyed, and one of them said that all this—what he was doing here, the beauty he had found and that now owned him—was forbidden, absolutely forbidden with no loopholes or exceptions. He would obey this law and never come here again. He would never enter the holy of holies again lest he be struck dead. As Gene would tell it, what led up to this moment was preparation; what followed was recollection.

He closed the foreskin back over the head or, rather, allowed it to close; he released it and it swallowed the stamen and hung slightly shorter than before—at about 80 percent. Gene hunkered down lower and was able to see up the wrinkled sheath to the tip, notched with a slit that had tiny red lips of its own. The intimacy of peeking at this mouth—cheating, when he had already allowed the stamen to return to its protective bell—gave Gene another bubble.

Then there was an awful rapping sound that made Gene want to cover his ears with his hands (he didn't, though, having learned years ago the law that said you should endure noise without closing your ears and hiding from it), and Gene turned to see Enrique in the window, pointing to the hallway. Gene dropped the robe over Jay and stood straight. Lina emerged from the hallway, her breasts swinging under her lacy nightgown. Upon seeing Gene, she drew back. "What are you doing here?" she said.

"I'm . . ." *Checking his pulse.* This lie would occur to Gene later as he spent the night alone, terrified, in his trailer. But he could never lie on the spot; it was one of the weaknesses that disabled him from navigating the world. His voice simply stopped.

"Go home, Gene," said Lina.

"I'm back," Enrique said, coming through the front door.

"Where did you go?"

"I was only gone a sec."

"I told you to sit with Jay!"

"I needed some air. Gene came over to eat, so I left him with Jay. I was only gone a minute."

Lina turned to Gene. "Go home, I said!" Gene quickly left, and Lina turned back to Enrique. "Can't I trust you to do one little thing?"

"Jeez, Mom, it's no big deal."

"It is a big deal, Enrique. Your brother's hurt!"

Jay stirred grumpily.

"I was only gone a minute," Enrique repeated quietly.

"He was *doing* something to him," Lina hissed.

"What?"

Lina was quiet, her eyes on Jay, watching him settle back into sleep. "I don' know," she whispered. "But that kid is *weird*. I don' want him coming here no more."

"*You're* the one who agreed to feed him."

Lina answered only with a shudder.

CONNIE AWOKE WITH a start and, from where she lay on this unusually firm bed, searched the walls unknowingly. The motel. She was in a motel in Utah. She sat up and looked at her watch. It was nearly midnight. Gene had certainly gone to bed already, but she would call anyway. Maybe he'd answer (a boy would take advantage of his mother's absence to stay up late watching TV), and if he didn't, she'd leave him a message. Connie picked up the phone's heavy, old-fashioned receiver, and pulled at the tightly coiled cord. There was no dial tone. On the phone's console was a sticker that said, "Dial 0 for Reception." She didn't dare wake up that man to ask him how to dial out.

She went and peeped out the door, thinking there might be a pay phone affixed to the motel's sun-bleached, yellow exterior, but all she saw was a line of lamps between the doors, some burned out, the others weakly illuminating the dust that blew in the air. Across the highway was only blackness. A few parking spaces down, the wind caused a strip of duct tape that hung from a pickup truck's side mirror to rattle, and coyotes barked in the distance. She closed the door again and locked it.

Quickly, quietly, as if someone were listening at the door, Connie washed up and put on her nightgown. She left the lamp over the sink on and closed the bathroom door, hoping the faint slice of light cast on the ceiling would be enough to keep her from being afraid. Then she slipped, shivering, into bed. What if Gene was waiting for her call, worried that she had been in an accident? He wasn't the type to worry, but what did she know? She had never left him alone before. Connie couldn't stop shivering, and although she knew it was from her nerves, she rose anyway, found the thermostat and turned it up, causing a ticking, springing kind of music to come from the electric heater that ran along the floor under the window. She got back in bed and began to cry. Was this how she would spend every night on this trip, alone and scared?

Why was she on this trip? What was the silly fantasy that had brought her here? In her giddy preparations, she had forgotten it, and now it brought her no joy. Why find Eugene? She had no one to marry.

Dear Lord, she prayed, *help me. We can be saved in a moment, Lord, like the flicking of a switch. I believe it because Your word says it.* Give me my moment. *I'm in danger of losing my faith. Thomas doubted You, and You forgave him. You did more than forgive him, You showed Yourself to him, let him feel the holes in Your hands. You helped him put away his doubt forever. Reveal Yourself to me, Lord, or at least send me a sign. I'm lost. I need to know if I'm heading in the right direction. I believe in miracles, and I may be one of Your last followers who does. Don't be angry at me for asking, Lord, just come to me as You did to Your disciples after You died on the cross. Put away my doubts, and I'll follow You forever.*

Connie drifted off, only briefly, then a rustling sound caused her to jump. The window curtain was shifting with intention—like a living being, it seemed. As she stared, it rippled and bulged in a way that could only be described as supernatural. She squeezed her eyes shut, so horrified she dared not even move, lest the sound she made cause the being behind the curtain, or the curtain itself, to awaken all the more. Then she remembered her prayer and opened her eyes. She breathed steadily to calm herself and watched the curtain as the shadows shifted, curled, and arranged themselves into shapes. The shapes came in and out of focus. Fascinated, Connie lost them as soon as she found them.

And then He appeared. Christ, life-size, watched her just as He had from the picture on her childhood bedroom's wall. As soon as she saw Him, her heart leaped into her throat, and He was gone again. A shadow of His form returned, and she squinted to see Him better, and this caused Him to disappear. She continued to stare at the curtain—and there He was again, smiling that gentle smile. Relief washed over Connie. Jesus was with her, and she had nothing to fear. Then He faded. It seemed the force of her desire to see Him could just as easily make Him go, so she relaxed her eyes and her mind and let Him come. This time He stayed, and the two gazed at each other. He had always been here, close at hand. He was here to remind her of that now, to answer her prayer and restore Connie's faith. "Thank you," she whispered.

In answer, Christ closed his eyes reassuringly, then opened them again.

In her mind, Connie begged, *Don't go.* She had never felt love for the Lord so intensely. Then Jesus moved, and Connie gasped. Now His arm was raised, the robe hanging from it in great folds. His finger pointed, but His gentle eyes remained on Connie. Home. He was pointing toward Eula. "Yes, my Lord," Connie whispered.

She lost Him for some seconds, and when He came back into focus, He stood as before, arms at His side. Again, Connie feared that He would go and this would end. Should she speak to Him? Should she ask Him something?

As if in response to this thought, Christ raised His hand in blessing. In the center of His palm was a dark spot. Overwhelmed, Connie heaved a great sob. A painful shudder went through her body, and with that Christ sealed up the wound that Bill had left, and there was no more pain. It had hurt so badly for so long that Connie had forgotten it until now, when she felt marvelously healed, whole, and at peace.

Once, when Connie was small, she had gone to sleep-away camp with some of the girls from church. Exhausted from a fruitless day of fishing, she had fallen asleep in the drafty cabin with her sleeping bag unzipped and one arm fully exposed. The temperature dropped during the night. Connie was awakened by her teenage counselor placing her arm, which was chilled almost numb, into the sleeping bag, and zipping it up. No sooner had she felt the awful cold than it was soothed; she was awakened to the pain by the cure itself, so pain became pain's opposite.

This was what Connie felt now. Christ himself had zipped her up and put everything right in a moment. With that, He was gone. It was only a window curtain now, moving slightly with the heat that rose from the electric heater.

Connie slept peacefully for a few hours, then rose before dawn and headed home.

CHAPTER 23

Wanda walked all through the night with the conviction that she was doing it for her health, which was the health of the baby. The town was at rest, and the odd car that passed her made a friendly sizzle against the pavement. At dawn, she realized why it was so much easier to carry the mobile in her left hand: her right shoulder, which had been jarred in that first swing of the pipe, ached. So did her side, where Hank had tackled her. Still, she walked. Homemade announcements on squares of cardboard, YARD SALE and FREE KITTENS, sandwiched signposts; dogs raced to the end of their chains to bark Wanda away.

Mid-morning she sat down at a graffiti-riddled picnic table in the park to rest. The lawn here was yellow at the corners where the sprinklers didn't reach. In the wide parking lot, a few trucks and vans started to arrive, driven by potbellied old men who unloaded miniature scooters from them. The men shook hands, then stood at a distance from one another, resting the backs of their wrists on their hips, looking up at the sky, and chatting. Then they revved up their scooters, fifteen in all, and, after a puttering overture, practiced formations: rings, cloverleafs, and braids—up and down the lot. The Shriners, Wanda realized, were practicing for Eula's Independence Day Parade, when they'd ride wearing fezzes and vests with tasseled trim.

While Wanda watched them, her legs seized up in cramps. She was suddenly hungry, ravenous with morning sickness. She hadn't eaten for a day. She left the mobile on the table, limped around the back of a shed where a group of mourning doves took flight, creaking with every stroke as if their wings were attached on rusty hinges, and coughed a thick, white web into the bushes.

Crisscrossing the town in the night, she had had momentum, and only infrequently had her mood slipped into a bog of despair; now she returned to the table and sat entrenched in it. Moments of hope were the rarity now, and she struggled to gain purchase on them like stones in the quicksand, but it was no use. There were two possible cures: to return to Gideon's and buy more of what she hated him for giving her, or to go someplace safe and beg sleep to come take her. But instead she stayed on the bench in the appalling sunlight and watched the Shriners practice.

It never came—whatever it was Wanda waited for, whoever it was that would save her—so she rose and, on aching legs, headed back to Coop's. Now her shoulder throbbed, and her ribs . . . her attention shied away from the ache. Had Hank really hit her from the side? He had, and hot waves of pain replaced the euphoric heaving of last night. How could she have been so foolish as to put her baby—Melissa and Randy's baby—in danger? Wanda put her hands to her belly to support him and keep him out of reach of the waves.

The kids were in rare form that afternoon. Maybe it was the brilliance of the weather or the fact that summer vacation was just around the corner. More than once, objects—not just spitballs, but objects with weight—bounced off Coop's head as he drove. It had been weeks since Enrique last rode the bus, and the back seats had again become a refuge for troublemakers. Today they leaped around, fighting, snapping training-bra straps, climbing and tumbling over seat backs, stealing Rubik's Cubes and comic books and throwing them out windows; and their victims, girls with braces and fat third-grade boys, wept openly. If anyone other than Gene cared to look, he would have seen that for the first time Coop wasn't smiling. That one piano-key tooth, the false incisor, was concealed behind a tight frown.

Only Gene noticed, and it made him so uneasy that he moved a couple of seats back.

Coop was ruminating on the fact that he had spent his life deceived. In his pity for Uncle Frank, he had lost many an opportunity. His only consolation now was that he hadn't lost Maria; she had been patient enough to wait year after year. Well, he wouldn't make her wait anymore. "Take it slow, old man." That had been her only words of advice in bed this morning, after a day of grumbling and a night of shifting about sleeplessly. The woman was a saint.

How could Frank not have known? How does a man tell another man to keep his suicide a secret, and still not reveal his intent? "With Cooper men you gotta read between the lines," Frank had said. Who was he to tell Coop about Cooper men?

A Cooper man.

"I'll be movin' along shortly," Frank had said.

Coop's heart froze, and he slammed on the brake.

They had reached the empty stretch, and the kids, having become used to the speeches given by Chicken Coop, barely took note.

He pulled the emergency brake and stood, but this time there was no speech. "Out!" he bellowed.

The din lowered a bit.

"Git the hell out, every one of you!"

Coop began to go down the aisle and grab kids—the good ones near the front—by the shoulder and fling them toward the door. "Out! Now!" The other kids began to leave of their own accord, rushing past Coop with frightened expressions, holding their backpacks over their hearts. They descended the three stairs and cowered in a group among the satiny milkweed at the roadside. "Out, God damn you!" they heard Coop yell, and the last of the boys stumbled out and fell on his knees in the gravel. They all watched the bus, growling and squealing like an angry monster, jerk back and forth in the awkward task of turning around on a road hardly wider than it was long. Then it was free and it roared away back toward town, leaving the children blinking in the sunlight. A few started to walk toward a silo, which, though distant, was the only structure visible over the corn.

Nothing in the world, no command or incentive, no promise of solitude and order, or unlimited access to all the scientific publications that existed or even a ride in a submarine, could have gotten

Gene to do what those children now did, which was to walk down that open road under that yawning sky. That bright Idaho sunlight everyone else seemed to love was, to Gene, a searing radiation. In it, objects shone blindingly, then purpled, as his retinas—and his brain—roaringly burned. Gene *heard* sunlight, though he would never tell anyone this lest he receive the ten-thousandth blank look of his life. It sounded like a brushfire in the wind, a firestorm.

But he didn't have to. Having seen before anyone else what Coop meant to do, he had crawled under the bus seat, and he cowered there now, his head hidden under his piled arms, his cheek pressed flush against the sticky floor. Gene was surprised but not frightened. He had ridden behind Coop for years, and felt between them a distant, quiet respect, which was all he wanted from anyone.

WANDA ENTERED THE house through the kitchen door, hoping not to rouse Uncle Frank if he was asleep. That way she could slip into the bedroom undisturbed. Yesterday's breakfast dishes were still on the rack. Coop must have spent the night at Maria's. Wanda went to the cupboard and found a box of graham crackers. She ate these greedily and washed them down with a glass of milk. Then, hoping to find Frank asleep, she eased the swinging door open and slipped into the living room.

The smell shocked and sickened her. It was that old smell that she knew so well, the caustic bile-smell of death. She put her hand over her face and passed quickly through the room. Despite her determination not to look, Uncle Frank appeared in the periphery of her vision, sitting among the cushions just as he had when he was asleep, his head rolled back. Wanda closed herself in the bedroom, went to the wastepaper basket by the desk, and coughed out a long, thick string festooned with lumps of cracker. She pinched it free from her mouth and turned. Frank, that poor old man. She had felt sweet toward him, a little, there at the end. But now she was in a race to get out of here, or else his death (or at least responsibility for the cleanup) would be pinned on her. She threw her things into her bag and placed the folded mobile, which had lost a couple of clowns without her noticing, on top. The toothbrush and creams she had left in the bathroom could stay here. Then she held her breath and charged through the living room and out the front door.

There was no other choice but to call Melissa. She'd make her understand. Wanda had enough money for a bus ticket; in fact, that was all the money she had. Randy and Melissa would give her another advance, and she would stay with them and be safe.

Wanda headed toward the bus station, heaving the heavy bag. It was a long way.

Halfway there, a pang of horror and ache rose in her side where Hank had hit her, and moved low in her abdomen, the baby's seat. She froze there in the road, holding her bag with one hand and her baby with the other, and began to cry. "*Don't*," she whimpered. "Please forgive me. Please, don't!" The wave passed and she walked on, as evenly and quickly as she could.

"You might as well come out from under there," Coop shouted as he entered Eula going faster than a bus should go. Back on the empty stretch, he had seen the boy drop quickly to the floor. He would have pulled him out and thrown him off if he didn't know how the boy cowered from the sunlight under the bill of his baseball cap. Coop pitied him.

Now Gene popped back up, eyeing him grumpily. "I ain't goin' far," Coop said. He stopped himself from adding, *Just sit there*, because what else did the boy ever do?

Coop drove down his narrow street, where he had never taken the bus before, and parked at an angle in front of his house. He killed the engine, yanked the lever sending the doors open, and jogged up the walk. The front door was ajar. He didn't bother calling out Frank's name as he entered—that's how certain he was of what had passed. "I'll be movin' along shortly," Frank had said. What else could he possibly have meant?

The rush was over now, and Coop, at somewhat of a loss, took his time. Walking quietly along the walls, he opened the windows to let the breeze clear the smell. Then he took his place on the couch, where he had sat yesterday, and, again, turned off the television. A finch's twitter outside was the only sound. Only now did Coop look at the man's face. It was frozen in a look of horror, mouth agape—the face of one of the salted herrings Coop's grandfather, Frank's father, used to eat. Coop bowed his head. He rested his elbows on his knees and pressed his palms together, wishing for once that he was a praying man. "Ya coulda waited," he whispered. Suddenly he was choked by sobs. "Ya coulda waited a couple days for me to cool off."

Coop cried for all those he hadn't cried for before—his father, his mother, Louis, and now Frank. He whimpered like a child, shaken physically as if punched by sobs, letting the tears and snot collect on his nose tip, then drip onto his sandwiched hands.

There was a sound behind him, and Coop turned to see the boy watching from the room's dim corner. Coop ducked his head in shame and took a deep breath. "You better call 911, kid," he said.

"They're already here," Gene replied.

Coop wiped his face, went to the door, and saw that two police cars—not an ambulance—had arrived, their flashing lights lost in the sunshine.

WANDA SAT FOR a long time in the blue plastic seat. Another pang had shot through her abdomen just as she reached the station, and she felt that she needed stillness now, to settle her body and think things through. Finally she rose, went to the phone booth, and called Melissa's work number, collect.

"What is it?" Melissa asked in her work voice once the operator patched Wanda through.

The calm, rational explanation that Wanda had planned—that Hank was causing trouble and she feared for her safety—crumbled, and Wanda broke out in sobs.

"Wanda, what's wrong?" Melissa said.

"I've got to come back. I can't stay here. Please, just for a while."

"Are you safe? Is the baby okay?"

"Yes, I—"

"Then come, Wanda, just come. Do you need money?"

Now at last Wanda could breathe. "No. I'm taking the bus."

"When can I pick you up?"

As she made arrangements with Melissa, Wanda felt firmly that once back in that house in the woods she and the baby would be fine. They just had to hold on till then.

A crackling voice over the loudspeaker announced the arrival of the 5:15 Salt Lake-to-Seattle. Wanda picked up her bag and went outside.

There, in the dappled, tree-filtered sunlight was the boy—Lucy's boy. *Wanda's* boy. He sat on the curb with his elbows hooked around his knees, making his back dome like a tortoise shell, and gazed toward the station with an expression that mirrored Wanda's own desolation. Wanda must have gasped, because the boy turned. His face lit for a moment, then dropped. *It's me*, Wanda wanted to say, but the boy quickly rose and picked up his bike from where it lay in the weeds. Wanda still had the drawing. She dropped her bag and reached into her pocket to show him—*Look, I know Lucy—I know you!*—but the boy sped away.

Wanda burst into tears. He was gone.

"Are you all right, ma'am?" The driver stood at the bus door. Everyone else had gotten on.

Wanda nodded. She couldn't speak. She picked up her bag and reached into her other pocket for the ticket. She avoided the driver's gaze as he ripped it in two.

Enrique had been watching the men's room door, but his mind was still fixed on his mother's shudder and the wordless disgust that had taken her over after Gene left last night. All morning, while tidying the house and tending to Jay, she had avoided Enrique's eyes. He had never felt so hated. He wished for a different mother, one who wouldn't cling to him for dear life, then cast him away when he failed her. These experiments—they really showed how the world worked.

But he couldn't help but suspect—then, as the idea developed, *hope*—maybe these experiments changed the world, or at least their subjects. Gene wouldn't have done what he did if Enrique hadn't guided him into it. And then Lina wouldn't have shuddered. Enrique feared he was like one of those bad scientists who manipulated his experiments to get the results he wanted. Or, worse, one who experimented on helpless animals, hurting them in the process. Enrique made one of his simple self-commands: *No more experiments.*

Then, in the corner of his eye, he had seen a woman come out of the station and recognize him.

Enrique's split-second reaction to being recognized by an adult was to inhale to say hello. But then he remembered where he was—watching the men's room door at the bus station—and leaped onto his bike.

He sped across town toward home. The fact that he had believed, for a moment, that he had been caught gave Enrique an awful realization: he had sat there on the curb, all those times, for all those hours, in plain view of all of Eula. What was he thinking? It didn't matter that the woman was some crazy-eyed drifter—no one he knew. He made the decision, and knew that this time it was for real: he would never go back there.

No more experiments; no more bus station. He had lost both his hobbies at once. Thank God he still had his bike.

"Mom!" Gene barked as he entered the trailer, breathless from the long walk.

Connie sat at the table, soaking in the cool and quiet of home after her trip. When she had pulled in an hour ago, Lina had come out onto her porch. "Back early," she had said.

"Yes."

"That's good, 'cause I don' want Gene coming over here no more."

Connie had responded to this only with a placid smile.

"I don' like the way he looks at my Jay."

This was a test, a Temptation. How best to respond? But before she could decide, Lina had gone back inside, letting the screen door bang.

"Sit down, Gene," Connie now said.

He inhaled to tell her about the corpse and the policemen who put the weeping bus driver's hands in cuffs—not for having killed the man, but for having dumped all the kids out on the road—and who told him, Gene, to skedaddle. Then he saw that his mother would hear nothing of it and shut his mouth.

He must see that I'm different, Connie thought when she saw Gene's expression shift. "Sit down."

He sat.

"We've never been much like mother and son, have we, Gene?"

He scowled and looked away.

"It's all right, Gene. Look at me. It's all right. We've just got to acknowledge it, that's all. I want to ask you something. What do you *need* from me, Gene?"

"Nothing," Gene said.

"Nothing? Nothing at all? You don't need food, or clothes, or a house, or a ride to the library?"

Gene gave one of his wild, exasperated shakes of the head. "Yes, I do need *those* things."

"Then those are the things you'll get, nothing more," Connie said, gently and with finality.

Gene rose and went to his room. He shut the accordion door between them and rattled the handle till the magnet caught, leaving Connie alone in the presence of Christ, as she had been before. There was no room for games and false niceties in this new life—only truth.

In the minutes that followed, the light faded in the house. Then the door opened again with a series of slaps, and Gene stood outlined in gold by the bedroom light, blinking his tiny eyes.

"Yes?" Connie said.

Gene put his hand to his chin. "It's getting scratchy."

It was true. Yesterday, when she tilted up his chin to say goodbye, Connie had noticed that his beard was no longer soft.

"You want me to teach you how to shave? Is that what you need from me?"

Gene nodded.

Had he come up with this in those minutes alone? So be it.

Connie didn't know, though, that the most upsetting thing about the corpse today wasn't its skin, speckled purple like granite, or the acid smell, or the foam that had dried to a crust at one corner of the gaping mouth, or the jumble of yellow teeth inside. The most disgusting thing had been the matted white beard that, since the head had rolled back, stood out from the man's neck like the fanned leaves of a Rolodex. Now more than ever Gene hated the texture of his own beard. It was like something alien that had taken up residence on his face, an invasion of needles.

"All right, then," Connie said.

They went to the bathroom, and Connie seated Gene on the toilet seat. She worked a bar of soap up into a lather, which she then spread onto his face, then took one of her pink disposable razors from its package under the sink and put it into his hand. She put the hand mirror in his other hand and tilted it so he could see himself. "You've got to open your eyes, Gene, or you'll cut yourself." Connie put her hand over Gene's and guided him in making short, gentle strokes at his cheek with the razor.

WANDA SHOVED HER bag onto the overhead rack and sat gingerly into the seat. The muscles of her legs were knotted, and her shoulder throbbed. The boy had run away. She shouldn't think about it.

The other passengers were arranging their belongings, rustling potato chip bags, cracking open pop cans. Beneath Wanda the idling bus made a comforting rumble. She liked how the tinted windows mellowed the world. She felt a little safer already.

The bus shuddered and began to move.

Another wave of pain racked Wanda's abdomen at the outskirts of Eula, and another after Payette, yet she sat frozen in her seat, worried that if she were so much as to acknowledge the pain with a wince, the baby might come loose. She felt the need to move her bowels, but resisted. These waves of pain were deceitful, begging her to push when that was the last thing she should do. But as the bus crossed the blank landscape toward the Oregon border, acid rose in Wanda's throat and, at last, she rose and made her way back to the bathroom, clutching one headrest, then the next.

She had been right—standing made it worse. She pulled the stiff door closed just as a wave went through her, causing her knees to buckle. Her hands were tingling, numb, as was the top of her scalp. This cylindrical metal room was like the inside of a pop can, and it smelled sweet, like pop; the thick blue liquid that swirled around the toilet bowl had successfully masked any foul smell. A thought occurred to Wanda: *Coop could use that stuff to cover the smell of death in the living room.* Nonsense. Her mind was doing its flipping-fish thing, resisting at all costs settling onto the hot-skillet fact that the boy had run away; that she was losing her boy—the two were one. *No!* If she made it to Melissa's house, if she kept him inside her body till then, they'd be safe.

She closed the toilet seat, sat down, set the miniature faucet to dribbling, and tried to fill the cup of her hand. Now a different pain arose: cramping, low down, like when she had her period. Wanda brought water to her mouth and began to cry. With wet hands she undid her belt and, without rising, scooted her jeans down. There, on her underwear, just as she had feared, was a speck of blood. "*No, no, no, no,*" she cried, as one would cry to a baby. "*Don't do this.*" She half-rose to pull some paper towels from the holder, and another cramp seized her and bent her into angles. She braced herself against the wall, put her towel-wrapped hand between her legs, and pushed up. It came away bloody, a black clot at the tip. "*No, please,*" she whimpered. This couldn't be happening. But it already had. The boy had run away. Sickly fascinated, in a miserable trance, she rubbed the clot between her fingers till it came apart.

There was a knock on the door.

"Go on!" Wanda shouted.

She heard the shuffling of feet, then, a minute later, another knock.

"I'm sick! Leave me alone!"

Wanda could hear voices outside the door—"Says she's sick"—followed by more footsteps. Then she heard a hiss of hydraulics and she pitched against the door with the slowing of the bus. "No!" she cried. The bus veered and stopped. More footsteps. "No!" she begged. "Keep going!"

Step Seven: *Presentation*

CHAPTER 24

The milking barn at Frieson's Dairy, spacious and dark inside as a warehouse, stayed in operation day and night. Fifty at a time, the cows filed into the barn and up a chute onto a great horseshoe-shaped catwalk—the milking parlor—where their udders were at eye level. They hardly needed guidance as they entered their individual stalls, because they did this twice a day for most of their short lives and knew that they would be let out the other side of the barn into the feeding lot afterward. A worker made his way swiftly around, attaching the milking-machine suction cups. No sooner had he hooked up the last cow than it was time to unhook the first, swab her teats with antibiotic, and send her off to breakfast with a slap to the rump. The suctioned milk traveled through tubes and pipes out to a gleaming steel vat that was refrigerated and insulated from the July sun.

Sprinklers tossed silvery arches over the mint fields beyond the dairy. It was eight a.m., and the water would soon be turned off until sundown, to avoid scorching the leaves with drops that evaporated on contact. A hot breeze periodically drew the mist of one sprinkler into a curtain over the road. Enrique and Tommy noticed this and ran faster to pass through one and be cooled.

"What's the time?" Enrique gasped. With every inhale it felt like his lungs would burst from their cage.

Tommy raised his wristwatch. "Ten after eight."

"Hurry!" was all Enrique could manage. If they didn't get to the dairy in time, they'd have to walk home.

The events of that weekend back in May had left Enrique with few options of how to spend his time. If he wasn't going to spend his after-school hours hanging around the bus station, if he wasn't going to perform experiments on his friends and family—what, then? Ride his bike in endless circles around Eula? So, the following Monday he swallowed his pride, found Annie Schiff in the lunchroom, and apologized for the cruel trick he had played at track practice. She forgave him and led him back into the good graces of the team. It was too late for Enrique to re-join, but he attended some meets as an observer.

At one of these, Mr. Dodd climbed the bleachers to where Enrique sat.

"May I?"

At Enrique's nod he draped himself over the bleachers, crossing his ankles on the seat below and propping his elbows on the seat above. They watched the meet in silence until Mr. Dodd said—coolly, as if the subject had already been broached—"If you want to join cross-country in the fall, you've got to train over the summer."

Early morning was the only time cool enough.

The boys reached the Frieson's Dairy sign and ran down the lane. Enrique noticed with relief that Jay's car was still there. He began to gradually slow his pace, and Tommy followed suit; their running shoes raised dust clouds in the lane as they braked. They reached the lot and walked around the car a few times with their hands on their hips, catching their breath. Tommy gathered the hair from his face and wrung it out like a rag. Both boys had grown their bangs long at the command of Miriam, who was spending the summer with Penny in California and periodically called with fashion alerts.

Jay emerged from the barn, squinting in the sunlight and unzipping his white coveralls to reveal a sweat-soaked undershirt. There was a gap in one of Jay's eyebrows, a narrow, naked scar that changed the shape of that eye, exposing it. His front tooth was chipped, and his arm still hadn't regained its color after hatching from its cast. But other than this, he had healed.

"What time did you guys start?" he asked.

"Quarter to seven."

"From home or from Tommy's?" Jay shrugged out of the sleeve to look at his watch.

"Tommy's. Not bad, huh?"

"Not good. What, did you guys skip the whole way?"

"Fuck you."

"Let's go."

They drove toward Eula. "I'll bet by September we'll be down to a six-minute mile," Tommy said.

"That still won't win any races," Jay replied.

"We'll be down to five," Enrique said.

"Tell you what. The day you get down to a five-minute mile, Enrique, I'll give you this car." Jay had put a down payment on a used Corvette in Boise and, given the increased wages he earned working graveyard, he'd be able to afford it by Christmas.

"What'll *I* get?" Tommy asked.

"A ride to school," Enrique answered.

Principal Campbell set out on a quick tour of duty before heading home for lunch. He was operating summer school with a skeleton crew and had to keep an eye on things himself. Better to have a figure of authority passing by the classroom window now and then to keep these summer-school students—delinquents, most of them—in line.

When doing tasks that required little expertise or attention to detail, Campbell liked to practice a speech he might someday give to a Rotary Club or Oddfellows meeting. *Great men*, he would say, *are not born great. That's the common misperception. Great men are regular fellas who come upon great positions and fill them. Any man can be great.* (With this he'd sweep the crowd with his gaze, making them all feel as if he had looked beyond their eyes and seen their inner lives.) *All it takes is the luck of finding the job and the gumption to do it.* He himself had been a less-than-average man, but he took the job, filled the position, *became* the principal. Now Eula High was operating below budget, test scores were up, dropouts were down, and, thanks to his zero-tolerance policy, there were few discipline problems. The board of education in Boise had been poking around for ideas, and Fred imagined a job offer would come after a year or two. Maybe someday he'd run for public office—who knew?

With his hands bulging in the pockets of his chinos, Campbell left the academic buildings and strolled across the lawn and through the woodshop. The janitor had found cigarette butts behind the table saw last week, and Campbell was itching to catch the perps in the act. But the room was empty, and a thin film of sawdust muffled his footsteps. Then he passed through the garage. Ironic, to remember that autumn afternoon when he had dreaded to come here and confront Coop about his beer purchases. Compare that to the day in the spring when he fired Coop, telling him with relish that leaving the kids out on a country road was nothing less than psychopathic, and that if it were up to Campbell, he'd send Coop to Blackfoot for an evaluation. Coop had patiently nodded through this, his eyes pinched at the corners and his lips drawn up in that hateful smile of his. That was the last Campbell had seen of the man, though he had overheard in the teachers' lounge that Coop had married some Indian out near Homedale and had become a truck driver. Good riddance. Shouldn't be around kids.

Why had Campbell feared people so? Once he achieved a single-minded vision of how the school would operate, everything fell into place, and tasks became pleasurable. Yes, Campbell felt he understood great men now: Joseph Smith, Ronald Reagan, and even (although he'd never say so to the Rotary Club) Jesus Christ.

He walked across the lawn, into Building D, and peeked into the room where Cafferty's speech class was convened. Here, speaking before class, was another example—that girl Abby Hall. The old Campbell would have let her be valedictorian, even though she hadn't completed her course load. He would have melted the moment she started crying in his office. But not the new Campbell. *One day she'll be grateful*, he thought, and moved on.

Inside the classroom, the mood was dreary. Mr. Cafferty, unhappy with having been given a summer school class, had turned the first assignment into a punishment for his students. The subject on which they had to speak was "Why I Am in Summer School."

Yesterday's speeches had been one after another contrite retelling of the school's policy that every graduating senior have speech class under his belt, full of excuses for why the speaker had failed on the first try. Today's started off a little better, with a girl's ironic claim that she hated sunlight and loved homework. And now Abby Hall was up.

To this point, Abby had not said a word in class. She had sat through Cafferty's lectures on the proper structure of a speech, argument-building, and voice projection, staring glumly down her long nose at her notebook. Now she took her place at the podium without notes and slowly raised her great, orb-like eyes to the class, the eyes of an old woman set in the face of a girl.

"Why I am in summer school.

"I was accepted to Stanford University, which is the best and hardest-to-get-into school west of the Mississippi. All I need now is a high school diploma, and I'm out of this crappy town for good. It doesn't matter what grade I get in this class as long as I pass and, Mr. Cafferty, you have no choice but to pass me as long as I show up and do all the assignments. I was supposed to be doing an internship at an engineering firm in California this summer. My best friend, Liz, is there already, doing her own internship at a newspaper. We were supposed to be roommates. But our principal refused to let me do the work for this class anywhere but here, as he says I have to give these speeches in front of an audience; otherwise it's a violation of school curriculum."

Here, she caught a glimpse of the very man at the door, turning away.

"Our principal, Fred Campbell, is an idiot," she said in a heightened voice, though he couldn't hear.

"So here I am, stuck in front of you losers, and there you are, forced to listen to my speeches, which I promise you, will all be made up as I go along.

"Why I am in summer school. I am in summer school because my mom died. She had cancer in her cervix—that's the opening into the uterus at the top of the vagina. First she had a hysterectomy. That didn't work. They did treatments where they stuck a needle up there and burned the area with radiation. That didn't work either. The cancer metastasized to her lungs. She had polyps, sores inside her lungs that produced fluid, and this fluid would fill up her lungs.

She'd start to drown without even being in water. Every week I'd take her to the hospital to have a long needle stuck into her back, through the tissue, into her lungs. They'd suck the fluid out and she'd be able to breathe again for a few days before her lungs started to fill up again.

"They gave her chemotherapy, which is where they hooked her up to an IV and fed poison into her bloodstream. This made her much sicker than the cancer did. I wiped up her vomit and bathed her when she was too weak to bathe herself. She was not the type of mom who liked her daughter to see her naked, but she had no choice. Her hair fell out and her mouth was so full of sores she couldn't eat. She lost her beauty, her happiness, her sense of humor, and I had no choice but to sit by her side and watch. And she lost her dignity. There were times I was holding her like a helpless baby, and I could see in her eyes that she was ashamed. I think that was the worst part. No, actually. In doping her up to ease her pain, we robbed her of the chance to say good-bye. *That* was the worst part. And after she died, everyone gathered around to tell me it was good that she was dead, because she was in heaven now—people who didn't really know her or me and hadn't seen the hell she had gone through."

Abby looked at the clock on the wall. The speech had to be at least five minutes long.

"Here's a little story that took place not long before she died: my mom wasn't vain, but she did like having nice fingernails. She'd go to Boise to get them done. They'd put these extensions on so they were medium-length and very hard—you'd never guess they were fake—and they'd paint them a nice color, sometimes two colors. Even when she was really sick and we were staying in Salt Lake, we'd still go get them done. It made her happy.

"Now, the chemicals they use in chemotherapy attack any cell that's breeding quickly, whether it's a cancer cell or one of your own. That's why your hair falls out. But it has other effects, too. You get mouth sores. Constipation, too, because the chemicals attack the cells in your intestines that push stuff through.

"One night, my mom had really bad constipation. She was waking up again and again and calling out for me like a frightened little girl. I'd come in and help her—carry her, basically, because she could hardly walk—onto the toilet. Then I'd wait outside the door and listen to her cry out in pain. Then she'd give up, and I'd carry her back to bed. Then, near morning, she actually got something out and was finally able to sleep.

"The next day, I kept smelling something. I thought she had had an accident in bed, but I couldn't find anything. I looked all through her blankets and I got her up to search the cracks in the easy chair, but there was nothing.

"Finally I found it. It was her fingernails. They were filthy, encrusted. And I realized what she had finally done the night before—she had reached in with her pretty fingernails to pull the shit out.

"It took a long time soaking her hands and working on her fingernails with Q-Tips to get them clean. My dad showed up, and he and my grandparents kept giving me these sweet looks, like I was giving her a manicure out of kindness or boredom."

Abby looked up at the clock again and said, "So that is why I am in summer school. The end."

When the sun moved past its crest in the sky, Coop nudged Maria. She quickly lifted her pole. "I got one," she said.

"That was me. You've been asleep for an hour. Your bait's long since washed away."

"I think this creek's been fished dry," she said, reeling in her line. "I don't know how you stay awake."

"Hope, my dear—pure and simple."

They slowly broke down their poles, sorted their sinkers and hooks, folded their chairs, and brushed off the seeds that had settled on their clothes. "I didn't tell you this before, Coop, because I didn't want you marrying me for the wrong reasons, but as a member of the Shoshone Tribe I'm allowed to fish certain protected stretches of the Salmon River."

Coop froze.

"And as my husband, well . . ."

"God damn," he said. They packed up the car. "How long were you gonna wait to tell me that?"

"About this long."

"Well, I think that calls for a trip upstate, soon as I get back from this Kansas run."

"Take it slow, old man," Maria replied. "We got time."

THE KITCHEN PHONE, if pulled to the farthest length of its cord, reached the front porch. Enrique often brought it here on these long summer afternoons to keep from waking Jay with his laughter.

"Check and see if they have penny loafers at Payless," Miriam said. "If they don't I'll bring you a pair."

"Penny loafers? That's, like, geeky."

"Yeah, but it's *good* geeky. It's *mod.* But don't put pennies in. Only nickels."

"Mod?"

A car pulled into Enrique's mother's spot. It wasn't his mother's car; it was a Cadillac.

"Miriam, I gotta go. Call me tomorrow."

Lina emerged from the passenger side and walked to the foot of the stairs, an imploring look in her eye. "Enrique, sweetheart, I thought we could all go to Sizzler together. Do you think that would be all right?"

Enrique looked again at the car. The only other time he had seen Mr. Hall was when he had been made frantic by Jay's stumbling into the house covered in blood and dirt. Now he got a good look at this plain, bald white man in a brown suit. When the man smiled shyly, his forehead broke out in wrinkles. Enrique suddenly remembered the little village inside, gathering dust on his bookshelf—Mr. Hall's things. Enrique had never returned them as planned, at first because he liked them too much, later because it no longer seemed important. He had inadvertently signed a contract to be nice to this man. Mr. Hall had won after all.

Then someone in the backseat moved from behind Mr. Hall to look out the window. Abby.

Her eyes had changed. They were patient, adult, ready for the worst. But as they turned in their deep pockets toward Enrique, one side of her mouth lifted in a detached smile. Enrique didn't smile—

he couldn't—he felt he might cry. Abby's smile sweetened, and she was rocked a little by laughter, as though Enrique was a joke she had forgotten, and to see him was a friendly reminder of the old life where she could be amused by such things. Then she drew herself up in her seat, her smile dimmed, and she squinted as if to see him better. It seemed to Enrique that they had a whole conversation in those few seconds. What had *he* said?

He looked back to Mr. Hall, then to his mother. They were all waiting for him.

"Okay."

"Maybe . . ." Lina hesitated. "See if Jay's awake."

Enrique understood: Jay would be more likely to come along if Enrique asked him.

He went into the house and quietly eased Jay's door open. Jay's long body intertwined with the sheet, and his gaping mouth emitted a long, rattling breath. His brow was knitted, and his cheek rested against his hand. Something coiled around one finger of this hand. Enrique stepped in to look closer. It was hair—brown hair much longer than Jay's, which had been twisted into a string and wrapped around his finger. Enrique retreated and eased the door closed.

He paused in the kitchen and looked out the window. In the car, the three waited quietly. He felt a stirring of his old hatred of Mr. Hall. He didn't want to do this, especially without Jay, but he had said yes.

Paradoxically, in order to make his feet move, to walk outside and get into the car, he had to *not* diminish the importance of the event. He had to *not* trick himself into thinking it was just another meal out with his mother and a nice chance to catch up with Abby. To make his feet move, Enrique had to go in the opposite direction, to explode the event's importance by imagining a future time, after he had gone away on that Greyhound bus and returned, when he was a grown-up and his mom and Mr. Hall were old. He imagined a lake house in the mountains, and three little children wearing inflatable water wings on their dimpled arms running up the grassy slope from the dock to the porch, where Enrique sat with his feet up. The oldest child, a girl, carried a shiny, dripping, dangling treasure in her hands: a weed, necklace, or tentacled thing—Enrique couldn't make it out for the flashes of sunlight from the lake. The children all had matching noses, long and narrow like Abby's—and they called out as they ran, "Lookit! Lookit! Look what we found, Uncle Enrique!"

Uncle Enrique. *How's that, Mrs. Cuddlebone?*

CONNIE LEFT THE Mennonite charity shop where she volunteered on her days off and drove to the mini-mart to pick up a few things for dinner. She had quit First Church of the Nazarene and joined the Mennonites. People had always assumed she was one, from the way she dressed, and now she considered this a sign she should have been one all along. There were signs everywhere now.

Mennonite services contained nothing vain. Simple hymns were sung in four-part harmony without even the aid of a piano. The preacher drew his teachings straight from the Bible. There was no mention of Ronald Reagan or Oral Roberts or Jim Bakker. The tithes went to feed the poor. The men dressed in the clothes from a simpler time and many sported Abraham Lincoln beards, and the women covered their heads.

Connie had been self-conscious about her uncovered head, but was too shy with her new friends to ask where they had bought their white bonnets. Then one day at the store, one of the older ladies had placed a neat pile, starched and folded, into her hand. "For you," she said simply. Since then, Eula had never seen Connie Anderson bare-headed.

She pulled into the mini-mart parking lot, got out of her car, and stood for a moment, contemplating the rich blue sky. There were two jet-trails: the newer was like a line drawn in chalk, the older like the smudge left when that line was erased. The Air Force base at Mountain Home was not far away, although to drive there took three hours. A canyon lay in-between that was not yet bridged.

Her thoughts were interrupted by a woman's voice. "Pardon me, ma'am. My mother's sick and can't leave the house. Could you maybe spare a dollar or two so I can buy her something to eat?"

Connie began to walk toward the store. "I can't spare a dollar or two to feed a mother who passed on twenty years ago, Wanda Cooper."

Wanda fell back.

Connie hesitated and turned. The girl's arms emerged like sticks from her T-shirt, and there were red sores on her hands, which she now balled in order to hide them from Connie's view. "I was in school with your sister Katherine when it happened. I'm sorry."

Wanda turned away.

"I could buy you some groceries, though."

Wanda's lips disappeared into her mouth, where she chewed on them.

Connie adjusted a hairpin and headed toward the store. Then she turned to Wanda again. "Come on, Miss Cooper. I won't take no for an answer."

THE SUN GREW red, the jets returned to their base, and the sky absorbed their trails. Farmers lifted dikes, and water charged through pipes to again be chopped by the sprinklers and tossed over the mint. The last of the pleasure boats left Lake Overlook, and its foamy green surface was still.

Jay rolled out of bed and carefully returned Liz's hair to the folded paper he kept hidden in his sock drawer. He dressed and drove across the fruited plain to the dairy. The first group of fifty cows lumbered up onto the milking parlor, and Jay attached that first cup and began his night dreaming of the Corvette—not of Liz, but of the Corvette. The tube glowed white in the dimness, went dark with a few bubbles, then white again as the milk flowed to its new steel home. Apart from a quick pass through hot pasteurization pipes, it would be a cold journey from here to the throats of Idaho's youth.

CHAPTER 25

There was no fanfare on the morning in the spring of 2001 when technicians opened a valve on a structure floating at the center of Lake Nyos's glassy surface, and a white plume shot a hundred feet in the air. No ribbon-cutting. The president of Cameroon stayed in the capital, and the villagers kept their distance. A small group of scientists on the lakeshore cheered, but that was all.

Gene had been right. The Lake Witch had been a massive bubble of carbon dioxide that gathered under Lake Nyos, overturned it, and rolled down the surrounding slopes, suffocating everything that breathed. Now engineers had guided a pipe into the depths and attached it to this floating structure. Through the pipe, carbon dioxide would escape continually, preventing another disaster.

By this time Gene worked for layaway in the vast second-floor warehouse at ShopKo, a discount department store. It was a sunless job that suited him. If a customer wanted to get something out of layaway—if, for example, a woman wanted to use her Christmas money to buy, at last, the fake leather coat with silver studs and tassels she had found on sale months ago—she would go to the layaway counter with her receipt. One of the girls would look up the woman's record in the logbook and call a number out to Gene over the loudspeaker. Gene would find the woman's box and send it down the conveyor belt. Conversely, if a man found that, after his hours were cut at the sugar factory, he could no longer afford that $200 Weedwhacker, he could come to layaway, get a refund, and Gene would send down his box to be re-shelved in Lawn and Garden. But the purchases outnumbered the returns three to one. All in all, Gene helped the poor people of Eula by keeping their things safe until they could afford to buy them, and he did it without having to look them in the eye. Using a numbering system of his own invention, he never lost a box. The girls at the layaway desk liked to call him Genius instead of Gene. They had brought in a cake on his birthday.

Gene lived in a little apartment above a lawyer's office in downtown Eula, where he had cable TV. On the science channel there was a show completely devoted to modern inventions, engineering, and problem-solving. This was how he learned the fate of Lake Nyos. He had been making dinner and missed the beginning, but now he sat on the couch, turned up the volume, and pulled a cat into his lap. Dinner could wait.

A simple solution, the type Gene could have come up with: they stuck a pipe into the lake and eased the pressure, the way a doctor lances a boil. Never again would the surface of Lake Nyos be still; no one else would die. The resulting fountain was pretty. If they wanted, they could view it as a memorial to the dead. *They*, to Gene, meant everyone in the world beside himself and his cats. They were, after all, fond of that sort of thing.

Acknowledgments

I wrote this novel with the generous support of the National Endowment for the Arts and the New York Foundation for the Arts.

For their hospitality I would like to thank the Blue Mountain Center, the Corporation of Yaddo, and the Patten family of Sedgwick, Maine.

I am deeply grateful to my agent, Mitchell Waters, my editor, Rakesh Satyal, and those who read my manuscript and offered their criticism: Jonathan Strong, Jason Tougaw, Casandra McIntyre, David McConnell, and Peter Cameron. And I am especially indebted to Michael Lowenthal for guidance and support at every stage of this novel's creation.

Finally, to my darling Tristan le Masson Bangard: Thanks for *everything.*